Cleat Cute

Also by Meryl Wilsner

Something to Talk About
Mistakes Were Made

Cleat Cute

A Novel

MERYL WILSNER

ST. MARTIN'S GRIFFIN
NEW YORK

First published in the United States by St. Martin's Griffin, an imprint of St. Martin's Publishing Group

www.stmartins.com

Library of Congress Cataloging-in-Publication Data

Names: Wilsner, Meryl, author.
Title: Cleat cute : a novel / Meryl Wilsner.
Description: First Edition. | New York : St. Martin's Griffin, 2023. |
Identifiers: LCCN 2023016959 | ISBN 9781250873309 (trade paperback) |
  ISBN 9781250873316 (ebook)
Subjects: LCGFT: Romance fiction. | Lesbian fiction. | Sports fiction. | Novels.
Classification: LCC PS3623.I577777 C57 2023 | DDC 813/.6—dc23/
  eng/20230413
LC record available at https://lccn.loc.gov/2023016959

Our books may be purchased in bulk for promotional, educational, or business use. Please contact your local bookseller or the Macmillan Corporate and Premium Sales Department at 1-800-221-7945, extension 5442, or by email at MacmillanSpecialMarkets@macmillan.com.

First Edition: 2023

10 9 8 7 6 5

For Ashley,
and so

You can't win a championship without gays on your team. It's pretty much never been done before, ever. That's science, right there.

—Megan Rapinoe

One

The vending machine takes the crumpled dollar bill Phoebe feeds it, then immediately spits it back out. Phoebe huffs, taking the bill and flattening it against the thigh of her spandex shorts.

"Don't let me down now," she murmurs as she tries once more.

When the dollar isn't smugly returned, Phoebe pumps both hands above her head in victory. She jams her index finger against buttons with only vague outlines of *C* and *4* left after years of use, and peanut M&Ms plummet to the bottom of the machine.

"How many blues in this bag?" she asks her brother, Teddy, who always times his break at the front desk for when Phoebe is between personal training clients.

Teddy picks at the chipped top of the lone table in the break room, legs splayed wide like that will make him taller. "What do I get if I win?"

"I'll share 'em with you," Phoebe says. "If I win, you buy my next bag."

"Is that just because you're out of cash?"

He isn't wrong—she'd had to dig through her drawstring bag, thinking all hope was lost until she found a bill in the bottom corner.

"It's because it's an equal bet," Phoebe says, then admits, "Or, well, it can be because of two things."

Teddy used to be her Mini-Me, before he'd chopped his hair and changed his name. Not that it affected too much—no one could look at their flaming red hair and fully freckled faces and think they're anything but siblings. Teddy leans into the messiness of their matching hair, always looking like he's just rolled out of bed, but somehow managing to pull it off. (At least Phoebe knows she'll look good if she ever decides to cut hers and go butch.)

"Ten," Teddy says. "And if I win, you take me to New Orleans with you."

"That seems like awfully high stakes for a bet about M&Ms."

It's better than Teddy's usual bet, though, which is to make Phoebe wash his binder. He always waits until after working out to collect, the asshole.

Still, she'd take him with if she could. Her only reservation about heading to Louisiana at the end of the month is how far she'll be from her family. College was one thing—Mapleton was close enough to bring her laundry home. Moving to NOLA will be her first time living outside of Indiana in her twenty-two years.

On the table, Phoebe's phone rings with a shrill melody. She got it out of her locker earlier to scroll TikTok during the half hour she waits for her next client to arrive. It's weird to have this long of a break between clients. Throughout college, she always scheduled an entire day of back-to-back sessions to make the thirty-minute drive from Mapleton worth it. Plus, it's the first week of January, when the gym is still full of people yet to give up on their resolutions. Phoebe typically shoots for 100 percent retention of New Year's clients, because it means she proved to them working out is *fun*, but she didn't take anyone new on this year. It wouldn't have made sense, since she'll be leaving for New Orleans in a few weeks.

"Why in God's name is your ringer on?" Teddy says with a grimace.

Phoebe hurls herself into the plastic chair beside her brother and looks at her phone. It's a Chicago number.

She didn't used to pick up numbers she didn't know. She didn't used to have her ringer on, either, given that she's not a boomer, but since New Orleans drafted her in December, there've been a lot of phone calls to set things up before the preseason starts next month. Granted, most of those numbers are from Louisiana, but just in case, she answers the call.

"Hello?"

"Hi, is this Phoebe Matthews?" The voice is accented—Phoebe doesn't know enough about the UK—Great Britain? the British Isles? whatever it's called—to place it exactly.

"Yup, that's me." Phoebe pins the phone against her ear with her shoulder so she can open the packet of M&Ms.

"Phoebe, hi. This is Amanda Greene with the US Women's National Team."

Phoebe's hands pause. Her heart slingshots around inside her rib cage. "What?"

"I wanted to congratulate you on being drafted last month," the person says. "You'll do well with New Orleans. But more specifically, I wanted to invite you to training camp with the national team in a couple of weeks."

"Shut the fuck up." Phoebe laughs, high-pitched and awkward. This has to be some kind of prank. She pulls at the edges of the bag of M&Ms again and says to her brother across the table, "Did you do this?"

"What?" both Teddy and the person on the phone say.

Phoebe swallows. "This is really Amanda Greene?"

Teddy's eyes go wide.

"It really is," the person on the phone says.

The bag in Phoebe's hands finally opens—but too enthusiastically, sending M&Ms skittering across the break room floor. Phoebe doesn't move to pick them up. She told the coach of the US Women's National Soccer Team to shut the fuck up.

"Oh my God, I'm so sorry for—I shouldn't have—I didn't mean that. When I said to shut up, it was just an expression. I'm—wait, are you really serious? You're inviting me to camp?"

"We are." The person—Amanda fucking Greene, apparently, coach of the national team—sounds like she's smiling. "I can't make any promises about the likelihood of getting called up again this year, but I'm looking forward to getting a look at you."

Phoebe grins. "I'm looking forward to earning another call up."

This might feel unreal, but Phoebe isn't lacking confidence in her talent.

Amanda chuckles. "Someone will be following up later this week to get you set up with everything you'll need to join us in Jacksonville. I'll see you soon."

"Thank you. I can't wait."

"You're fucking with me, right?" Teddy says as soon as Phoebe ends the call. "That wasn't Amanda Greene."

Phoebe gulps down a couple of breaths. "That was Amanda Greene."

"You're going to January camp?" If it were a text message, the comment would've been in all caps with twenty question marks at the end of it.

"I'm going to January camp."

Phoebe can't seem to do anything but parrot her brother's words in answer form.

Teddy leaps out of his chair, his hands tugging at Phoebe's to pull her up, too. She stumbles to her feet while her brother jumps up and down beside her.

"You got a call up! You got a call up!"

Teddy is shouting, but Phoebe's head is filled with the sound of blood rushing through her veins or static or the Lake Michigan waves at Indiana Dunes State Park. Her heart thumps against her sternum.

"Tell me everything she said. Verbatim."

Phoebe can't remember. "I didn't even think it was her. I thought it was a prank call, that you or Alice had put someone up to it."

"We're rude but we're not that rude."

She relays what she can remember of the conversation to her brother. It happened. It *just* happened, but it doesn't feel real. Like a dream that you thought made sense, but as you explain it to someone, the surreality unfurls.

Getting drafted into the American Women's Soccer Association was a dream come true in and of itself. Phoebe had sat in that hotel conference room in December, a week out from graduating college, wearing a tailored navy-blue suit that cost as much as the rest of her wardrobe combined. The expense was made worth it when the New Orleans Krewe picked her in the first round of the draft.

At the time, it was the best thing that had ever happened to her.

This is better.

The national team has multiple camps throughout the year. The best American players from all over the AWSA—and sometimes even farther (Becky Ewing plays in Europe)—come together for training and often games before going back to their club teams. Being called into camp is the first step toward making the national team roster. When you're on the roster, you not only get a chance to play for your country, but—more importantly to Phoebe—you get bonuses.

A lot of things are more important to Phoebe than "playing for her country," actually, but the national team is the route to all of them. Beyond the money, making the national team is about playing on the biggest stage. It's about being the best.

"You're on the fucking national team!"

"Okay, I mean, I'm not like—" Phoebe hedges. "There are no games during this camp. It's just training. And she specifically said she couldn't promise me anything about future call ups this year, which obviously makes sense because it's a World Cup year. It'd be wild to make the team right now. She's gotta have the lineup mostly figured out already, right? Or at least the options narrowed down?"

"Maybe she does, and you're one of the options."

Phoebe sucks in a breath at the thought. How is this her life?

"I have to get back to the front desk, but I'm so fucking proud of you, dude."

Teddy hasn't stopped grinning since Phoebe got off the phone. He throws his arms around her shoulders even though she's got five inches on him. They squeeze each other tight.

After pulling back, Phoebe looks at the floor and says, "So I have to clean up the M&Ms you jumped on top of?"

Teddy, obviously unrepentant, makes the face of the grimacing emoji. "Pretty please?"

"You suck so bad."

"Thanks, love you!" he says, flicking her off over his shoulder as he leaves.

Phoebe pulls her scrunchie out of her hair. She combs her fingers through the messy red waves and wrestles them back into another ponytail. The vacuum in this place only works half the time, so Phoebe starts by picking up the M&Ms that didn't get crushed in the celebration.

Twenty-three players make the roster for the World Cup. More than that are called into most training camps, to give Amanda and the rest of the coaching staff a chance to evaluate each player close-up. Of course, they're also evaluated by their club play.

Phoebe intentionally graduated early so that when—she always said *when*, rather than *if*, even though non-NCAA players rarely got drafted—*when* she was drafted, she could join her AWSA team in the spring. She planned that part of her career out. She'd never thought to add the national team as a goal.

Or, of course she had considered it—making the national team has been her goal since she was twelve years old, sitting too close to the forty-two-inch TV that only got four channels, stars in her eyes, while Grace Henderson subbed on for the national team for the first time. Her first career appearance—first cap, as it's called—came before she'd gotten her driver's license, according to the announcers. To this day, a poster of Grace Henderson hangs on the wall in Phoebe's bedroom at her parents' house.

But being Grace Henderson is not a realistic career goal. It never made sense for Phoebe to expect to make the national team right out of college. Not in a World Cup year. Instead, once she got drafted, her plan became about playing so well while the biggest stars of the league are away at the World Cup that she'd have a chance to make the Olympic roster next year. Sure, it'd be *amazing* to make the World Cup roster, but it isn't realistic. Even someone like her, who barely passed her stats class last semester, can recognize the probability of making that roster, having never been called up before, is minuscule. Better to plan for things that might actually happen. Things she can have a hand in making happen.

But now that she's gotten called into a training camp? This gives Phoebe some control. This gives her some power.

This gives her too big of a head and she's getting so far ahead of herself. She's not about to make the World Cup roster; she is vacuuming the break room—it's working for once—at Planet Fitness in Buttfuck Nowhere, Indiana, with five minutes until her next client arrives.

She puts the vacuum away, shoves the still half-full M&M bag into her locker, and tells herself not to get carried away. A single call up doesn't mean too much, except that she got noticed. The camp in two weeks is her time to make sure they keep noticing her.

Two

The practice field is silent when Grace arrives. The fences cast long shadows across the grass, still damp with dew. The team won't even be out here today. First day of camp means being indoors—weights and cardio equipment and the like. But Grace likes to start at the field. It helps her remember why she's here. She loves a soccer field.

That is what this is supposed to be about: doing what she loves. Of course outcomes matter. She wants to win. But at its core, playing with the national team is about just that: playing. It's supposed to be fun. Most of the time it is, but any year with a major tournament makes Grace tense. They've won three World Cups in a row. Anything less than winning is failing.

So Grace will make sure they win.

Even with the side trip to the pitch, she's the first to the locker room.

Other players arrive in groups. Grace focuses on organizing her locker so she doesn't have to say much more than hello. Returning for January camp is like the first day of school: chaotic and too loud. The AWSA season doesn't start for another month, and the last national team camp was in November. For those who arrived early enough last night, there'd been a team dinner, but otherwise, no one has seen each other since before the holidays.

"Hey, Captain," Kayla Sorrell, one of Grace's teammates on the Krewe, greets her.

"Not captain here," Grace says. She can handle being the captain of New Orleans, but captain of the US Women's National Team is too much. "I don't want that kind of responsibility."

A heavy hand claps on Grace's back. "Plus, my shoes are too big for you to fill, Baby Spice."

The national team's actual captain, Courtney Trout—better known as Fish—grins down at Grace. Her microbraids aren't pulled back into a ponytail yet.

"Big and old, that's Fish in a nutshell," Sorrell teases. "You know I had to look up the Spice Girls the first time I heard you call her that?"

"I refuse to believe that's true," Fish says. "I'm gonna make them play 'Wannabe' while we lift and you're both gonna sing along."

Grace shakes her head. Not that she doesn't know the song—it may have come out the year before she was born, but she doesn't live under a rock—she just will not be singing in front of anyone. Fish knows that. The whole team knows that. Except the two new players, who both got their first national team call ups after being drafted to the Krewe earlier this month.

Grace doesn't know anything more about the rookies than what she saw in the draft: their names, positions, and headshots. Forward Gabriella Rodriguez is changing on the other side of Sorrell. Grace glances around the locker room. The other new girl, Phoebe Matthews, is a midfielder with bright red hair that's hard to forget. But it's nowhere in the locker room.

• • • •

When Matthews does finally arrive, she makes a scene.

The rest of the team is already in the weight room. Amanda is halfway through her welcome speech when someone slams into the doors of the room from the outside.

"Shit!" The person grunts for a second before pulling, rather than pushing, and finally getting the doors opened. The other new girl. "Sorry! Sorry I'm late. I couldn't find—" Her mouth snaps shut. "Sorry," she says once more, quieter this time, almost demure.

Amanda nods. "Matthews."

"Hi," Matthews says, head down, shoulders up. She slinks farther into the weight room, coming to stand behind Sorrell on the side of the team.

Not being the captain means it's none of Grace's business if Matthews is late. She doesn't need to care. She doesn't care, really, except that she can't imagine being late on your first day with the senior team. If Grace remembers correctly, this is Matthews's first day with any national team. She hadn't been in the Olympic Development pipeline. She came from some nowhere school after growing up in some nowhere town. And she's still willing to throw away her shot by being late on the first day of camp.

Grace isn't impressed.

Matthews's freckles are evident from across the room. Her hair is even redder in person. It's still down, too, or had been when she arrived. By now, she's combing her fingers through the mess, which is thick and full of tangles. Grace wants to get her hands in it. After years of experience with her younger sister, she's been the designated hair braider on the team for almost as long as she's been on it. Grace can get Matthews's hair in order. Two french braids, starting on either side of that middle part and connecting to a ponytail. It's more practical than the squirrel's nest of a bun Matthews manages to secure with a lime-green scrunchie.

Amanda goes on explaining the plan for the day. Most of the players would rather be on the field, but the coaches make sure they ease into training. Elite athletes are too competitive for their own good.

Cardio machines—bikes, ellipticals, and treadmills—are mainly used for warm-ups and testing. You can't outcompete a heart rate monitor. Pulse ox, VO2, heart rate: Grace likes these numbers. She likes things you can measure. They aren't the be-all, end-all—a better lung capacity doesn't score goals—but they're concrete.

Grace has the unknown quality, too, the thing that makes her the one who other players turn to when they're tied in the eighty-fifth minute of a knockout game and no one wants to go to overtime. She has grit, perseverance, drive, whatever you want to call it. But she can't explain it. Fitness numbers, on the other hand, make sense.

Before cardio, Grace has her one-on-one with Ilse. The team's fitness expert has one-on-ones with every member of the team at the beginning of the year. They're an analysis, really, assessing each player's range of motion and flexibility through a variety of stretches, both static and dynamic. But Ilse always makes it seem like a conversation.

"Anything been bothering you lately?" she asks as Grace goes through the required movements.

"No," Grace says.

Nothing more than usual, anyway. She's had a twinge in her hip for months, but Ilse doesn't need to know that. Grace has seen too many aging players sidelined by the smallest of failures of their body. That's what getting older is: your body falling apart. At least it seems that way.

"You're not working too hard?" Ilse asks.

"We're not even in season, Ilse."

They aren't even in *pre*season; the Krewe doesn't have players report until the end of the month.

"Like that has ever stopped you."

It isn't bad to stay fit in the off-season. Grace has spent the last ten years taking the best care of her body that she can. The right food, exercise regimen, sleep schedule. It's paid her back in spades, but she's always known there'd come a point when she wouldn't be able to bounce back like she used to. She was a teenager when she'd started on this team; of course her body has changed.

Ilse mostly stops lecturing Grace. Their conversation is more about catching up than catching Grace in her lie. For the last movement, Ilse directs Grace to an open area in the middle of the gym, about ten yards long. Butt kicks one way, high knees the other. Grace steels herself. High knees bother her hip. It isn't too bad, but it isn't comfortable.

"I promise I'm being good, Lil Il," Grace says midway through the high knees, employing the nickname she knows will distract the trainer.

Ilse rolls her eyes. "You might not be working yourself to death, but you're gonna be the death of me. Get outta here. Phoebe, you're up."

Grace moves on to the stationary bike. She might as well have stayed for Matthews's assessment—the redhead talks loudly enough that Grace can hear the whole conversation.

"Nope. No pain. I had Osgood-Schlatter's in my right knee as a kid and it still sometimes aches when it rains, but not, like, every time it rains. And even then it's not bad or limiting, just a little achy, I just wanted to make sure you knew."

She wants to make sure Ilse knows a lot of things, apparently, like how she has a younger brother named Teddy and an older sister named Alice and no pets right now but she's more of a dog person than a cat person, though she loves both. Grace tries not to listen. She didn't know it was possible for someone to talk more than Fish.

Grace has never liked the constant proximity of national team camps. It's one thing to be on top of one another in training, but then there are team meals and assigned roommates. At least with the Krewe she can go home at the end of the day and sit alone on her screened-in porch.

Of course, there are benefits to camp. Not being captain is one. Getting to see her teammates' baby after dinner is another. Half the team crowds into H and Madeeha Wilson's room when their nanny brings Khadijah by once the day is over.

Grace met the little peanut last fall when the Krewe played Philadelphia. Khadijah was still bald then, but her hair has since come in, black fuzz now covering her head. Grace tries to be patient while her teammates who have yet to meet Khadijah coo over her, but eventually she decides they've had enough time and scoops the baby out of H's arms.

She retreats to the corner with Khadijah while the rest of the group rehashes their day. Babies are the perfect conversation partners: cute as hell and not too talkative.

"What did you think about the newbies?" H asks.

Grace further tunes out. She doesn't gossip about her teammates. She makes faces at Khadijah instead, scrunches up her nose, waggles her eyebrows, gives the girl an open-mouthed smile.

Grace's eyes are crossed and her tongue out when she hears, "How about Grace's protégé?"

She looks away from Khadijah. "What?"

"What do you think about your new fangirl?" Kelsey asks, smirking.

There are only two brand-new players, and Grace has spoken to neither. She should've, probably; they're both rookies on her club team, too. But she doesn't want the responsibility of being their captain yet, so she's avoided them.

"Oh my God, do you not know?" Kelsey laughs. "I'll pull up the video. You have to see this."

"Gimme that baby," Fish says. She takes Khadijah off Grace's hands. "No screens before she's two."

"Seriously, look at this," Kelsey says, thumbs flying over her phone screen.

Amber and Kelsey crowd on either side of Grace, close enough that the end of Kelsey's high blond ponytail tickles Grace's shoulder. Grace tries not to prickle while they wait through an ad on the video. She never knows how much Kelsey is pretending. Kelsey acts like she didn't break Grace's trust, or at least like it isn't a big deal that she did. Grace doesn't know if it's acting, really, or if what happened between them mattered so little to Kelsey she really did forget about it. Meanwhile, it still gets under Grace's skin every time Kelsey sidles up beside her. She used to do it because she liked being close to Grace; at least that was what she'd let her think.

It doesn't matter. This isn't about Kelsey. It's about Matthews, apparently, who is on Kelsey's phone once the ad ends, an AWSA press screen behind her. She's breathless, her cheeks as bright red as her hair. Grace would think she just played a game if she wasn't wearing a navy-blue suit that fits her perfectly. Her face splits into a wide grin.

"Are we sure this isn't some fever dream?" she says on the screen.

The person holding the microphone laughs, and Matthews's grin grows.

"Is it possible I'm still fourteen and having the best dream of my life? Getting drafted to Grace Henderson's team? Not only do I get to play soccer—not only is someone going to *pay me* to play soccer, but I get to play with my *idol*? It absolutely does not seem real. How could I have gotten this lucky?"

Grace can feel Kelsey looking at her, glancing between the screen and her face, checking for her reaction. The reporter in the video asks what it feels like to be one of only a few non-NCAA players ever drafted.

"There's one more thing she says at the end," Kelsey says over Matthews's answer. She skips ahead to the end of the video.

"When I was a kid, all I wanted to be was Grace Henderson," Matthews is saying. "God, I'm going to embarrass the hell out of myself the first time I meet her. And quite possibly every time after that."

The reporter congratulates her again, and the video ends.

"Somebody's got a crush," Amber singsongs.

Grace tries not to grimace. How is she supposed to react?

"Who doesn't have a crush on Grace?" Madeeha says.

"Look at that face," H says. She catches Grace by the chin. "How could you not have a crush on that face?"

Grace shrugs H off and uses the movement as an excuse to get away from Kelsey and Amber.

Fish doesn't look away from Khadijah to say, "She's not called Baby Spice for nothing."

"She's not called Baby Spice at all," Grace grumbles.

"All right, I thought she was smiling at me but she's definitely pooping," Fish says. "This baby is no longer mine."

Madeeha takes her child back, and the conversation turns to diapers.

Grace will have to buy Khadijah another book for getting her out of that. There's still a smirk on Kelsey's face, though, like she's waiting for the chance to say more about the Matthews video. While Madeeha and H jokingly bicker over whose turn it is to change the baby, Grace slips out of the room without saying anything.

So Matthews is a fangirl. Great.

It'll be annoying, but not a big deal. It might help, actually, at least on the Krewe when Grace will be her captain. The ones who look at Grace with stars in their eyes are usually the easiest to lead. Very Grace says *jump* and they say *how high?*

· · · ·

That's what Grace thinks of the next morning, the entire team save one on the pitch.

Training hasn't *officially* started when Matthews barrels up the sideline in slides, her cleats dangling from one hand, but in Grace's opinion, if you're not early, you're late.

"I'm here!" Matthews shouts.

Grace sighs. She can't imagine being late in the first place, much less announcing it as she arrives.

No one else seems to care. Matthews didn't get lectured for being late yesterday, and she doesn't get so much as a side-eye this morning.

Coaches are gentler on young players than they used to be. It's a good thing, for a lot of reasons, including that it means Grace doesn't have to be. Matthews has enough people being nice to her. Grace can be the hard-ass.

"Matthews," Grace says without looking at her. "With me."

*Ooh*s go through camp. Amanda turns away, but not before Grace sees her smile.

Either ignoring the ominous *ooh*s or oblivious to them, Matthews bounds to Grace's side, beaming. "I'm Phoebe. Matthews. You know that already, obviously. Hi. Nice to meet you."

She offers her hand. Grace doesn't take it.

"Training starts at nine. That means you're dressed and ready at nine."

Matthews's smile dampens. "Right. Yeah. I'm not super great at time management. I have a couple of different alarms, but now that I know how long it takes to get to the field, I can set one with a different noise for when I have to leave my room, and that way—"

"I don't need your morning routine," Grace says. "Just need you here on time."

"Yes, ma'am," Matthews says. She tilts her head like she's considering something. "Not ma'am. You're, like, barely four years older than me, I don't think I should be calling you ma'am."

Fish snorts to Grace's left. Grace ignores her. She ignores Matthews, too, who still has to change her shoes while the rest of the team starts warm-ups.

They begin with dynamic stretches halfway across the width of the field and back. Grace puts on her game face. Even in training, she isn't willing to show weakness, and she never knows when her hip might send a shock of pain through her. Better to look angry and unapproachable than to let the pain show.

Sorrell, who is used to Grace's game face, has no problem approaching her as they wait for their turn to lunge across the field.

"Thought you weren't captain here," she says.

Grace shrugs. She'll be Matthews's captain on the Krewe, might as well act like it here, too. She has a feeling Matthews is going to need a firm hand.

Three

Grace Henderson gave her advice.

Okay, granted, yes, it was maybe a little condescending, grow-up-and-be-on-time type advice, but still. Phoebe *needs* to grow up and be on time anyway. And Grace noticed her. And spoke to her. And is even hotter in person than on the TV, but that isn't the point.

As they do leg swings, Gabby Rodriguez, who Phoebe made friends with yesterday, catches her eye.

"Are you still freaking out?" Gabby asks out of the corner of her mouth. "I'm still kinda freaking out."

"I'm . . . not really freaking out," Phoebe says.

"What?!"

She was nervous for the AWSA draft. She was nervous arriving at the camp, getting her roommate, meeting the team. She was nervous in the weight room yesterday. She isn't nervous on the field.

Phoebe knows what to do on the field. She's always known what to do on a soccer field.

"How are you not freaking out?" Gabby asks.

Phoebe shrugs. "We're actually playing today. And I really love soccer."

"Okay but we're still playing with like . . . all of these people."

Gabby isn't wrong. A part of Phoebe wants to leave training so she can call Teddy and tell him all about it. But she *doesn't* want to leave training, obviously, especially not when she's training with *Grace Henderson*. And Courtney Trout and Madeeha and Sarah Wilson, for that matter. These are players she grew up watching, and she's here, on the field with them.

Gabby is the only person on the field who didn't intimidate Phoebe from the start. Not only is it her first time in camp, but she got drafted by New Orleans, too. She'll report to the Krewe's preseason with Phoebe next month. Thank God she's nice.

There are other players who are nice, too, obviously. Sorrell is also on New Orleans, and Gabby has already made friends with her. And Michi—the newest call up other than Gabby and Phoebe—was super friendly when they were lifting yesterday. Phoebe talked to her a lot. Maybe too much. She talks too much for most people, but she needed a distraction so she could stop eyeing the veterans like a starry-eyed little kid.

After warm-ups, goalies separate off for their own training, while all the position players stay together.

"Okay, two lines facing each other. One here, one over there," Amanda says, gesturing toward the other side of the field. "We're tackling."

Grace steps up to start the first line. Phoebe sprints to be at the front of the second line. Her first actual soccer drill with the national team, and she's going to go up against Grace Henderson. Too excited to stay still, she bounces in her cleats while Amanda explains what they'll be doing. It's simple: the player from one line begins with the ball, and the player from the other line tries to get it.

Phoebe forgets about the extra energy in her limbs once they start the drill. This is how it always goes—soccer makes Phoebe's mind go quiet. Her brain normally boomerangs around at top speed. She's always had terrible focus, easily bored and distracted by anything that moves and most things that don't, too, to be honest. But on the pitch? In a game or a scrimmage or even a drill, there's nothing else. Phoebe's focus narrows to what is right in front of her.

Today that's Grace Henderson, dribbling toward her.

It doesn't matter that it's her first national team camp or that she's about to take on her childhood hero. Phoebe's brain is quiet and her body knows what to do.

She slides at the perfect time, one foot connecting with the ball almost delicately, just enough to change its momentum without sending it flying. Then she's back on her feet, the ball in front of her, and she races toward the line of players Grace came from.

Kelsey comes at her.

When Phoebe was growing up, more often than not, she had a soccer ball at her feet. Other kids had fidget spinners for their extra energy—Phoebe had her soccer ball. She zipped it in her backpack every morning before sprinting to make the bus. After school, she'd dribble it the entire mile-and-a-half walk home. She had a few teachers who would let her keep it beneath her desk during class, as long as it didn't get away from her. Phoebe got really good at not letting it get away from her.

Just as Kelsey is about to go for the tackle, Phoebe jukes and crosses her up, slipping past with the ball while Kelsey tries to stay upright.

The next player Phoebe faces is Fish, and Phoebe might have good footwork, but this is Courtney Trout, AWSA Defender of the Year four out of the last five years. Phoebe doesn't even mind how easily she loses the ball. She jogs back to the sideline, grinning wide.

"That was great," Phoebe says as she takes her place behind Grace in line.

"Getting the ball from Grace or getting wrecked by Fish?" Madeeha asks.

"Both."

Grace peers over her shoulder and Phoebe beams at her. When she looks away, Phoebe redirects her smile to Madeeha.

"I know this is going to make me sound like the new kid, but I am, so"—she shrugs—"oh well. I truly can't believe this is a job? Like people are paying us to play a game? It's pretty great."

"It is," Madeeha agrees. "And it's good to have new kids around to remind us every once in a while."

Now that they've started, it feels like a normal practice. Phoebe *loves* soccer. How could practice be anything but fun? She'd rather play an actual game, sure, but anything that gets her feet on a ball makes her smile. So does winning every defensive tackle she makes the entire first drill.

She grins most of the day, really. They cycle through exercises with different focuses: passing, agility, explosive speed. They scrimmage, seven-on-seven. After lunch, Amanda announces they'll be doing a team-building drill.

"Trust falls?" Phoebe suggests, tipping herself backward.

Madeeha isn't ready for it, but she manages to catch Phoebe anyway, her hands under Phoebe's armpits.

"This might be a little too much new kid energy," Madeeha says, but she laughs as she pushes Phoebe back to her feet.

The drill ends up just being two truths and a lie, which is a lot less fun than trust falls, even if it is cool to learn that Jess did 4-H as a kid, Becky has never been on a roller coaster, and Madeeha and Sarah were secretly married for six months before their official wedding. She also learns that more often than not Sarah is referred to as H, as in "Sarah with an H." Sara Dowling, on the other hand, is called Pants, and Phoebe has yet to figure out why.

After everyone has their turn, Ilse blows her whistle.

"Hate to break it to you, ladies," she says. "But it's beep test time."

The entire team groans as one. Except Phoebe.

"Don't tell me you have so much new kid energy you like the beep test," H says.

Phoebe glances around. "So, like, I've heard of the beep test. But I've never done it. I actually don't really know what it is."

"Oh my God." Kelsey laughs. "That it is the *newest* new kid energy."

Phoebe sinks into herself. Kelsey is laughing. It's a joke. She's teasing. Phoebe understands bonding through teasing—her family does it all the time. But for some reason her stomach dropped to her feet at Kelsey's comment. Obviously, Phoebe missed a lot by not taking the same route to the national team as the rest of the players, but she has never felt out of place until right now.

Before Phoebe can be too embarrassed, Grace appears at her side.

"It's a way to measure aerobic capacity," Grace says. "We run back and forth between two lines twenty yards apart. A beep starts the test, and you have to make it to the other line before the next beep. The first time you don't make it, you get cautioned. The second time, you're out. Every minute, the beeps get closer together. So the longer it goes on, the harder it is."

It's more words than Phoebe has ever heard Grace say at once, including in postgame interviews. Phoebe could comment on it, but she isn't going to look a gift horse in the mouth.

"Sounds fun," she says instead.

"Girl, are you crazy?" Becky asks. "How does it possibly sound fun?"

"What's not to like? I love running and being better than everyone."

Becky laughs and Phoebe grins, no longer feeling like a fish out of water.

"Better than everyone, huh?" Becky says.

"What do you wanna bet I last longer than you do?"

Becky shakes her head. "I'm not taking a bet from someone who thinks the beep test sounds fun. And anyway, Grace is the one who's gonna be your competition. She's won this thing three years running."

"Is that right?" Phoebe says, turning her smirk on Grace. "What do you say we make this interesting?"

"No."

Apparently Grace is back to her usual taciturn self.

"That makes sense." Phoebe nods, all faux understanding. "I probably wouldn't take a bet I know I'd lose."

"I'm not going to lose, and I'm not betting."

Her staunch refusal only eggs Phoebe on.

"C'mon, Henderson," she needles. "If you're so sure you're gonna win, there's no harm in making a bet, right? It'll be win-win for you, then."

This morning, Phoebe was ready to call home about being on the same field as Grace Henderson, and here she is badgering her into taking a bet.

"Good luck getting Grace to have fun," Amber says. "She's been too serious for years."

She giggles like she's made a joke. The only other player who joins in is Kelsey.

"Fine, let's make a bet," Grace says, stopping to tie her shoe.

She had been leading the way toward the goal line, where Ilse and other staff have set up cones twenty yards apart. The rest of the team seems to slow as they part around her, like they're trying to wait and see what happens without it being obvious they're invested.

"If I win, you don't talk outside of drills for the entire day," Grace says.

"Okay, ouch!" Phoebe laughs loudly. It's easier to pretend to be in on the joke than to admit you're the punch line. "So what—if I win, *you* don't talk outside of drills for the entire day? That doesn't seem much different than right now."

Grace scowls. "No. It doesn't have to be reciprocal. You can pick whatever you want."

Kelsey replies before Phoebe even begins to think of something. "How about a kiss?"

The rest of the team fully stops now. Grace is still down on one knee, tying the lace of the shoe on her other foot. Phoebe can't help the grin that takes over her face.

"That's not something I usually have to bet for."

No one laughs. And like, it wasn't *that* funny—it was more true than funny, really—but it was better than Amber saying Grace never had fun, and Kelsey laughed at that. Phoebe looks around. Everyone's eyes are on Grace, who is focused on her shoelaces.

"I think we can come up with something better than that," Phoebe says. She's never gonna make anyone kiss her who doesn't want to, even if she's not encountered many people who don't in her life.

"No." Grace double knots her laces. "It's fine."

Phoebe offers Grace a hand to pull her to her feet. It's not supposed to be a move—it's instinctual, to Phoebe, when a teammate is on the ground to help them up—but when Grace takes it and stands, they end up face-to-face, close enough Phoebe realizes Grace's brown eyes have flecks of gold in them. Grace steps back, ducking her head and glancing at their teammates, who Phoebe forgot still surround them.

Grace's hands go to the hem of her tank top, her tan fingers dark against the lighter strip of skin that was revealed when the shirt rode up. She tugs it down.

"It doesn't matter anyway," she says. "I'm going to win."

"Here's the thing," Phoebe says, and Grace absolutely looks at her mouth. She looks at her mouth and then immediately away, before making eye contact once more. Phoebe smirks. "You're not gonna win."

Grace rolls her eyes. "The only way you're going to beat me is if I die, so have fun kissing my corpse."

She takes off at a jog toward the cones at the end of the field.

"Oh my God," Kelsey guffaws. "You have to win now. That would be so funny."

"I'm not gonna make her kiss me," Phoebe says.

She's not. By the way Grace looked at her mouth, Phoebe's not going to have to *make* her do anything. But also: if Grace *does* pay up on the bet, Phoebe's gonna leave it up to her whether anyone else knows that.

It's not like Phoebe didn't expect to be distracted by the thought of kissing Grace Henderson—she's daydreamed about kissing Grace Henderson for almost half her life by this point—but it didn't seem like something that could actually happen. It's still not, she reminds herself, unless she wins the beep test.

The team has mostly caught up with Grace by this point, and Phoebe's glad, because she wants her to hear this.

"I'm gonna win the beep test because I can, not to make Grace kiss me," she says.

Doing well in camp is more important than kissing pretty girls.

Well, both are important—soccer and kissing girls are Phoebe's two favorite things—but she's not focused on girls right now. She's focused on making this roster.

And anyway, Grace will never kiss Phoebe if she doesn't take camp seriously. Phoebe doesn't even know Grace that well yet, but she knows that.

• • • •

The beginning of the beep test, it doesn't seem so bad.

Phoebe can talk, and she does, telling some of the cringiest jokes she knows. *Why wasn't Cinderella good at soccer? Because she ran away from the ball.* At one point she tells Grace her shoes are untied, just to mess with her. It doesn't even get Grace to look down.

As the beeps get closer together, though, Phoebe stops talking. She needs her breath. Other players start getting cautioned, then dropping out. She tries not to pay attention. Your best performance is just that: yours. It doesn't matter how the people around you do.

Well, it does matter how *one* person around her does. She has to beat Grace. She can't make a bet like that and then *lose.*

Phoebe has a song in her head. It's a trick her mom taught her when she was a kid. She has a few go-to songs that she knows most of the lyrics to, and if she's doing a drill or taking a test or doing anything stressful, really, she can always take a moment, hum along to the song, and feel better. She doesn't have the breath to hum, but she goes over the lyrics in her mind. She focuses on them instead of the way her muscles burn.

She tries to, anyway. As time goes on, the burning gets harder to ignore.

Normally, Phoebe loves her body. Not in an *I'm hot* way—though yes, that way, too—but for what it can do. She loves dancing with her feet on the ball. She loves taking set pieces, curling a corner into the box. She loves running, normally. The thwack of her soles against the pavement, or the swish of her cleats through the grass. She loves a sprint, going balls to the wall on a breakaway or speeding back to help the defense.

She hates it all right now.

Everything burns. Her lungs, her legs, even her feet are cramping. The only thing she wants to do more than stop running is win this damn bet.

"That's a caution, Grace," Ilse says.

Phoebe just turns around and keeps running. It doesn't matter if Grace got a caution.

But it does.

Because three beeps later, a whistle sounds. Grace hasn't crossed the line.

"Someone finally dethrones Grace," Amanda announces. "Wait, Matthews, where are you going?"

Phoebe barely hears. There's a trash can by the benches, and when Phoebe reaches it, she finally, finally, *finally* stops running. The only reason she's still standing is so she can vomit. Making it in the trash can is embarrassing enough, she'll die before she throws up on the field in front of everyone.

Once everything she's eaten today comes back up, she collapses on the sideline.

The sky is a wide expanse of blue. Phoebe hears another whistle. She'll rejoin the team eventually, she just needs a minute. She'll celebrate her win, too, when her brain has enough oxygen to think about it.

Eventually Yoni, one of the equipment managers, appears in her view.

"Are you . . . alive?" Yoni asks.

Phoebe tries to shrug but her body seems to be done moving. "Not clear," she manages to say.

"But you're not having, like, a medical event, right?"

"M'fine."

"Clearly." To someone she can't see, he calls, "She says she's fine."

Ilse comes to stand next to Yoni, both of them looking down at Phoebe, who is still spread-eagle in the grass.

"Up, Matthews," Ilse says. "Come do cooldown."

"I'm up," Phoebe says, though it takes her a moment to actually push herself into a seated position. "I'm up," she repeats as she gets to her feet.

When she rejoins them, her teammates make sure she's okay before congratulating her. Fish claps a hand on her back so hard Phoebe momentarily loses her breath again.

Kelsey doesn't even say good job, just puts an almost singsong teasing lilt in her voice when she says, "So Phoebe wins the bet."

Grace either doesn't hear or does a really good job pretending she doesn't.

"Yeah, somehow I think vomiting probably voids a bet when it's for a kiss," Phoebe says.

Kelsey looks like she's going to protest, but Becky speaks up first.

"You still think the beep test is fun? Even with the vomiting?"

"Hey, I won, didn't I?" Phoebe says.

Madeeha shakes her head. "Definitely too much new kid energy."

"You're the weirdest person I've ever met," Becky says.

Phoebe grins. "I get that a lot."

The entire cooldown, Grace doesn't look at her once.

Four

Grace doesn't go see baby Khadijah after dinner that evening. She doesn't join Sorrell and the other Krewe newbie, Rodriguez, who are watching *Bend It Like Beckham,* or her roommate, Jess, and some others, who are checking out the pool. She doesn't do anything but hole up in her hotel room, sitting cross-legged on top of the blankets, computer open in front of her.

She needs to know more about Phoebe Matthews.

Not that Grace normally would have joined the other activities, anyway. Every camp, she spends more time alone than anyone else. She's happier doing a crossword in the corner of the bus than getting into any team shenanigans. If there are ever an odd number of people needing hotel rooms, Grace is the one who doesn't have a roommate. It isn't that she doesn't like her teammates—she does. She just appreciates her space and she appreciates the quiet.

She tries not to feel guilty about it. After a game, the team does recovery. There are ice baths and foam rollers and rest. Grace has to do the same thing after being around people. Mental recovery, rather than physical. She needs to recharge.

Tonight, it's about more than recharging.

She searches for "Phoebe Matthews AWSA draft." There's the video.

It's less weird to watch alone, without everyone's eyes on her reaction. Rewatching it, Matthews doesn't seem so much like a fangirl. She looks good. Charming, even. She answers the reporters' questions and makes them laugh. She is *likable*.

Grace wants to be annoyed. She *should* be annoyed, the way Matthews never stops talking, the amount of space she fills up. Even when they're on the pitch, her presence is huge—you can hear her laughing from across the field.

That's another thing about her: she laughs all the time. She's constantly joking and having fun. Like the trust fall thing—what *was* that? Where does her mind come up with these things? Grace wants to be mad, and she would be, normally. Normally if someone is clowning around, it means they aren't paying attention, aren't working hard enough. But Matthews worked hard today. Harder than Grace expected, given her penchant for tardiness. She got the ball from Grace's feet more successfully than anyone has in years. And she spent half of training laughing.

Grace doesn't understand this girl at all.

The next video autoplays. It's highlights from a game. Matthews is hard to miss, that red ponytail flying behind her as she streaks down the field and sends the ball toward the goal. Faster still, she chases down a forward on a breakaway and executes a perfect slide tackle.

There are a surprising number of videos for this girl, most of them from her college, which is some tiny school Grace has never heard of. Someone there must have really liked her. The school even put together a playlist. "Phenomenal Phoebe" has fifteen videos of Matthews.

It makes sense, Grace supposes, as she clicks on the next video. Matthews needed to be seen somehow to get drafted. Givhan and the rest of the coaches probably did exactly what Grace is doing now, watched the whole playlist of Phoebe Matthews videos. Sometimes they are game highlights, but there are also videos separated by skill: set pieces, slide tackles, even headers, which makes sense given how damn tall Matthews is. She's good, too. Really good.

At the end of the playlist, Grace clicks one of the suggested videos:

"Fancam of Phoebe Matthews's dimples." Shot after shot. Videos and still pictures, both. Matthews grins, dimples bracketing her smile, even when the ball is in play. She looks like she's having the time of her life.

Grace loves soccer. She's always loved soccer. She can't remember the last time she smiled like that.

The door to the room opens, and Grace jumps. She squints against the lights when they turn on. Jess comes around the corner and pauses.

"You're just sitting here in the dark?"

"I . . . ," Grace starts. "I didn't realize how dark it had gotten."

"What are you doing?"

"Watching some stuff on YouTube." She shifts her laptop to ensure Jess won't see the screen. "You?"

"The pool was fun, but I gotta condition my hair and get the chlorine smell off me," Jess says, wrinkling her nose.

She grabs pajamas from her suitcase and disappears into the bathroom.

Grace looks back at her computer. Matthews is still smiling on the screen.

Phoebe Matthews is incredibly attractive. It's not the first time Grace has noticed, just the first time she's admitting it to herself. She noticed from the moment Matthews shoved through the weight room doors yesterday—tall enough it seemed like she had to duck through the doorway, though Grace knew intellectually that she hadn't.

But Grace hadn't let herself notice, because this isn't high school. Not that Grace finished high school. She got her GED while playing for Lyon, already focused on her career. What matters is how hard she works, how good she is, not who she's attracted to.

Grace may not talk about her sexuality, but she isn't closeted. Her teammates know, or at least they could guess. She may not have dated since Kelsey—if what happened with Kelsey even counts as dating in the first place—but some of these women have known her since she was fifteen. Not publicly talking about her identity doesn't make it a secret. Her sexuality has nothing to do with her career. Sure, sometimes Grace looks at Madeeha and H and thinks about how they're normalizing teammates being married with a kid. Sometimes Grace thinks about

Briana Scurry, the first openly gay player on the USWNT. Sometimes Grace wonders what she could be doing, what she could mean to quiet gay girls across the country.

But being a public figure is hard enough. A celebrity. A role model. She gives so much of herself to her fans, and gives all of herself to her teams. Her identity is hers alone.

So of course Kelsey suggested a kiss. Of course she did something that was at best thoughtless and at worst intentionally antagonistic. Of course Grace couldn't back down.

The bet was stupid, but Grace absolutely would have collected had she won. The idea of Matthews having to work so hard to stay quiet, just because Grace said so—it sends a little thrill up her spine even now. And if she would've collected, she should pay up. That's how bets work. She can't just renege because she doesn't like that she lost.

Matthews tried to let her off the hook by claiming throwing up voids a bet. It was nice, but Grace doesn't want to be indebted to her. Grace is an adult. She pays her debts. She doesn't need to be protected from a stupid kiss that isn't going to mean anything anyway.

Matthews is in room 321 with Pants. She'd announced it when inviting Rodriguez over after the team dinner yesterday. Not that Grace was paying attention, her voice just carries.

The room is down the hall. Grace could retrace her steps to the elevators, go right instead of left, and get this whole thing over with.

Before she can further overthink it, Grace closes her browser, then her laptop, and climbs out of bed. The water in the bathroom is already running, and she'll be back before Jess is out of the shower. No one needs to know she's doing this, but she couldn't live with herself if she didn't. She's a woman of her word.

The hallway carpet is thin and quiet beneath her socked feet. It takes fewer than thirty seconds to reach room 321. Grace takes a breath, lifts her hand, and knocks three times.

Phoebe's long red hair has left big wet spots where it touches her charcoal-gray sweatshirt. She wears blue plaid pajama bottoms and no shoes. The pink polish on her toenails has mostly chipped off.

Her eyebrows raise as she takes in Grace, then the corners of her mouth do the same, and she's grinning that stupid grin Grace saw in all those videos, swimming-hole dimples and a gleam in her eyes.

"Hendy." She calls Grace a nickname only veterans use for her. "To what do I owe the pleasure?"

Grace thinks of the YouTube playlist. Phenomenal Phoebe. "Phenom."

It's supposed to be a demeaning nickname. The way Matthews's smile goes even brighter indicates she does not take it as such.

The TV plays quietly in the room behind Matthews. Grace can't tell if Pants is there or not. Either way, she isn't going to invite herself into Matthews's room. Yet standing at the door feels too exposed. Grace tilts her head toward the VENDING/ICE sign that sticks out a few doors down. Matthews keeps looking at her. Grace raises her eyebrows and gestures with her arm instead. Matthews looks down the hall but her feet stay rooted to the floor. With a huff, Grace leads the way to the alcove where the ice and vending machines are, not bothering to see if Matthews is following. Of course she is.

The alcove provides privacy, but Grace doesn't feel any safer with Matthews still smirking down at her. The rookie has at least six inches on Grace. Her self-satisfied grin is maddening. Even more infuriating— it's sexy. Grace rubs the pad of her index finger against her thumb and tries to remember why she came here. This is business. Something to get taken care of.

"You won the bet," Grace says.

"I did."

That's all she says. Of course the one time Grace wishes she would lead the conversation, Matthews says nothing.

"I pay my debts," Grace says.

"And that's what this is? A debt?"

"We made a bet. You won. I owe you what I owe you. I know you said throwing up voids it, but it doesn't. As long as you brushed your teeth."

Matthews laughs softly. "I brushed my teeth," she says. "But are you sure you don't just want to kiss me? You don't have to use a bet as an excuse."

What Grace wants is to be in her own room, under the top sheet, a book of crosswords in front of her. She wants to be in an ice bath, refusing to think about how cold it is. She wants to be on her screened-in porch in New Orleans, in the chaise where no one can see her from the street. She wants to be anywhere but looking up at the smirk on Phoebe Matthews's face.

It's possible Grace actually wants to kiss her.

Her bottom lip is plump, even when her mouth is stretched wide with a smile. Matthews leans backward against the vending machine. It probably should be more awkward than sexy, but the sight makes Grace's breath catch anyway. Phoebe's face is a mask of freckles. Too many to count. She even has them on her lips. Grace can't stop looking at her mouth.

The ice machine hums to life and Grace jumps. Matthews lets out a chuckle that is deep and warm and sends tingles along Grace's nerve endings.

"Let's just get this over with."

"Whenever you're ready." Matthews's voice is a low murmur.

Grace scowls. "I'm ready."

She steps closer but then doesn't do anything.

She doesn't know why she's being so ridiculous about this. It's just a kiss. It's not like it'll be the first time she's kissed a teammate, and it can't go as poorly as the last time. She doesn't want to be thinking of Kelsey right now. This only has to be a peck, nothing more. But now she's been standing close to Matthews for so long the air is humid between them.

Matthews doesn't look at all concerned with the delay. Instead, she waits, those absurdly long legs crossed at the ankle. The smile has even disappeared from her face. She is the picture of patience.

Grace really needs to get this over with.

She takes one more step into Matthews, ready to finally close the distance between them.

"It doesn't have to be on the mouth," Matthews says.

One corner of her lips turns up in a lopsided smirk. She looks inordinately pleased. So proud of herself, to have thrown Grace off her game. That's it. Grace is going to put this rookie in her place.

"Oh, it doesn't have to be on the mouth?" Grace says. "Okay."

She leans closer still and brings her lips to the pulse point under Matthews's jaw. The skin is so soft there. Matthews lifts her chin and arches her neck, her hands coming to rest on Grace's hips. Grace sucks more than she kisses. It isn't strong enough to leave a hickey, though she's tempted, just to make Matthews try to explain it at training tomorrow. She draws Matthews's skin into her mouth and bites it, gently but not too gently. Matthews groans. She pulls Grace closer.

Before their hips can touch, Grace steps backward. Matthews makes a noise of protest, but Grace is already out of reach. Matthews's eyes open, glassy, her pupils blown wide.

Grace cocks an eyebrow at her like a challenge, then spins on her heel and heads back to her hotel room.

In the empty hallway, where no one can see her, she presses the back of her hand to her mouth.

Fuck. What did she just do?

Five

Being an AWSA rookie might not pay much, but at least it comes with housing. And while the rest of the team reports at the end of January, the Krewe's front office arranges for Phoebe to move in a week early. The building is new, but cheap. Generic. The apartment itself has low-pile brown carpet everywhere except the bathroom, which is outfitted with a wobbly toilet and a tiny shower stall. It'll take a lot to make this place feel like a home. The twinkle lights that hung on the walls of Phoebe's dorm are buried in one of her suitcases. They'll be the first step, but that will come later.

For now, Phoebe drops her suitcases—clothes in the bedroom, non-clothes in the living room—and logs into the Wi-Fi that came with the place. A tab is already open, mapping the route to the stadium.

Phoebe's body has yet to recover from the twenty-hour bus trip from Indiana to New Orleans. A fifteen-minute walk will stretch everything out. Who cares that it's dark and everything will be locked? There's an email from Stuart, the facilities manager, in Phoebe's inbox, telling her where to meet him tomorrow to get her first tour of the place, but Phoebe wants to see it *now*. A bus trip and an empty apartment doesn't feel real enough. She wants to see the stadium she'll be playing in.

Phoebe digs through her clothes suitcase for a new pair of black joggers and the first top she finds, an orange Mapleton hoodie. Once dressed, she stands frozen between her living room and bedroom for a moment. New Orleans in January isn't warm, but it sure isn't anything like Indiana in January. There's a puffed vest on the top of her suitcase, the last thing she put in before sitting on it to get the zipper closed, but even that is probably unnecessary, right? *Fuck it,* she decides, and leaves in what she has on, locking her apartment door behind her.

Her headphones ran out of juice on the bus ride, but she wouldn't have them in even if they hadn't. It feels meaningful, or something, to listen to the sounds of her new city. She really moved, more than a half day away from her family, to a city where she knows no one. Well, not quite no one, obviously. There's Grace and Sorrell and Gabby, but Gabby isn't coming to New Orleans until team training starts next week, and Phoebe hadn't gotten either of the other two's phone numbers.

She has a feeling Grace won't want to hear from her anyway.

They haven't really talked since their kiss—or not-kiss, as it turned out. Because the bet was for a kiss, but that wasn't what Grace did. Phoebe tried to be a little bitch, smirking and telling her it didn't have to be on the mouth, and Grace turned it back around on her. She didn't kiss Phoebe's neck; she bit it, sucked the skin into her mouth, let her tongue brush against it. She drove Phoebe crazy and it didn't take more than ten seconds. Phoebe hasn't stopped thinking about Grace's mouth since.

Well, of course she has, because her brain tends to jump from topic to topic, but the spirit of the phrase is true. She thought about Grace more than she thought about anything else, including her move, which is why her family will have to bring her favorite sneakers when they come to visit for the first game of the season.

Phoebe reined herself in during the rest of camp. She'd wanted to chase Grace down the hotel hallway. She'd wanted to smirk at her at practice the next morning, act like she was interested but not, like, affected or anything by Grace's mouth on her skin. She'd wanted to spend the rest of camp seducing Grace. But she didn't.

Phoebe is stupid and horny, but she isn't *that* stupid and horny. She couldn't spend her first camp with the national team trying to get into Grace Henderson's pants. It was too important, too consequential. She had to prove her worth.

And she had, she's pretty sure. She worked hard, not just on the soccer side of things but on the personal side. She made people laugh. She made them like her, made them remember her. She did everything she could so when Amanda is thinking about who to call in for the sHeroes tournament at the end of next month, she'll think of Phoebe.

It will be different, with New Orleans. Not that she doesn't want her teammates here to like her, too, but she is—well, not guaranteed a spot, obviously. But they drafted her. First round. They want her here. She is here to learn and grow. She'll still make people laugh and prove her worth, like always, but the ground beneath her feels firmer here. Feels like she has a firmer grasp on . . . something. Her dreams. What she's doing here.

Phoebe could spend a lot of time trying to figure out what's going to happen next.

The World Cup starts in six months. Is there room for her on the national team right now? Is Amanda even still considering new players for the roster, or does she have the pool of players she'll pick from figured out already? What if someone gets hurt? If Phoebe does well with New Orleans, will Amanda take notice? What, if any, roles need to be filled with the national team? How can Phoebe prove she can fill them?

She doesn't know any of the answers. And it isn't a matter of puzzling until she figures them out—she *can't* know the answers. What she can do: play well. The only thing she can control is her performance, her behavior, her attitude. So, she'll play out of her cleats and be hilarious and charming, like usual, and not overthink it.

Even from three blocks away and with only half of them on, the stadium lights are blinding white. Phoebe bounces as she walks, her strides lengthening. This is her park. She's gonna play here. The stadium seems to tower over the buildings around it, though Phoebe knows it isn't even close to the biggest in the AWSA. That honor goes to San Francisco, which averages more than ten thousand fans a game. Phoebe can't wrap her head around the idea of regularly playing in front of ten thousand people. At Mapleton, their crowd size was rarely in the triple digits.

As she waits for the walk sign across the street from the Krewe stadium, she looks up. They call it the Swamp. Even the five-thousand-fan crowd New Orleans averages sounds huge to Phoebe. This is where they'll be, behind these walls, fans decked out in purple and yellow, wearing scarves they definitely don't need in Louisiana—Phoebe has never understood why team scarves became a thing. It probably started in England, where they love soccer—*football*—and the weather is cold as fuck.

Phoebe drags her hand along the brick exterior of the stadium. Of her home stadium.

The main gate is a wrought iron fence topped with fleurs-de-lis. The field beckons her—the part she can see, anyway, a slice of green between seating sections rising on either side. As she gazes out, thinking about her cleats in that grass, about the stains it will leave on her jersey—oh God, she's going to get a *jersey* with her name on the back and everything—a figure runs across her line of vision. A familiar figure. Phoebe recognizes that run. What the hell is Grace Henderson doing here at—Phoebe checks her phone—nine o'clock at night?

Grace crosses the field again, upright with her head down, running the same way she seems to do everything—serious and focused. This girl is ridiculous.

Phoebe looks up at the points of those fleurs-de-lis. The fence isn't even that high. If they really want to keep people out, they should try harder. Without another thought, she takes a three-step start and hoists herself over the fence.

"Fuck."

Of course the part of her that gets scratched by the top of the fence is her boob. Now safely inside the stadium, she rubs at her chest. She'd like to keep her nipples, thank you very much.

It isn't until she's already hopped the fence that she wonders about security cameras. But whatever. It isn't like the team is gonna have her arrested, even if breaking into the stadium is probably not the best first impression. Honestly, they probably don't have anyone actually *watching* the security cameras. They might check them if someone vandalizes the place, but a team that doesn't have the money to pay all its players a living wage probably isn't employing twenty-four-hour security.

To Phoebe's left are concessions. The silver roll-up door is closed. To the right is the team store, fully dark. That she'll check out tomorrow—they gave her a shirt when they drafted her, but she wants a snapback with the crest on it.

She cared enough about seeing the stadium to come directly after getting off a twenty-hour bus ride, but now that she's here, the stadium itself doesn't matter as much as the person on the pitch.

Her focus on Grace breaks when Phoebe makes it through the tunnel to the edge of the field. It feels like a theater, two levels of seats rising on all sides, orchestra and balcony. The lights rise even higher. They're not all on but still, the field is bright, lit up like a stage. Sponsor ads line the front of the second level. It isn't silent—the city makes too much noise around them—but it feels quiet, Phoebe unable to pick out any sound but the blood rushing in her ears.

She turns in a slow circle, taking it all in.

The sight of Grace, who has yet to notice her and is still running what appear to be suicides, jostles Phoebe out of her reverie.

This girl.

Maybe Phoebe shouldn't be calling a woman four years older than her "this girl," but . . . this girl.

"Hey!" Phoebe calls.

Grace keeps running.

"Hey!"

Still no reaction.

Why not be obnoxious? Phoebe waves her arms over her head like her top half is doing jumping jacks. The next time Grace turns around at the eighteen, she stumbles back instead of continuing to run. Caught sight of Phoebe, then. Grace's hand comes up to her ear and removes an AirPod.

"Phoebe?"

It's the first time Grace has ever called her by her first name.

"What are you doing here?"

"Asking you that exact question." Phoebe comes farther out, onto the actual field, stepping in bounds from the end line, no flag up to mark the corner during the off-season. "Why the fuck are you running suicides at night?"

Grace doesn't answer the question. "How'd you get in? I thought Stuart was showing you around tomorrow."

Phoebe grins. "Oh, so you've been talking about me, huh?"

"What—no, I—Stuart told me. I didn't ask."

"No, yeah, you're right. I was technically just coming to see the place." Saying it out loud, Phoebe remembers her original purpose and looks up at the stadium around them. This will be her view. "But then I saw you, and I had to jump the fence to tell you how ridiculous you are."

She wants to kiss the scowl right off Grace's face.

"Do you only train after sunset like some kind of vampire?"

Grace rolls her eyes. "You've seen me in sun before."

Phoebe remembers. The shine of Grace's hair, always in some kind of elaborate braid. The tan of her skin, which Phoebe swears deepened with every day of sunshine at camp. Her smile, which seems brighter than the sun itself, even if Grace doesn't show it often.

Grace's hair is simpler this time, parted in the middle, a french braid going down each side. Does it count as pulling on pigtails if her hair is in braids? That's what Phoebe wants to do, or the grown-up equivalent, anyway. Maybe the *too* grown-up equivalent, as a vision of clenching those braids in each hand while grinding against Grace's face pops into her head. Phoebe can't help it—Grace is too sexy in her spandex leggings and cropped black tank top. Her hips cutting a V like an arrow pointing to where Phoebe wants to go. Phoebe looks at the seats of the stadium instead.

"I didn't mean to interrupt your workout," she says. "Even if it is ridiculous you're working out at night."

"It's not a problem, Phenom." Grace ignores Phoebe's teasing. "I was finishing up, anyway. I can walk you out."

"How chivalrous of you."

"I can't let one of my players get arrested for jumping the fence."

"One of *your* players?" Phoebe laughs. "You the owner now? The coach?"

"I'm the captain," Grace says flatly. "Anything dumb you do reflects back on me."

"Oof, you're in trouble, then, 'cause I do a lot of dumb shit."

"I've noticed."

God, Grace is fun to bother. She takes herself way too seriously, as evidenced by this whole "my players" thing, even if Phoebe doesn't really mind being called Grace's in any capacity.

This is the first time they've been alone together since Phoebe collected on the bet—since Grace *made* Phoebe collect on the bet. For the rest of camp, Grace avoided her, and Phoebe let her. She also caught Grace looking at her mouth on more than one occasion. The thought bolsters Phoebe, even as Grace acts like this is no big deal, like being alone with Phoebe is normal and natural and doesn't throw her off her game in the least. She leads Phoebe to the other side of the field, where she toes out of her cleats, casual as you please, and slides into sandals on the sidelines.

"So you just come here whenever you want?" Phoebe asks. "Do we all have unlimited access to the stadium or is that a Grace Henderson special?"

"Keycards stop working after ten," Grace says. "I'm sure Stuart will tell you all about it tomorrow when he gives you the full tour."

"Oh, is that not what you're doing?"

"My stuff's in the locker room, but that's as much as I'm showing you."

The thought makes Phoebe's heart race. The locker room. *Her* locker room. Her own locker, where a jersey with her name on it will hang every game day. She takes small steps to walk with Grace up the locker room tunnel, through one set of doors, and then they're there.

The lockers are purple, and not so much lockers as—closets, sort of? Each easily two feet wide—there will be no trying to shove your winter coat in just right so it fits and you can close the door—which wouldn't happen anyway given that you don't need the kind of winter coats Phoebe's used to in New Orleans. There aren't even doors on any of the lockers, just open cubbies.

"I think this is the longest I've ever been around you without you talking."

Phoebe blinks. Right, Grace is there, too.

Should she be embarrassed—to be so in awe of a room that's probably boring to Grace? Grace has been in fancy soccer locker rooms since she was a teenager. The only locker room Phoebe is used to—besides the one at Planet Fitness—is her college's, and that was just the general gym locker room. Two rows of lockers everywhere, no way to get to the pitch for the game without winding through the gym hallways, passing the weight room and all the coaches' offices. Phoebe kept the same locker all four years. Learning a new combination each year was hard enough; she hadn't wanted to have to learn a new locker number, too.

Grace gathers her things from the only locker with stuff in it. Though some of the empty lockers manage more personality than Grace's—they don't have any belongings in them, but they're decorated, at least. Phoebe's eyes catch on a Philadelphia Eagles pennant in one and she knows it must be Sorrell's. Besides the pennant, there are various pictures of the midfielder and other people—some players, some with the same skinny nose who Phoebe assumes are family. When Grace takes her coat off the hook in her locker, Phoebe sees that she does at least have some pictures up. Phoebe can't make out what they are, but she wants to know. What's important enough to Grace to tape to the back of her locker?

"Ready?" Grace asks, like Phoebe is doing anything other than taking this place in.

"Sure."

Grace leads the way out of the building. Phoebe doesn't bother looking around too much. She'll have plenty of time tomorrow.

Out on the sidewalk, Grace asks, "Where'd you park?"

"Oh, I don't have a car," Phoebe says. "The apartments they put us up in are walkable."

"Right."

Grace glances toward a parking garage where Phoebe assumes her car is. There's a moment where Phoebe thinks maybe Grace is going to offer her a ride, but right as Phoebe gets her hopes up, it passes.

"I'll, uh, see you later."

"I'll be here tomorrow at nine, but you probably already know that from Stuart." Grace rolls her eyes and Phoebe grins. "Maybe I'll see you?"

"I don't know my schedule for tomorrow yet," Grace says.

Phoebe doesn't know Grace that well yet, but she's pretty sure that isn't true. This girl seems like the type to have shit planned. She doesn't call her out on it.

"See ya when I see ya then."

"Right," Grace says again. "Bye."

Phoebe watches her head toward the parking garage. Her oversize jacket hangs well past her butt, or it'd be a lot more fun to watch her leave. While Phoebe wasn't stupid and horny enough to spend her first call up to the national team trying to sleep with Grace, she is exactly stupid and horny enough to spend her first AWSA preseason doing it.

They have a week until the rest of the team shows up. Phoebe has seduced people in a lot less.

She hopes Grace will show tomorrow. She can't get enough of her. That smooth skin and those angry eyes—or not angry, exactly, but alert. Wary. That's what Grace Henderson is: wary. Phoebe loves winning people over. That's why she enjoys being around Grace so much.

Phoebe likes to succeed, but it's always more fun with a challenge.

Six

The sun is high in the sky by the time Grace makes it to the stadium. It's still technically morning, if only by a few minutes. It makes sense for Grace to have gotten a late start—she doesn't normally work out at night. She can't very well wake up for her normal morning workout when she worked out the night before.

Her timing has nothing to do with Matthews.

When she walks into the locker room, Grace freezes for a half second. Kelsey's locker has a bag hanging in it, slides haphazardly discarded in front of it. Grace takes a breath, coming back to herself. Kelsey is with Phoenix now. Grace is just confused since it's the first time in months that her own locker isn't the only one not empty.

Matthews must have gotten Kelsey's old locker, and she's obviously still at the stadium. So even if Grace was trying to avoid her, it looks like it wouldn't work, unless she wants to turn around and head to the ice bath room for a while. Matthews probably won't find her there.

Not that Grace needs to avoid her. They're adults. Matthews doesn't necessarily always act like one, but she is. They can be professional. If they can't, Grace has bigger problems than seeing her in the locker room. They're teammates. They *need* to be professional.

Grace keeps her New Orleans teammates at more of a distance than those on the national team. She has to lead the Krewe. She needs their respect and their trust more than their friendship. She can't have favorites. She certainly can't sleep with any of them.

She didn't have these rules before Kelsey. But she was young and stupid then. Plus, she and Kelsey didn't even actually sleep together, and that still blew up in her face.

Grace wonders, not for the first time, if her response to Kelsey's betrayal—if calling it a betrayal in the first place—is an overreaction.

The door to the field bursts open, a beaming Matthews striding in.

"Hendy!" Matthews greets her. "You're out in the daylight!"

Grace has dealt with people like Matthews before. People who think they're funny. Who like to push buttons. She never yields an inch.

"Phenom."

Matthews grins wider. "We gotta get our timing figured out."

It's so strange to see her approach Kelsey's locker as her own, it takes Grace a moment to process her words.

"Excuse me?"

"We keep catching each other at the end of workouts," Matthews says. "It'd be much more fun to be workout buddies. Tomorrow I was thinking I'd run Lafitte Greenway—is that how you say it? La-feet? I know you pronounce stuff weird down here. Like Bur-GUN-dee Street."

Matthews pulls off her shirt as she talks. Grace is pretty sure it isn't even a move—she isn't undressing to flirt; she's just casually comfortable with her body—which, to be fair, who wouldn't be, when they look like that? Matthews's stomach is ridged with a perfect six-pack. Her skin glistens, and Grace's tongue wants to follow the arrow made from the muscles above Matthews's hips. She chews the inside of her bottom lip instead.

"Anyway," Matthews says and Grace realizes she never responded. "Yeah. I'll be running Lafitte Greenway at nine tomorrow, if you wanted to come? Starting from the south side."

Grace has no interest in a workout buddy. The only reason Stuart even told her that Matthews would be arriving today—it isn't because she *cares,* she wasn't *talking about* Matthews—was to warn her, since she usually has the facilities fully to herself until the rest of the team arrives.

"We'll see," Grace says, because it feels too rude to admit she isn't interested.

"Awesome!"

Matthews tugs the hair tie out of her ponytail and shakes out that mane. Grace can't quite figure out this girl's hair—it's somewhere between curly and straight and wavy and a tangled mess.

"Well, I gotta shower," Matthews says. "Have a good workout! Maybe I'll see you tomorrow!"

Grace walks to the field and doesn't think at all about Matthews in the showers.

For all the ways Matthews is annoying, at least she hasn't brought up the bet. She never said a thing about it, actually, after Grace practically gave her a hickey and then fled. Grace thought for sure Matthews would bring it up the next day, tease her and needle her and just be a general pain. It seems to be her MO. Grace planned to avoid her as long as possible, but of course when Amanda told them to partner up for a one-touch passing drill, Matthews appeared beside her. Grace steeled herself for whatever the rookie had to say, but then Matthews said nothing. She focused, and worked, and when she smiled at Grace, it didn't seem to be anything more or less than friendly.

That's how it went for the rest of camp. Grace was grateful but confused. She couldn't make sense of Phoebe Matthews.

She couldn't stop thinking about her, either.

While Matthews is apparently unaffected by whatever happened between them, Grace can't get the other woman out of her head. Matthews *was* affected, Grace knows, because the memory played back in her own brain on repeat for days afterward. Matthews might be over it by now, but she was affected at the time.

Grace is still affected.

That's why she was at the stadium last night. Yes, New Orleans is hot and evening workouts make sense, but that wasn't what drove her there. She was thinking of Matthews. She was annoyed as hell at her stupid, traitorous brain, which loves to fixate on that moment beside the hotel vending machine. The way Matthew's skin tasted, her intake of breath, her step forward, trying to get closer, to get more. For a moment, running suicides last night, turning around and seeing Matthews waving her arms on the side of the field—Grace wondered if she'd thought her into existence. Like Matthews popped out of her thoughts and into the stadium.

It's just hormones. Grace hasn't slept with anyone since before getting involved with Kelsey—it's been almost four years of solo orgasms. Grace doesn't have a problem with that, but apparently her body does. She's accustomed to telling her body what to do. She works out through pain, sprints back on defense while her lungs beg for a break, ignores the way her hip twinges when she changes direction. She is in control. For her entire life, she's maintained her performance through regimen and discipline.

Then Phoebe Matthews shows up and her body rebels.

Grace needs to remind it who's in charge.

That's why she decides to meet Matthews for a run the next day. It'll be good cardio, and Grace can wrestle control back from her libido. Like exposure therapy. She's simply unaccustomed to being hit on—by gorgeous women, anyway. There's always some overconfident white man after a game, getting an autograph and offering his number. Grace usually pretends she can't hear him.

Grace will spend more time with Matthews to show her body there's nothing to obsess over. She has to get used to the girl—they'll be seeing each other every day in training next week. Grace needs to be more in control by then. She's the captain. She has responsibilities. Daydreaming about one of her teammates is a distraction. It's embarrassing. She's better than that.

• • • •

Matthews didn't give a specific location to meet her. Somewhere on the south side of Lafitte Greenway. She didn't give Grace her number. Nine o'clock.

It's 9:15, and Matthews is nowhere to be seen. Grace shifts on her feet, trying for some dynamic stretching while standing in place. She shouldn't have come. She definitely shouldn't have waited this long. What if Matthews was fucking with her when she extended the invitation?

Grace would do the run by herself, but Matthews might've started early without her. Passing the other woman on the green is too embarrassing to risk. Instead, Grace will head to the stadium, get her workout in there, like usual. As she turns toward her car, a storm of red hair appears in front of her.

"You came!" Matthews crows.

Grace almost stumbles at the size of her smile. And then again at the highlighter-yellow fanny pack she's wearing.

"You're late." Matthews's smile dims, and Grace keeps talking before she can stop herself. "Do you not have six different alarms like you did at camp?"

That wide, dimpled grin is immediately back. "I thought you didn't need my morning routine, just needed me on time?"

Perhaps it means something that they both remember such a trivial interaction enough to quote it. Or it means nothing, but Grace's libido is looking for something to latch on to.

"You're lucky you're here now, Phenom. I was about to leave."

"Thanks for waiting." Matthews looks down, smoothing her hair into a low ponytail. "I really am sorry I'm late. I'm trying to work on that."

"It's fine," Grace says. She doesn't need to know what Matthews is working on. Why her voice went soft and sincere. "You ready?"

"Sure!"

Grace gestures for Matthews to lead, and the redhead takes off. She's starting much too fast—Grace had fifteen minutes of bouncing on her feet, warming up, but Matthews didn't. And yet the rookie starts at a clip. Grace intentionally hangs behind, making Matthews slow to match her pace. Grace isn't gonna let this girl pull something the week before preseason begins.

"I didn't think you were gonna show," Matthews says.

Grace doesn't mention that she thought Matthews was going to be the no-show, was going to stand her up even though she'd been the one who extended the invitation. Does it count as being stood up if the plans were never confirmed?

"I needed the cardio."

"Yeah, same," Matthews says. "I'm ready to get back into the season. I definitely wasn't in good enough shape with the national team. I wish I'd been called in for November camp, right at the end of the college season. I was way more fit then."

"You still won the beep test."

Grace wants to slap herself. Just yesterday, she'd thought how nice it was that Matthews hadn't mentioned the bet, and here she is, bringing up the beep test.

"I remember," Matthews says.

Grace refuses to look and see if she's smirking. She speeds up instead. It wasn't a long enough warm-up, but she doesn't care anymore. Matthews stays in step beside her.

"I probably should've asked before I invited you, but do you like to run in the city? Or, like, does your workout get interrupted when you get recognized?"

"Please," Grace says. "No one cares about me enough for me to get recognized."

It isn't altogether true—she does get recognized sometimes. But it happens more often around the national team than New Orleans. It's an instinctive response, to deny celebrity. Grace knows she's famous among a certain crowd. Matthews had obviously known who she was. She's one of the most recognizable faces in women's soccer by this point, but given the size of the WoSo community in the US, that isn't necessarily saying that much.

"Bullshit." Matthews calls her on the minimization. "I'll buy your breakfast if you're not recognized this morning."

"What?"

"I bet you get recognized. Loser buys breakfast."

Grace doesn't want to make another bet with Matthews. She doesn't want to *not* make it and draw attention to their last bet. She doesn't want to go to breakfast with Matthews, even though she knows she'll be starving after the run. She doesn't even want to be on the run. What is she supposed to be proving to herself again?

"Fine," she huffs. "Have fun buying my breakfast."

"We'll see." Grace doesn't have to look at Matthews to hear the smile in her voice.

Grace tends to downplay her fame, not because she's humble so much as because she doesn't want it. She wants to be the best in the game, yes, but she doesn't want to be the most known. She likes her privacy. She likes quiet.

Matthews, it seems, has never heard of the concept.

"One of the reasons I wanted to run here instead of laps at the field or whatever—I really wanna see the city," she says. "Obviously I'm not gonna have a ton of time, but I want to explore. Do you have a favorite place? Or thing to do?" She doesn't wait for an answer. "I don't just wanna do the tourist stuff like Bourbon Street or whatever. But I've never lived outside of Indiana before. It's really different here. And cool. And like, thanks for running with me, because I don't know anyone else here. I mean, I know the team will be here next week, and I'm starting my second job later today, so like, I'm not worried about making friends, really. It's just nice to not be completely alone in a new place."

That's too sincere for Grace to engage with.

"You've been here two days and you've already got a second job?"

"Yeah. It's a twenty-four-hour diner, so I can schedule shifts around training. I waitressed a bit in college. It's not great money, but it's something. Especially if you get good tips."

Grace can imagine Matthews gets good tips.

"But, yeah, they had a sign in the window about needing a server, and when I went in to ask about applying, someone quit right in front of me. So I was like, 'Can I finish their shift?' and they basically hired me on the spot. It's over on—shit, I already forgot what the street was called. I'll look it up after our run and let you know. See if you've been there before. It's probably not classy enough for you, kind of a dive-type diner. You probably eat at fancier places, right? Like, what's your favorite restaurant in New Orleans?"

When Grace doesn't reply quickly, she feels Matthews's eyes on her. "Or just, like, one of your favorites? If you can't pick a single favorite."

"Oh, you actually want me to answer?" Grace says. "Earlier you asked a question but then kept talking, so I wasn't sure."

"Sorry." Matthews lets out an uncomfortable chuckle and ducks her head. "I know I talk a lot."

"It's fine," Grace says. She doesn't know how Matthews can have an arrogant smirk one minute and seem like a wounded puppy the next. Guilt turns her stomach. "I was kidding. We can go to one of my favorite restaurants after the run, if you want."

Immediately, Matthews is grinning again. "That'd be awesome."

Grace keeps the pace fast enough after that, Matthews mostly stops talking.

• • • •

Later, though, once they've cooled down and are standing in line at Pagoda Café, which has the best breakfast tacos in the city, Matthews is back to talking way too much. She asks questions about the menu— which isn't big enough to need questions asked about it—and marvels over the outdoor-only seating and how *This place literally couldn't exist for half the year in Indiana.* Grace doesn't have to reply for the most part. Matthews can keep up a conversation all by herself.

"Excuse me," someone other than Matthews says.

Grace glances at them, ready to step out of the way. The line is out the door, as usual, and she figures they need to get by.

But the stranger isn't asking her to move. The stranger is a young white girl, maybe thirteen years old, holding a tiny spiral notebook and a pen, looking at Grace like she's a goddess.

"Could I have your autograph?" the girl says. "Please. Sorry. I meant to say please."

Matthews lets out a hoot. "I *told* you." To the girl, she says, "Thank you. You just got me free breakfast."

"Ignore her," Grace tells the girl, who hasn't taken her eyes off Grace to begin with. "What's your name?"

"Rowan."

Grace learns Rowan plays forward and her favorite thing about soccer is either scoring goals or her friends on her team. She's been trying to convince her parents to buy season tickets for the Krewe but she plays travel soccer in the summer and they don't have their schedule yet, so they might miss too many games for season tickets to be worth the money.

Grace signs a piece of notebook paper for her. *Rowan. Keep scoring goals and making friends.*

"If your parents are okay with it, what do you say I leave four tickets at will call for you for the home opener? That way you can bring a friend, too."

Rowan's eyes somehow get even wider. "Really?"

It takes a minute to get it all figured out—Rowan's parents finally coaxing her away when it's their turn to order.

Matthews gets a bacon taco and a sausage roll *and* one of every flavor of cookie, but Grace doesn't complain, just pays. They sit at one of the seafoam picnic tables to wait for their order.

"That was some of the cutest shit I've ever seen," Matthews says.

She was unusually quiet during the whole thing. Grace knew it was too good to last.

"I was surprised you didn't jump in to tell her you played, too," Grace says. "You seem to love being the center of attention."

Matthews's grin is cocky. "I'll have her attention when she comes to the game and sees how good I am."

Grace isn't sure if Matthews is trying to be annoyingly conceited, but she actually appreciates the confidence. Making the move from college to professional soccer can be tough—more fans, harder competition, more pressure. Grace skipped college herself, but she's seen plenty of rookies whose lack of confidence ended up being a self-fulfilling prophecy.

"Seriously, though," Matthews says, "that was cool. Do you always give people tickets? Do we all get tickets to give away?"

"There's a friends and family section, but I usually buy tickets and leave them at will call if they're for people I don't actually know."

A worker calls Grace's name from the order pickup window, and Matthews scrambles to her feet without saying anything and goes to grab their food.

"You paid," she says when she returns, sliding Grace's taco in front of her. "I figured I could at least carry the food."

"I paid because I lost a bet. You didn't owe me anything."

Matthews rolls her eyes. "Oh my God, dude, I know I talk too much, but you are impossible at small talk."

Grace sighs. She isn't usually so awful at small talk—she doesn't like it, but she can do it. Matthews sets her on edge, though. Trust isn't easy for Grace, especially with someone she barely knows. Her body would like her to trust Matthews, but her brain knows better.

At least Matthews doesn't seem to hold a grudge.

"Oh my God, these are amazing," she says through a mouthful of taco. "See, this is why I asked you. You gotta find a local rather than just googling shit. You're always gonna find the best stuff that way."

"I'm not a local," Grace says, though she's been here long enough to almost think of herself as one. "I'm a transplant."

"Right," Matthews says. "You're from New York, right?"

Grace is used to it—people knowing random facts about her because they watched some documentary or behind the scenes of the USWNT or something. She usually lets it go, but she doesn't want Matthews to think she knows her.

"Born there, but my mom and I moved to California when I was eleven so I could work with the best Olympic Development team."

"Wow, I can't imagine. What was that like?"

It was hard. Her parents sacrificed so much for her, living apart for six years. Her dad raising her younger sister alone. They never made Grace feel like it was hard, but she knew. Other kids' parents didn't move across the country so they could play a game.

To Matthews, though, Grace simply shrugs. "It was what it was," she says. "It had to be done for me to get where I am today."

"Did you always know you wanted to play soccer?" Matthews asks. "Like, what would you do if you couldn't play soccer?"

"I don't know."

Grace doesn't like to think about the question. Soccer is what she does. She loves it. She's great at it. She has to be. It has to be worth splitting her family up for so long.

"I don't, either," Matthews says. "Like, sure, I'm waitressing, and I've worked as a personal trainer, but my parents always wanted me to have, like, a 'real job,' whatever that means. But I can't imagine having to sit in an office all day. I have too much energy."

She's halfway through her taco by now. Grace picks up her own to take the first bite. She thought she'd gotten out of small talk when Matthews scolded her about it earlier, but apparently not. As they eat, Matthews continues to pepper her with questions. Grace isn't rude enough not to answer, but she keeps her responses short. Matthews is never deterred.

Once Grace finishes her taco, she decides to address the situation head-on.

"You know you're not going to get more playing time by being my buddy, or whatever, right?"

Matthews squints at her. "What?"

"You wanted a 'workout buddy.'" Grace uses finger quotes around the term. "You always wanted to partner with me at camp. You're asking me all these questions. But I'm not going to talk you up to Eric or Amanda or anything. There's nothing to be gained here, Phenom."

"You mean, except, like, friendship and camaraderie?"

Grace rolls her eyes.

"Seriously, Grace—asking all these questions? This is called getting to know you. It's a normal thing people do."

It's a thing Kelsey had done. Gotten Grace to talk about herself, to open up. Acted like she'd cared.

"And at camp? Your obsession with me there?"

Matthews throws back her head and cackles, which is not the response Grace expected.

"You're good at soccer, Henderson," Matthews says. "Better than me. I want to get better. That's why I partnered with Madeeha for the settling drill, because she has great technique. But you're one of the best midfielders in the world. I wanted to learn from you."

Of course it comes down to soccer. That's always why people are interested in Grace. And why wouldn't it be? It's the only thing she's good at. It's her whole life. That's why she didn't know what to say when Matthews asked what she'd be doing if not playing.

"Also, like, yeah, you're hot," Matthews says with sheepish dimples. "That might've played a role, too, I admit it."

Grace feels the tops of her ears go red. She hopes she still looks flushed from their run.

"But I invited you for this run because I like you," Phoebe continues, "and you're also the only person in town who I know. Even if you've decided I'm obsessed with you or whatever and never want to talk to me again, this was so worth it." She gestures with the taco toward the café. "Like I said, asking a local—sorry, transplant—is way better than Google. I'm not obsessed with you—I just want to know the secrets of this place. I've never lived outside of Indiana. I need some tips. With training and the diner, I'm not gonna have time to explore like I'd like. Going on a run and stopping at an amazing restaurant afterward is probably my best chance to see the city."

Grace hasn't made a new friend in a while. Did she forget how? She thought her concerns made sense, but Matthews laughed at her. It was a nice laugh, loud and unselfconscious, but it was *at* Grace, even if it doesn't seem like Matthews meant it meanly.

Perhaps Grace can try not to take everything Matthews says in the worst way possible.

"If it makes you feel better, I asked other people stuff, too," Matthews continues. "Like Stuart told me I had to get—what's it called? King cake? From Randazzo's. It's not Mardi Gras for like a month, but I guess it's a Mardi Gras thing?"

"First of all, in New Orleans, Mardi Gras starts January sixth," Grace says. "Secondly, never listen to Stuart. Randazzo's has way too much icing. Dong Phuong has the best king cake in the city."

Matthews grins, those dimples sparkling. Grace's stomach flips. She should've gotten another taco.

"See? This is why I'm asking you stuff. How was I supposed to know Randazzo's has too much icing? Should I also not trust his recommendation of Café du Monde?"

Grace shakes her head. "There's something to be said for the du Monde experience, but Morning Call is the better choice for beignets."

"I should be taking notes."

Friends, Grace thinks. Or if nothing else, exposure therapy. The more she is around Matthews, the less the other woman will affect her.

"We'll go tomorrow," Grace says.

"Tomorrow?"

"Weights in the morning and beignets after. It's not exactly the best post-workout meal, but we're still technically in the off-season. It'll be fine."

"Geez, you wanna work out again tomorrow? Why are you so obsessed with me?"

This girl.

"Do you want me to show you the city or not?"

"I do, I do! I'll be good," Matthews promises.

Grace doubts that.

Seven

Phoebe rushes into the stadium the next morning fifteen minutes after Grace told her to arrive. The locker room is empty. Grace probably started without her. Phoebe's footsteps on the linoleum echo down the hallway as she makes her way to the weight room, already formulating an apology for her lateness. But every machine is empty.

She heads back to the locker room, then peeks her head out the door toward the field. A wave of humidity hits her in the face even though it's the end of January. The pitch is empty, too.

Phoebe slumps onto the bench in front of her locker. Grace probably got annoyed and left. It's what Phoebe deserves—how hard is it to be on time? For normal people, anyway, not hard at all. Phoebe had five alarms this morning—to wake up, to get out of bed, to finish breakfast and get dressed already, to get out of the apartment, and no, seriously, you really have to leave right now to be on time—and still, she was late. Of course Grace didn't want to wait around for her.

As Phoebe considers punishing herself with suicides in the humidity, she's startled by a voice.

"Morning."

It's Grace, dressed to work out, sunglasses still on and messenger bag slung over her shoulder. Phoebe stares blankly at her as Grace hangs the bag in her locker and sets her sunglasses on the top shelf.

"You ready?" Grace asks, turning to her.

"You're late?"

Phoebe cringes as soon as the words are out of her mouth. People love to point out her tardiness to her, and it's never helpful. She always feels guilty enough.

Grace, though, smirks in response. "I'm early, actually. I told you a half hour earlier than I planned to start so we'd make it at roughly the same time."

Phoebe has been chronically late as long as she can remember. Even when she intentionally gives herself more time—waking up early or whatever—she still somehow finds a way to be late. She'll get caught up watching TikTok or there'll be traffic or she'll take longer to get ready than she expects. She's tried to use the same trick Grace did—tell herself events start before they actually do—but that never works; her brain knows the truth.

Punishments never work, either. Detention, push-ups, extra chores—nothing has ever been enough to overcome Phoebe's poor time management. She's never had anyone understand and work with her instead of just resigning themselves to the fact that she won't be on time. She can't help the smile that takes over her face.

"Only our second workout together and you're already figuring out how I tick," she says. "Are you always this observant or do you just like paying attention to me?"

"Keep telling yourself that, Phenom."

She doesn't have to tell herself. Grace is showing her.

Grace tries to come off so prickly—like, that nickname is probably supposed to be rude and patronizing, but how could *Grace Henderson* giving her a nickname be anything but amazing? And Grace *is* paying attention. She cares enough to figure this out.

The weight room still kind of blows Phoebe's mind. She lifted her first workout, that first day after Stuart gave her the tour, but she hasn't gotten used to this place. The walls are purple, with LAISSEZ LES BONS TEMPS ROULER! in yellow along one wall, the Krewe's shield on another.

She's been working out in shitty school gyms and Planet Fitness and friends' basements her whole life. It's still surreal to be in such a well-equipped weight room. There are machines she's never used in her life—she doesn't even know what some of them are for.

"Do you have a particular circuit you want to do?" Phoebe asks. "I don't want to mess with your routine."

Grace takes a moment before responding. "Yeah. I like to start with hips and work my way around."

Today's leg day, apparently.

One of the downsides of being a lesbian athlete is other women are always doing hot things around you.

Okay, maybe it isn't a downside, but it sure makes focusing difficult. The sweat beading on Grace's brow. The perfect sculpt of her arms. The way she taps her foot to the beat of music she's somehow connected to the room's speakers.

Phoebe follows Grace's lead. She even tries to stay mostly quiet. Grace literally thought she was—what? ingratiating herself to her or something yesterday, when she was just asking questions.

But Phoebe only lasts so long before speaking up again.

"I've been thinking," she says between sets of calf dips. "What counts as being obsessed with you?"

Grace sighs. "Look, I'm sorry. Sometimes younger players sort of see me as some kind of celebrity. Grew up idolizing me, had posters of me on their wall as kids—that sort of thing."

"Oh no, yeah, if that's the criteria, I'm definitely obsessed with you. Your poster is still on my wall, actually, in my room at my parents' house."

"What?" Grace wrinkles her nose, and even from a machine away, it makes Phoebe want to kiss it.

"Oh yeah, you were absolutely one of those formative celebrities, you know? Like, I didn't know if I wanted to kiss you or be you."

Grace stares at her, slack-jawed.

"Both, it turned out," Phoebe says with a wink.

Phoebe has always had a lot of game. Not in the soccer sense—or not *just* in the soccer sense—but in the flirting sense. It's one of her favorite hobbies. It's fun to figure out how to flirt with different people. Phoebe can woo someone with compliments or by laughing at their jokes or even by pretending to be a damsel in distress. The way she flirts with Grace is her favorite, though: annoying but charming. Irresistible.

She lets Grace digest the thought of Phoebe growing up with a crush on her until they get to the last exercise: the leg press.

As Grace is adding weights to hers, Phoebe says, "I bet I can press more than you."

But she's seen Grace's thighs, and to be honest, she isn't actually sure this is a bet she would win. She's pretty sure it would be worth losing, though.

Grace sighs. "Are you not able to do things without betting on them?"

"I've managed most of this workout, thank you very much," Phoebe says.

Of course she can do things without betting on them; it's just more fun to make bets. Boring activities are made immediately more fun once something is on the line.

"Aren't you competitive?" she asks.

"Yeah, Phenom, I'm a professional athlete and I'm not competitive." Phoebe can hear the eye roll in Grace's voice. "Anyway, if you're so competitive, why do you insist on betting on things you're going to lose?"

"I seem to recall you thought you were going to win our first bet, too. And the one yesterday, for that matter. Did you forget how you bought me breakfast? In fact, I've never lost a bet to you."

"Yeah? What are you going to bet this time?"

The weight of their first bet hangs in the air between them. Is this Grace flirting back?

"I mean, I've got some ideas."

Phoebe swears she can still feel Grace's mouth on her. It felt like Grace gave her a hickey, even though Phoebe looked in the mirror in her hotel room afterward and there was no mark. It just felt like there was, like Grace had left behind proof of her presence.

The pulse in Phoebe's neck throbs.

"God," Grace says with yet another sigh, "I can't wait to finish this set and get away from you."

That is a cold bucket of water dumped over Phoebe's head. She must have leaned too far into the annoying side of her flirting.

"Okay but . . ." She almost doesn't continue. Maybe it's better to forget about their plans than be outright rejected. "Aren't we supposed to go get beignets?"

Grace shakes her head, but she's smiling. "It's unfair how easily you can do puppy-dog eyes to get what you want. But yeah, we're still getting beignets."

She sits and starts the exercise. Phoebe pretends whatever puppy-dog look she gave Grace was on purpose instead of because she hates the idea of Grace wanting to get away from her.

"It's a middle child skill," she claims. "Gotta find some way to make sure you're not forgettable."

"You certainly managed that, Phenom," Grace says.

Eight

When Grace first moved to New Orleans, she thought Café du Monde was everything when it came to beignets. They must have better marketing, or maybe they're better known simply by virtue of being in the Quarter. And it isn't like Café du Monde's beignets are bad, but Morning Call is better—plus you never have to deal with crowds of tourists.

"They used to have the spot in the park, too, but Café du Monde took it over." Grace rolls her eyes.

"For someone who claims they're not a local, you're pretty uppity about your NOLA restaurant opinions."

"It's called having good taste."

Matthews giggles, seemingly delighted.

They split one order of beignets and each get an iced coffee. Grace pays, out of habit or politeness, but of course Matthews has to make a big deal of it.

"I could get used to pretty girls taking me on dates around town," she says with a grin.

Grace hasn't been on a date in years. It sounds nice, maybe, but it isn't what's happening here. This is about exposure therapy. And it's working—Grace only thought about following a drip of Matthews's sweat with her tongue twice while they lifted weights. She's sitting across from the woman now and her libido isn't in fight-or-flight-or-fuck mode.

The beignets arrive on a small plate piled high with powdered sugar. Matthews looks like a kid on Christmas morning, her green eyes even wider than her smile.

"I gotta take a picture of this," she says.

Grace sits back and doesn't touch anything. Matthews arranges the plate and both of their drinks according to some unknown order before unlocking her phone to take pics.

"You wanna get in one?"

"Absolutely not," Grace says.

Matthews's smile dampens. "Okay," she says, drawing out the word.

"Sorry," Grace says, but she isn't. "I'm not wild about getting my picture taken."

It isn't a lie, even if it isn't the whole truth. Grace doesn't need Matthews to have "proof" they're friends. Not that the other woman would necessarily use any photos that way, but it's better to not have to worry about it. The fewer pictures of Grace, the less she has to worry about them cropping up somewhere.

"I got a picture of the important stuff anyway," Matthews says.

She's teasing, but Grace doesn't disagree.

"So can I drink my coffee now?" Grace asks.

"Feel free."

With that, Matthews carefully lifts the top beignet off the plate. It doesn't matter how careful she is; powdered sugar is going to get everywhere.

"Oh yeah," she moans after her first bite. Her lips are painted white with sugar. "I could definitely get used to this."

Another benefit of Morning Call instead of Café du Monde: there's no one around to hear Grace tell Matthews, "This isn't a date."

"Whatever you say, Henderson." She's more focused on the beignets than on Grace.

Grace hates the arrogant certainty in her voice. This girl doesn't know her, hasn't played with her. Grace's sexuality might be an open secret to her teammates, but Matthews is a rookie. They've barely been teammates yet.

"What even makes you think I'm into women?"

Matthews's eyebrows go up, her hand frozen halfway between the plate and her mouth. "You're saying you're not?"

"That's not what I said at all, actually."

Matthews shoves what is somehow already the last bite of her first beignet into her mouth. "No one kisses like that if they're not interested in women."

"I didn't technically kiss you," Grace says.

"Oh, excuse me. No one sucks on another woman's neck like that if they're not interested in women. Not kissing me is not a point in your favor." Matthews arches an eyebrow at her. "Especially since the bet was for a kiss."

"Okay, whatever. It counted." That's a can of worms Grace is not going to reopen.

Matthews lets her off the hook. "Also, like, I was a teenage lesbian who was into soccer, and the internet exists. There are entire L Chat boards dedicated to how gay you are."

Grace curls her lip. This is why she doesn't talk publicly about her sexuality. It's no one's business, but being in the public eye makes people think it is. Her sexuality is not entertainment, not something to be consumed.

"What does L Chat think is the gayest thing I've ever done?"

"I mean, I assume slept with a woman, but that suit you wore to the ESPYs in 2020 is pretty up there."

Grace presses her lips together instead of smiling. Even she can admit it was a pretty gay suit. She picks up her beignet and takes a bite so she doesn't have to respond.

"Also, to be honest, even if you supposedly were straight"—Matthews shrugs like she's brushing arrogance off her shoulders—"that hasn't always been an obstacle for me in the past."

"You've slept with straight women?"

"That's what some of them called themselves."

It would be nice to say that doesn't make any sense, but Matthews is so magnetic, it doesn't surprise Grace.

"Well, regardless, I'm not interested in a relationship."

Matthews smirks. "Who said anything about a relationship, Henderson?"

"Well, I'm not interested in that, either. Casual sex, I mean. That's not really something I do."

"Really?" Matthews's brow furrows. "But you're hot and famous. You could have anyone you wanted."

She says it so casually. Like it's a fact. Maybe it is. But Grace is not the type to have casual sex.

"Well, I don't want anyone. Not like that, anyway."

"Oh shit," Matthews says. She holds up her hands, palms facing Grace. "My bad. I tend to just assume everyone's down to, well, you know. Only platonic bets from now on, I promise. And no more flirting."

She draws an X over her chest with her pointer finger, literally crossing her heart. Grace doesn't know anyone like her. Matthews hadn't even been the one to name the stakes of the first bet to begin with. That was all Kelsey. Matthews had tried to let Grace off the hook.

She finishes the last beignet silently, then says, "You're still gonna show me all the best parts of this city, though, right? Remember, without you, I could've been led astray by Randazzo's."

Grace nods. "Yeah, fine. We'll get Dong Phuong's at some point."

"Not just that, though," Matthews says. "For real, I want to see your favorite things in the city. Restaurants, yeah, but parks, buildings, I don't know. I'm still getting used to living someplace other than Indiana, but I want to love it. You seem like you love it."

"I do."

"And again, my bad on the whole . . . other stuff. I read things wrong and that's on me."

Grace can't pinpoint any specific change, but it's like Matthews turned her charm down several levels.

"Anyway," Matthews says, and Grace is grateful they aren't talking more about casual sex, "safe to assume you probably don't want me to tag you when I post the pictures, right?"

Grace shudders. "I really wish that you wouldn't."

"So, like, can people not know we're friends?"

Grace takes a moment before responding. "Social media is full of people who think they know everything about you. I prefer to keep mine strictly professional."

"You don't even have a private one or anything?"

She used to, when she was a kid. Then she made a travel team over one of her friends, and the so-called friend took screenshots and shared them everywhere. They weren't of anything that bad; Grace had simply talked about her feelings about not starting. But everyone acted like she was rubbing it in people's faces who hadn't made the team in the first place. The whole point of the private account was because she was posting something personal. It wasn't supposed to be for everyone to see.

Grace knows she probably seems overly distrustful. But better safe than sorry. She's been sorry too many times. Even so, against her better judgment, Grace has enjoyed Matthews's company. The girl is surprising, and surprisingly disarming. Grace isn't about to make the same mistakes she did with Kelsey, but she can be friendly with Matthews, as long as they both know where they stand. No one needs to think this is anything other than what it is.

"In terms of showing you the city," Grace says rather than answering Matthews's question, "are you interested in going to a Mardi Gras parade?"

Matthews beams. There's powdered sugar on her cheek that Grace's fingers itch to wipe away.

"Totally. I googled them actually, but there's so many. I didn't know which one to check out."

"There's a good one on Saturday. I'll take you."

Grace hasn't been to a Mardi Gras parade in a couple of years. The Krewe du Vieux parade goes through the Quarter and is always raunchy and political. It isn't necessarily Grace's favorite parade, but it is perfect to take someone to. It's what people tend to expect from Mardi Gras in New Orleans: booze, boobs, and beads.

Nine

Phoebe stands on the sidewalk in front of her apartment building, waiting for Grace to pick her up. She's already been in Grace's car for the trip to Morning Call, and it's exactly what Phoebe expected: a forest-green Subaru Impreza, cleaner inside and out than any car Phoebe has ever driven. There's nothing personal about it, not even a Krewe shield decal like the one Phoebe already plastered onto her water bottle.

Grace texted—yeah, Phoebe has Grace Henderson's phone number now—when she left her house, so Phoebe is ready and waiting when Grace clicks on her turn signal and pulls over in front of Phoebe's building.

"Hey," Phoebe says as she slides into the passenger seat. "Is this okay?"

She gestures to her clothes. An hour and a half ago, she frantically texted first Teddy, then Grace, asking what she should wear. Having also never been to a Mardi Gras parade, Teddy was no help. Grace wasn't much better. Whatever you want, was her first answer, eventually followed by Anything green, gold, or purple. Phoebe chose camouflage joggers and a cropped sweatshirt that's more highlighter yellow than gold, but she hopes it's close enough.

"It's fine." Grace turns on her other blinker and pulls back onto the otherwise empty street. "There will be people there literally dressed as genitals. There's not really a wrong outfit."

Phoebe cannot imagine Grace in a crowd including people dressed as genitals, but after they park a few blocks from the parade route, she doesn't have to imagine. There are plenty of people, all walking in the same direction, and Phoebe fits in better than Grace does. Absurd costumes and/or a lot of skin seem to be the dress code. Grace wears black skinny jeans with a black biker jacket over a white shirt. Her resting bitch face—which is a term Phoebe isn't wild about, but that definitely fits Grace Henderson—doesn't match the rowdy crowd, either. Everyone is boisterous, loud laughter ringing out, and someone even plays a trumpet as they walk. Phoebe suspects she and Grace are the most sober people headed for the parade. Within a block, someone gives them both bead necklaces.

"I thought you had to show your boobs to get beads," Phoebe whispers to Grace, who shrugs.

"I'm sure they wouldn't object if you wanted to."

Phoebe opens her mouth to ask if Grace would object, but for once her brain works fast enough to stop her before she says something stupid.

Grace was clear. She isn't interested in Phoebe. Honestly, it's probably smarter not to get involved with her captain anyway, no matter how Phoebe can't get that moment next to the vending machines out of her head. So, Phoebe won't flirt, because it doesn't count as flirting when the other party doesn't want it.

"Maybe later," she says instead. "I am an oversharer, but not quite in that way."

By the time they find a place to set up, at a high-top table barely off the sidewalk, in a bar that is basically open air to the street, they've collected necklaces in every color. Grace orders a beer with gator in the name, and Phoebe orders a hurricane. It's a New Orleans tradition, right?

Phoebe doesn't know where to look. There are people everywhere. The bar is full, and the sidewalk, too. Revelers crowd balconies in the upper levels of the buildings lining the street. They throw beads to the people below. She can't believe the size of the crowd when Mardi

Gras isn't technically for weeks still. Grace wasn't lying when she said it was a whole season. Everything is purple and green and gold: clothes and beads and bunting hanging from the balconies. There's someone selling glow stick necklaces that are probably way overpriced but Phoebe craves anyway.

A harried waitress delivers their drinks as the beginning of the parade must be making its way up the street—the crowd noise starts to get louder.

Sure enough, it isn't long before a mule pulls the first float into view. The float is a giant book, 2023: LET'S OVERDUE IT BY KREWE DU VIEUX written on the cover. A rainbow flag flies from a pole at the top.

"You brought me to a gay parade," Phoebe says.

Grace rolls her eyes. "It's not a gay parade. It's a banned books parade."

Phoebe gestures to the next float. "That is literally just two women making out."

"Because queer books have been getting banned. Not because it's a gay parade. Each krewe gets to interpret the theme however they want. That's who makes the floats—krewes. And where the team gets our name, obviously."

Phoebe knows that already, but she isn't about to interrupt Grace.

"Each year they have a different theme," Grace explains. "This parade is always raunchier and more political than most."

It's like nothing that Phoebe has ever seen. Her hometown has a Fourth of July parade every year, but that's mostly fire trucks and the middle school band, designed for families with small children. The bands in this parade are jazzy, older, no awkward military-esque uniforms. And this parade is definitely not for families—though Teddy would fucking love it.

Grace gives her more info about the parade, most of which Phoebe already learned from her googling, but there's some new stuff, too.

As Grace tells her about how the first Mardi Gras festival in the US wasn't even in New Orleans, a woman stumbles on the sidewalk. Without thinking, Phoebe is off her stool and catching the stranger before she can come face-first with the cement.

"Oh my God, thank you!" the woman says, her Cajun accent thick.

Phoebe holds her by the elbows until she seems steady on her feet again. The woman's grateful smile grows when her eyes land on Phoebe's.

She giggles. "My knight in shining armor."

"I do my best," Phoebe says. She lets go, but with the crowd around them, the woman doesn't step back. "You okay?"

"Thanks to you," the woman says. "I'm Lindsay."

"Phoebe." No one else stopped with Lindsay. "Are you here alone?"

She pouts, sticking out a bright red bottom lip. "My friends bailed on me."

"Well, why don't you join us? This is Grace."

Phoebe steps back toward their table, and Lindsay comes with her. Grace barely manages a smile. Of course. She obviously isn't wild about meeting new people, if the way she treated Phoebe at the beginning is any indication. But this is just a cute stranger at the parade all by herself. Besides, Phoebe is pretty sure Grace doesn't need to worry about Lindsay becoming obsessed with her anyway. She barely takes her eyes off Phoebe to greet the brunette.

There aren't enough stools for the three of them, and every other table is using their own, so Phoebe offers Lindsay hers and stands instead. Her hip bumps Grace's and she apologizes with a grin. Grace finishes her beer.

"I'll get the next round," Phoebe says. Grace bought the first, but Phoebe checked her bank account this afternoon—she can afford three drinks. "What are you drinking?"

The waitress is nowhere to be seen, so Phoebe works her way to the bar and flags down the bartender. He tries to get her to open a tab, but her bank account isn't *that* full. Especially once she learns how much three drinks cost.

Back at the table, Grace and Lindsay look like they haven't said a word to each other. With how bad Grace seems to be at small talk, Phoebe isn't surprised.

"You better enjoy these," Phoebe says, setting the drinks in the middle of the table. "They cost more than most of my meals."

"Bars in the Quarter can get away with that, especially during Mardi Gras," Grace says.

Phoebe isn't usually much of a drinker, but she wants to go to Grace's favorite bar. Before she can ask, Lindsay says, "Are you not from around here?"

"Me?" Phoebe shakes her head. "Nah, I'm a Midwestern girl. Brand-new in town."

"Ooh, a Mardi Gras virgin. How fun."

Phoebe didn't plan on picking anyone up, and it isn't like she's going to take Lindsay home or anything, but this provides a nice outlet for the way attraction buzzes under her skin from being so close to Grace. She can't flirt with Grace, but she can flirt with Lindsay. She grins like she knows exactly what Lindsay wants and lets her eyes linger. Sure enough, Lindsay's cheeks go pink.

Lindsay kind of looks like Grace, actually. Well, a poor man's Grace, even if Phoebe feels mean thinking that. Her skin is slightly paler, probably from not spending so much time on a field under the sun. Her hair is darker, too, none of the highlights that run through Grace's straight locks. She's skinnier and slightly taller, gangly where Grace is sturdy. Sturdy doesn't sound like a compliment, but Phoebe means it as one. Grace is strong. She can probably snap Lindsay like a twig.

But whatever. That isn't the point. The point is Phoebe has someone new to flirt with. And Grace can't even be mad that Phoebe invited a stranger to join them, because Lindsay doesn't pay Grace a single glance of attention.

They do the typical getting-to-know-each-other questions. Lindsay is a kindergarten teacher, born and raised in the Big Easy. When she learns Phoebe plays soccer, she lets out a low whistle.

"Wow. A professional athlete. Are you any good?"

"I'd say I'm pretty good." Phoebe slides a smile toward Grace. "What do you think, Henderson?"

"You haven't played in a single game beyond the college level. Don't get ahead of yourself."

Apparently Grace doesn't want to be Phoebe's wingman. Not that she really needs one.

"She's just grumpy because I beat her at the beep test."

Lindsay seems enthralled as Phoebe explains what the beep test entails. Phoebe has a feeling Lindsay would seem enthralled with whatever Phoebe talked about. She even giggles when Phoebe recounts puking in the trash can, which is objectively disgusting.

Honestly, Lindsay is cute, but someone so clearly into her is less interesting to Phoebe than someone like Grace, whom Phoebe has yet to make laugh. It always feels better, more genuine, to make someone like Grace laugh. It makes her feel powerful. The way Lindsay looks at her just makes Phoebe feel hot, which is also nice, but not quite *as* nice.

Grace, of course, is silent, her mouth a thin line. Even when Phoebe tries to include her in the conversation, she gives the shortest responses possible. Phoebe would tease her for being such an introvert if she wasn't sure that Grace would *not* appreciate being teased in front of a stranger.

As the night goes on, with more inappropriate floats, wildly talented bands, and—Grace was right—a surprising number of people dressed as genitals, Phoebe feels . . . well, maybe she's a little homesick. The night is fun, and interesting—different from anything she normally does. It isn't that she doesn't like it, just that she feels like she has to be on her best behavior. She and Grace are becoming friends, yeah, but it's still that beginning period where they are feeling each other out—*Not like that,* she tells her dirty mind. She isn't supposed to be thinking of Grace like that. Especially not with Lindsay in front of her, running a finger along the rim of her own glass and batting her eyes.

Phoebe knows what it looks like when someone is angling to get kissed, but she isn't going to do that in front of Grace. Lindsay doesn't seem to feel the need for discretion. She leans closer.

The table wobbles as Grace hops off her stool.

"Restroom," she says gruffly and disappears into the crowd in the bar.

"Nice of her to give us some privacy," Lindsay says.

She leans in again, but Phoebe puts a hand on her shoulder, not firm but certain.

"We just met," she says. "And we've both been drinking."

Lindsay's smile widens. "That's half the fun."

"I don't want to be drunk if we're going to—" Phoebe cuts herself off. Because she isn't *drunk,* exactly, and because it'd be a lie to act like she doesn't love drunk kissing. "I prefer clearer heads when starting anything."

She prefers not having carpooled with someone else she would like to kiss.

Just like that, Lindsay isn't smiling anymore. "So you've been leading me on?"

"No, that's not it at all." Phoebe tries to backtrack. "I'd love to get your number and maybe we could—"

"I'm good." Lindsay snatches her clutch off the table. "Thanks for wasting my time."

She leaves without another word. Phoebe stares after her long past the time she disappears into the crowd on the sidewalk. That was . . . not how she expected that to go. When did Phoebe get so bad at reading people she flirts with? Not that she can even blame Lindsay for being upset. Mardi Gras seems like the perfect time to tipsily make out with a girl she just met. If Phoebe knew Grace a little better, maybe she wouldn't have stopped Lindsay—she's abandoned friends for a hot stranger during nights out before, but it seems rude to do to Grace, who did her a favor by bringing her tonight.

On the bright side, at least she doesn't have to stand up anymore. She reclaims her stool as Grace returns.

"Where'd your date go?" Grace asks.

Phoebe doesn't want to admit how thoroughly she was rejected. "She had a thing. But she took my number, so like, maybe some other time."

"Great."

Phoebe hopes Grace will loosen up with Lindsay gone. She was talkative at the beginning of the night—talkative for Grace anyway. The parade is over by now, but for some people that seems to mean the party is just getting started. Phoebe somehow doubts Grace is the partying type.

"So, what next?"

"I finish this," Grace says, tipping her beer bottle toward Phoebe, "and we go."

"Right," Phoebe says. "That's what I figured. I just—yeah, just wanted to be sure. No reason to stay out when I might already be hungover at my breakfast shift at the diner. Did you ever say if you knew the place? Bourré Café?"

"Nope." Grace sips her beer.

Apparently the talkative Grace ship sailed. They finish their drinks in silence. Phoebe wishes she never invited Lindsay to their table—clearly the company used up all of Grace's social energy. Phoebe had fun flirting, but she's pretty sure she would've had more fun bothering Grace.

On the way back to the car, she has to ask, "Did you have fun?"

"Of course," Grace says. "Why wouldn't I have had fun?"

"Just making sure," Phoebe says. "I had fun."

"Yeah, Phenom, I could tell."

Phoebe's laugh comes out more like a giggle. She likes that Grace is comfortable enough with her to give her a hard time.

Ten

Grace doesn't sleep well. She lies in bed staring at her ceiling, telling herself to stop thinking about Matthews. About the way Matthews smiled at that other woman. The way she stood so close to her, the way she let her hand find the other woman's skin to emphasize a point or laugh at a joke—any excuse, it seemed, just so she could touch her.

It isn't that Grace is jealous. It simply confirms that Matthews didn't really care about her, wasn't really interested in anything other than sleeping with a famous person. Grace was right to tell Matthews she isn't interested. Grace has no desire to be involved with anyone who can just swap out partners without caring.

Knowing she made the right choice doesn't lessen the anger simmering in her veins. Grace doesn't like being used. She's had enough of that in her career, being a spokesperson where companies literally pay to use her fame, celebrity, name recognition. She refuses to accept it in her personal life.

In fact, she's going to tell Matthews that. Matthews seemed blissfully unaware about how irritated Grace was last night. The woman clearly skates through life without thinking about other people. That is unacceptable if she is going to be a part of the Krewe. It's Grace's responsibility, as the captain, to hold Matthews to a higher standard than that.

The rest of the team comes back tomorrow for the official start of the preseason, but Grace doesn't need to do this in front of everyone. Anyway, she knows where Matthews is right now: hungover and serving breakfast at Bourré Café.

• • • •

It isn't until Grace is inside the diner that she realizes she didn't plan her speech. She should've. She needs something to focus on other than the pile of red hair trying to escape the hairnet Matthews has haphazardly tugged over it. Matthews wears a little white apron over a teal polo shirt tucked into black shorts. She's tall enough that, even with tables between them, Grace can see too much of the skin of her thighs peeking out from underneath the apron.

"Grace!" Matthews exclaims upon their eyes connecting. She immediately cringes, like the noise was too loud even though she's the one who made it. Much more quietly, she continues, "Did you come here to see me suffer?"

"I want to talk to you," Grace says.

"Okay. Booth or table?"

"I'm here to talk, not eat."

"Right, but my manager is back there and it's my first week and he's kinda strict. Like, I kinda get why so many people quit. So, like, maybe you could just take a seat?"

"Booth," Grace grumbles.

"Right this way."

Matthews sits Grace on the opposite side of the room from any of the other patrons. It wouldn't be efficient, were Grace actually ordering, for Matthews to have to walk so far to serve her, but it gives them privacy to chat.

"Can you order coffee or something, too? Just so it doesn't seem like you're taking up a table and not buying anything."

"You really think they're worried about me taking up space when there are only three other occupied tables?"

"I don't know! I just don't want to get in trouble for having friends visit me."

There's that word again: friends.

"Fine." Grace turns over the mug in front of her. "Coffee's good."

Matthews pours her a cup from the pot in her hand. "I'll leave you a menu to look at. Gotta go check on my other tables, one sec."

"Matthews, can we just—"

But she's already gone, checking in with other customers about their food, laughing loudly at something one of them says.

Grace frowns and rips open a packet of creamer. But she does need the caffeine, what with how poorly she slept.

She's halfway through her cup by the time Matthews returns to her table.

"You sure you don't want food? Dallas—that's the cook—makes amazing stuffed hash browns."

"I told you I didn't come here to eat."

"Right," Matthews says. "What did you want to talk about?"

"The way you flirted with that woman last night."

Matthews's eyebrows jump up her forehead. "What?"

"At the parade."

"Yeah, I know where we were last night. But you want to talk about *what*?"

"You flirted with her. After flirting with me for the past week."

Matthews tilts her head, her brow furrowing. "Right, but you told me you weren't interested."

"I'm not!"

"So what's the problem?"

"I was clearly nothing more to you than a celebrity notch in your bedpost."

Someone whistles, and Matthews's head snaps to look to the counter where another worker stands. He must be the manager, the way he nods toward a recently vacated table like Matthews should already be busing it. The customers aren't even out of the diner yet. Matthews leaves without a word. Apparently she was right to worry about a friend visiting if that's how her manager operates.

Not that Grace is a friend—she's Matthews's captain. This is a professional conversation. Grace nurses her cup of coffee, watching her thumb rub back and forth over the smooth ceramic.

When Matthews returns, she continues their conversation without preamble. "You weren't a notch in my bedpost? We didn't even do anything."

Grace sighs. "It's the principle of it."

"Which is what, exactly?"

"You can't just use people."

"I didn't use you! I flirted with you!"

Grace keeps her voice level. "You obviously didn't actually care about me, with how easy it was for you to find someone new to flirt with."

"You specifically said you weren't interested in a relationship, nor anything casual. So, I quit flirting. I don't understand why this is a big deal?"

"You didn't notice that I was unhappy with your behavior last night."

"My *behavior?*" Phoebe sputters, but Grace speaks over her.

"You clearly were only paying attention to what you deemed important. In a social situation it's one thing, but as your captain, I want to tell you that will be unacceptable when the rest of the team arrives for the preseason tomorrow."

Matthews stares at her for a moment without responding. Grace doesn't break eye contact.

"You're here as my captain?"

"Yes."

"To tell me you're mad I flirted with someone else?"

"Yes." Grace blinks. "Well—no. I'm not mad."

"You seem mad."

"No. I'm just—"

"'Unhappy with my behavior' were your words."

Grace doesn't need Matthews to remind her. "Yes. I'm—"

"Jealous."

"*What?*"

"You're obviously jealous I was flirting with someone else."

That's so off base, Grace opens and closes her mouth twice before she is able to formulate a response. "No, I am not. As I told you, I'm not interested in a relationship."

"I didn't say you were," Matthews says. "But you're sure not interested in me flirting with someone who isn't you."

"No. I am here as your captain."

"You tracked me down at work to tell me not to flirt with other people."

"No. I tracked you down—" This conversation is getting away from her. Matthews is interrupting and twisting her words and driving her off track. "Actually, I didn't track you down—you told me you were going to be here. I stopped by to discuss what is and isn't appropriate behavior when the team arrives."

"And it's not appropriate for me to flirt with people who aren't you."

"I didn't say that. I—"

"I know I said I was obsessed with you, but it seems like maybe it's the other way around," Matthews says. "This is pretty weird."

Grace scowls. "No weirder than leaping a fence to come talk to me during a workout."

"You're right." Grace appreciates the words but not the way Matthews smirks. "I guess we're both a little weird for each other."

Matthews stands with her hip leaning against the booth where Grace sits. From under the apron, her shorts are short enough that her legs seem bare, just *skin skin skin* all the way down to a faded pair of Toms. Grace must have had too much caffeine, the way her heart goes double time in her chest.

A bell chimes from the kitchen.

"Order up!"

"I'll be right back," Matthews says, pointing a finger at Grace. "We should keep talking about this."

She goes to deliver food to other customers. And when her back is turned and her focus elsewhere, Grace throws too much cash down on the table and flees.

Eleven

When Phoebe returns to the booth, Grace is gone. Two ten-dollar bills sit on the table. A cup of coffee costs two dollars. At least Grace left a good tip.

Phoebe wants to laugh about this. It's funny, Grace barging into her workplace—*as her captain,* of course. That's just—Phoebe isn't always good at understanding her feelings, but that is ridiculous. Grace is jealous and doesn't want to admit it or maybe doesn't even know and Phoebe absolutely wants to make fun of her for it.

But also, Grace is Grace. Phoebe wants to make fun of her for it because it's hilarious and adorable, but Grace doesn't really seem the type to enjoy being teased. Not in that way, at least. And if Phoebe is going to find out if Grace likes to be teased in any *other* way, she has to play this right.

Which—maybe Phoebe will never find out. Just because Grace is jealous doesn't mean anything is actually going to happen. She said she wasn't interested in a relationship, nor in casual sex. Phoebe doesn't understand that, but she isn't about to disrespect it. But if seeing Phoebe talk to another woman made Grace change her mind . . . If Grace hadn't fled, they could have talked about this. Instead, Phoebe is left to wait other tables while her brain churns. She has no freakin' idea how to handle this.

In the lull between breakfast and lunch, Phoebe leans against a sink in the kitchen and talks to Dallas, her favorite coworker. Her only co-worker, at the moment, now that their manager has left. Dallas has a ponytail of locs, a scorpion forearm tattoo, and their pronouns on their name tag.

"Dallas? Are you into women?"

Dallas shrugs. "I'm not really into anyone."

"Good for you." Phoebe points at them. "Girls are way too con-fusing. It's a much better idea to not be into them. Not that—I didn't mean to imply it was like a choice or whatever to be into them or not. To be into anyone or not. And like, I realize being aro or ace isn't all sunshine and rainbows. Not that you necessarily identify with either of those labels. I just mean—"

"Take a breath, ginger," Dallas says. "I know what you meant."

"Okay good. I don't mean to offend—"

"So you're having lady problems?" they ask rather than let Phoebe babble more.

Phoebe drops her head into her hands. "I'm having confusion."

"You wanna talk about it?"

"Oh, you don't have to—I'm sure you have better things to do."

Dallas gestures at the now-empty diner. "Not really."

"Oh. Right."

Phoebe does want to talk about it. Rather desperately. But she wants to talk about it with *Grace*. Plus, like, Grace likes her privacy. It still isn't clear if she's out to anyone. But it isn't like Dallas is a huge women's soccer fan or anything. It probably won't matter if Phoebe tells them.

But what is Dallas going to tell her anyway? Phoebe can't get an-swers from them, so it won't even be a productive conversation—it will just be Phoebe ranting.

"Nah," she says. "There's better things to do with your time even if this place is empty. Like—tell me an interesting fact."

"About me or?"

"About anything."

With no hesitation, Dallas says, "Trees use mushrooms to communicate."

The rest of shift is pretty slow, with a slight uptick for lunch service. Phoebe and Dallas spend the whole time talking about mushrooms. Phoebe was right—it's a much better use of their time.

• • • •

After work, Phoebe goes home and showers before passing out. She isn't hungover anymore—Dallas's stuffed hash browns with over-easy eggs on top pretty much cured that—just tired. When she wakes up, she scrolls through her phone instead of getting out of bed. Her suitcase, still mostly packed, beckons from her open closet. The non-clothes suitcase is still in the living room, also mostly packed. She only unpacked things she immediately needed: the one pot and one pan that make up her cookware, enough workout gear that she's only done laundry once in the week she's been here, twinkle lights to hang on the top of the wall in her room, and her snapbacks and the over-door rack for them that Teddy bought her a couple of birthdays ago.

She's had time to unpack. She knows she should, and even wants to, really. The dingy apartment provided by the team will feel a lot more like home with her pictures on shelves and shit. But there's just always other, more interesting stuff to do. Maybe tonight she'll put on Bob's season of *Drag Race* and work on unpacking. She wrinkles her nose at the thought. There's definitely other stuff she could be doing tonight.

Sometimes, to Phoebe, sex is like soccer. Though it's generally more one-on-one than having a whole team involved, and it isn't that Phoebe has *never* done it in front of spectators but—that isn't the point.

Sex is like soccer in that Phoebe is good at it.

She likes it. It's a game, and Phoebe knows it doesn't necessarily matter that much in the long run, but sometimes it feels like the most important thing in the world. Phoebe doesn't *need* sex, but if it's an option, she's unlikely to say no, just like she's almost always down for a pickup game.

Sex and soccer are the type of games that Phoebe is good at, but when it comes to being into people, she's never understood playing games. She doesn't want to make Grace uncomfortable, but she wants to be honest. Because Grace *is* into her, clearly, even if she doesn't want to be. Normally, Phoebe would push that—if she's into someone who's into her, there shouldn't be anything holding them back. But Grace said she wasn't interested in casual sex, nor a relationship. Where does that leave them?

Phoebe could go back to flirting. She likes flirting. It's fun. Grace doesn't have to want to fuck her to want to keep flirting, right? It wouldn't be overstepping boundaries.

Again, if Grace didn't flee that morning, they could've *talked about this,* but no.

It's stupid to let something fester when they can just talk about it. And somehow she doesn't think Grace will be the one to break the silence between them.

The next time she sees Grace, they'll be surrounded by other people. The rest of the Krewe report to preseason tomorrow. If they're going to get on the same page, it has to be tonight. Unpacking can wait.

Phoebe unlocks her phone and opens her messages. Teddy texted last—an update about Phoebe's favorite personal training client, Mrs. Frankenberger—and her conversation with Grace is right beneath that.

There are so many things she could say. *Why'd you leave?* and *I kinda like that you're jealous* and *Can we please figure this out before the rest of the team shows up?* Honestly—she totally wants to hook up with Grace, but not at the expense of the delicate friendship that's growing between them. Phoebe likes Grace separate from the whole thinking-she's-really-hot thing. She was afraid at Morning Call the other day that she fucked up their chance at a normal friendship by flirting too much. She's still—not walking on eggshells exactly, but trying to tread carefully. Grace is Phoebe's captain, and her teammate, and she is cool and interesting and fun. Phoebe doesn't want to mess anything up. She just wants to get on the same page, to make sure things are okay between them.

> I'm like a dog who needs to go run around at a dog park sometimes

Twelve

Matthews said that her phone has been randomly dying, so Grace doesn't text when she arrives at the stadium. Instead, she drops her gear in the locker room and goes straight to the field. Matthews is spread-eagle on her back in the middle of it, looking up at the sky. Grace chews her bottom lip, her feet dragging through the grass as she makes her way toward midfield.

What can Grace say? What does she want to say? She doesn't have anything prepared. When Matthews texted, Grace didn't let herself think too hard before agreeing. A soccer field makes sense to her, even if the woman lying in the middle of it doesn't.

Everything about Matthews's outfit is bright: neon-green shorts that barely make it past the hem of her top, which is a purple Krewe T-shirt that she's already cut the sleeves off of. As Grace approaches, her eyes flick between the long expanse of Matthews's legs and the highlighter-yellow sports bra visible through the giant armholes Matthews cut in her shirt.

"You were right," Matthews says, her eyes landing on Grace, though she stays flat on her back.

Grace swallows. "Was I?"

or I get restless. Except instead of
a dog park it's a soccer field. You
wanna kick a ball around?

Phoebe has never had a dog of her own, but she was the neighborhood dog walker before she was old enough to get a real job. Babysit-
ting was way too much responsibility for her, but she could handle
dogs. Grace is probably going to think the message is ridiculous, but
whatever. It has the benefit of being both true and an olive branch, a
way to move on from whatever made Grace flee that morning.

Phoebe knows better than to watch the three little dots as Grace
types. She watches them anyway. They appear, disappear, reappear, and
disappear again without anything coming through for long enough
Phoebe has to touch her phone screen so it doesn't lock. Of course
Grace is thinking about this too hard. She thinks about everything too
hard.

Finally, a reply comes.

Meet you at the stadium

"Working out after sunset is smart, not ridiculous."

"You call this working out?"

Matthews laughs. "I was doing laps waiting for you. I'm just taking a break."

"I thought you wanted to kick a ball around, not run laps."

"Yeah, but—" Matthews pauses, like she doesn't want to admit the next part. "I forgot where the balls are."

"Get up," Grace says. "I'll show you."

Matthews leaps to her feet, suddenly too close for Grace's comfort. Grace steps back but Matthews follows. Right. She's supposed to follow. She has to, if Grace is going to show her where the balls are. Grace rolls her shoulders back.

The silence is awkward, but Grace has nothing to say. The last time she tried to explain herself, it didn't exactly go well. She can admit by now that perhaps she is a little jealous. But that doesn't change anything. She still isn't interested in a relationship, nor in casual sex. Matthews is her teammate and could possibly become her friend; anything other than that is asking for drama. Grace doesn't do messy. She isn't about to embarrass herself again by opening the door to any potential feelings.

So she says nothing as Matthews follows her through the hallways to the equipment room.

"They're here," Grace says, and she opens the door, but when she turns to Matthews behind her, the redhead is typing away on her phone, which apparently didn't die.

It isn't jealousy that flares in Grace's chest; it's frustration. Yes, the first thing that pops into her mind is that Matthews is probably messaging the woman from the parade, but who she's talking to doesn't actually matter. She's the one who texted Grace to meet here, and now she can't even be bothered to focus.

"Look, do you want to kick a ball around, or do you want to play on your phone?"

Matthews's whole face goes red under those freckles. She shoves her phone into the tiny pocket in her shorts. "I was, uh, just writing down where to find the balls so the next time I forget I can look at my notes."

"Oh," Grace says. "That's a good idea. I'm sorry for being rude."

Matthews blinks at her. "It's okay. No big."

Honestly, it works better when Grace doesn't talk. That seems to be the only way to prevent her emotions from getting the best of her. She hands a ball to Matthews and gestures for her to lead the way back to the field.

As they head down the hallway, Matthews says, "Did you know trees can share nutrients through mushrooms?"

"What?"

"It's true. Not like the part of the mushroom that actually grows out of the ground or anything, but mushrooms are like icebergs, there's a lot more underneath the surface than what we can see. It turns out they have all these little threads that connect entire forests of trees together through their roots. And so, like, especially for little trees that can't get enough sunlight, the older trees send nutrients through the threads of mushrooms to the little trees."

Grace hates it when people talk in metaphors. They never make sense to her.

"Why are you telling me this?"

"Oh." Matthews shrugs. "I learned it recently and thought it was cool. It's wild how some of them are delicious food, and some you only have to eat half a cap of and it can kill you."

Maybe this isn't a metaphor. Matthews is actually just sharing facts about mushrooms.

"To be honest," Matthews continues as they push out the double doors leading to the field, "you know how some people don't like to eat meat or, like, specifically pork because pigs are really smart? With that criteria, I'm not sure we should be eating mushrooms."

She drops the ball into the grass, dribbles a few feet away, then turns and passes it to Grace.

"You think mushrooms are too smart for us to eat?" Grace passes the ball back.

"I mean, I don't think so personally, but I also eat pork." She sends a pass a little in front of Grace, making her jog to get to it. "But mushrooms do share more DNA with people than plants."

"How do you feel about bananas? We share fifty percent of our DNA with them." Grace read that somewhere and never forgot it.

"Neat," Matthews says, then she grins and takes off down the field with the ball.

Without a thought, Grace chases her.

In a game, Grace has to think. She's captain of the Krewe; she is in charge of talking to the refs. She has to pay attention to how everyone else is playing, know when to give a player a pep talk or a kick in the ass. During a game, Grace has responsibilities. But here? Nothing but her and Matthews and a ball? Grace can let instinct take over. That's what playing soccer feels like: instinct. Something she can't remember not knowing how to do. She works hard, yes, but it's best when it comes naturally. The games when she makes amazing plays are the ones she can't describe afterward—she can't explain what happened or how she did something, she'd just done it.

On the field with Matthews, no stadium lights on to counteract the slowly darkening sky—Grace doesn't know how she gets the ball, but it's at her feet, Matthews pressing against her back. Grace dances to keep her away from the ball.

They go back and forth like that, over and over again. At some point, Grace strips off her top layer, and they both kick off their shoes and socks. They're a tangle of bare feet and long arms, playing more physically than they would be allowed to in a game. It's the first time Grace has had physical contact with another person since January camp. Every time their bodies come together, it gets a little bit rougher.

Eventually, Matthews hip checks Grace hard enough to lay her out. Rather than leap to her feet, Grace shoots a hand out and catches Matthews by the ankle to bring her down, too. Matthews laughs as she sprawls out on the grass, so Grace doesn't even feel guilty about it. They both lie there for a moment, breathing hard and looking up at the sky, where the first stars are battling the city lights to emerge.

"So, are we going to talk about it?" Matthews asks once she catches her breath.

Grace considers it.

She still doesn't know what she wants to say.

"No. We're not."

Matthews laughs quietly. "Okay."

Grace didn't expect it to be so easy. Matthews is always pushing back, challenging Grace in ways other people don't. Grace is a veteran, captain, professional, superstar talent. It's how people always see her. She doesn't know what to make of this rookie who acts like none of that matters. It *doesn't* matter, Grace knows, but no one else ever seems to. She's just a person. Most of the time she wishes people recognized that instead of acting like she's *special*. But that's exactly what Matthews does, and Grace doesn't know how to handle it.

After a while, they both make it to their feet and back to the locker room. Grace planned on showering at home, but Matthews pulls her muscle tank over her head, revealing that damned bright yellow sports bra. Grace busies herself with arranging things in her locker, even though everything is already in its place.

Matthews sits on the bench. She uses the shirt to mop sweat from her body.

"I can't believe the whole team is gonna be here tomorrow," she says. "The first day of my first season as a professional soccer player."

Grace's first professional game was almost a decade ago. She'd had to get a waiver to play since she wasn't yet eighteen. Matthews isn't that much younger than her, but it feels like they come from different worlds.

"Do you think betting on me being on time tomorrow will help me be on time?" Matthews shakes her head at her own question. "Okay, to be honest, I know the answer to that because I've already tried it in the past; it does not work. But we should try it anyway. Maybe the nineteenth time's the charm."

Grace speaks without thinking. "If you get here early, I'll braid your hair."

Phoebe practically guffaws. "Okay, I know you said we're not talking about it, but that is *flirting*. That is good flirting. Hendy, you got *game*. You didn't even show me this before—well, I guess with the whole kissing-me-not-on-my-mouth thing. That was game, too."

Grace breathes through her nose and keeps her eyes on her locker.

Matthews feels like the sun, like if Grace looks too closely, she'll go blind. That smile is even brighter.

"Yeah, okay," Matthews says. "That's gonna work better than telling me the wrong time, honestly."

Grace presses her lips together instead of grinning. She'd wager that Matthews doesn't even remember the name of the woman from the parade, but the idea of Grace's hands in her hair will get her to training early.

Not that Grace is in competition with a stranger. It just feels nice.

That's the thing about Matthews: spending time with her isn't like spending time with anyone else. If you told Grace last month that there'd be a rookie who interrupted her preseason training, who asked for a tour of the city, who infiltrated Grace's life like this, she would've hated it. In theory, Matthews sounds terrible. She's everything Grace is not: loud and talkative and playful. Quick to trust and quicker to flirt. Grace usually hates the class clown, but tonight was fun. Beignets were fun. Matthews is . . . unexpected.

She also seems to have forgotten she's undressing. She's still half naked on the bench in front of their lockers, scrolling on her phone. Her abs are unreal. The perfect sculpture of Matthews's muscles contrasts with the mess of hair she's let out of her ponytail. Grace's body thrums from their workout, or maybe just from the physicality of it, the contact, those abs pressed against Grace's back while Matthews tried to body her away from the ball.

Grace should say good night. She should go home and do her nightly routine and get as much sleep as she can to prepare for tomorrow. She knows this.

When Grace was nine years old, she learned to french braid.

When Grace was eleven, she and her mother moved across the country so she could play soccer.

When Grace was sixteen, she gained thousands of followers after playing for the national team for the first time, and understood her performance was not just about her.

Grace has spent her entire life controlling herself. Patience, discipline, responsibility. She's an eldest daughter, a captain, a veteran of any team she is on. A leader. A role model. She knows what she is supposed to do.

Instead, she leaves her keys in her locker and walks over to Matthews.

Matthews doesn't seem to notice Grace's approach until she's right in front of her. Grace steps closer, and Matthews leans back, making space for Grace to put one knee on the bench on either side of her hips. She tosses her phone aside without looking to see where it lands. Grace wraps her arms around Matthews's neck.

Matthews grins, dimples as deep as the Grand Canyon. "I thought we weren't talking about it."

"Who's talking?" Grace asks, and kisses her.

Matthews doesn't miss a beat. Her hands cradle Grace's waist, and she tilts her head for a better angle. She's somehow still smiling, even as they kiss. When her mouth opens and their tongues touch for the first time, Grace feels it in her toes. Matthews kisses like she flirts, like she plays, like she seems to live: as though she has never experienced a moment of self-doubt. And why should she? There's nothing to worry about when it comes to how she kisses, at least. Thirty seconds of lips and tongue and occasionally teeth, and Grace didn't think everything through before she first straddled Matthews, but she sure has now. They aren't leaving this bench until she makes Matthews lose control.

Matthews breaks the connection between their mouths to kiss along Grace's jaw. "I bet I can make you come first."

"You're talking," Grace says, answering her own question from earlier. "Of course you're talking. Shut up and put your mouth to better use."

Matthews does as she's told, sucking the pulse point in Grace's neck. Grace groans and rolls her hips. It's been too long since she's done this, and her body seems desperate, like it's moving of its own accord, without clearing it with Grace's brain first, sliding a hand into the mess of Matthews's hair and grinding her hips down again, wanton and insouciant.

Grace is glad she and Kelsey never—Matthews slides her hands around to cup Grace's ass and Grace stops thinking about Kelsey.

Matthews kneads Grace's ass as they return to kissing. Her hands are strong. A minute of making out and Grace already feels wild. Matthews breaks away to suck at Grace's neck again.

"Matthews," Grace murmurs, and it's supposed to be encouraging, but the other woman stops instead.

It takes Grace a moment to realize she's laughing.

"You're really gonna call me Matthews while we do this?"

"Would you prefer Phenom?"

Matthews huffs out one more laugh before putting her mouth back on Grace's skin. Her hands find the hem of Grace's tank top and slowly slide it up. Too slowly—Grace reaches down and pulls it off herself.

She's shirtless in the lap of a shirtless woman. Perhaps she can start calling her by her first name.

Phoebe—the name feels weird even in Grace's mind—is being too gentle. It isn't that Grace wants her to leave marks—in fact, she appreciates that she's being careful, especially given that the rest of the team arrives tomorrow. Wearing cover-up while training in the New Orleans heat is not a recipe for success. But Grace wants more, wants teeth instead of tongue, wants to *feel this,* because it's been too long since she felt anything like it.

"I want my mouth on your tits." Phoebe sounds breathless.

Grace's head spins. Her sports bra is tight; she probably looks more absurd than sexy as she struggles to get it off. But Matthews—Phoebe—whoever the hell she is—doesn't have any snarky comments. For once, she doesn't have any comments at all as she stares hungrily at Grace's chest. Grace has been naked in this locker room more times than she can count. But this is different. No one has ever looked at her like this in the locker room before. It's possible no one has ever looked at her like this in her life. Grace feels warm all over.

"I thought you wanted to get your mouth on them."

"Fuck yes."

Phoebe wraps her lips around one of Grace's nipples and Grace's hand shoots to the back of Phoebe's head, holding her in place. She said she wasn't interested in casual sex, and she knows her reasons, she does, but right now she can't remember a single one.

"You're so hot."

"Thanks, Phenom, but didn't we just establish there are better things you could be doing with your mouth than talking?"

Phoebe chuckles but doesn't have a smart-ass reply. She returns her attention to Grace's chest. As she sucks the other nipple into her mouth, her hands move, fingers tracing the waistline of Grace's shorts, then teasing at the bottom where they fall against her thighs. Grace can't decide what to focus on. Phoebe's mouth is amazing, but her hands are like a promise Grace wants her to immediately fulfill.

Grace keeps shifting her hips, trying to get Phoebe's hands where she wants them, but Matthews must not get the message, because instead of cupping Grace's center, she feels the need to pull away and ask, "Can I touch you?"

"You'd better."

Phoebe grins so big that when Grace leans in again, her kiss lands more on teeth than lips. Not that it matters, because when Phoebe rubs Grace through her shorts, Grace can't focus on kissing anymore. She whines, sparing a moment to consider that she'll be embarrassed about making that noise later, and rolls her hips in an effort to get more friction. Phoebe doesn't make her wait, rubbing hard and fast while doing ungodly things with her tongue against Grace's neck.

"You like this?" Phoebe asks. "Or do you want my fingers in your cunt?"

Grace whines louder. Her answer to both questions is *yes*. She never wants Phoebe to stop but she wants her clothes out of the way, she wants Phoebe to feel how wet she is. Phoebe pulls Grace's earlobe between her teeth and Grace wants the other woman's mouth on her clit instead.

"C'mon, baby," Matthews murmurs directly into Grace's ear. "Tell me how that feels."

"Good," Grace pants. Phoebe's fingers rub just right. "Jesus fuck. Good. So good."

"Yeah? You wanna come for me like this?" Once she finds that perfect spot, she doesn't move away from it, giving Grace the exact pressure she needs. "I want you to. Can we get you there?"

Of course Matthews is a talker—when is she not? It doesn't normally work for Grace, but something about Phoebe's smooth voice or the way she's making it about Grace or simply the way she's touching her— Grace likes it this time. She tries to say yes, but it comes out as a moan.

"That's it." Phoebe sounds like she swallowed a handful of gravel. "Let me hear you."

Grace isn't focused on doing what Phoebe wants. She can't even process the request. She can't think beyond *more* and *please,* saying them not with her mouth but with her body, rolling and pushing and grinding against Phoebe's fingers. Phoebe flips her hand to use her knuckles instead and Grace jerks. She lets out a hiss of pain, her leg must've moved in a way she didn't expect, but she doesn't care, she only cares about chasing the feeling coiled in her center. Phoebe slows the movement of her hand.

"Whoa," she says. "You okay?"

"Don't stop."

"I'm not." She speeds up again. "I just—"

"Don't stop. Don't stop. Don't stop."

Grace keeps her eyes clenched closed. She doesn't want to see Matthews smirking as Grace begs her.

But when Phoebe speaks again, it's soft—sweet, even—not cocky. "Go on, baby. I got you."

Grace sees stars. She shudders and shakes and Phoebe keeps rubbing, her other hand pressed flat against Grace's lower back, holding her in place on her lap as Grace comes with a quiet whimper.

It always takes Grace a moment to return to herself. When she does, Phoebe is kissing her.

"Okay, you're right," the redhead says. "I'm definitely obsessed with you. I gotta make you do that again."

"It's my turn," Grace says.

But when she tries to climb off Phoebe's lap, the other woman holds her in place.

"Just one more," Phoebe says. "Then it'll be your turn, I promise."

Grace is not used to not being in charge during sex. Truthfully, she isn't that used to sex in the first place, but when she was younger, she had been in control. She's always in control, in bed and out, on the field and off. Grace doesn't even know if she *can* come again, but it's not exactly a hardship to let Matthews try. She supposes she can not be in charge this once.

Phoebe is looking at her, hands tight around Grace's hips. She doesn't move until Grace nods. Then Matthews kisses her, slow and deep, and Grace wonders if she'll use her mouth this time. But Phoebe makes no move to adjust their positions. Grace stays on her lap, fully topless, while Phoebe takes so long with the kisses that Grace stops being worried she won't be able to come. Her first orgasm feels less like release and more like a warm-up, like her body hasn't gotten enough, like she would take every last thing Matthews would give her.

By the time Phoebe's right hand finally migrates to the top of Grace's shorts, Grace can't help the little whine she lets out. She's splayed her legs wider than necessary and has to straighten up so Phoebe has enough room.

"Is this okay?"

Grace doesn't know what else she can do to indicate this is absolutely okay. She nods, burying her head in the crook of Phoebe's neck as the other woman's fingers find purchase.

"God, you're wet," Matthews says, not like she's stating a fact, more like she's amazed. "I love it."

Grace whimpers and Phoebe presses a kiss to the side of her head.

"I love it so fucking much."

Grace loves it, too. Loves the way it makes Phoebe's fingers slip and slide around her clit. Phoebe focuses her attention there at first, never too direct or offering too much pressure, just enough to drive Grace mad.

Right into Grace's ear, she whispers, "Can I go inside?"

"Please."

Phoebe slides one finger in and out, then does the same with another before pushing them both back in.

"Fuck."

She and Grace say it at the same time.

"Your cunt feels so good."

Grace whimpers again.

Matthews pumps her fingers, slowly at first, but she got Grace too worked up for slow. Grace bounces in her lap, trying to control the pace herself. Phoebe takes the hint and speeds up.

"Is this what you want?"

It is. It's exactly what Grace wants. Why the hell did she say she wasn't interested in casual sex when it feels this good?

Phoebe keeps talking. "You're so fucking hot when you come. Your eyes closed and that little pink mouth open. I can't wait to feel it like this, feel your cunt clench around my fingers."

Fuck is this ever working for Grace. Her skin is hot all over.

"Can you take another?"

Grace shakes her head. She *could,* but she doesn't want it. She doesn't want anything but this, two fingers thrusting up while Grace grinds her hips down. Phoebe's thumb hits Grace's clit every time.

"Yeah, just like that, you're so good," Matthews murmurs. "You're so hot fucking my hand, look at you."

Grace opens her eyes even though she doesn't have the vantage point. She can't see Matthews's fingers as they move inside of her, but she doesn't need to, the look on Phoebe's face is enough. When she realizes Grace is watching, Matthews surges forward to kiss her. The movement takes her even deeper, and Grace moans into her mouth.

Grace has gotten pretty good at getting herself off the last few years. It doesn't feel like this. It must be that someone else is touching her. That she can't predict the way Phoebe's fingers are going to twist, the way she's going to nip at the sensitive skin of Grace's neck, the way her voice slides down Grace's spine and embeds itself in the center of her pelvis.

It never takes Grace this long when she does it to herself, but it never feels this good, either. And she certainly never comes twice. It's usually more about release than anything. Grace doesn't know what this is about. She could get lost worrying about it—about what it means and what happens next and how this is going to affect the team—but Phoebe somehow doubles the strength behind each thrust, and Grace's runaway brain comes to a screeching halt.

"Yeah?" Phoebe says like it's a question. "You gonna come for me, baby girl?"

If you asked Grace beforehand if she'd like being called *baby girl,* she would've said absolutely not. But she must, because she doesn't have words, but her body answers Matthews all the same. The tight coil inside her snaps or releases or *something*—she doesn't know how to describe the way pleasure crests like a wave, then breaks, crashing and churning and flowing around her. She vaguely recognizes that Phoebe is still talking, but she can't make out anything she's saying over the sea-foam froth of satisfaction coating her brain.

It is without a doubt the best orgasm Grace has had in years, maybe in her entire life.

She breathes heavily, willing herself to recover quickly, but she feels truly lost. Phoebe stays motionless, her fingers still in Grace's cunt, nothing moving but her mouth, which presses the occasional kiss to Grace's cheek. At some point, she pulls her fingers out, quietly shushing Grace when she whimpers in response.

Grace shakes her head to try to clear it. It's embarrassing, lolling in the lap of this rookie. She has to get it together, has to pay back the favor, to show Matthews she can give just as good as she can take. It's another moment before Grace is sure she can move, but as soon as she can, she climbs off Phoebe's lap. She doesn't acknowledge the wobble in her legs, like that will stop Matthews from noticing. When Grace looks at her, though, Matthews isn't smirking—instead she looks almost devastated.

"It's my turn," Grace says, and Matthews is already grinning again.

Grace lifts Phoebe's legs and spins her entire body with them, turning her so she's sideways, straddling the bench.

"Yes, ma'am," Matthews says, lying back when Grace pushes at her shoulders.

But Grace pulls her up again immediately. She needs to be more naked. Grace yanks at Phoebe's sports bra. Finally, somewhere Phoebe doesn't have quite as many freckles. They fade out on this skin that never sees the sun, fewer and fewer on the way to dusty pink nipples. Grace lets Matthews deal with actually taking the bra off, because as soon as she has the chance, she gets her mouth on those nipples.

"Oh fuck," Phoebe groans.

The peaks stiffen in Grace's mouth, first one, then the other. Matthews tastes salty, and Grace knows rationally that it's sweat, that maybe she should be disgusted, but she loves it. Phoebe's boobs are so small

Grace can almost fit one in her mouth if she opens wide enough. She sucks in as much as she can and Phoebe's hips come up off the bench.

"Fuck. Fuck fuck fuck. God, that feels good."

Grace pauses. "You don't have to . . ."

Phoebe blinks up at her like she has no idea what Grace is going to say.

"I don't need a performance."

Grace puts her mouth back on Phoebe's skin so they don't have to talk about it.

"Performance?" Matthews gasps as Grace closes her teeth around a nipple. "Fuck, Grace, Jesus. It's not a performance. You're just making me feel really fucking good."

Grace's whole body flushes at that. She slides her hand into Phoebe's underwear and doesn't mind the way the redhead whispers *yes yes yes please yes.*

If her wetness is any indication, Matthews is not lying about how Grace is making her feel.

Grace keeps her mouth on Phoebe's chest while her fingers play. She doesn't go inside yet—there's plenty of time. Except when she gets the pads of her middle and index finger on either side of Phoebe's clit to rub, Matthews clutches tight at her shoulders. Grace didn't realize she was so close, but she's coming then, hips thrusting upward, and finally she's not talking, but that doesn't mean she's quiet, just that her mouth can only make vowels. Grace pulls a nipple between her teeth and Matthews gets louder still.

After, Grace eases up. She doesn't *want* to, but she doesn't know how sensitive Matthews gets after coming, so she releases Phoebe's nipple and slows the movement of her fingertips. The breath Phoebe takes makes her chest heave. It turns out Matthews did not deal with her bra at all; it's still on, cutting a line above her breasts. The blissful smile on her face makes Grace pretty sure she doesn't mind.

Grace feels powerful making Phoebe feel this good. But it doesn't seem fair that she didn't get to go inside. Not fair at all, so she remedies the situation by sliding her fingers backward. In the moment Grace pauses to check in, Phoebe nods so frantically there's no doubt of what she wants. What they both want. Grace buries two fingers in her.

"*Fuck*," Matthews whines.

Grace doesn't usually use the word *cunt,* but the way it sounded coming out of Phoebe's mouth earlier was everything. And Phoebe's cunt is everything, too. Molten wet heat. So tight Grace doesn't have much room to move her fingers, but the whine Phoebe lets out when Grace curls them makes her do it again and again.

"Shit. Feels so good. Grace, you're so good."

Grace has never slept with anyone who talks as much as Phoebe does during the act. She hates how much she likes it. Phoebe's voice has gone deep and scratchy, and if it were possible to touch a sound, Grace would rub her entire body against it. She can't get in her head wondering if the other party is enjoying it when Phoebe is constantly saying how much she does. And it's not just what Grace is doing that Phoebe compliments—it's Grace herself.

"You're so good. You fuck me so good. Oh *fuck,* right there, yes. Fuck, Grace."

Grace *wants* to be good for her. She never wants to stop fucking her. She wants to give Phoebe everything she wants. She was supposed to be keeping Matthews at a distance, protecting herself. There's no distance between them now, Matthews beneath Grace on the bench, two of Grace's fingers anchored inside her. Grace never should have let herself do this. Anything that feels as good as Phoebe complimenting her must be dangerous.

"Right there. That's perfect. Fuck, you're perfect. Yes, Grace, please. Grace. Please."

Phoebe opens her eyes to look up at Grace. Her brow is furrowed, pupils taking up most of her green eyes. She looks so desperate, Grace can't do anything but curl her fingers one more time and finally say something herself.

"Come."

Phoebe follows directions.

Grace was too busy with Phoebe's chest to watch her face the last time she came, but she watches now. She sees the soft way that it breaks open, the flush under all those freckles, the O of her open-mouthed moan. Phoebe's skin glistens, wisps of her hair sweat-stuck to her forehead, the rest of it billowing around her, cascading off the bench toward the floor. She is absolutely gorgeous, and Grace was right: this was a terrible idea.

As quickly as she can without being obvious, Grace extricates herself from Matthews. She stands, topless, beside the bench, in front of their lockers. Matthews continues to lie there, feet on the ground on either side of the bench, her sports bra still not all the way off, smiling with her eyes closed as she catches her breath.

Grace shifts from one foot to another and almost gasps at how wet she is. *This is a terrible idea,* her brain says, but her body wants to come again, wants to make Matthews come again.

Phoebe opens her eyes. When they find Grace, her smile goes even wider.

"Can I eat you out in the showers?" Then: "Unless you want me to use a dental dam, because I don't have one on me, so in that case maybe we could go back to my place and I could eat you out there?"

Of course she doesn't have a dental dam on her. Who carries dental dams?

"But, I mean, I got tested last month, and I'm good to go if you are," Phoebe says since Grace apparently took too long to respond.

"I . . ."

"No pressure either way. I just really wanna get my mouth on your cunt."

Grace should say no. Grace should never have straddled Matthews in the first place. She should never have shown up at the stadium tonight.

"Pretty please?" Phoebe says, batting her eyelashes.

Grace doesn't say no.

Thirteen

"I've never had showers this nice," Phoebe says as she turns on the water.

Grace shifts her weight back and forth on her feet.

Right. Talking about crappy shower facilities isn't exactly arousing. It's true, though—at Mapleton, Phoebe used to wager her place in the shower line. It was an important bet, given that the hot water usually ran out before the team finished.

The water here, though, warms with ease, and Phoebe is confident it will last. She catches Grace by the hips and turns her under the spray.

Grace Henderson is the most beautiful woman Phoebe has ever seen. Her dark brown hair falls in tangled waves over her shoulders, the strands remembering the braids they were in ten minutes ago. Her tan skin stands out against the white tiles of the shower. Phoebe likes where it goes pale, down across Grace's chest. She has bigger boobs than most soccer players—her bras must cost an exorbitant amount, but that's not really what Phoebe's thinking about right now, because she's tracing Grace's crisscrossing tan lines with the tip of her index finger, following the lighter skin down, over the swell of her breast, to her already pebbled nipple. Phoebe wants to study her, wants to research the exact color of her areolas. They're some kind of rosy brown, with layers of peach or salmon or maybe even coral pink. Phoebe pinches one, and it blushes pinker, what a party trick. Goosebumps prickle along Grace's arms even though the water sluicing over her body is warm. Phoebe easily loses focus when something is not interesting to her, but she could look at Grace forever.

"You specifically asked if you could go down on me." Grace breaks the reverent silence between them.

Phoebe drags her eyes back to Grace's. "Yeah?"

"Are you going to or are we just going to stand here?"

Phoebe cackles. She can't help it. It makes Grace furrow her brow, which makes Phoebe laugh harder.

"Grace Henderson," she says when she has her breath back, "not interested in foreplay. Noted."

Grace rolls her eyes. "I didn't say I'm not—"

The rest of the sentence is lost when Phoebe kisses her. If Grace wants her pussy ate, Phoebe is not about to let her down. She plasters her body against Grace's, nudging her backward until she breaks the kiss with a gasp when her back touches the wall.

"Cold," she says.

"Sorry," Phoebe says, but that gasp was so sexy, she's not really.

She further apologizes by ducking her head and taking one of Grace's perfect nipples in her mouth. The noise Grace makes sounds like she forgives her.

Phoebe loves sex. She loves it. She loves another body against hers, loves the different levels of give—sucking on the hard line of Grace's collarbone with her hand squeezing Grace's boob. Phoebe drops to her knees—she doesn't want another critique from Grace—and she loves this the most. Phoebe likes to come—obviously, like, she's pretty sure most people who like sex like to come, because orgasms are great—but she likes making people come more. Not just *giving* them an orgasm but *making* them. Being so good at flicking her tongue or pumping her fingers—or both—that the other person doesn't have any option but to come.

Grace's legs are still closed, but Phoebe, kneeling on the shower tile, can smell her cunt anyway. God, this is going to be fun.

Grace winces as Phoebe pushes her left leg wide.

"What was that? Are you okay?"

"I'm fine," Grace says.

But she winced in Phoebe's lap, too. Phoebe wants to make her feel good, not to hurt her.

"Are you sure? Is this a comfortable position?"

Phoebe's hand is on Grace's thigh, holding her leg up and open.

"It'd be a lot more comfortable if you put your mouth on me already."

She's deflecting, but Phoebe lets her get away with it for now.

"Like this?" Phoebe asks, sucking the wet skin of the inside of Grace's knee.

"Matthews." Her last name sounds like a warning.

"Is this not what you wanted?"

Phoebe slowly moves her mouth up Grace's leg. She bites just below the crease where Grace's leg meets her torso, the skin so soft and pale. It's hard to tease when all Phoebe wants to do is bury her tongue in Grace's cunt. The scent is deep and musky and Phoebe wants it all over her face.

She leans away instead, because it's the only thing she can think of that will help her last. She switches hands holding Grace's leg up so she can bring her mouth all the way to Grace's ankle. The thin skin over the joint is like butterfly wings, like if Phoebe's not careful, her teeth will tear right through it. She drags her tongue up to Grace's calf and bites, and the contrast is stark: there's no give, the muscle solid and strong.

"How are your legs this long when you're so short?" Phoebe asks as she continues her path upward.

Grace always wears the shortest shorts, so Phoebe can't leave marks the way she'd like to. She wants evidence of her mouth all over the inside of Grace's thighs, but she's gentle instead, careful. Grace's hips are doing these little stop starts, forward then back, like she wants more but refuses to ask for it. Phoebe doesn't make her. Instead, she wraps one hand around Grace's right knee, the fingers of her other hand digging into the thick cords of Grace's left quad. Water from the shower splashes against Phoebe's side, but she's forgotten about it—it's nothing compared to the woman open and exposed in front of her. There's a mess of curls between her thighs, wild but so soft; Phoebe knows from slipping her hand down Grace's shorts earlier. That was good but this is better, getting to see everything.

"What a pretty pussy," Phoebe murmurs, more to herself than anything.

On the first lick up the center of Grace's cunt, Phoebe moans almost as loud as Grace.

"You taste so fucking good," she says.

There's no way Phoebe doesn't love fucking women—fingers rubbing or grinding on thighs or snapping her hips while strapped up—but this might be her favorite. It's the most personal, maybe even vulnerable. Phoebe's slept with women who claimed she *didn't have to,* like it's a hardship instead of her favorite part. She's slept with women who wouldn't let her unless they'd just showered, like they were afraid of being dirty. Grace, thank God, doesn't seem to have any qualms. They're in the shower, but haven't showered yet, not really; there's still sweat on her skin from a half hour of keep-away, but that doesn't stop her from rolling her hips downward toward Phoebe's mouth.

Phoebe is equally enthusiastic. She tries to stay focused, to not lose herself to the satisfaction of cunnilingus. Just because it's her favorite part doesn't mean it's *about* her. Grace is slick from her first two orgasms, and Phoebe laps at her, paying attention to what makes Grace gasp or clench. She winces, actually, when Phoebe pays too much attention to her clit, apparently still too sensitive for that right now, which is no problem for Phoebe, who dips down and curls her tongue into Grace's opening instead.

Grace lets out the loudest noise she's made this whole time, a moan that reverberates off the walls. Immediately, Phoebe wants to hear it again. Grace has been quiet, mostly, throughout—quiet enough she'd assumed Phoebe's noise was a *performance*—Phoebe is gonna have to address that more later—and Phoebe wants to make her scream, to completely take her apart. Grace Henderson, always put together, knows exactly what she wants, total badass, and Phoebe wants her messy, lost, splayed open. To make her feel better than she's felt in her entire *life*. She wants Grace to know exactly how perfect she is.

"That's it, baby," Phoebe says, except Grace probably doesn't understand, because Phoebe refuses to ease up with her tongue to say it. She keeps chasing Grace's taste to where she's wettest, dipping in and out until finally Grace's hands come down to hold herself even wider.

Phoebe pulls back, then, and blows a stream of air over Grace's clit. Grace lets out a noise somewhere between a whine and a shriek.

"You taste *so good*," Phoebe says. "You're perfect."

She licks a stripe up Grace, bottom to top, full and deep, swirling around her clit at the end. Grace doesn't wince this time, doesn't pull away. Instead, her leg goes out wider still, barely grounded enough to hold herself up.

"You like that?" Phoebe says, and does it again.

Grace's eyes are clenched closed, her head tilted back against the shower wall. She adjusts to help spread herself wider, like she can't be open enough for Phoebe. Phoebe fucking agrees. She licks Grace again and again while Grace twists her hips and whimpers. For half a moment, Phoebe considers stopping, going slower, making it last even longer. Maybe she should, especially if this is going to be the only time she gets to do this, but she can't stop making Grace feel good.

"You want my fingers, too, baby, or just my mouth?" Grace nods desperately and Phoebe doesn't know which she was saying yes to. She slides her fingers up next to where Grace opens for her, and asks again. "Fingers?"

"Yes, Matthews, fuck me, Jesus."

It only takes one finger actually, slid inside and curled while Phoebe's tongue does cursive over Grace's clit, and Grace lets go of her own body to hold on to Phoebe's, one hand clutching at her shoulder while the other tangles in her hair. It's Grace's loudest orgasm yet. Phoebe wants to talk her through it, but she wants to keep her tongue on Grace's clit more. She plans to stay on it until Grace pulls her away, but then Grace's legs give out, and Phoebe has to stop licking her cunt to catch her instead. Phoebe wants to laugh—Grace is sort of folded in half over

CLEAT CUTE | 105

her shoulders—but figures it's impolite to tease someone still gasping for breath.

Phoebe has never been very good at estimating time, but it's gotta be at least a full minute before Grace gets her feet back underneath her. She straightens up and combs her fingers through her wet hair. Phoebe is still on her knees.

"You good?"

Grace nods. "Fine. Yeah. Good."

They've been mostly out of the spray this whole time, the shower-head above and to the right of Grace, but when Phoebe stands, she gets a face full of water. She sputters and laughs and steps backward. That's what she gets for paying more attention to Grace than to her surroundings.

"Are *you* good?" Grace asks.

"Gonna do my best not to drown, yeah," Phoebe says.

Instead of crowding closer to share the water, Grace turns on the next shower. Phoebe chuckles quietly.

Maybe Phoebe should be nervous or embarrassed or at least concerned by the way Grace goes silent as they shower, separately, but she's not. Sex endorphins, maybe, but Phoebe is happy. She's never fucked someone until they lost their balance and had them regret it. And Grace is Grace, standoffish and distrustful to the point Phoebe basically had to bully her into being friends. Of course she's going to be weird about this. Maybe she's not being weird; she's just returned to her previous stance regarding talking about this. But whatever, the sex was good, and fun, and so when they're back in the locker room, towels wrapped under their armpits, and Grace is looking anywhere but at her, Phoebe just grins and faces the awkwardness head-on.

"Is this where you tell me you had fun but . . ."

Grace still doesn't look at her. "I haven't changed my stance on relationships. I am not interested."

"Okay," Phoebe says, pulling her duffel out of her locker. She shoved a set of clean clothes in it earlier—and a toothbrush, just in case the night went *really* well and she ended up at Grace's place. "But have you changed your stance on casual sex? Because when the sex is that good, it seems like you should."

"I didn't say it was that good." Grace immediately backtracks, finally making eye contact. "No, I'm sorry, you're right. It was great."

"It's a good thing you took that back." Phoebe smirks. "Otherwise, I might have to remind you that I gave you three orgasms, and you couldn't even stand after the last one."

Grace rolls her eyes. "And yet you're still reminding me."

"Yeah, sorry," Phoebe says, not sorry in the least. "I'm proud of making your legs not work."

Grace's cheeks go the cutest shade of pink.

"Actually, speaking of your legs"—Phoebe reaches behind herself to do up the hooks on her bra—"what's wrong with your left hip?"

That cute blush turns into a glower immediately. "What do you mean? Nothing's wrong with me."

"Uh, you definitely winced multiple times. You must be in some kind of pain."

"It's nothing. I'm fine." Grace turns to her locker to start dressing. "Anyway, you're right. It would be a shame to say no to sex that good."

"It'd be a fucking travesty, an affront to Sappho herself, but don't think you can distract me from the fact that you're obviously injured by agreeing to sleep with me again."

She could *absolutely* distract Phoebe, but she doesn't need to know that.

"I'm not injured," Grace says. "I'm just getting older. It's natural to have aches and pains."

"Grace, seriously. You're twenty-six. That's hardly ancient."

"Fine, if you don't wanna sleep with me again, you can just say that."

"Oh my God." Phoebe laughs. "I never came close to saying that. But you're being ridiculous about this, which makes me think you know it's a big deal. What did the trainer say?"

Grace stays focused on her locker.

"You haven't told the trainer?"

"I told you it's nothing."

Phoebe is fully dressed by now, and Grace is still in a bra and underwear. The way Phoebe takes a second to enjoy all the skin on display makes it incredibly clear how easily Grace could distract her if she really wanted to.

"Okay, look," Phoebe says. "I absolutely want to sleep with you again. But I'm not going to until you talk to the trainer."

"Oh, you really think I want to fuck you so badly that withholding sex is going to control me somehow?"

The affront in her voice reminds Phoebe of their moment in the hotel at January camp, Grace trying to one-up her with that not-kiss.

"I guess we'll see."

Phoebe says it with a shrug and a smirk, and Grace scoffs like she's infuriating, but that doesn't mean she's wrong.

Fourteen

"You know you don't have to be here this early, right?" Scott, an assistant coach, says as he hands Grace a cup of coffee.

"And yet you got me coffee," Grace says. "Mixed signals."

"I knew you'd be here and I'm nice. Doesn't mean you *have* to be here."

It's true. Most of the team isn't due in for an hour, but new players report early to get everything set up—a locker assignment, ID cards to get into the building, Krewe gear to practice in, and measurements taken for jerseys. Grace doesn't *need* to be here, but she's the captain. New players need to know they can count on her. Orientation is never too busy, either; it's a good way to ease back into her captain duties.

"Someone has to give the rooks the behind-the-scenes tour," Grace says.

"The team quite literally employs people for that," Scott mutters before taking a sip of his coffee.

He knows it's a lost cause; they have this conversation every year.

"Rodriguez!" Grace puts on a smile. "Good to see you again."

Their new forward practically jumps when she realizes Grace is talking to her. "Oh! Hi!"

Grace isn't tall, and still Gabby Rodriguez only comes up to her nose.

"Go ahead and get checked in, and once you get your picture taken, I'll take you on a tour."

"Okay! Thanks!"

This is what Grace is used to from new players. Even though they spent an entire national team camp together, Rodriguez is obviously eager to please. She's nothing like Matthews.

Not that Grace is thinking of Matthews.

To Scott, she says, "Thanks for the coffee. See you on the pitch."

He salutes her with his to-go cup, and she's off to captain duties.

· · · ·

Grace is in the middle of showing Rodriguez where her locker is when someone squeals, "G-Rod!"

Rodriguez squeals right back. "Matty!"

Grace didn't recognize the first voice, but she recognizes the lanky limbs and wild red hair as Matthews and Rodriguez hurl their arms around each other.

"I guess Phoebe Matthews requires no introduction."

The rookies giggle.

"We met at national team camp," Gabby says.

Right. Of course. Grace knows that. After their bet, Grace avoided Matthews, but she didn't manage to avoid watching her. Phoebe made friends easily. Her first national team camp and she won over Madeeha and even Fish without much effort. But it was Rodriguez she was usually next to during meals, laughing loudly enough to get Grace's attention even if she hadn't already been looking.

"You two are going to give me trouble this year, aren't you?"

"No guarantees," Phoebe says with a wink.

Rodriguez goes to bump her hip against Phoebe's, but she's so short her hip only hits Matthews mid-thigh.

"I'm so freakin' excited for this season," she says.

Matthews beams. "Bet I beat you in Rookie of the Year voting."

"Oh my gosh." Rodriguez laughs. "I'm gonna go get my measurements taken for my jersey and come up with a good wager for that, since I'm definitely gonna beat you."

"I'll walk you," Grace says.

"That's okay! I saw the sign on the way down here. I can find it." She flutters her fingers in a wave. "See you in a bit!"

And so Grace and Phoebe are alone in the locker room.

The last time they were alone here, Phoebe was spread out on the bench not three feet away. Grace clears her throat.

"Did I get here early enough to get my hair braided?" Phoebe asks.

Fuck. Grace forgot that little deal, what with all the orgasms she had after it.

"I've been helping get the rookies oriented," Grace says. "I should check in with Scott."

"Doesn't this count as helping a rookie get oriented?"

She holds out a brush and hair tie like an offering.

It's fine. Grace has done the hair of pretty much everyone on this team. There's no reason this time has to be weird simply because she and Phoebe slept together yesterday.

Phoebe sits on the bench where they had taken each other apart and scrubs a hand through her hair. She has more than anyone Grace has ever seen. It's thick and heavy as Grace examines it. She could create artwork with the amount of hair Matthews has, but there's no reason for that. Two braids, she decides. Simple. Quick.

"When I was nine, my coach told the team if we missed a play because we were pushing our hair out of our faces, we'd be benched for the next game," Grace says.

"Jesus," Matthews mutters.

"That's when I started learning how to braid."

It's a story Matthews has probably heard before—Grace trots it out whenever anyone asks. Grace had practiced french braiding on her sister's dolls, then on her sister, before figuring out how to adjust the technique to do it on herself. It was still easier for her on other people, even more than a decade and a half later.

Grace has a collection of similar stories: crowd-pleasers that don't reveal more about herself than she's willing to share.

"When I was nine, my team was lucky if we all knew what direction we were supposed to be kicking the ball in."

"I don't believe you," Grace says, separating Phoebe's hair in the center. "You're trying to tell me you weren't a phenom as a kid, too?"

Matthews sits up a little straighter, like she's preening. "I didn't say *I* didn't know what direction we were supposed to be kicking it in. Just that the team as a whole wasn't exactly Olympic Development quality."

"ODP didn't start until I was eleven."

"Oh, excuse me for getting the facts of your life wrong. You'd think someone obsessed with you would've known that."

Grace tugs the brush through Phoebe's hair harder than required.

Like she's retaliating, Matthews asks, "Have you met with the trainer yet?"

"I told you I don't need to. I'm fine."

"You're obviously not."

The brush gets caught in tangles and Grace forces herself to extricate it rather than yank it out.

"I've been busy, Phenom. I don't even know if Dawn is here yet."

"But you're going to talk to her?"

There's no one else in the locker room, but Grace lowers her voice to almost a whisper as she secures half of Phoebe's hair with a hair tie to keep it out of the way. "Why? Do you already want to fuck me again?"

It's supposed to throw Matthews off her game, but it doesn't.

"I mean, yeah, absolutely," Phoebe says. "I wanted to fuck you again immediately after we stopped."

She talks loudly, like always. Grace doesn't know why she herself spoke more quietly about them sleeping together than about going to Dawn—it's the latter she's more worried about anyone discovering. No, she doesn't want her sex life broadcast, but at least that wouldn't affect her playing time.

"How many times did I beat you last night?" Grace changes the subject. Exposure therapy went a little too far; her body seems reluctant to forget that Matthews is great in bed. This morning, Grace startled awake from a dream about her. Three orgasms and still Grace's subconscious wanted more. "Clearly this is not something that affects me on the field."

Phoebe scoffs. "What—because you could handle a game of keep-away with me? You know that's not real game play."

"Well, I did just fine at the end of last season, didn't I?"

"Your leg has been injured since last season?"

Fuck. Grace should not have said that, but Matthews is under her skin.

"I told you, I'm not injured." The bump in Phoebe's hair is so amateurish Grace undoes her work and starts over on the braid. "I'm getting older is all. And no one needs to know about it, because it doesn't slow me down on the field."

That's mostly true. And anyway, it's natural for players to get slower as they age. Grace doesn't need to draw attention to the fact that she isn't some young superstar anymore.

"I don't believe you," Matthews says. "And you don't know if it slows you down on the field when you've made no effort to fix it."

"Well, we still won the championship last year, didn't we?"

"How can you act like this doesn't matter? It's a World Cup year. You really want to be not at your best during the World Cup?"

Grace doesn't answer.

"For fuck's sake, Henderson," Phoebe practically growls. "If you won't do it for yourself, do it for your teammates. You think it's fair to them that you're not at your best? How are you gonna have their backs?"

For the first time, Grace considers going to the trainer. Not because Matthews made a good point—she'd actually made Grace's point for her. *Of course* Grace has her teammates' backs. They have no reason to doubt her, and she isn't going to give them one by whining about typical aches and pains. But Phoebe is so worked up about this, it's clear she isn't going to let up. It might be worth going to Dawn herself, if only to stop Matthews from turning her in.

The thought of whining rubs Grace the wrong way, even if she'd probably score points with Dawn. Trainers always want to know absolutely *everything* about you. The first time Grace got her period, she told Ilse, the national team trainer, before she told her mom. But this simply isn't a big deal. Dawn would tell coaches and staff, and Grace would have to either tell Amanda herself or tell her agent and let him handle that. If she gets benched—which she most likely will, in the name of *rest*—people notice, reporters start asking questions, suddenly the entire WoSo world is debating whether or not she'll be well enough to make the World Cup roster.

Even though it's a fake situation in her head, the possibility is annoying enough that Grace accidentally pulls the sections of the second braid a little too tight, and Phoebe gasps. Memories of the night before envelop Grace. She can hear other noises Phoebe made: her pleased chuckle at how wet Grace was in her lap; her whine when Grace bit her nipples; her voice every time she said how good Grace was, how perfect.

Fucking in the locker room was the worst idea.

"Oh man, I miss that," a voice says, jolting Grace from her filthy reverie.

Looking over her shoulder, Grace sees Ash, the Krewe's starting goalie. Sorrell is beside them. Having so many eyes on her makes Grace want to step away from Matthews, but she isn't finished. Not that it's weird for her to be doing someone's hair—but she feels obvious being so close to Phoebe. Like people will take one look at the two of them and know what happened last night.

"The only bad thing about having short hair is Grace Henderson can't give me braids." Ash runs their hand through their white-blond buzz cut.

See? Totally normal for Grace to be braiding Phoebe's hair.

"The only bad thing?" Sorrell asks. "What about when you first shaved it and didn't put on sunscreen?"

"I did put on sunscreen," Ash says. "I always put on sunscreen. I just didn't realize I needed it on my scalp."

Grace remembers. Ash is Welsh, with the palest skin of anyone on the team, except that day, when the top of their head burned bright red. They started keeping their buzz a little longer after that.

"Enough about me," Ash says loudly as Sorrell continues to tease them. "Who's the newcomer in our midst?"

Matthews turns her head to say hello and Grace has to turn with her.

"Hi. Phoebe Matthews. New to your midfield."

"A rookie and you've already got Henderson doing your hair? You must learn quick."

"When you have a leader like Grace, it makes it easy," Matthews says.

Sorrell snorts, and Ash throws their hands in the air.

"Oh my God, ew, what a suck-up. I take back my previous compliment."

Phoebe laughs along with them, like she's never found a group she didn't fit in with, then tilts her head back to look at Grace, which isn't helpful for a number of reasons. First of all, her smile is frustratingly distracting, and second, Grace's hands are still in her hair.

"Stop moving," Grace says. "I'm not done."

"Yes, ma'am," Matthews says.

Grace ignores the way the other two snicker. "Ash, how's that finger?"

"This one?" Ash asks, flipping her off.

It *is* the right finger, though—they jammed it in the semis last season and spent the entire second half on the verge of tears.

"It's fine. It's been four months."

"I know, but injuries can linger," Grace says.

Matthews does a poor job of disguising a snort in a cough.

How many times does Grace have to say she's not injured? There's a difference between an injury and aging. She's been hurt before, tore her ACL when she was nineteen. She can still remember the audible pop when her foot stayed planted instead of turning with her leg. That's what an injury is—sudden and jarring. Aging, on the other hand, is a slow simmer, like a frog in a pot of water, not realizing it's boiling until it's too late.

There's noise outside the locker room, voices unintelligible in anything except their excitement. The rest of the team must have begun arriving. Grace can't help her grin; she loves her team.

She finishes the second braid in record time. It's a lot easier without Matthews bothering her.

"Now get out of here before anyone sees and I'm roped into doing everyone's hair."

"Thanks, Captain," Phoebe says and flounces off.

Grace isn't annoyed by how easily she leaves. Grace *wants* her to leave; she wants to get away from Matthews, to prevent anyone from noticing anything. It's *good* that Phoebe acts like there's nothing going on between the two of them. Because there isn't. It doesn't matter that they slept together. It doesn't matter what Phoebe thinks she knows. She's just the same as any other teammate. And after Grace does the hair of any other teammate, they say thank you and go on their way.

And anyway, Grace doesn't have time to think about Matthews. She has a practice to run.

Fifteen

Phoebe spends most of training trying to talk to anyone who isn't Grace. She laughed at the idea that she's obsessed with Grace, but growing up, she definitely was. She wanted to be her. When they were alone last week, it was easier to see Grace as any other person. Seeing her running a drill, leading by example, being a captain—Grace gets a little of that celebrity mythos back. It makes Phoebe feel like a kid, in that good, childlike-sense-of-wonder way, but also in that embarrassing, young-and-inexperienced way. She doesn't want to be seen as having a crush on the veteran.

It doesn't help that another reason Phoebe is avoiding Grace is to avoid jumping her bones. Grace's hands in her hair had driven Phoebe crazy. She cannot be *horny* at her first team practice.

She is, though. It's competence porn, watching Grace. Or, like, leadership porn, or something. Phoebe likes it, is the point. Not that she will be acting on it. Not until Grace gets her leg looked at.

At least there are plenty of other things to pay attention to. Phoebe only met two coaches at the draft—head coach Eric Givhan and his assistant Scott Kramer. There's another assistant coach and the goalkeeper coach, plus multiple trainers and a PA and someone called a performance specialist. Phoebe forgets most of their names almost immediately after shaking hands, but she remembers Dawn, the head trainer. The one Grace is avoiding. Phoebe does a little better with the names of her teammates, though it helps that she's watched the majority of them play in the AWSA. Plus, there's Kayla and Gabby, whom she knows from January camp. It turns out Gabby lives on the same floor as Phoebe at the apartment building. Then there's Ash, their goalie, and Phoebe has to be careful not to seem too obsessed with them either, because they were one of the first openly nonbinary players in the league, and so Phoebe's kind of obsessed with them. Queerness equals coolness, in Phoebe's opinion.

Which—speaking of—Phoebe can't even tell if Grace is out. Okay, sure, maybe training is not the place Grace feels like sharing her identity, but Phoebe and Ash have a heated discussion about the hottest Charlie's Angel—from the original to the early 2000s remakes to the most recent—and Kayla and a couple of other teammates weigh in, too, so some people are okay sharing how queer they are here. (The correct answer is Lucy Liu, obviously.)

Not that it matters. Grace doesn't have to be out. Phoebe is much more interested in why Grace refuses to admit she's injured. What's the point? Why would you want to play hurt? Well, okay, that isn't exactly the right question. Phoebe has absolutely played injured when she didn't wanna leave a game. Like when someone's cleats gashed open the skin of her knee, and she covered it with gauze at halftime so she could go back in. And there was the memorable—or not so memorable, as it turned out—time she played with a concussion, swearing she was fine after her head connected with the goalie's on a corner kick. Apparently, she ended up scoring the winning goal, but she couldn't read or look at her phone or do anything without wearing sunglasses for two full days afterward.

But it isn't like they're in the middle of a game. They weren't even in the preseason until today. And if it were any other player, Grace would tell them to go to the trainer. Phoebe knows because, in addition to inquiring after Ash's finger, Grace asks Colleen about a nagging ankle injury. It's only her own problems she chooses to ignore.

As for Phoebe, Grace isn't ignoring *her,* exactly. She can't tell if Grace actually goes out of her way to avoid her, or if Phoebe herself is just paying Grace so much attention that it feels like it.

During drills, at least, Phoebe is sufficiently distracted. Every moment of downtime, though, her eyes find their way to Grace. She simply commands attention. It's almost like she became a different person when the rest of the team arrived—she isn't Grace anymore, she's the Captain. She seems taller somehow, even though Phoebe still has seven inches on her. It's like on the field, her presence is so big you forget she isn't quite 5'4". Or—well, that's what the internet says, anyway. Not that Phoebe looked her up after their not-kiss or anything.

Her hair, in a single french braid leading to a braided ponytail, is neat. Perfect. Proper. Phoebe wants to ruin it. She wants Grace's hands in her hair like they were last night, not this morning. There's something about the idea of taking a woman so put together completely apart.

Yeah, Phoebe cannot be thinking these things at her first AWSA practice. She does manage to survive the day with no overt displays of horniness. Choking on water when Grace pours a little of her own bottle over her head doesn't count.

Every soccer team Phoebe has ever been on, the team stretches together at the end of practice. Stretching together is always Phoebe's favorite part of practice. It's where you get to know your teammates, where someone inevitably starts taking off their cleats and socks and whoever's next to them complains about the smell, where after hard practices everyone's too tired to even lean over and stretch, where leaders—and sometimes even rookies—give inspiring speeches about what you've been through together and what you have ahead of you, where you're not worried about winning or losing because you have your team with you. Phoebe has always said soccer is her favorite thing in the world, but deep down, the game itself has always been second to her team.

It's no different with the Krewe—neither the stretching, nor Phoebe's attachment to her teammates. Even now, when she barely knows most of them, she's ride or die. Practice felt normal because practice *is* normal, similar drills and lectures and the same type of cleats on her feet since she was thirteen, but stretching afterward, even though it's what always happens at the end of a training session, Phoebe can hardly believe this is her life. For the entire season, she gets to practice and play and win and lose and stretch with this team.

Unless she makes the national team, but for once, that's not what she's focused on.

She's focused on trying to wrap her hand farther over her toes than Gabby is managing to do beside her.

"God, you're fucking flexible," Phoebe mutters.

"To be fair, your legs are much longer than mine," Gabby says.

There's a full foot of height difference between the two of them.

As they switch to the butterfly stretch, Gabby asks, "You wanna hang out later?"

"Absolutely," Phoebe says. "I've gotta tell you about my week of New Orleans adventures."

She's not going to tell Gabby *everything*, of course. She's not going to tell anyone everything, not even Teddy. She's gonna keep her big mouth shut for once. But Grace isn't the only good thing about New Orleans.

"Wait, you've already been here a week?" Gabby asks.

"Yeah," Phoebe says. "I came in early to find a part-time job and succeeded. Got a serving gig at a diner."

Gabby groans. "Please don't remind me that I probably need to get a second job."

"Okay, okay, sorry. Less draining things are also happening! Like I've been exploring the city a bit. With Grace's help."

"Really?"

"Yeah, she has excellent taste in restaurants. We went to a beignet place—not the one in the French Quarter but the other one—and another day got the most amazing breakfast tacos. I forget what it's called but we should go sometime, it was so good." Phoebe's mouth waters just thinking about it. She's always starving after practice. Grace is across the stretching circle from them, so Phoebe raises her voice to ask: "Hey Grace, what's that place that you took me to get breakfast tacos at?"

She doesn't mean to shout, but there's a lull in the conversation around them right as she speaks, and it comes out louder than she meant it to. More than one of her new teammates turn to look at her. That's fine. It's only embarrassing if she acts like it is. She pretends not to notice, just waits for Grace to answer.

Grace makes it more awkward by staring blankly at her for a good five seconds before finally replying. "Pagoda Café."

"Right, yes, Pagoda," Phoebe says, turning back to Gabby. "They were fucking delicious."

"Grace took you for breakfast?" Kayla joins the conversation, sounding almost incredulous.

"Yeah." Phoebe shrugs like it's no big deal, but she's getting the feeling that maybe it is. "She's helping me explore the city."

Grace apparently decides to be less of an awkward weirdo about things. "Took her to Krewe du Vieux's parade on Saturday. Since she's a Mardi Gras virgin and all."

Was that so hard? Phoebe wants to ask.

"Popped your parade cherry, did you?" Ash grins. "What'd you think?"

"I didn't know you could get beads without showing your boobs."

Ash laughs. "Did you learn that before or after showing them?"

"I never flash and tell," Phoebe says with a wink.

She means it as a joke, not a loaded statement, but she catches Grace looking at her, and the eye contact feels heavy. Not that Grace needs to worry. Phoebe isn't about to out her about anything—not her sexuality, nor her injury. Though, if making her nervous about the latter means she's more likely to talk to Dawn herself, well, that certainly wouldn't be the worst thing in the world.

"So where you gonna take her next, Henderson?" Ash asks.

Phoebe tries not to look too invested.

"Where would you take her?" Grace shoots back.

"Yeah," Phoebe says. "To be clear, I'm happy to get shown around the city by anyone, not just Grace."

It's true, even if she's a pretty big fan of being shown around by Grace.

"You should know she'll make you pay for her food, though," Grace says.

"Excuse me." Phoebe fakes affront. "You lost that bet fair and square."

They don't mention how Grace paid for the beignets, too.

"Take her on the ferry," Ash suggests. "At least that's cheap."

"And a great view of the city," Kayla says.

Grace nods. "That's true."

"Does that mean you're gonna take me?" Phoebe asks.

"Sure, Phenom. We can go on the ferry."

"Tonight?"

Ash snickers. Maybe Phoebe shouldn't be so enthusiastic. She just likes hanging out with Grace, and any time Phoebe says she'll do something "sometime," she never ends up doing it. Always better to make a plan.

"Thursday," Grace says in a way that doesn't sound like she's offering the day as a possibility so much as it's been decided.

"Sweet."

"Can I come, too, Captain," Ash asks, "or is this a private date?"

Phoebe can see Grace's eye roll from across the circle. "It's not a date but you can't come simply because you're obnoxious."

"Yeah, that tracks," Kayla says, and Ash throws their shin guard at her.

• • • •

"So, what's it like being *friends* with *Grace Henderson*?"

Thank fuck Gabby is focused on unlocking her apartment door—Phoebe doesn't need her noticing how she flushes in response. It's a normal question. It's a question Phoebe would be asking Gabby if their roles were reversed. And anyway, she and Grace *are* friends. Gabby doesn't need to know they've had benefits, too.

"It's . . . surprisingly normal, actually?" Phoebe says. "I mean, if I think about it too much, yeah, it's fucking wild, but it's also just like at camp—she's one of my teammates. One I've bullied into hanging out with me."

"So, what you're saying is she's just like me?" Gabby asks once she finally gets the door open.

"No, you're so uncool you actually *want* to hang out with me. Much worse."

"Ooh, yeah, that is embarrassing for me."

Gabby's apartment is a mirror image of Phoebe's—but where Phoebe's living room is empty but for the furniture that came with the place and a half-empty suitcase, Gabby's is decorated. There are extra bookshelves lined with books and plants and pictures in frames. A huge bi flag takes up half the wall above the TV.

"How did I not know you're bi?" Phoebe asks.

"Oh, I'm not, I'm just a big supporter."

"Oh." That's pretty weird, but. "Okay. Cool."

Gabby cackles. "Jesus, Matty, I'm kidding. Of course I'm bi! I don't just have a huge bi pride flag on my wall because I'm such a big ally. What is this, middle school, before I figured my shit out?"

"You never know!"

"*Please* tell me you didn't think I was straight!"

"No, I—"

"This is so embarrassing," Gabby says. "This is way worse than voluntarily hanging out with you. Do I look *straight*?"

"Oh my God, stop."

"I mean, I have been thinking of getting an undercut."

"Okay wait, don't stop, definitely get an undercut."

"Yeah?"

"For sure," Phoebe says. "But for real, how did I not know you're bi? I talk about being queer all the time. Why didn't you join in the conversation about the hottest Charlie's Angel?"

"Um, because you were already about to fight Kayla for saying Kristen Stewart, so I wasn't gonna chime in with Naomi Scott."

Naomi Scott is fine as hell, but Phoebe shakes her head. "How can you say that when Lucy Liu exists?"

Gabby shrugs. "I haven't even seen those versions. Didn't they come out before we were born?"

"The first one did, but like a good lesbian, I immediately became obsessed with the franchise and have watched all the way back to the Farrah Fawcett version."

"Wow, you're goofy as hell."

Phoebe preens. "Very much, thanks for noticing."

"Wait, you might be goofy, but you're also tall," Gabby says, like that has anything to do with anything.

"What?" Phoebe asks her retreating form as she disappears into the kitchen.

"C'mon, I need your help with something."

The something she needs help with is putting a pitcher and four huge margarita glasses on the top shelf in her kitchen.

"Okay but now you won't be able to reach them when you need them," Phoebe says as she puts them away.

"I'm only gonna need them if I have friends over, so you can get them then."

"Am I your only friend? How depressing."

Gabby rolls her eyes. "Yeah, it's just gonna be you and Grace Henderson and me, hanging out."

"You gotta stop full-naming her if you wanna be her friend," Phoebe says.

If Phoebe hadn't hooked up with Grace, she might flirt with Gabby. In fact, if Grace were anyone else, Phoebe probably would still flirt with Gabby. Phoebe and Grace are friends, and they could have benefits again if Grace would go to the trainer. But regardless—there's no commitment, no exclusivity. Phoebe has had more than one hookup buddy at once plenty of times. But it's different with Grace. Phoebe doesn't think she'd get to fuck Grace again if she fucked someone else. And Gabby's hot, and will only be hotter if she gets an undercut, but Phoebe is not giving up the chance to sleep with Grace again—once she goes to the trainer, of course.

Phoebe has never had much trouble combining friendship and sex, but some people do, she knows. So, it doesn't hurt to keep Gabby securely on the friend side of things.

Really, it'd be nice to have a friend to talk to about everything going on with Grace. Girl talk or bragging or both, maybe. *Can you believe she straddled me?* and *She couldn't stand up after that last orgasm* and *She's so frustrating, not taking care of herself.* But again, Phoebe doesn't even know if Grace is out to anyone but her family. Plus, she's the most private person Phoebe has ever met. When it comes to things with Grace, Phoebe isn't even telling *Teddy,* who she knows would take it to his grave if she asked.

She doesn't usually kiss and tell anyway, but it's different when it's a *celebrity.* Phoebe wasn't lying to Gabby about how it's normal to be friends with Grace—she never thinks about Grace's fame when they hang out. It's only thinking about it now that it feels strange. She *hooked up* with *Grace Henderson.* She knows what Grace is like in bed, knows the noises she makes and the way she tastes, knows what Grace's fingers feel like inside of her.

"This is just . . . our lives now," Phoebe says to stop thinking about Grace fucking her.

"Do you think we'll ever get used to it?" Gabby asks.

"I really fucking hope so."

Sixteen

Grace agrees to take Phoebe on the ferry because she doesn't know how to say no. The redhead asked in front of the entire team. Even if she hadn't, Grace doesn't actually have a good reason to decline. What is she going to do, refuse to take Matthews anywhere unless she promises not to tell Dawn about Grace's so-called leg injury? That's an unnecessary escalation. If Matthews doesn't bring up Grace's leg, Grace isn't going to, either. It's not a big deal. She doesn't want Phoebe knowing she's thinking about it.

She is, though. Each practice, she's thinking about showing no weakness, about not giving Matthews too much attention, but not fully ignoring her, either. Grace dreads partner drills, expecting Matthews to pair up with her, but even when she does, Phoebe stays focused, professional. She doesn't say anything about Grace's aging body. She doesn't drop hints or look at Grace the way people do sometimes, like she's supposed to know what they're thinking just by their eyes. She works, and plays, laughing as much with the Krewe as she did at January camp.

Perhaps Grace doesn't have to worry about whatever Phoebe thinks she knows.

That's not her only problem when it comes to Matthews, anyway.

The bigger issue is that exposure therapy worked too well. Grace's body would like to continue to be exposed to Phoebe's, thank you very much. Her libido is out of control. She can keep a lid on it in practice, because she has to focus, to work, to lead. Afterward, though . . .

On Thursday, before they head to the ferry, Grace's mouth goes dry at the curve of Phoebe's bicep as she twists her still-wet hair into an unusually low—for her—bun. She'd worn the braids Grace gave her for two straight days, flyaway hairs frizzing out like a halo, before showing up Wednesday with the long ponytail Grace had seen in all those You-Tube videos. Grace wanted to tame it again. She kept the thought to herself. Now, Phoebe's wet hair makes Grace think of the showers, the bench in front of their lockers, the places they'd touched each other.

Getting away from the location of the memory should help, but having Matthews in her car reminds Grace of Mardi Gras, the strip of pale but still freckled stomach that peeked out from under Phoebe's cropped sweatshirt.

She's more covered up tonight—baggy black joggers and a hooded bomber jacket over a white T-shirt. Her bun is low to make room for a black snapback on top of her head, GAL PALS embroidered in white thread across the front.

The entire way to Canal, Phoebe talks. She doesn't need much from Grace, more of a running commentary than a conversation. Not even a full week of training, and Matthews is strategizing lineups like she has a say in them. Grace lets her babble.

Of course Matthews wants to talk to Grace about soccer. They're not sleeping together again—they'd made that clear—so why else would she want to hang out with her? Too bad for Matthews that she doesn't know Grace doesn't gossip about her teammates. Though, as the one-sided discussion continues, Grace realizes Phoebe isn't exactly gossiping, either. She has something nice to say about everyone. *Gabby's so fucking fast* and *Colleen doesn't have to be showy because she's dependable* and *Has anyone studied Sorrell? Because the accuracy of her passes is legendary.*

More annoying than how much Phoebe talks is how *not* annoying she is. Grace knows how she's supposed to feel, how she would usually feel in this situation, but the emotions simply aren't there. Acting as

Phoebe's tour guide hasn't been much of a burden. Grace hasn't spent this much time out and about in the city in a long time. She loves New Orleans. It's not a hardship to go to her favorite restaurants, even if she has to take Matthews. Grace hates the *idea* of spending so much time with this rookie, but she finds actually doing it isn't so bad.

Tonight is the same. Grace didn't want to go on the ferry—it's for tourists and commuters, and she's neither—but now that they've bought tickets and are climbing the steps to the second level, she's kind of excited. No one else seems to have come to see the city, but with sunset before six, there are plenty of commuters heading home from work.

Grace doesn't look at Phoebe's ass as she follows her to two seats toward the back of the boat, as close to the side as they can get. Nothing obstructs their view.

"For dinner in Algiers, we can either do typical New Orleans fare or a legit English pub," Grace says. "I haven't been to either in a long time, but I remember loving them."

"Wait, we're doing dinner?"

"Of course. As long as we're going over there, I figured you should see the neighborhood a bit rather than turn around and get right back on the return ferry."

Phoebe takes her hat off and readjusts it. "We didn't say anything about dinner. I've got mac and cheese I was gonna make at home."

Grace doesn't understand. "Do you not want to get dinner?"

"I, uh—no, you know, it's fine."

The ferry pulls away from the dock, then, and Phoebe goes quiet.

Grace hasn't been on the river in a long time. She counts in her memories—three years. When her parents and sister came for the opening game that year. They're usually the people she shows the city, though her dad is always more knowledgeable about it than she is, having torn through books about New Orleans as soon as Grace signed. He recites facts about the history of the city while Grace avoids her mother's questions about her love life and her sister's questions about anything Harmony thinks will annoy her.

It's different with Phoebe. Quieter, which Grace never would've expected. There's less pressure to entertain her, given Matthews invited herself, basically. The biggest difference, though, is Grace looks at the city through new eyes as it stretches out before them. It's not so much like she's looking at it for the first time, because she recognizes St. Louis Cathedral and the Crescent City Connection bridge behind them and even though she hasn't been to the river recently, she can tell it's high, the golden light of the setting sun making the water look almost pearlescent—but she's imagining what it must look like to Matthews. Trying to remember what it looked like to her, the first time she took this trip.

They pass a tugboat pushing a barge in the river, and then the *Natchez,* still docked on the bank, its huge rear wheel bright red in the evening light.

"That boat does basically the same thing as the ferry," Grace tells Phoebe. "Except for way more money."

Phoebe *mmm*s in response. It's so out of character Grace almost asks what's wrong, but then, what does she know about Phoebe's character? Maybe the girl gets seasick. Grace should be thankful for the reprieve, rather than disquieted by the lack of chatter.

Of course, right as Grace thinks it, Phoebe speaks up.

"Grace," she says, then pauses, tentative.

This might be the first time Grace has seen her anything but completely confident. "Yeah?"

Matthews must make a decision, because her voice is stronger when she continues. "You have to realize not everyone is like you."

Grace almost laughs. That has to be a joke. Most of the time it feels like *no one* is like her.

"We don't all have the allocation money that comes with being on the national team, or sponsorships, or honestly just not league-minimum salary," Phoebe says. "Some of us actually have a budget we'd like to stick to. You can't just spring dinner on us."

Grace hadn't considered that. "I'm sorry," she says. "I'll pay."

Matthews rolls her eyes. "I'm not asking you to pay. I'm saying—"

"I will," Grace says. "I insist."

Of course she should pay. She should always be paying if she's taking Matthews out. Not just if she loses a bet, but because she has more money than Matthews. Grace paying doesn't make their time together a date. It doesn't mean they're anything other than friends.

"Grace," Phoebe says.

She says her name a lot.

"No, you're right. I should've recognized. I'll pay."

"I mean, I'm not gonna fight you on that," Phoebe says. "But I'm serious, is all. You get that I have a second job, right? I don't waitress for fun. Like, yeah, I could probably survive on my salary because housing is free, and I'm used to budgeting so I'm pretty good at it, but Teddy needs top surgery and of course it's not covered by my parents' insurance. Plus, I'm trying to have an emergency fund, so if something goes wrong—for me or my parents or Teddy or Alice—like, they've taken out those shitty payday loans before, and I don't want them to ever have to do that again. So, I'm just. Trying to save. But yeah, you can pay. Just also recognize most of your teammates are not in the same boat as you."

"I'm sorry," Grace says again. "I wasn't thinking."

She thinks about a lot of things when it comes to Phoebe—her hair and her dimples and the way her freckles fade out on her chest. The way she kissed. Her voice when Grace touched her. Phoebe is *distracting*. That's why Grace didn't think through dinner. That and the fact that Grace doesn't really know how to make friends. She supposes she's lucky Matthews excels at it.

Phoebe seems to excel at forgiveness, too, if the smile on her face is any indication. Obviously she isn't holding anything against Grace.

"You know," she says, her dimples deepening, "taking this ferry at sunset is pretty romantic. If I didn't know better, I'd say you were trying to woo me."

"Uh," Grace says.

That is not what she's doing. She thought she was clear.

Before her brain figures out how to let Matthews down gently, the redhead is laughing. Cackling, more like.

"God, you should see your face," she says. "I was joking, and it was totally worth it for how terrified you just looked."

Grace lets out a sigh of relief. The last thing she needs is this rookie getting romantic ideas.

"Has anyone ever told you that you have a dumb sense of humor?"

"Literally all the time." Matthews beams. "But I don't let that stop me."

The ferry ride itself takes less time than it took to buy tickets. Five minutes on the muddy river and then they're in Algiers. Grace doesn't remember much from her dad's lecture on the neighborhood three years ago, but she takes a roundabout route to the restaurant anyway, lets Matthews see the sights.

Phoebe certainly seems to enjoy it, wide grin and the way she greets every stranger they pass. At the restaurant, she chats up their server, a woman with warm brown skin. She's probably not trying to flirt, not even when she winks her thanks as their drinks arrive. That's just Phoebe's default state. Not that Grace cares who she flirts with.

"How am I supposed to choose?" Phoebe asks, eyes darting over the menu. "What's the best thing here?"

Grace bites back the suggestion that she ask their server. "It's been a while since I've been here. But I remember everything being good."

Matthews talks her options down to red beans and rice, a catfish platter, or one of three different po'boys. She goes with the shrimp po'boy, beaming when the waitress compliments her choice.

Then Grace orders an oyster po'boy, plus a side of red beans and rice and catfish. She won't have more than the oyster po'boy—won't have more than half of it, probably; po'boys are delicious but always too much bread for her—but Phoebe can take the leftovers. Maybe they'll make up for not thinking about her financial situation.

"Grace Middle Name Henderson," Phoebe says.

Grace does not offer her middle name. Phoebe is not deterred.

"You tried to be so tough that first day on the field at camp, but you're actually very sweet."

Grace doesn't know what to do with that comment, so she stays silent. Phoebe lets her, changing the subject instead of pushing it.

"Living in New Orleans is so wild to me," she says. "I mean, I guess it's not New Orleans specifically, but like, any city. There's so much to do. If you ever wanted a tour of the best places in my hometown, I'd take you to the one five-screen movie theater, where I got my first shitty job as a fourteen-year-old. There's a coffee shop, too, I guess. And a dead-end road where kids go to make out. But yeah, that's really it." She takes a gulp of her water, then chuckles. "It must seem ridiculous to you, 'cause you've been, like, everywhere."

"I've been everywhere?"

"Playing for the Krewe, and for Lyon in France, plus the national team? You've been to more countries than I've been to states, probably. Until Mapleton made the tournament, I hadn't been outside of the Midwest. I've had such a boring life compared to yours."

"You've done plenty I haven't done," Grace says. "I never had a crappy job as a teenager. I've never graduated from high school or been to prom." She shrugs. "Different people have different experiences. That doesn't make you weird."

"Okay, to be honest, you really didn't miss out by not going to prom," Phoebe says, cringing. "Though maybe that's just the experience of a lesbian teenager in Middle of Nowhere, Indiana."

If Grace hadn't moved to play, she would've been a lesbian teenager in Middle of Nowhere, Upstate New York. It might not have been much better.

"Being so focused on soccer probably saved me from a lot of conversations about boys when I was growing up," she says.

"Right. But like"—Phoebe glances around like she's making sure no one can overhear, which Grace appreciates—"your family knows you're queer, right?"

Grace decides to fuck with her, just a little. "Who says I'm queer?"

"Oh my God. You cannot be one of those people who thinks queer is a slur. Like I am going to walk out of this restaurant and leap into the river if you say that to me right now."

Grace laughs. "No. But I had to get you back for joking about the ferry ride being romantic."

Phoebe blinks at Grace, her face gone slack. Grace wonders if there's something in her teeth.

"You okay there, Phenom?"

Phoebe shakes her head quickly. "Yeah. Sorry. I was just really thrown by the possibility that you had bought into TERF rhetoric about *queer*. It's really important to me as a word that includes trans people in my community."

"Of course," Grace says, immediately embarrassed that she'd joked about it. "I also like it because it doesn't tell anyone too much about your business. Obviously, as a"—Grace grimaces, wishing there was a better word, but—"celebrity of sorts, there are parts of my identity I keep to myself. Very few people need to know what specific label fits me best."

"Lesbian is important to me," Phoebe says. "The world likes to act like it's a porn category, not an identity. It took me a while to realize it wasn't. I want other girls like me to know it's a beautiful word."

That hits Grace in the chest. She's never thought about it like that before, but Phoebe's right. Grace has a clear memory of seeing two women holding hands and thinking, *I hope I'm not a lesbian.* She hates the memory; it feels like a betrayal of who she is, even though she was maybe seven years old at the time. It wasn't her fault. She knows that, but still.

"I've been out pretty much since I knew what a crush was," Phoebe continues. "In elementary school, I declared I would never have a crush on a boy. Some adults in my life did that heteronormative thing where they were like, 'Oh, wait until you're older.' But I'm older now and it still hasn't happened, so."

She somehow manages to make her shrug violent, like she still wants to fight those adults. Grace doesn't have that fighting spirit—she'd rather ignore assholes than bother fighting them—but she likes it.

Their food arrives then, and Phoebe's eyes go wide at the sight.

"Holy shit, this looks good."

She doesn't even smile at the server when she says thanks, too awed by the spread in front of them. Together, the dishes barely fit on the round high top. Before Grace so much as reaches for her sandwich, Phoebe holds up her arm.

"Can I just—can I take a picture first?"

Grace nods. And while Phoebe arranges the plates on the table and takes photos from different angles, Grace thinks.

She could let this go. She could focus on her food and let the conversation move on. There is nothing she needs to share. But there's a pull in her stomach that has served her well for most of her life. She has two AWSA championships, an Olympic bronze, and two World Cups. It's her gut she listens to on the pitch, more than her coach or even her brain. Right now, Grace's gut is telling her to share her own coming-out story.

"Okay, let's eat," Phoebe says, and wastes no time taking her first bite of shrimp po'boy. She might say *Oh my God* afterward, but there's too much food in her mouth to be sure.

Grace listens to her gut.

"I came out at Christmas when I was eighteen," she says. "My little sister, Harmony, had come to me asking for advice about coming out as pansexual to our parents. I had zero advice. I'd known I was gay for a couple of years by then, and I hadn't figured out how I was supposed to come out. But I wasn't going to let Harmony do it herself. All alone? Not knowing how they were gonna respond? No. I told her I'd go first, if she wanted me to, because she'd still have to live in their house for a few more years. I mean, not that we thought they'd kick her out, but you never know, better safe than sorry. So I came out. And as my parents were telling me they loved me, Harmony shouted out she was pan. It was an eventful holiday."

"That's the fucking cutest coming-out story I've ever heard."

Grace blinks. "What?"

Phoebe's po'boy is frozen halfway between her plate and her mouth, which is split open in a smile. "Seriously. Like, noble and shit. What a good older sister."

Grace shrugs. She had just done what any older sister would have. Plus, it helped her. It solved her own problem of how she was going to come out. It had hardly been noble.

Phoebe is the noble one. The way she talks about her identity, the way she cares about the queer girls who come after her. Grace has too much on her plate to add being a role model in that way. It feels wrong, though, to shirk that responsibility, feels like there should be something else she can give up so she can take it on.

Rather than think about it, Grace shifts focus back to Matthews.

"So have you just always been publicly out?"

Phoebe shrugs. "It was never anything I thought about, being publicly out. There was never really any 'public' for me to think about until recently." She uses air quotes around the word public. "Even in college, until my senior year, we didn't get media. Not really. But I think I would've anyway, even if it was a conscious choice. Because this is who I am. And it's not that I think not being out is hiding at all. Who you're out to and when is always your own decision, but I don't know. I'm loud and obnoxious and gay. It's like my brand."

Grace hates that. The brands they have as players are one thing, but in general, they aren't brands; they are *people*. They get treated like brands, but they're so much more than that.

"My brand is who I am as a soccer player, not as a person," Grace says. "I don't like strangers thinking they know me."

"That makes sense," Phoebe says. "For me, it's just that I like sharing a part of myself with the fans. So my brand as a player and as a person are kinda the same."

On the ferry ride over, Grace told herself she didn't know Phoebe's character, but that's not true. And Phoebe's brand, as a player or a person, is not loud and obnoxious and gay. Phoebe is fun. She's the class clown until you realize how hard she works. She's an unabashed flirt who is somehow also absurdly respectful, backing off the moment Grace said she wasn't interested. Phoebe clearly loves being the center of attention, and yet from everything Grace has seen, she's more likely to pass the ball than take a shot.

Calling Phoebe loud and obnoxious and gay ignores all her layers and contradictions. That's Grace's issue with fame—people take you at face value. Nobody bothers to look for the person beneath the brand. To most people, Grace isn't a person; she's a soccer player. Even to her family—they come visit for the first game of the season. Her dad calls after every game. She's used to it by now, but that doesn't mean it's not frustrating. It's absurd to her that Matthews is talking about herself like a brand, like that's a good thing. But then, she's a rookie; she doesn't know fame yet.

Grace realizes the conversation has stalled. Because that's what had been happening: a conversation, not just Phoebe talking Grace's ear off. But Grace had gotten lost in her own thoughts instead of responding. Has it been too long for her to pick the conversation back up?

Normally when Grace gets lost in her thoughts, the silence she comes back to is awkward, but it doesn't feel like that with Phoebe, who is sopping up red beans and rice with a piece of Texas toast in one hand while the other pops the last bite of a hush puppy into her mouth.

Phoebe doesn't give her a weird look or ask where she disappeared to or anything of the sort. She just continues the conversation, talking around the food in her mouth.

"Plus, like, Briana Scurry was a little old for me, but I remember what it was like when I was barely a teenager and Abby Wambach came out. My family had never made me feel like being a lesbian was gonna hold me back or anything, but it was different to actually see someone like me doing what I wanted to do. Ever since then, it feels like women's soccer has gotten more gay, and I, for one, am here for it. I almost wish I wasn't out just so I could do something hard-core like come out by announcing my engagement."

That was something, when two of Grace's former teammates announced their engagement with a photo shoot in *People* magazine. Grace would quite literally never. Not that she's anywhere close to being engaged anyway, but there are some things that strangers just don't get to see.

Seventeen

The sun has long set by the time they board the ferry for the return trip. Phoebe still heads to the upper deck, and Grace follows, though it's cold enough now that Phoebe zips her jacket up to her chin.

They take the same seats, but everything looks different in the dark. The lights of the city twinkle at them. The sight makes Phoebe's breath catch. It does legitimately seem romantic, especially given the night as a whole.

"Thanks for buying me dinner," Phoebe says.

"No problem," Grace says. "Sorry again that I—"

"Stop apologizing."

"Right," Grace says. "Sorr—wait, fuck."

Phoebe laughs at her.

She can't help it. Grace is funny, even when she's not trying to be. To be honest, tonight is maybe the first time Phoebe has ever seen her try to be—with that joke about not being queer. Phoebe's not even sure she'd seen Grace laugh before that moment. It struck her speechless, the way Grace's face lit up like—like—Phoebe still can't come up with the right word for it. Inexplicably, it made her think of the first spring crocus after an Indiana winter.

Another first of the night: Grace actually, like, volunteering personal information about herself. Sure, she'd told Phoebe about how she started braiding hair, but Phoebe knew that already. Countless articles about Grace have included that story, or the one about when she played for Lyon and was still learning French, and she said she was pregnant instead of full. Grace seems to have carefully curated what people are allowed to know about her.

Her sexuality is not included. Even if Grace ever went to the trainer, if there's ever anything between her and Phoebe, they can't be open about it. Not that Phoebe needs to be public about who she's sleeping with, obviously. Sometimes the sneakiness is part of the draw. Granted, with Grace, the draw is more about that skin and those muscles and the face and the things Phoebe already knows Grace can do with her fingers.

Phoebe understands why Grace isn't publicly out, though it's not something she herself could ever do. She might envy Grace's fame when it comes to soccer, but not everything else that comes with it. The idea of L Chat boards about your private life is kind of a lot—enough that Phoebe feels bad she'd been one of the people posting on them.

As they approach the dock, Phoebe looks away from the city lights— and catches Grace looking at her mouth.

It would be easy to let her lean in. It would be so easy to kiss Grace on this romantic-ass ferry trip after she paid for dinner. To act like this is a date. But neither of them wants a relationship, and for once, Phoebe has more self-control than she gives herself credit for. Before their mouths get too close or the tension too high, Phoebe clears her throat.

"So it seems like you haven't gone to see Dawn yet."

Talk about ruining the mood.

"It seems like none of your business."

Grace stands suddenly and heads for the stairs at the front, like she's going to be able to go anywhere. Phoebe follows her. No surprise, they have to stop at the base of the steps—the boat isn't docked yet.

It *is* Phoebe's business. She is Grace's teammate. Grace not being her best absolutely affects Phoebe. Even if it didn't, Grace is her friend.

Phoebe doesn't want Grace playing hurt because Phoebe doesn't want Grace hurt. That is enough of a reason for it to be her business.

Undeterred, she continues. "Why does injury only count as weakness when you're the one injured?"

"I didn't say it was weakness. I said I was fine."

"Right, but that's a lie. I'm just trying to understand why you won't go to the trainer. Especially when doing so means . . ." She lets her eyes drag slowly up Grace's body. "We could have a lot more fun if you would have it looked at."

The tops of Grace's ears go pink. She takes a moment before responding.

"Is the ferry not fun enough for you?"

"Not the kind of fun I'm talking about," Phoebe mutters.

The ferry is fun. This whole night has been fun. But it'd be a lot more fun if Phoebe could push Grace up against her car when they get back to it. Which of course she *could* do, and Grace would probably let her, but Grace clearly needs some kind of incentive to get her leg looked at.

If flirting with her won't work, annoying her is probably the next best bet.

"You're gonna break eventually, even if you are stubborn as hell."

"What makes you so confident?"

Phoebe smirks. "Well, last time I stopped flirting with you, you didn't last very long."

She throws in a wink to really grate on Grace's nerves. Sure enough, she earns herself one of those Henderson scowls.

"I'm not driving you home," Grace says.

"Liar." Phoebe laughs. "As though my *captain* would leave me stranded. But anyway, you aren't driving me home. You're taking me to work."

"What?"

"Yeah. I've got an overnight shift."

"When are you going to sleep?"

Phoebe shrugs. "After training tomorrow?"

"Matthews." Grace's voice is full of warning.

"How about this? You can give me shit about my sleep schedule when you go to the trainer about your leg."

. . . .

Overnight shifts aren't that bad in general. It's never packed for one thing, and even working at 2:00 A.M. isn't as bad as some lunch shifts. Phoebe is a good waitress—as long as she can have a notepad to take orders and doesn't have to remember them. She likes meeting new people and can chat up anyone from a family of five to a lone male who looks like a creep until you get him talking about his German shepherd. She can deal with the actually creepy customers, too—not always in a way management might prefer, but it works.

Phoebe worked in a twenty-four-hour diner just off campus at Mapleton, but even on weekends, with drunk college kids wandering in at all hours, it wasn't like this. She's never been to New York City, so maybe it really is the city that never sleeps, but New Orleans seems to give it a run for its money.

"Be glad we're not actually in the Quarter," Dallas says. "Too many messy drunks over there."

The restaurant isn't packed by any means, but when Phoebe took an overnight shift between two practices, she'd expected a fair amount of downtime. Instead, it takes until three for service to slow. By then, she's dragging. At the start of the shift, Dallas put on some album full of soft, mellow music. They claimed it was to calm down drunk patrons, but it calmed Phoebe, too, like a murmured lullaby.

"Is this what you listen to all the time?" Phoebe asks when the diner is finally, blissfully empty. She yawns wide, forgets to cover her mouth until the end. "How do you stay awake? How are you staying awake right now?"

"I took a three-hour nap this afternoon," Dallas says. "And I listen to a lot of different stuff."

Phoebe *mmhmm*s and slumps onto a stool at the counter. What she wouldn't do to be horizontal right now. Her feet ache. Maybe Dallas will make her breakfast before her shift's up.

. . . .

Phoebe jolts when the bell rings over the door.

"Hi!" Her voice is too chipper for—what time is it again?

She blinks a few times but can't read the clock on the wall, eyes still blurry from sleep. Wait, why had she been sleeping?

Luckily, the couple who came in are too wrapped up in each other to notice Phoebe having an existential crisis at the counter. They sit in the same side of a booth, and Phoebe tries to shake her brain awake as she goes to get them water.

After taking their order—though they look like they'd rather eat each other than anything on the menu—Phoebe hovers near Dallas in the kitchen.

"When did I fall asleep?"

Dallas cracks an egg into a bowl and tips their head, considering. "About an album ago?"

"What?" Phoebe hadn't noticed that the music was different. It's still more peaceful than anything she listens to. "And you just let me sleep?"

"Why wouldn't I?" Dallas asks as they scramble eggs with a whisk. "We didn't have customers."

"I can't sleep at work!"

"Why?" Dallas's dark eyebrows are furrowed. "Are you a capitalist or something? Like what the fuck?"

Her entire life, Phoebe has been disciplined at work for everything from talking too much to being disorganized. She's never had a coworker like Dallas before—they're the best. Especially because, two hours later, they send her off with a to-go box of their stuffed hash browns.

Even with an album-long nap, all Phoebe wants to do when she gets to her apartment is sleep. But training starts in thirty minutes, and it's a fifteen-minute walk to the stadium. She doesn't have time to sleep. She doesn't even have time to wash the grease smell out of her hair.

Twenty-seven minutes later, Phoebe shuffles into the locker room. It's basically empty this close to practice, most everybody already out on the field. Phoebe doesn't quite *collapse* onto the bench in front of her locker, but she's too tired to come up with a more precise verb.

"Hey, you okay?" It's Kayla who asks. Phoebe didn't even see her when she came in.

"Good." Phoebe offers a smile she can tell doesn't look real. "Great. Just a little slow this morning."

"You sure?"

"A hundo p," Phoebe says, then cringes. The phrase is an inside joke with her college team, but she's aware she probably sounds unhinged to Kayla. "Hundred percent. For real."

"Okay. See you out there."

Phoebe can't close her eyes or she might not open them again. She rests her hands on either side of her on the bench, and it's not until then that she thinks about how Grace laid her back across it. How can she be so tired she didn't think of that immediately?

The memory wakes her up a bit, at least. She puts an ear to her shoulder, stretching out her neck, then switches sides as she pulls the hair tie from her ponytail.

It snaps in her fingers.

"Fuck!"

Of course she only brought one. And the team is already on the field, so she'll have to go out there, in front of everyone, to ask if she can borrow a hair tie from someone. She's late, and exhausted, and now she's unprepared, and everyone is gonna know.

Phoebe jumps as the door to the field opens. Grace rounds the corner, eyes finding Phoebe immediately.

"How was work, Phenom?"

Phoebe grits her teeth. "Great. Thanks for asking."

Grace probably has a hair tie she could borrow. Or Phoebe could just tie the snapped hair tie back together. Then at least she wouldn't have to ask Grace for anything. She knows Grace thinks of her as a rookie, and a clown, probably, and normally Phoebe is fine with that— she likes clowning around, really—but right now she is just too tired to deal with anything.

"I'll be right out," Phoebe says, standing to—she's not sure what, exactly. Standing to look like she's awake and in the middle of something and really will be right out so Grace can just leave her alone.

"No," Grace says. She points to the bench. "Sit."

"You're not the boss of me," Phoebe says, but she sits.

Grace gets a brush and a ring of hair ties out of her locker.

"Practice is about to start," Phoebe says.

"And you can't practice with your hair like this."

Normally, Phoebe might push back, if for no other reason than to annoy Grace, but she's tired and she needs her hair done. She'll argue with Grace when she has enough energy to make it flirty.

Phoebe can't help but make a noise—not quite a moan but not *not* a moan—at the first pull of the brush through her hair. She had a ponytail all night, and Grace is being gentle. So sue her for enjoying it, okay?

It feels too good, actually, to be sitting down while someone plays with her hair—not that Grace is *playing* with Phoebe's hair, she's *doing* her hair, but still. Phoebe doesn't remember closing her eyes but she's looking at the backs of her eyelids instead of the lockers. She could fall asleep right here. Her breathing starts to even out, and she pinches her own thigh to stay awake.

Grace silently, efficiently finishes the first braid.

"I know, I know," Phoebe says. "You don't have to say anything."

"I'm not saying anything."

"Yes, you're not saying it very loudly."

"That doesn't make any sense," Grace mutters.

If she does actually say anything, Phoebe is ready. Any lecture Grace could give her, the captain should give herself instead. *Soccer should be your priority* and *Showing up exhausted isn't professional* and *How can your teammates rely on you?* Phoebe will turn any one of them back around on Grace.

But Grace stays silent until she's wrapping the end of the second braid with a hair tie.

"Let's get out there, Phenom."

Phoebe hustles the best she can. They're both late by this time, but Givhan doesn't do more than shout, "Thanks for joining us!" before continuing.

Practice is gonna suck today.

• • • •

At college, they had a trainer. Singular. One person who worked for both soccer teams, women's and men's, plus a few student volunteers who wanted to go into some kind of medicine career. They had team dinners sometimes, the night before a game, but they were mostly left to fend for themselves.

New Orleans has more people on staff than Phoebe can keep straight. There are at least three trainers, plus a chiropractor and a massage therapist and a nutrition specialist. What that means is throughout practice, there are too many people commenting on the bags under her eyes. But it's fine. She survives. Training ends, and all she needs to do is get out of this building and make it however many blocks home. Then she can sleep.

So of course she passes the head trainer, who comes to a complete stop in the hallway when she lays eyes on Phoebe.

"Yes, I know, I look tired. I'm fine," Phoebe says.

She's walking the opposite direction Dawn was, but the trainer turns and falls into step beside her.

"Are you getting enough sleep?" Dawn asks.

"Don't worry. Grace has already lectured me about it."

She didn't, really, but she tried to last night, and her silence this morning spoke volumes. Phoebe knows Grace judges her for pulling an all-nighter, which would be fine if Grace had a leg to stand on. A *noninjured* leg to stand on.

"Well, Grace is right," Dawn says. "And I'm sure it wasn't a lecture so much as looking out for your well-being."

"She should worry about her own well-being and take care of her damn hip," Phoebe grumbles.

"Excuse me?"

Phoebe's eyes snap up from the pattern of the tile in front of her to lock onto Dawn's. "What? Nothing. She should mind her own business is what I said."

"I don't think so. What about Grace's hip?"

The front door is fifty feet away. Phoebe was so close to freedom and safety and sleep, and she had to mess it all up.

"Nothing," she says. "Seriously. I said nothing. You can't know that."

"I'm in charge of the health of this team, Matthews."

People have been calling her by her last name her entire life, but after a week of only spending time with Grace, somehow it feels like their secret. Phoebe keeps grimacing when she hears it from other people. Not that that's the only reason she's grimacing, here.

"Tell me about Grace's hip," Dawn says.

"I don't know," Phoebe says. "Honestly, I don't. All I know is her left hip gives her trouble sometimes. It's just, like, something I noticed when we trained together last week. I've been trying to convince her to come see you. Please please *please* do not tell her I said anything."

"You've got other things to worry about. Promise me you're going to get some sleep."

"Promise," Phoebe said, not worrying about her sleep schedule at all.

The adrenaline pumping through her veins makes her forget that she's exhausted. Outside, she sprints for a block and a half like she can outrun her big mouth.

No. She did not just do that. No no no no no no. Nope. Absolutely not.

Except it's fine, actually, Phoebe decides as she slows to a walk. Totally fine.

It isn't bad that she said something. Someone had to, and it certainly wasn't going to be Grace. Grace was so concerned about Phoebe getting enough sleep, or Ash's finger, or Colleen's ankle, and yet she wasn't taking care of herself. It's *good* Phoebe said something, as a matter of fact. Even if it was an accident.

Eighteen

Grace doesn't remember leaving the stadium.

She doesn't remember the drive home.

Lilly meets her at the door like always, chirps turning to meows when it takes Grace longer than usual to get the key in the lock. Once inside, Grace hangs her keys on the hook by the door, toes out of her shoes, and heads to the pantry, Lilly winding between her legs with every step. It's Grace's own fault her cat is so obnoxious—she's the one who conditioned him to expect treats every time she comes home from practice.

She drops one treat to Lilly, then tosses a couple more for him to find on his own. As he hunts, the cat goes quiet. Grace's mind is anything but.

Three to six weeks.

She's out three to six weeks. Dawn seems to think it'll be closer to six.

Grace hasn't been injured since she tore her ACL at nineteen. Coaches have kept her out if they saw her wince in warm-ups, like one awkward landing meant she couldn't play a game. But that was always precautionary, never long-term. It certainly wasn't three to six weeks.

She's on the couch in her living room, staring at the TV, even though it's off, when Lilly finds her again. The cat pushes his head into Grace's hand for pets. Lilly has never been subtle about what he wants, and he always gets it. She runs a hand along his long, cream-colored fur and his blue eyes close.

Grace can't believe she let Dawn notice. Obviously, her hip isn't a big deal—she's been playing with it since last fall, doing just fine. But Dawn, like any coach who ever saw Grace wince, immediately sidelined her.

She can't quite fathom her situation. She understands it, rationally; she knows what a muscle strain is, knows how long three weeks is. But the idea of not playing soccer for that long doesn't make sense. Worse, Dawn said she couldn't train at all. No weights. No running. No agility drills. What is she supposed to do? Watch film for a month? How is she supposed to help her team?

If Grace can't do anything for three weeks, she'll miss the sHeroes tournament with the national team. The tournament doesn't mean anything but bragging rights, but Grace still doesn't want to miss it. It's about getting time together, time to gel as a team. Their last camp before the World Cup roster is announced, and she won't even be there. If she's out much longer, she'll miss the start of the AWSA season. This team she is supposed to be leading will open their season without her. Matthews will probably fill in for her, both for the Krewe and the national team.

Not that it matters who plays in her spot, just that it isn't her. For the next three to six weeks, Grace Henderson doesn't matter.

Her stomach hurts with something she can't name. Too many feelings she doesn't want to admit, doesn't want to address. All she wants is the one thing she's not allowed: to play soccer. It's all she's ever wanted. She puts up with so much—captain duties and media responsibilities and meal plans and always being on her best behavior, always a role model—in order to play soccer.

She should order takeout. Something rich and unhealthy. Drown her sorrows in booze or chocolate.

But Friday night is pizza night.

So Grace does what she does every Friday: takes the pizza dough she made yesterday out of the fridge to rest while she thinly slices red and yellow bell peppers and ribbons basil. Grace likes cooking recipes she knows. There's a cadence to it, a rhythm—the knife against the cutting board, the stretch of the dough as she rolls it out. Tonight, she makes her pizza smaller than usual, doesn't have the patience to get the crust as thin as she likes.

She stays in the kitchen after putting the pizza in the oven, watching her fingers drum against the countertop. Her mind is either blank or too full; she can't decide. Her phone lights up with a text, and Grace swipes to unlock it.

> Gabby told me she saw you talking to Dawn. How did it go???

Of course Matthews wants to know. The longer Grace is out, the better it is for Matthews. Grace's injury opens up a spot in the midfield.

A follow-up text comes almost immediately.

> At least this means we can really have some fun, right? ☺

Grace can't deal with Matthews right now, no matter how much her libido perks up at the idea. She locks her phone without responding.

When Matthews learns how long Grace is out, she'll stop texting. She'll stop trying so hard to be friends. Grace is old and injured and sidelined. All she has to offer Matthews is king cake recommendations.

Her timer goes off. Grace burns her thumb getting the pizza out of the oven, doesn't bother running it under cold water.

Pizza night is always a reprieve after a long week of work.

Tonight, Grace barely tastes it.

The crust is too thick.

• • • •

Grace never wanted to be famous. Celebrity itself makes her uncomfortable, but she deals with it, because at least it means she's good enough at soccer that strangers know who she is. But there's a difference between knowing who she is and knowing *her*. A lot of other players cultivate that parasocial relationship, for some reason. Colleen is constantly roping people into her TikToks. One couple who used to play for the national team released an entire video of their wedding day. Grace can't imagine.

When Grace was seventeen, she flew to LA to film her first commercial, an ad for a streaming music platform long since defunct. Her agent was with her on the set, as was her dad. Even then, it felt weird that anyone thought her endorsement would sell a product. But that's how celebrity works; Grace wants people to know her for her skill and success on the pitch, nothing more, but her endorsement *does* sell products. Someone took a picture of her eating her favorite power bar on the sidelines at a game, and she's had a long-term deal with the company ever since.

She has a commercial to shoot Saturday morning. This time, the film crew comes to her. They rented a soccer field on the outskirts of New Orleans, and it's in Grace's contract that they won't take more than three hours of her day. No one joins her on the set, which is good, given that she has yet to tell her agent about her injury. She will, but there's no reason to cancel filming. Less than three hours on a field before the air gets too muggy. She'll run a little, kick a few balls, and tell her agent tomorrow. Dawn doesn't know about the commercial and Grace's agent doesn't know about her hip, and what they don't know can't hurt them. It can hurt Grace, supposedly, but she's been playing through it since last season.

Sure, her so-called injury would've been the perfect excuse, but Grace keeps her word. Plus, the production team was likely already in New Orleans by the time Dawn benched Grace. It would've been such an inconvenience to cancel, even if she wishes she could. She considers it, sometimes, considers canceling everything, giving it all up—commercials, captain responsibilities, playing professionally. She could retire, maybe change her hair in an effort not to be recognized, and then play in some recreational league. The thought seems ungrateful, though. Her family gave up so much for her to get here—the amount of money spent on gear and trainings, the fact that she and her mother lived across the country from her sister and dad for six years—she can't just walk away. She'd never leave her teammates behind like that, either.

That's why she never said anything about her hip. And now here she is, abandoning the team for three to six weeks, right before the start of the season.

Not that she can think about that right now; the parking lot attendant is waving her through to a parking space amid three trailers and countless people rushing around looking very busy and important, which seems to be a prerequisite for every set she's been on.

Grace parks her car and takes a deep breath. Flips the visor down to look in the mirror. They'll do her makeup, of course, but she did her own hair, two perfect braids. She practices her *I'm so happy to be here* smile while no one is paying attention, then flips the visor back up.

Time to get this over with.

Nineteen

It's fine that Grace didn't text her back. Of course it's fine. Grace was probably busy, or maybe just sad, and she didn't want to talk. She doesn't owe Phoebe anything. It's good, really, that Grace enforces her boundaries.

Just like it's good Phoebe said something to Dawn.

At least that's what Phoebe told herself all weekend. That's what she keeps telling herself as she and Gabby walk to practice together Monday morning.

When Grace isn't in the locker room, Gabby elbows Phoebe. "You know, Dawn didn't look super happy when they were talking Friday."

"Maybe we're early," Phoebe says, knowing they're not.

"I guess we did leave before your *okay you're gonna be late* alarm went off," Gabby says.

She doesn't say anything else about Grace, thankfully, because Phoebe isn't sure she can talk about her without it being obvious that she's freaking out a little.

It's not even that weird Grace didn't reply to Phoebe's texts. It's not like they text that often, unless they have plans. But Phoebe doesn't want to fuck things up with her. She doesn't wanna fuck things up with anyone on the team, but especially not the captain, and especially not the captain she had excellent sex with a week ago. She'd tried to distract Grace with that in her text. She knows this sucks. Nobody ever likes being injured. But Phoebe said that after Grace went to the trainer, they could hook up again. It seems like a natural silver lining.

Obviously, Grace didn't think it was funny, or maybe she doesn't even want to sleep with Phoebe again. Maybe she somehow knows Phoebe was the one who told Dawn. Or maybe Phoebe is just spiraling and needs to get it together.

Except then Grace shows up, and any hope Phoebe has evaporates.

The rest of the team is on the pitch, warming up, when Grace arrives in joggers and a Krewe polo. Coach Givhan calls them all together, and Phoebe tries to catch Grace's eye. Grace looks anywhere else. It's clear that whatever has been growing between them is gone. Phoebe's stomach turns.

Eric announces Grace is out three to six weeks, much to the team's dismay. Grace doesn't accept any of their sympathy. She still doesn't look at Phoebe.

Phoebe is off all practice—too slow or not in the right place or both. She gets winded too easily, her chest tight. It's worse every time Grace's eyes pass over her like she isn't even there.

If it weren't so embarrassing, Phoebe might claim she's too sick to keep practicing. But she isn't actually ill, just unwell. Rejected.

Toward the end of practice, as they run a set piece drill, Gabby sending the ball in from the corner, Grace seems to finally notice Phoebe exists.

"Matthews!" she shouts from the sidelines. "Be patient!"

It might be better to have Grace ignore her than criticize her in front of everyone. A headache starts building behind Phoebe's eyes.

The next time Gabby sends the ball in and Phoebe makes a break for it, she can hear Grace groan.

"You're leaving too early, Matthews!"

Phoebe is the tallest on the team—besides Ash, who's in goal— that's why they're practicing finding her head on set pieces. But she feels about two feet tall.

"Excuse me," Coach Givhan begins, and Phoebe is ready for more criticism. But it turns out he's talking to Grace. "Are you running this practice or am I?"

"Well, someone had to tell Matthews that she was making her move way too early."

Is Phoebe being punished? She doesn't even know if she's actually doing this drill wrong. Nobody's gonna say anything against Grace. And if Grace is mad at her about talking to Dawn or about the text message or about who knows what, maybe this is how she's getting back at Phoebe. No one will contradict her. Phoebe's second week of practice and she's already fucked things up so much she's about to cry in front of the whole team.

"Again!" Givhan calls. "And this time, Matthews, be a little more patient."

Phoebe tries. She does. She wants to go but she waits one, two seconds longer before making her move. She still doesn't manage to get her head on the ball. She doesn't look to the sidelines afterward, doesn't want to see Grace's reaction, or Coach's, either. She just wants to get this right. Then she can stop feeling like such an idiot, such an unwelcome presence at practice.

"That was better," Sorrell says quietly, but the kind comment is overshadowed by Grace's voice.

"I'm not gonna do anything," Grace is saying. "I'm just gonna show her how to do it. I swear I won't use my leg."

When Phoebe wasn't looking at her, apparently Grace was making her way onto the field. Phoebe's feet stay rooted to the ground while the players around her part to let Grace through. Grace marches right up to her, stands so close Phoebe wants to take a step back.

"Get into position," Grace says. "And don't move until I tell you to."

If Grace responded to her text Friday, or looked at her at all today, Phoebe might make a joke. If she weren't feeling dumb and useless, she might make some allusion to bondage just to see Grace blush. As it is, she ducks her head and gets into her starting position.

Grace follows right behind her. Phoebe squeezes her eyes shut briefly,

CLEAT CUTE | 153

swallows down her nausea, and waits for Gabby to send in another corner. She's the one to avoid Grace's eyes this time, unwilling to see rejection in them.

But then, as Gabby is getting the ball set just right on the corner
grass, Grace stands behind Phoebe and puts both hands on Phoebe's
hips.

"I want you to stay right here." Grace is close enough she doesn't
need to do anything more than murmur. Phoebe feels like her entire
body goes up in smoke. She's too hot all over, but especially where
Grace's hands hold her. "You're not going to move until I let go."

"Yes, ma'am."

Grace tightens her grip, and Phoebe tries not to shiver.

This is . . . not rejection. Other people have to notice, right? The
air around them has gone thick. Their teammates are moving nearby,
jockeying for position, but the two of them stand stock-still. Phoebe
is a rubber band stretched taut. Every muscle in her body is tense. She
sucks in a ragged breath.

Gabby kicks the ball.

"Patience." Grace's voice is velvet, or hot fudge, or a Jacuzzi, something soft and warm and sweet, and Phoebe wants to bathe in it. "Wait
for it. Now."

She punctuates her last word with a squeeze of Phoebe's hips before
letting go. Phoebe barely remembers she's supposed to be running. But
when she does, it's like time slows down. Her feet take her right where
she's supposed to be. Two minutes ago, she felt small, but now she tow-
ers over her defender, leaps even higher, and heads the ball into the back
of the net.

"Fuck yeah," Kayla says, even though she's on defense for the drill.

Phoebe's teammates pat her on the back and Gabby runs in from
the corner to leap into Phoebe's arms like they're celebrating a real goal.

But Phoebe only cares what one person thinks.

Grace isn't quite smiling but she looks happier than she has all day.
"That's how you do it, Phenom."

Phoebe blooms.

"On that high note, let's call it a day," Givhan says. "Well done, Matthews, Rodriguez."

. . . .

Phoebe chases Grace into the parking garage after taking the fastest shower she's ever taken in her life. Her hair is dripping everywhere—she barely even attempted to dry it—but her skin is still buzzing at her waist, like Grace left electric handprints behind. She doesn't care if she seems too enthusiastic. It's worth it to catch Grace before she gets to her car.

"Hey."

"Hi," Grace says, face unreadable.

"Thanks for your help today," Phoebe says. She scuffs her worn-out sandal against the ground. "Clearly I needed it."

"Go easy on yourself, Phenom," Grace says. Phoebe wonders if she ever takes her own advice. "Your balls-to-the-wall attitude is great in a lot of situations, but you have to learn patience."

Phoebe lets out an unamused laugh. "If I had a dollar for every time I've been told that in my life."

"We'll get you there." Grace's voice leaves no room for doubt, no matter how many times Phoebe has failed thus far.

"Yeah," Phoebe says. "You seemed to have a pretty good method of teaching me today."

Grace's eyes flash.

Phoebe lowers her voice. "Can I buy you dinner? You can tell me about what Dawn said."

"Matthews," Grace says quietly. She scans the parking lot, though no one else is even out of the locker room yet.

"Say yes," Phoebe says. "If anyone asks, you're just giving me a ride home."

No one is going to ask, but Phoebe can tell Grace needs the excuse, just in case. God forbid anyone see them together.

"What are we eating?" Before Phoebe can even smirk, Grace huffs. "I mean for dinner."

"You're the one who knows the restaurants around here," Phoebe says. "But, uh, I can pay this time."

It's the beginning of the week; she can budget for one meal. It feels like it matters, somehow. Like it might shift their relationship, like it isn't just Grace being older and wiser and richer and more knowledge-able, about soccer and New Orleans both, and Phoebe tagging along. Like she has something to offer, too.

"I'm paying," Grace says. "You like Chinese food?"

Okay, so what Phoebe offers will have to be something other than money.

They order in the car before leaving for Grace's house. Phoebe's leg bounces in the passenger seat. She sneaks a glance at Grace, who is focused on the road. Phoebe clenches around nothing.

This is *not* the time to be so ready to go—Grace is sad, probably, and frustrated, and Phoebe knows that, she does. She gets that. It's just Grace also *put her hands* on Phoebe *in front of people*. Phoebe spiraled out, over the weekend and also throughout practice, about how Grace probably hated her now and why did she ever think it was a good idea to text Friday to check in and couldn't she do anything right? But here they are, in Grace's car on the way to her house, the air between them thick with silent tension.

Phoebe wants to make sure Grace is okay. She wants to make sure *they* are okay. She just also wants Grace to pull over on a quiet street and climb into Phoebe's lap. She wants to kiss her as soon as they get inside Grace's house. She said no sleeping together until Grace went to the trainer, and Grace—well, she didn't *go* to the trainer, exactly, but she *saw* the trainer. She's finally being treated for her injury, which was the point of Phoebe's terms, so it counts. It wasn't hard not to sleep with Grace—it's barely been over a week, for one, and a busy week at that, and Phoebe is pretty good at sticking to her guns when it matters—but now that she *can*? Yeah, she's fucking ready.

When they arrive, though, Phoebe is distracted by the gorgeous, fluffy, cream-colored cat who greets them at the door.

"Who is this *angel*?" Phoebe's voice goes up the way people's voices do when they talk to babies. "Aren't you just the most beautiful kitty in the whole wide world? Yes, you are, little baby."

"That's Lilly," Grace says.

"Lilly!" Phoebe exclaims. "What a perfect sweet baby girl."

"Boy," Grace says. The cat follows her as she goes farther into her house. "He only cares about treats. Don't be offended."

"You have a boy cat named Lilly?"

"I thought he was a girl when I found him," Grace says. She shakes the bag of treats and Lilly meows louder. "Named him after Kristine Lilly, most capped American woman."

Phoebe snorts. "I know who Kristine Lilly is."

"Thought you might be a little young for her."

"I'm literally only four years younger than you, Henderson."

Grace always acts like she's *so old*. Sure, she's been on the national team for a decade, but she's still in her midtwenties.

"You're gonna pass her, aren't you?" Phoebe asks.

Grace freezes, open treat bag in her hand. The cat twines between her legs, meowing, but Grace just stares at Phoebe.

"Kristine Lilly had 354 caps," Grace says.

"Yeah, but I mean, like, you're on track." Phoebe shrugs. She doesn't know why Grace is being awkward about this. "Obviously there's a long way to go. But you both debuted at sixteen, so you totally could."

Grace turns away. "Maybe."

Phoebe finally pays attention to Grace's house instead of her cat.

The house is nothing like what Phoebe expects. Well, Phoebe doesn't know what she expected, not really—she's no good with interior design, no good with organization in general. But Grace seems put together. Adult. If Grace isn't in team-branded clothing, she's in black or white.

Grace looks good, all the time, and that's not to say that her house doesn't—it's just that she's clearly opted for comfort over style when decorating. The furniture is massive and occupied—not by people but by pillows. Grace owns more throw pillows than anyone Phoebe has ever met. There's a couch with at least a dozen, with more piled on the two chairs on either side of it. Even the coffee table has two pillows stacked on top.

After feeding her cat, Grace marches over and efficiently removes pillows from the couch until there's room for Phoebe to sit.

"Sorry for the mess," Grace says, shoving the pillows into a basket that slides under the coffee table. "I wasn't prepared for company."

On the coffee table is a lone, mostly empty glass of water. Over the back of the reclining chair is Grace's leather jacket—or one of them, anyway. Phoebe has only seen one, but she wouldn't be surprised if Grace had more. The rest of the room is spotless. The rest of the *house* is spotless, from what Phoebe can see, and since it's an open floor plan, she can see a lot. There's a dining room table only big enough for four, and beside that is the kitchen, with basically empty granite counters. Phoebe can't even see any dishes in the sink. With half the pillows hidden away in the basket under the coffee table, there's nothing even approximating a mess.

"If this is a mess, you're literally never allowed to come to my apartment." Phoebe throws her arms out and leans back into the couch, three pillows of varying firmness behind her. "This is so cozy."

"Yeah," Grace says. She's perched on the edge of the opposite side of the sofa from Phoebe. A pillow sits in her lap, tassels coming off each corner. Grace rubs the fringe between her pointer finger and thumb on both hands. "That's what I was going for."

Grace's cat trots into the living room and hops onto the couch between them. He ignores Phoebe in favor of pushing his head into Grace's palm as she pets him. Phoebe watches for a full thirty seconds without saying a word. How is it that Grace's cat has less prickly cat energy than Grace herself?

When Lilly has apparently had enough, he leaves the couch for the recliner, which still has a pile of pillows on it. He curls himself into a ball on a pillow that's so fluffy it looks like a cloud.

Their food arrives then, and Phoebe watches Grace as she meticulously plates it. Phoebe would've just eaten out of the take-out carton, but she says nothing. Not about the plates or all the questions she has. *Are you okay?* and *Why didn't you respond to my text?* and *You don't hate me, right?* She's pretty sure she knows the answer to that last one. Grace wouldn't have touched her if she hated her. Grace wouldn't have let her come to her house if she hated her.

Phoebe knows better than to ask, regardless. In the locker room on Sunday, Grace didn't want to talk. Actions speak louder than words anyway, right? Phoebe doesn't need to say *I'm worried about you. I am glad you're taking care of yourself.* This, being there—she's showing it. Plus, she always talks too much anyway. She can learn a thing or two from Grace's quiet.

Just in case, though, just to be sure, after they finish eating, Phoebe asks, "You wanna talk about it?"

Grace sighs. "Are we really doing this?"

"Doing what?"

"Talking about my feelings?"

"Why not? I wanna make sure you're okay."

"We're not dating," Grace blurts out. Phoebe raises her eyebrows. "You're not my girlfriend. Or my captain. Or my mom."

"Are those the only people who are allowed to make sure you're okay?"

Grace huffs. "I don't need to talk this out with you."

"Okay." Phoebe shrugs. "I'm fine getting right to the good stuff."

She slides closer to Grace on the couch, a wolfish smile taking over her face. Grace, though, just blinks at her.

"What?" they both say at once.

Phoebe tries not to shrink. "Do you not want to make out?"

"That's what you came here for?"

"Well . . . ," Phoebe hedges. "Not exactly, but also kind of?"

She came to be there for Grace, however Grace needs her to be. But this is a way to be there, too. Grace does *not* put herself first. Phoebe can help with that.

"I guess you did say that once I went to the trainer . . ."

"I did, didn't I?" Phoebe pushes her hand into the soft fabric of the couch. "Plus, this sofa is a lot more comfortable than anything in the locker room."

"There's also a bed," Grace says.

"Eh, we'll get there. We should start here first, though."

"Yeah?"

"Yeah."

This time when Phoebe encroaches on Grace's space, Grace is almost smiling. Phoebe feints for Grace's lips but then lands a kiss on the pulse point in her neck, the exact spot Grace first kissed her. It makes Grace chuckle, and Phoebe feels the vibrations under her mouth. She sucks the skin there so, so gently, hyperaware that she won't get the chance to do it again if she leaves a mark. This has to be secret. No one can know but the two of them.

Phoebe kisses her way up Grace's neck and jaw until their mouths finally meet. She stays soft at first, all wet lips but no tongue. She wants to take her time with Grace, like they're teenagers exploring someone else's body for the first time. That's what Phoebe likes about the sofa, too—she feels young as she presses Grace into the arm of the couch, like she's in the basement of her best friend's house with no one due home soon and they are quiet and uncertain and learning.

Grace doesn't seem quite so timid—she slides her legs up onto the couch, adjusting so she can lie back with Phoebe on top of her. Her fingers are already slipping under Phoebe's tank top.

Phoebe catches Grace's hands in hers. "Just . . . let me take care of you?"

"You're saying I can't touch you?"

She sounds almost outraged, and Phoebe can't help but smile.

"I'm saying nothing of the sort. I just want this to be about you right now. I don't want you to worry about anything."

"I'm not *worried*," Grace says. "I wanna see your boobs."

Phoebe laughs loud and bright. "You will. I promise. Can you just trust me?"

Grace's nostrils flare. Phoebe didn't realize that would be a hard ask. Grace lies back on the couch and laces her fingers together behind her head, elbows out. "Fine, Phenom. Do your worst."

"I'm tempted to make you regret telling me that," Phoebe says before surging forward for a kiss. A few moments later, after taking Grace's earlobe between her teeth, she murmurs, "But I'm gonna do my *best*. I'm gonna treat you so good, baby."

Saliva clicks in Grace's throat as she swallows.

Phoebe's best? Working slowly down Grace's body. Slipping her fingers under Grace's tank while her tongue is still tracing the brunette's clavicle. Slowly, slowly. Soft. Gentle. Warm. Punctuated by only the occasional nip of her teeth. Taking a moment to stare once Grace's shirt finally comes off. Grace wears a simple off-white bra, no lace, nothing fancy. Her nipples are already hard enough to strain against the fabric. Phoebe's best means she loses track of time while she mouths at Grace's chest, first through the bra and then gentler once it's off. She sucks and licks and uses her fingers on whichever nipple her mouth isn't on in the moment. Grace squirms, her breath gone ragged.

"Yeah?" Phoebe says. She rolls both nipples between her thumbs and index fingers. "You like that?"

"Jesus."

"I'm serious. You like that?" Phoebe repeats.

She only sees the whites of Grace's eyes as the other woman rolls them. "Yes, God, obviously."

"Not obviously," Phoebe says. "I don't know how to best make you feel good unless you tell me."

Grace shifts beneath her, frowning. "You really can't tell unless I actually say it?"

Phoebe lets herself smirk, just a little. "I mean, I can tell it's good. But I want to know exactly how you want it. You had no problem telling me what to do in that drill today. Do the same thing here. If I'm not getting it, don't hesitate to put your hands on me."

Grace brings her hands down to Phoebe's fingers, which are still playing with her nipples. She squeezes.

"Harder."

Phoebe pinches Grace's nipples and Grace closes her eyes, sucking in a shuddering breath.

"There you go," Phoebe murmurs. "You look so good."

A flush is settling onto Grace's tan skin, spreading from her cheeks down across her chest. Phoebe follows it with her mouth. When she reaches Grace's nipples again, she leaves gentle behind, biting until Grace rolls her hips up and into Phoebe's body.

"I wanna go down on you," Phoebe says.

Grace nods, her eyes still closed. "Yes."

"Yeah?" Phoebe's hands are already pushing Grace's joggers down. "You just lie back and let me lick your cunt, baby."

"Honestly, do you ever shut up?" Grace says, like that's gonna hide the way her whole body shivers at Phoebe's words.

"You don't want to hear about how I'm gonna eat you out?" Phoebe traces the edge of Grace's underwear without letting her fingers stray anywhere too interesting. "You don't wanna know how I'm gonna tongue at your clit until you come all over my face?"

Grace shivers again. Her hips keep chasing Phoebe's hands as they drag across her skin. She says nothing.

Phoebe smirks. "That's what I thought, baby girl."

She slides farther down the couch. Grace is short, but there still isn't room for both of them lying like this. Phoebe's knees rest on the arm of the sofa, feet in the air so her legs don't hang over the edge. How they're arranged isn't particularly important to her as long as she can get at Grace's center.

Like her bra, Grace's underwear is simple. Heather-gray cotton, and between her legs there's a spot that's darker. The thought that she got Grace this wet already makes Phoebe clench. She inhales, licking her lips at the deep, musky scent. One day, Phoebe swears she'll take it slow, but today is about making Grace feel good, not making her beg. So when Grace adjusts, spreading her legs wider, Phoebe leans in and puts her mouth on that wet spot of Grace's panties.

Grace's legs go so wide one is fully off the couch, her foot dropping to the floor.

She likes it a little rough on her chest, but Phoebe isn't sure about down here. The panties, though, offer enough protection that she doesn't hesitate to find Grace's clit and bite at it.

"Oh fuck."

"You taste so good." Phoebe's words are muffled as she sucks the taste out of the thin layer of cotton.

Grace moans and Phoebe matches it, moaning right against Grace.

Phoebe can't do this for long. She doesn't want the muted, protected feeling. She wants her tongue dragging directly through Grace's wet folds. She wants to bury herself in Grace's smell and taste and the sounds she makes. She hooks her fingers in the sides of Grace's panties and pulls them down.

Twenty

Grace jumps when Phoebe puts her mouth on her again, no barrier this time. Her knee hits the coffee table as she tries to spread her legs wider. It doesn't hurt. Neither does her hip, not that Grace is thinking about that. Phoebe runs her hand down Grace's thigh and cups it over her knee like she's protecting it, all without taking her mouth off Grace's center. Grace rolls her hips.

They were supposed to have gotten this out of their systems. Grace doesn't do casual sex, and she's certainly not interested in a relationship, so what is this supposed to be? She has no idea, but she is letting herself have it. It feels too good not to. Before Phoebe, Grace hadn't had sex in years, and she's never had sex this good. Phoebe is singularly focused on Grace's center. Grace grabs a handful of her own hair and tugs.

Phoebe's tongue is as relentless as she is when she's playing, or when she's decided to make friends with you. Matthews is always relentless, as far as Grace has seen. Once she learns to balance it with patience, she'll be unstoppable. Maybe she'll figure it out while Grace is on the bench. Maybe she'll get so good Grace won't have a spot in the lineup to return to.

Even as Phoebe is lapping at her clit, Grace is thinking about soccer. In

the locker room, she let go. Phoebe managed to make her stop thinking. She wants to stop thinking again. Phoebe's fingers trace the lightest
shapes over the skin of Grace's knee. Grace pulls her own hair again,
tries to focus. Every muscle in her body feels tense, ready to snap.

Phoebe uses her teeth and Grace groans.

"Does that feel good?"

Grace nods. "I want . . ."

She doesn't finish her sentence.

"Tell me," Phoebe says. "What do you want, Grace?"

"I want to come."

Phoebe chuckles. "Yeah, I want that, too."

"Phoebe." Grace drags out the last syllable of her name. "I wanna
come. I'm trying. I'm close."

Phoebe pulls fully back and Grace gasps, her eyes flying open.

"Matthews," she snaps.

Phoebe gets this dopey smile on her face, and fuck, she's probably
going to make fun of Grace for using her last name. But she doesn't.

"I don't want you to try," she says instead. "You're not supposed to
be trying to do anything. You're just supposed to be enjoying this."

"I am," Grace protests.

It's not a lie. Phoebe is excellent with her mouth, and Grace loves it.
And she'd really like to come. Phoebe leans back in, and even though
Grace doesn't mean to, she clenches everything.

Phoebe doesn't put her mouth where Grace wants it.

"You deserve this," she says, then sucks a hickey onto Grace's inner
thigh. "You work so hard all the time." She switches to the other thigh.
"You deserve rest, baby girl. Always taking care of everyone else. Let
me take care of you." At last, she licks straight up Grace's slit, finishing
with her tongue circling her clit. She keeps her mouth close when she
says, "Relax, Grace. Let yourself feel good. I'll get you there, I promise."

When she puts her tongue back on Grace's cunt, Grace takes a deep,
reverberating breath, and she tries to relax. To let her body go loose. It
sounds easier than it is.

She's not used to lying back and letting things happen, even when
those things are good, like a gorgeous woman going down on her. She's

used to being in charge, being *intentional*. The point of sex is to come, so that's what she wants to do. Matthews told her she's not supposed to be trying, not supposed to be doing anything but feeling good.

And it *does* feel good. Matthews knows what she's doing. Grace has never really believed the phrase *Variety is the spice of life*, but Phoebe keeps changing what she's doing with her mouth, from licking Grace's clit to sucking her labia to planting kisses on the insides of her thighs, and the variety is *good*. It gets Grace wetter, even if it doesn't necessarily bring her closer to orgasm. Phoebe keeps talking to her, too, every time her mouth isn't otherwise occupied, telling her how good she tastes, how good she is. Grace lets herself like it. She lets herself like all of it, doesn't try chasing what feels the best. Eventually, though, she can't help but whine when Phoebe's tongue stops circling her clit.

"Yeah?" Phoebe says. "You like that?"

Grace doesn't admit it verbally, even if her body already has.

"Tell me, Grace." Phoebe punctuates the command with a nip to the soft skin of Grace's inner thigh.

Grace's chest heaves as she looks down at Phoebe between her legs. "I thought I was just supposed to be enjoying it."

Phoebe's smile is pleased. "I wanna know what you like best."

"All of it," Grace says, because it's true. She thought she was supposed to come quickly, but this is better. Phoebe has slowly tightened the tension coiling in Grace's center so much it makes it hard to talk, hard to breathe. "You're so good with your mouth. Everywhere. But . . ."

"But what?"

"Am I allowed to be ready to come?" Grace asks. "I'm not trying. Just ready."

That smile goes feral, like Grace couldn't have said anything better. "Yeah? You wanna come with my tongue on your clit?"

Grace nods, and Phoebe doesn't hesitate before leaning back in.

"Oh, fuck."

It's so good, and more focused, now. Phoebe doesn't break away or pull back or give Grace a single moment of respite. Grace tips her head back, the top of it butting up against the arm of the couch, but she doesn't care. She barely even notices, really, because there is nothing other than Phoebe's tongue, strong and wet, and Grace isn't trying to come at all; she just can't help it.

Phoebe doesn't let up, keeps at her for so long Grace has to press her thighs together to get her to stop.

"W-Whoa," she says.

Phoebe bites the muscle of her thigh instead. She whimpers and swears she can feel Phoebe smile against her.

It takes a moment for Grace to get it together to make actual words.

"Time to move to the bed?"

Phoebe laughs. "Not yet. I'm not even close to being done with you."

"Matthews," Grace says. "It's my turn to make you come."

"Who said anything about turns? How about this—what if we forget about reciprocation? Don't think about how it should be my turn, or that after this orgasm, you'll touch me."

That's how sex works, though. Each party is supposed to make the other feel good. That's always been Grace's understanding, anyway. Sex should be reciprocal. Orgasms don't exactly have to be tallied to ensure equality, but there's a give-and-take. This—Phoebe's full, focused attention—it feels too much like she's trying to take care of Grace, and that's not what this is.

"Who says I'm going to have another orgasm?" Grace asks.

"I mean, you had three last time."

"I didn't have as much on my mind last time."

She shouldn't have said that. Matthews doesn't need to know that. It's embarrassing, the way Phoebe's smirk disappears, the look on her face going soft. Grace doesn't want to hear what she has to say to that.

"Why won't you let me touch you?" Grace asks.

"I will. I will." Phoebe shrugs. "But I like touching you. And you deserve extra because you haven't had the greatest day."

"You're the one who did so poorly in that drill."

"Oof," Matthews says, but she's laughing. "Saying you haven't had the greatest day is me being nice, not judging you. You don't have to attack me for it."

Grace is hardly attacking. But she doesn't need Matthews to be nice to her because her stupid aging body landed her on the injury list. She props herself up on her elbows and looks down at Phoebe.

"This is about you, Grace. I want to make you feel good."

"I want to make *you* feel good," Grace snarls.

"Then relax," Phoebe says. She caresses Grace's thighs with her fingertips. "Nothing feels better than making you feel good."

Grace arches an eyebrow at her. "Nothing?"

She expects Phoebe to laugh, but the redhead is serious.

"Nothing. Not to me."

Oh.

In that case, Grace supposes she can let Phoebe put her mouth back on her. It's about Phoebe. Grace is reciprocating by not reciprocating—or by not doing it yet, anyway. Because she still wants to touch Phoebe. It's not that she won't, just that she'll wait. She can be patient while Phoebe sucks and licks and kisses. She can let Phoebe make her feel good.

"Fine," Grace says, lying back on the couch again. "But I seriously might not come again."

"I seriously don't care, as long as you feel good."

She does. *Fuck,* she does. Phoebe is *so* gentle, which she has to be, because Grace is sensitive. Everything is warm and wet and so, so good. Grace doesn't even try to keep track of what exactly Phoebe is doing. She doesn't do anything except let herself feel good.

Eventually, and Grace doesn't know how long it's been, just . . . eventually, she gets a hand in Phoebe's hair and pulls her away.

"Okay," Grace says, and she's aware she's panting. "It feels great. You did good. Can I *please* touch you now?"

"I don't know."

Phoebe drags out the last word. Grace knows she's fucking with her, but it's still working.

"It's not about turns." Grace gasps when Phoebe sucks hard on her inner thigh. "It's not about reciprocation. I just really want to touch you."

"Well, when you put it like that . . ."

Finally, Phoebe relinquishes her spot between Grace's legs.

"Bedroom," Grace says before Phoebe can climb back on top of her. "You're too tall for this couch."

Phoebe stands and offers a hand to help Grace to her feet. Grace feels like she should put her clothes back on. Obviously, there'd be no point, they wouldn't stay on for long, but it's awkward walking through her house naked while Phoebe is fully clothed. Or maybe it's not awkward, but she feels like it is. Grace leads Phoebe to her bedroom in the back of the house, and Phoebe never stops holding her hand. Grace worries her palm is clammy. Phoebe seems perfectly comfortable, but that's not unusual for her. Just like discomfort isn't unusual for Grace.

She expects it to get worse when they get to her bedroom. She's never brought anyone there before. But Phoebe doesn't even take any time to look around the room once they arrive. She finally drops Grace's hand, then pulls her shirt over her head and steps out of her shorts. The speed at which she gets naked is impressive, actually, and Grace certainly isn't complaining when Phoebe catches her by the hip and presses their skin together. Grace tries to steady her breathing. She feels out of control with how much she wants Phoebe. Phoebe was so good to her, and Grace wants to return the favor. Not because she is supposed to. Not because that's how sex works. Because she *wants.*

Grace can't pick a favorite part, but she couldn't do without this. It's not about reciprocation; it's about how wet Phoebe is when Grace drags two fingers between her legs. It's about the way Phoebe's voice is immediately desperate.

"*Fuck,* Grace."

Phoebe knocks Grace off-balance. She confuses her. She's not like anyone Grace has ever met. Touching her gives Grace some control back, makes her feel powerful.

Phoebe does the same thing she did in the locker room, babbles about how good it feels, how good Grace is at fucking her. It's less off-putting this time around. Grace doesn't wonder if it's a performance. In fact, she almost wants to say something back. But she's not Phoebe; everything she thinks of sounds embarrassing.

She's not Phoebe, and Phoebe is not her. Phoebe is not thinking too much to come, doesn't have too much in her head for multiple orgasms. Phoebe comes the moment Grace's fingers are inside her, then again when Grace slides down her body to lick at her clit. The taste is strong on Grace's tongue as Phoebe shudders, and she chases it deeper. Does Phoebe love being told her pussy is delicious as much as she likes telling Grace hers is? Maybe next time, Grace will be comfortable enough to find out.

Grace has fully lost it, whatever *it* is. Control. Her sanity. Or maybe just her commitment to not having casual sex. She's already thinking about doing this again while Phoebe comes a third time, her body pulsing up into Grace's mouth.

After, Phoebe tugs Grace back up the bed for a kiss. Grace's face is wet, and Phoebe moans. Her kisses are open-mouthed, catching Grace's lips but also her chin, her cheeks, sucking her own taste from Grace's skin.

That should be it, but then Grace remembers how many times Phoebe has smirked about giving her three orgasms, so instead of being done, she flicks her fingers back and forth over Phoebe's clit until the redhead has her fourth.

While Phoebe gets her breath, Grace lies on her back and stares at the ceiling. She was so focused on making Phoebe come, she didn't think about what they'd do after. Now it's after, and she doesn't know what happens next. Phoebe still has her eyes closed, a blissed-out smile on her face. Grace wants to wash her hands.

She forces herself to wait, counts out a full sixty seconds in her head. But Phoebe is still just lying there, so Grace extricates herself from the bed.

"Mmm," Phoebe says, more a noise than a word. "Where are you going?"

"Bathroom," Grace says.

"Right. Yes. Good idea." Phoebe has still not opened her eyes.

Grace slips into the bathroom connected to her bedroom and closes the door. She takes a breath, turns on the warm water.

What are they supposed to do now? They've eaten—actual dinner and otherwise. It's nine o'clock. Normally, Grace would be going through her evening routine: she'd have already finished the crossword, lying on the chaise lounge on her front porch while Lilly watched the birds. This is worse in her own house than in the locker room. At least there, the next steps were obvious; they had to shower, had to get dressed and leave. What is she supposed to do with Phoebe in her house, in her bed?

Grace is not used to having someone in her home. It's big enough that she could have company, but she doesn't usually. Her parents and sister stay with her—her parents in the guest bedroom and Harmony on an air mattress in the den—when they come to visit, but that's really it. Madeeha and H used to stay when the Belles played the Krewe, but now that they have Khadijah, that's over.

Grace likes having her own space. Doing whatever she wants with it. She can have twenty-five different throw pillows on the three pieces of furniture in her living room without having to explain how, depending on her mood, she needs different textures and levels of softness and colors. She can eat the same meals every week without anyone asking if she gets bored. Her home is the only place that's all hers. Once, *Homes & Gardens* magazine wanted to do a feature on her house. They were going to come in and take pictures and they wanted Grace to provide little sound bites about why she decorated the way she did. It is one of the few media opportunities Grace has ever said no to.

Grace's clothes are still in the living room, but she doesn't want to go back to her bedroom naked. The oversize T-shirt she wears to bed is draped over the towel rack. Grace dries her hands on the hand towel before putting the shirt on. It covers enough, even if she'd rather have underwear.

She opens the door to the bedroom but then makes no move to go inside.

Matthews looks up at her from the bed and grins. "Did you know elephants can hear through their feet?"

Phoebe is rolled on her side and propped up with her elbow, her cheek resting against her palm. The sheet is only pulled up to her waist. Grace doesn't let herself get distracted by Phoebe's small breasts and pink nipples.

Then again, if they just keep fucking, she'll never have to figure out what to do after.

"Is that so?"

"Well, like, it might not technically be hearing," Phoebe says. "But it's, like, feeling vibrations and knowing what they mean. They can hear another herd of elephants from ten miles away, through vibrations in the ground."

"How do we know that?"

"They've been observed, like, changing direction."

Grace narrows her eyes. "Changing direction proves they can hear through their feet?"

"No, like, changing direction specifically to meet up with another herd," Phoebe explains. "And I mean, I'm not the scientist involved. I don't remember all of the documentary I watched. Just that they can hear through their feet. Oh! And that the bottoms of their feet are so soft they can step on a twig and not break it."

Grace is still standing in the doorway to the bathroom.

"Anyway, come over here," Phoebe says.

She's already only on one side of the bed, but she slides farther onto it, pushes the sheet back, and pats the mattress. Grace climbs into bed. She lies on her back, arms tucked tight to her sides.

"Roll over," Phoebe says.

"What?"

"Like, on your side? I want to spoon you."

Grace does as she's told, even though she's never been much of a cuddler. Phoebe is up against her back immediately. Grace's head turns when Phoebe slides one arm awkwardly under it.

"Sorry," Phoebe says as Grace adjusts. "This okay?"

"Mmhmm."

What's Grace supposed to say—no? That seems rude. She can just deal with this for however long Matthews wants to do it. Hopefully not too long. It's awkward. Too hot. Grace doesn't know what to do with her arms. How do people fall asleep like this? Does Phoebe want to stay like this the whole night? Not that Phoebe is staying the night. That's not something you do with casual sex, Grace is pretty sure.

She counts silently in her head to 180. Three minutes seems like a reasonable amount of time. She clears her throat, and Phoebe, whose breath had begun to go deep and even, stirs behind her.

"So, what happens now?"

"What?" Phoebe's voice is thick with sleep.

Grace rolls over, because she can't have this conversation while sweating and spooning. She doesn't know what comes next, and she needs to. Phoebe blinks at her, pulling her arm back to her side of the bed.

"As I said, I'm not looking for a relationship."

"Oh yeah, me neither," Phoebe says. She immediately amends, "Or, like, I'm not *not* looking, but I'm never really looking, either. I got other stuff to focus on, and to be honest I've never been that great at relationships anyway. I'm not looking to date you and let you down or anything." Phoebe shakes her head. "What I'm trying to say is I came here to check in on you and continue our friends-with-benefits situation. That's all."

"Okay," Grace says, even though that doesn't really answer her question.

"Can we veg out for a while, though? Your bed is so fucking comfy."

"Um," Grace says. "Sure."

"Sweet."

Phoebe rolls onto her back and sighs happily. Before Grace has to figure out what to do next, Lilly meows from behind the closed door to her bedroom.

"I should"—she gestures toward the door—"get him. He'll be obnoxious otherwise."

"Oh yeah, let him in. I'll cuddle the shit out of him."

"Do you need anything?" Grace asks as she gets out of bed. "Water or . . ."

"Water would be *great*."

Grace opens the door to let Lilly in, but then continues on to the kitchen. She feels like a stranger in her own home. Not that Phoebe is anything but perfectly pleasant. Grace simply has no experience with this.

She gets them both glasses of water and finds her clothes in the living room. Her underwear is a lost cause, soaked from Phoebe's mouth—and, admittedly, from Grace herself. Grace would prefer not to wear shorts without underwear, but it's better than nothing. Especially since she has to go to the front porch to grab the newspaper. Nobody gets a newspaper anymore, but Grace likes it. Doing a crossword on her phone isn't the same. There's a clock up in the corner in the digital version, and it stresses her out.

Back in the bedroom, she learns having someone in her bed as she does the crossword in the paper also stresses her out. Phoebe hasn't put her clothes back on, but she must have gotten up while Grace got the water, because she has her phone now, is watching videos on it with Lilly curled into her side.

"I don't have my headphones," she says as Grace climbs back into the bed. "Is that okay?"

"Fine," Grace says.

Phoebe keeps the volume as low as possible, but it still takes Grace too long to finish the Monday puzzle.

Phoebe cackles at a video, then turns to Grace. "So, you know that TikTok trend where people kiss toads to 'Rainbow Connection'?"

Grace shakes her head. "I don't really do TikTok."

Younger players usually make fun of her for that. Grace always refers to "younger players" like she's a wizened old vet when really, some of them are barely younger than her. If they aren't calling her old, she is weird, or technologically deficient, or overly private, but Phoebe doesn't seem to care. She just launches into an explanation of the TikTok trend, giving Grace the background necessary to appreciate the video before showing it to her.

It still doesn't seem that funny to Grace, but she appreciates Phoebe's effort.

"I should probably head home at some point," Phoebe says. "Or, like, now, since it's getting late. Can't show up to practice tomorrow in the same clothes I left in today, right?"

"Right."

That makes sense, assuming they don't want anyone to know about this. Grace has accumulated enough Krewe gear over the years that she's not sure anyone would notice if she wore the same clothes or not, but Phoebe is new.

"I mean, I'd be happy to stay." Phoebe grins. "But I'd definitely want morning sex, and that'd be *so* early so I could get home and switch clothes before practice. I don't want to make you get up early when you don't have to."

Grace doesn't want to think about sleeping in. It's one thing when it's a weekend or holiday, but staying in bed when the rest of the team is training—she already knows it isn't going to sit right with her.

"Okay" is all she says.

What comes next? *See you later?* She doesn't know when they'll see each other again now that Eric has banned Grace from practice, even though she *helped* today. Are she and Phoebe even friends outside of soccer? Does Grace have any friends outside of soccer?

Phoebe gives Lilly one last pat before getting out of bed and finding her clothes.

"I'm gonna give you some time to settle into being injured, yeah?" she says as she pulls shorts up her long, freckled legs. "But the way friends with benefits works is we do this again."

Grace can't deny that she'd like that. Phoebe is almost alarmingly good at sex. Even the part when Grace didn't come was so good she wants to do it again.

"So, like, keep in touch. Text me when you're bored or whatever."

"For a booty call?"

Phoebe smirks and gives a half shrug. "For whatever you want. Friends with benefits includes the friends part, not just the benefits part. Plus, you don't get out of being my tour guide just because you're not playing."

"I've never had a friend with benefits before," Grace admits.

"Seriously?"

Grace scowls instead of blushing. Phoebe's certain confidence always makes her feel embarrassingly unsure.

"Why is that so surprising?"

"Uh, 'cause you're hot and athletic and not looking for a relationship? You're, like, the perfect friend with benefits." Phoebe says it all so nonchalantly, like it's obvious. "No worries, though. I've got enough experience for both of us."

She's fully dressed finally. It's easier to breathe now that Grace can't see so much skin, though Phoebe's arms are still bare.

"Are you walking home?" Grace asks, though she knows the answer. Matthews doesn't have a car. "I can drive you."

She can't let the girl walk. It's a ten-minute drive to Phoebe's apartment.

"You totally don't have to," Phoebe says. "Honestly, I'd rather walk."

"Matthews, it has to be more than two miles," Grace says, getting out of bed. "You'll be cold."

Phoebe shrugs. "I'm okay. Really."

God, she is frustrating.

"If you're not going to let me drive you, at least take a sweatshirt."

Grace gets one out of her dresser and holds it out to Phoebe, who, for a moment, stands there beaming at her rather than taking the shirt. It's an absurdly big smile in response to being offered an old Krewe hoodie.

"Thanks," Matthews says, finally taking the sweatshirt and tugging it over her head.

It's a little short on her, but she grins down at herself like she doesn't mind at all. The purple fabric and yellow text are faded from so many washes.

"I'll wash it before I bring it back," she says.

"Sure."

Grace will wash it herself, anyway. She's particular about the way her clothes smell, but Phoebe doesn't need to know that.

Grace walks her to the front door because that seems like the right thing to do.

"So chivalrous," Phoebe says.

Grace doesn't know if she's serious or teasing her, but then Phoebe leans down to kiss her, so she supposes it doesn't matter.

Twenty-One

Injury reports go out Wednesday afternoon, so Wednesday morning, Grace picks up her phone. She'd rather not tell her family about her hip, frankly, but it's always worse if they learn something through the media. So, no matter how much she doesn't want to talk about herself and her so-called injury and deal with her family's well-meaning but intrusive questions, she calls her parents' home phone.

Her dad picks up. "Gracie! What are you doing calling in the middle of the day? Shouldn't you be running around on a soccer field?"

Grace knows exactly what she should be doing. Givhan has run practice the same way every year she's been on the team. Wednesday just before lunch, the team plays some kind of game, soccer tennis or keep-away. Givhan likes something fun before breaking for lunch, as if the players won't want to come back afterward, especially on a Wednesday, since it's the middle of the week.

Her dad doesn't need to know any of that.

"That's actually kind of what I was calling about," Grace says. She's always been one to rip off a Band-Aid. "I'm fine, but I've got a bit of a hip thing, and I'm gonna be out for a couple weeks."

"What? Honey, are you okay?" Then, muffled, she hears him yell, "Maggie! Pick up the phone! It's your eldest!"

Her mom picks up immediately. "Hello, beautiful. You never call during the day. How are you doing?"

"She's *hurt*," her dad says, still on the line.

"I'm *fine*," Grace insists. Of course the first thing both of her parents notice is that she's not at practice. Like Grace is a soccer player before she's their daughter. "It's a minor strain. I'll be back on the field before you know it."

"Are you okay?" her mom asks, like Grace didn't lead with the fact that she's fine.

"It's honestly not a big deal. I'm not limited in any daily activities outside of soccer and exercise."

"That sounds like most of your daily activities, sweet'ums," her dad says.

He isn't wrong, but she wishes he saw her as more than a soccer player. Maybe she can spend her time off the field figuring out how to see herself as more than a soccer player.

"I suppose you're bound to get injured as a professional athlete, but gosh, I don't like it," her mom says. "You haven't been hurt since you tore your ACL."

Grace is well aware of that, thank you. She remembers how hard it was to come back from, and she was younger then.

"I'm not particularly wild about it, either," Grace admits. "But I'll be fine."

"How long will it be?" her mom asks. "Will we still be able to see you play in the home opener?"

The Krewe's first home game is five weeks away.

"I don't know yet," Grace says. "I'd rather we not plan anything until I'm back."

"But we always come to the home opener," her mom says.

"Maggie, it's fine. The rest will be good for you, Gracie." Her dad says it like he has decided it, so that's how it will go. "You'll be back on the field before you know it."

What if I'm not? she wants to ask.

Instead, she lets them fuss over her for a while before insisting she has to go. Not that she actually has any commitments now that she's benched, but they seem to believe her.

After they hang up, Grace unloads her dishwasher. Depending on how much her mom talks, she figures she has between ten and twenty minutes before her sister calls. It only ends up being seven minutes before Harmony appears on her phone.

"Hi, Harm," Grace says.

Her sister, as expected, launches right in. "So, according to Mom, you're dying. How much is she exaggerating?"

"Well, I have a minor hip flexor strain, so. I'd say a lot."

Dawn hadn't called it minor, but Grace is. She can play through it—she knows she can, because she's been playing through it since last season—so it can't be that big of a deal. She still doesn't believe it's anything except her body getting older.

"Then why won't you let us have our weekend in NOLA?" Harmony asks.

Grace sighs. "I'm not doing all the work of planning the whole weekend when I might not even be able to play yet. We can do it for some other game."

"I don't care about the game," Harmony says. "I wanna eat really good food and maybe go to that jazz place you took us to last time and I guess seeing you is nice, too."

"Well, I need to focus on my recovery, not planning your fun weekend vacation."

"So I'll plan it," Harmony says. "C'mon, that weekend is like the only time I see you outside of holidays. Honestly, it's better if you're not playing, because—"

"We'll do it for a different game," Grace snaps.

She doesn't need to hear about how her sister likes to invade Grace's house and have her as a tour guide for a weekend. And sure, Harmony can offer to plan it, but she's always been more likely to improvise than organize. Grace doesn't want to waste time arguing over where to eat. It's easier for her to schedule their time, not minute by minute, but rigidly enough that they don't have downtime to get on one another's nerves.

She doesn't even fake an excuse to get Harmony off the phone—being annoyed is enough to make her sister annoyed, and Harmony offers vague well-wishes before hanging up.

• • • •

That afternoon, Grace's phone buzzes. She ignores it, focused on the crossword she's halfway through. A minute later, another buzz. Then another. Her phone vibrates itself right off the table.

The injury report must be live.

Grace only gets social media notifications from people she follows, but there are still too many to keep up with. Not to mention texts and emails, too. At least no one tries to call her—not that she would pick up for most people. She ignores the emails and only replies to the texts, figuring if someone has her phone number, they probably deserve a response.

Until an email comes in that she can't ignore.

A responsible player would've told their national team coach themself, but Grace had delegated that duty to her agent. Regardless, it got done, because a notification banner pops up with an email from Amanda Greene. Grace swipes it open, unsure if she's grateful to avoid having an actual conversation, or hurt that she isn't even worth a phone call.

Grace,

I'm so sorry to hear about your injury. You've never been the type to take it easy, but please do. There is no rush for you to return. We'll miss you for sHeroes, but it shouldn't even be on your mind as you recover. Take your time, and we'll see you for the send-off games.

Best,

Amanda

Grace already knew she'd miss the sHeroes tournament, but somehow it's worse reading it in the email. There's still a squeezing pressure in her chest. They don't need her. All the work she's put in her entire life, and Amanda doesn't want her to think about sHeroes. This is why Grace never said anything about her leg. Trainers and coaches are always certain they know what's best, making unilateral decisions like they're good for Grace. Who's to say Amanda won't decide that the team doesn't need her for the World Cup, either? That she's too much of a liability now that her body is falling apart.

Grace wants to turn her phone off, or maybe throw it into the Mississippi. It's warm in her hand from how often it's vibrated. She hasn't replied to a fraction of her messages, and already she's sick of acting optimistic or cheerful or doing anything other than wallowing.

At least when Fish calls, Grace doesn't have to pretend to be cheerful.

"Hey."

"Well, this fucking sucks, doesn't it," Fish says instead of hello.

Grace doesn't laugh, but she almost smiles. "It does."

"How are you doing?"

She sighs. "Out three to six weeks and Dawn seems to think it'll be on the longer end. I'm definitely out for sHeroes and maybe for opening day, too."

"I didn't ask about the prognosis," Fish says. "I asked how you're doing."

"Fine."

"Henderson, I know you don't like to talk, but tell me how the fuck you're doing."

Grace huffs. Her phone buzzes in her hand, and she pulls it away to turn on Do Not Disturb before answering Fish.

"Is this what I'm like as a captain?" she asks. "It's fucking annoying."

"I considered giving you some time to come to terms with it, but figured you'd just be pissed and wallowing instead. Good to know I'm always right."

Grace supposes she's predictable. Usually, she prides herself on that. It's another way to say she's reliable. Responsible. There when people need her, instead of out for three to six weeks at the beginning of the season.

"I'm fine," she tells Fish. "It is what it is. Ask me in three weeks."

"You are actually going to take it easy, right?"

"Yes." Grace is aware that she sounds petulant. "They won't even let me watch practice anymore. Even though I *helped* last time."

"I think we all know you could run that team better than Givhan does, but seriously. Rest. Do some shit that has nothing to do with soccer. Hell, take a vacation."

She doesn't need a vacation. She did New Year's in Belize. With the season starting, vacation time is supposed to be over. For the past five years, since Grace switched from Lyon to New Orleans, she's had the same schedule for her year. Even before that, her calendar revolved around national team camps. She's not supposed to have free time in February and March. She doesn't want to take a vacation anyway. Spring is the best time in New Orleans, when the azaleas bloom and the humidity isn't yet obscene.

"Whatever," Grace says. "You don't have to worry. I'm doing what I'm supposed to be doing and you're free of me until at least after sHeroes."

"I'm not free of you until sHeroes because I'm not calling just as your captain, dumbass," Fish says. "I'm not going to make you talk about your feelings every day or anything, but I am still going to check in on you separate from soccer."

Separate from soccer, Grace is fine. Separate from soccer, it doesn't matter if her body is falling apart. But separate from soccer is nothing. Grace has never been separate from soccer, and has never wanted to be. She doesn't want to be now, either—that's the problem. But she appreciates the sentiment anyway.

"I guess that's fair, but only if you're serious about not making me talk about my feelings."

"Deal," Fish says. "How did your team look first week back, anyway? Think y'all are going to manage a three-peat?"

They spend the next thirty minutes talking new players and AWSA rivalries. Grace feels normal for the first time all week.

• • • •

The next day Grace stays in bed as long as possible, but it doesn't even feel luxurious, just lazy. She goes grocery shopping and makes herself a chef's salad for lunch, then finally turns her phone off Do Not Disturb. The chaise on her front porch is as good a place as any to answer well-wishes sent by everyone from national teammates to her parents' neighbor. The activity is only survivable because she copies and pastes a generic *Thank you. I'm okay. Can't wait to get back on the field!*

She's still on her porch in the late afternoon when her mail arrives. There's a thick manila envelope with *H&M* scrawled in the upper left corner, above an address in Philadelphia that Grace memorized years ago when Sarah and Madeeha first moved there. Grace rips the envelope open. It's stuffed. There's a crossword puzzle book, a book of sudoku, a photo of Grace holding Khadijah, and a get-well-soon card, which Madeeha signed *Take care of yourself!* and H signed *Sorry this sucks!* They must have paid for overnight shipping.

Why can't everyone be as good as H and Madeeha?

Lilly curls up on the empty discarded envelope for a nap, and Grace breaks into the sudoku book. Normally she'd start with the first page, but normally she'd be leading cooldown at the end of practice right now, so she lets herself open to the middle of the book to work on a more challenging puzzle.

She's on her third sudoku when her phone buzzes yet again. She considers getting a new number while she's out. She certainly has the time, and the fewer people who can contact her, the better.

It isn't someone from her past wishing her a speedy recovery, though; it's Matthews, asking what she's up to. Another message comes in as Grace reads the first.

> If you aren't busy you could come over? Or I could come over, if you want

> I've got dinner plans, but I got time to eat first 😊

Sometimes Grace doesn't catch innuendo, but Phoebe makes it obvious.

Grace is absolutely not going to Phoebe's team-issued apartment. Other players live in the building, for one, and unless they've significantly upgraded from the last time Grace visited, the furniture is less than comfortable. Besides, Grace never takes an opportunity to leave her own space if she doesn't have to.

Matthews does seem like a good distraction, though. Grace texts come over, without thinking too hard about it.

Matthews is an *excellent* distraction—all messy red hair and kissing Grace as soon as she arrives. Sleeping with Phoebe is a lot more fun than answering text messages. It's more fun than doing a crossword puzzle. Grace has even become used to how much she talks during the act.

After, Phoebe grins up at Grace from between her legs.

"I hate to eat and run," she says, "but I'm going out with Gabby."

"Right," Grace says as Matthews clambers out of bed. "Sure."

Grace isn't used to the abruptness of friends with benefits. It's not that she wants Phoebe to stay; it's simply that she's bored. She doesn't always like all her responsibilities, but having none, it turns out, is worse. After the initial few days of constant notifications, her phone has gone silent. Her house is silent. Her schedule is empty.

Friday night pizza night is almost as bad as last week—it can't be a reprieve from a long work week when there was no work week to begin with. Grace can't revel in sleeping in Saturday morning when she hasn't had a reason to set her alarm the past four days.

Change makes Grace's skin itch, even when it's objectively good. But this? What could be the death knell of her career? She wants to fight tooth and nail against it, though there's nothing to fight. There's nothing to do but be bored and itchy.

When she gets a *you up?* text from Matthews on Saturday morning, Grace doesn't take time to plan before sending her knee-jerk reaction.

> It's not even 9 AM. I'm not in the mood for sex

Grace watches the three little dots appear and then disappear twice before Phoebe sends another message.

> Okay . . . does that mean we can't even hang out? Bc I have two king cakes from Dong Phuong that aren't gonna eat themselves

Oh.

Sorry, Grace texts. Yes. I'm up. And we can hang out.

The reply comes much more quickly this time.

> Good bc I'm outside your house but can't really knock on account of holding a king cake in each hand

Grace goes to open her front door rather than ask how Phoebe's texting.

"Hello, hello, hello," Phoebe says from the steps outside the porch.

Grace opens the porch door for her, too. "Hi."

Phoebe strolls in, dimples deep enough to fall into.

"I can't believe you thought I was just using you for sex. Obviously I'm also using you for your soccer knowledge." She laughs, bumping her hip into Grace's as she passes. "Seriously, though, I do have a soccer question."

Phoebe heads right to the kitchen, so she misses the way Grace grimaces.

Of course it comes down to soccer. It always comes down to soccer. With her family, her friends, even herself—Grace hasn't been able to function this whole week because she doesn't have soccer. And while she doesn't particularly enjoy the idea of Phoebe using her for her soccer knowledge, talking about the sport she can't play anymore might be better than trying to pretend it doesn't exist.

Twenty-Two

Phoebe considers asking where the plates are, but opening all of the cabinets in Grace's kitchen seems like the perfect way to gently annoy her.

"Stuart brought Randazzo's yesterday," she says as she begins opening cupboards. "And it was fucking delicious, so this better live up to your hype, Henderson."

"There's no accounting for bad taste."

Phoebe grins. "It's not fair that you're hot, talented, *and* funny. Like leave something for the rest of us, would you?"

"Yeah, since you're so lacking in talent and hotness," Grace mutters.

"You think I'm hot?" Phoebe winks at her.

Grace rolls her eyes.

Phoebe opens a cupboard to find five plates and five bowls on one shelf, with five glasses and five mugs lined neatly on the next. Phoebe's dishes are a mishmash collected over the years—chipped plates, a couple of bowls she made in the pottery class she took in college, and more empty food jars repurposed as cups than actual glasses. Grace's dishes all match, a soft cerulean blue.

Phoebe grabs plates, then sets her sights on the two boxes she set on Grace's counter.

"I felt like I had to get original, to get the full experience, you know?" she tells Grace, who is standing by the kitchen island watching her. "But they also had *coconut*, which sounds super fancy, so I got that, too. Also, let me first say that this is already winning over the Randazzo's cake because it's not some huge, awkward, donut-looking thing."

"The ring shape is traditional for king cakes," Grace says.

"Well, that's *dumb*, 'cause this way you get way more cake."

Instead of a ring, the center of the Dong Phuong cakes are filled in so they look more like giant cinnamon rolls, covered in frosting and decorated with green and yellow and purple icing sugar.

Grace has one of those fancy knife blocks on her kitchen counter. It takes three tries for Phoebe to find the long serrated bread knife. She cuts small slices, two of each cake. The inside looks like coffee cake mixed with the flaky layers of a croissant. Her mouth is already watering.

Grace gets them forks before Phoebe can open every drawer in the kitchen. Phoebe holds hers up, and it takes a moment before Grace realizes she's trying to clink the silverware together like they're making a toast.

"To supposedly the best king cake in New Orleans," Phoebe says before taking a big bite of the original flavor.

Smooth and buttery with a bite of cinnamon—she almost moans over how delicious it is. She takes a bite of the coconut king cake. Holy shit, it's even better.

"As much as I hate to admit it," Phoebe says, "this is better than Randazzo's."

Phoebe expects Grace to be pleased to have been proven right, but her smile is strained.

"You said you had a soccer question?"

"Yeah," Phoebe says.

She takes another bite instead of asking it, though. God, this is good. But as she savors the cake, she realizes Grace is staring blankly at her. Of course Grace is more focused on soccer than on food.

"Who do you think is the weakest player on the national team?"

Grace blinks at her. "What?"

"If I'm going to make the World Cup roster, I have to prove I'm better than what Amanda already has," Phoebe says. "I wanna figure out whose spot would be the easiest to take."

Phoebe continues devouring her king cake while Grace considers the question. But the veteran doesn't actually give an answer.

Instead, she says, "I'm not going to denigrate my teammates to you, Matthews."

Phoebe rolls her eyes. "Stop being so dramatic. You don't need to denigrate them. Obviously none of them are *bad*—they're on the national team. I just want to know where you think the roster could be stronger."

Seriously, the king cake is *so* good. Why did she cut them such small pieces? Is it weird if she gets seconds? Grace pokes her fork at the slices on her own plate without taking a bite.

"Look, I'm probably gonna make sHeroes just because you're injured, but obviously you're gonna be back by the World Cup." Phoebe is trying to explain it so Grace is less disgruntled about saying mean things about her teammates, but the veteran's eyebrows furrow deeper. Phoebe continues: "I gotta figure out where the roster is weakest and demonstrate how I would make it stronger."

"You're a professional soccer player. Figure it out yourself."

Grace shovels a bite into her mouth like she's done speaking on the matter.

Okay, fair. Phoebe can figure it out herself. It isn't like she and Teddy haven't gone over rosters four hundred times before. She just wanted a little of Grace's expertise—but as she cuts herself a second slice of the coconut king cake, she remembers what Grace said the day they'd gotten tacos together. Being her friend isn't going to do Phoebe any favors when it comes to soccer.

Which is fine. She doesn't need Grace's help to make the roster anyway.

• • • •

Phoebe and Teddy text every day, but it's different from getting to see him in person. It's different even to see him on her computer screen, but it's better than nothing. Something in her relaxes at the sight of his smile. His hair points in every direction.

"Hello, hello, hello," Phoebe says.

"Hey." Teddy drags out the end of the word.

"Have you ever heard of brushing your hair?"

"Who says I didn't brush it this way?"

"You're saying you want it to look like you stuck your finger in an electrical socket?"

"Gotta catch the eye of the girls, the gays, and the theys somehow."

"Speaking of, Alice said you won't shut up about some girl in your stats class."

Teddy groans. The best part about having a sibling is annoying the fuck out of them. After they shoot the shit for a while—and Phoebe further teases her younger brother—she brings up the roster.

"So," Phoebe says, the rest of her sentence dangling to create some anticipation, "you know how sHeroes is in a couple of weeks?"

"Shut up!" Teddy yells before Phoebe even says anything else. "Shut up, shut up, shut up. You're on the roster?"

Phoebe couldn't stop the smile from taking over her face if she wanted to—but she really doesn't want to. "I don't know yet, officially, but I'm really hopeful—especially with Grace out."

"Bitch, you're going to the World Cup."

"Okay, no, that's what I want to talk to you about, though," Phoebe says. "I asked Grace this morning whose spot I should try to go for on the roster—like, obviously, I have to replace someone to make it, so as much as I'd love to be like, 'Oh, the team is a family, these girls are my sisters,' these girls are actually my competition. And Grace basically told me to figure it out myself, which, like, fair. So who do you think is the weakest—or not just the weakest, but the weakest in things I'm strong in—who do you think I can replace?"

Teddy cracks his neck and stretches both arms in front of his body, fingers interlaced and palms out. "Let's do this."

They spend the next hour and a half going over everyone on the January roster—Phoebe doesn't know who will make sHeroes, so it's the most recent dataset they have. (Teddy's the one who calls it that—a dataset—because he, the musical theater nerd, is somehow excelling in stats at college. Probably to impress that cute girl Alice says he won't shut up about.) They go through every player, every position, advantages and disadvantages and style and history. When do fresh legs outweigh veteran presence? Where is the team the weakest?

Phoebe sets her computer on her bed as they talk, angles it so Teddy can still see her. She has to shove clothes aside to clear an area on the floor—she would put them in her hamper, but it's full of clean clothes she hasn't folded yet—just a three-by-five rectangle she can dribble back and forth in. A ball at her feet helps her think.

It's an imprecise science, what Phoebe and Teddy are trying to do. Phoebe googles every roster she can find. There were seven midfielders at January camp. There could be more at the World Cup, could be less. You always take three goalies to the World Cup.

"You have played goalie before, though," Teddy says.

"Yeah, in *high school* for *one game.* The only way I'm playing goalie for the national team is in a Mia Hamm/Briana Scurry red card–type situation."

The forward had filled in when Scurry got a red card in the 1995 World Cup, which was well before Phoebe was born, but she knew her team history. The US lost in the semis that year, then won four years later. When Phoebe turned eight, her parents gave her a DVD with every game of the '99 tournament. She watched it until the DVD skipped from wear.

After all of their analysis, Phoebe is left with a couple of possibilities, then a variety of increasingly less likely options.

"You basically have to decide what you want to focus on," Teddy says. "Show off your attacking skills, be a brick wall on defense, or be a jack-of-all-trades."

"I can always be a jack-of-all-trades," Phoebe says. "You're the one who said I could play goalie."

"Bet," Teddy says, and Phoebe rolls her eyes. "So, offense or defense then?"

Given that choice, the answer's easy.

Twenty-Three

The bell above the door is the only sound in the diner when Grace arrives late Sunday morning. It must be a slow day.

Phoebe bustles out of the kitchen, her customer service smile morphing into a real one upon seeing Grace.

"I'm so glad you're here," she says. "I need your opinion on something."

She reminds Grace of her sister. Since getting on ADHD meds, some of Harmony's more impulsive tendencies have been quelled, but she still loves to start a conversation with no hello, no small talk, just diving right in. Honestly, Grace likes it better than small talk.

"Do you think D. B. Cooper is alive?" Phoebe asks.

Grace's brow crinkles. "D. B. who?"

"D. B. Cooper. The only successful air pirate."

"Doesn't count as successful if he didn't survive," Dallas calls from the kitchen.

"That's why we need another opinion. So I can prove you wrong," Phoebe yells back. To Grace, she explains. "Hijacked a plane in 1971. Leapt out with two hundred thousand dollars. Do you think he's alive?"

"I guess that depends," Grace says. "How old was he in 1971?"

"I don't know. Why? You think he was more likely to survive jumping out of the plane if he was a certain age?"

"Not necessarily. But just because he may have survived the jump doesn't mean he's alive today."

"I see your point. But the crux of the matter is you think he survived the jump?"

"I didn't say that. I need more information."

Phoebe sighs. "Okay, c'mon, where do you wanna sit?"

"Wherever's easiest."

Phoebe sits her at the counter on one of the spinning stools covered in turquoise leather that's probably fake. "Coffee?"

"Yes, please," Grace says.

Phoebe pours it silently.

"So give me more about D. B. Cooper." Grace hadn't expected to have to prod her to keep going.

"He's dead," Dallas says through the window into the kitchen.

"He is *not*," Phoebe avows. "But knowing Grace, she's gonna have to know *everything* before she makes a decision, so I gotta do some research first so I can present my best argument."

Grace can't deny it. Apparently, Phoebe does know her.

"Okay, but at least tell her your ridiculous trans theories," Dallas says.

Grace stirs creamer and one sugar into her coffee and raises her eyebrows at Phoebe, who sighs again.

"They're not ridiculous," she mutters, her brow furrowed.

"No, you're right," Dallas says. "Honestly, I kind of love them. Even if he definitely didn't survive the jump."

A smile teases at Phoebe's lips. Grace finds herself fascinated watching her interact with someone other than one of their teammates.

"I'm just saying there are *options*," Phoebe says. "He could've been a trans man, and that was one of his first times debuting in public, so of course there was no record of a man by the name of D. B. Cooper anywhere. Or, *she* could be a trans woman, and so afterward she lived as herself and no one ever thought she might've been the hijacker because she was a woman!"

Grace is pretty sure *ridiculous* is the right word for those theories, but they *are* fun. Those are good descriptors of Phoebe in general: ridiculous and fun. That's certainly what Grace thought of her when they first met—Matthews bursting into the weight room five minutes late with messy hair. Then she worked her ass off, beat Grace more often in drills than anyone else. It's not that Grace expects everyone to fit an archetype, but Phoebe is unlike anyone she's ever met.

"Anyway," Phoebe says. "I'm assuming you're finally gonna take my recommendation and have Dallas's stuffed hash browns?"

Grace nods. Dallas retreats to make the food, and Phoebe leans against the other side of the counter from Grace.

"Oh!" she says like she's had an epiphany. "I got distracted by D. B. Cooper, but I meant to tell you: Kelsey Cleary."

Grace almost spits out her coffee. "What?"

"That's whose spot I'm going to take."

Grace takes another sip. The coffee isn't that hot, but her throat still burns as she swallows. "Kelsey's a defender."

"A defender who Amanda pushes forward," Phoebe says. "If I establish myself as a defensive mid, I can take her spot."

Grace does not want to talk about Kelsey.

"Plus, I played right back my entire freshman year after our starter tore her ACL."

"There's a bit of a difference between NAIA college soccer and the World Cup."

"Uh, yeah, bitch, I know," Phoebe says, softening the curse with a laugh. "But I do have experience, and I'm more versatile than Cleary. I remember the disaster of an experiment with a three back where she was supposed to play DM. I can do it."

Grace believes her.

Grace tries not to have opinions about rosters or lineups. They aren't her decision. Whether she likes them or not, she has to play with them, has to succeed with them. If she cared about lineups, she'd have to be sad that Eric plays her as a box-to-box midfielder every game. She'd rather be a playmaker, but that's not her choice, so there's no use wasting time being disappointed. Last time she had something to say about a roster, New Orleans signed Kelsey, and that obviously didn't work out.

If Grace did let herself have an opinion, she'd love the idea of Phoebe taking Kelsey's spot. There are other players Grace trusts more on defense, and no other people she trusts less in general. She doesn't know Phoebe well enough to trust her fully—on the field or off—but it's hard not to. The girl is just . . . earnest. Obviously, she has an agenda; she wants to make the national team. But she's never hidden that. And when Grace refused to help her by telling her where the team was weakest, Phoebe went and figured it out herself. Of course Phoebe *would* use her and her knowledge to make the team if Grace let her, but she's never tried to do it duplicitously. That has to be worth something.

Like she's proving Grace's point, Phoebe says, "Anyway, you don't have to say anything. I know you don't want to *denigrate* your teammates or whatever absurd way you put it, but yeah. I'm gonna take Kelsey's spot."

"Good luck," Grace says, and means it.

A bell dings—Grace's breakfast is ready, Dallas setting the plate in the window. Phoebe transfers it eagerly to the counter in front of Grace.

"You're gonna fucking love this."

Grace does. Maybe Phoebe really is trustworthy.

• • • •

Grace is still getting used to having anyone in her home.

Phoebe does not seem to need to get used to anything.

Monday evening, after practice, wearing only boxers and a bralette, Phoebe yanks pillows off Grace's couch. "Where's the fuzzy blue one? I love that one." She spots it tucked under the coffee table. "Aha!"

Grace watches from the armchair as Phoebe punches the pillow a couple of times, then plops down on the couch. She doesn't even put the pillow behind herself—she hugs it to her chest.

"It's so soft," Phoebe says, to herself, maybe. Grace is never 100 percent sure when Phoebe expects a response and when she's just talking.

Grace supposes it's reasonable that Phoebe tends to be in a state of undress when she's over, given their typical activities. Today she texted after practice asking if she could try out Grace's rain showerhead. Then once she arrived, she convinced Grace to join her. It wasn't an exact replay of their first time in the locker room showers, but it was close.

"If I watch TikToks, is that gonna annoy you?" Phoebe asks. "I have the volume low but my old knockoff AirPods broke so I don't have any headphones."

She'd watched them in bed the first time she came over, and Grace had survived that.

"I'm good," Grace says.

She is. She can be comfortable with Phoebe in her house. Maybe not as comfortable as Phoebe is, sitting cross-legged on the couch and still clutching that fuzzy blue pillow, but comfortable nonetheless. She can work on a crossword and not be bothered by Phoebe's giggles when she likes one of the videos she's watching. She's not *bothered,* but she is a little distracted. Phoebe has a nice laugh, is all.

Grace's phone vibrates on the arm of her chair. She glances down, not planning to pick it up until she sees the notification. An email from her agent, subject line: FWD: Grace Henderson interview request. She angrily swipes at the notification. When she told her agent she was injured, she specifically said she would not be doing any media.

She forgives him slightly when the email begins: I know, I know, but it's Megan Thrace.

Grace doesn't know if other professional athletes have favorite reporters, but women's soccer doesn't have a huge pool of media. Over the years, she's learned who's fair, who manages to be condescending even when complimenting you, and who looks for *good* stories instead of just big stories. Megan Thrace knows the ins and outs of the whole league. And while she might be a Boston fan, she never lets that allegiance sway a story—sometimes to the dismay of other Rooks supporters.

Grace didn't want her agent to send her media requests because she always has a hard time saying no. It feels even worse with Megan, who she'd almost categorize as a friend by this point. But as much as she knows Megan wouldn't go too hard on her, the thought of talking to *any* reporter—or anyone at all, really—about her injury feels like she's being stabbed with tiny needles.

She compromises.

Tell Megan she can have an exclusive upon my return.

This helps Grace in more ways than one: she doesn't have to technically say no to Megan; and now that she's offered an *exclusive,* she has no choice but to say no to any other interview request when she's back on the field.

That she doesn't yet feel like she'll *ever* be back on the field is a problem she's not thinking about right now. Instead, she looks at the newspaper in her hand, trying to figure out a seven-letter word for *made of clay.*

"Oh my God," Phoebe says from the couch.

"What?"

Oh, obviously. It's *earthen.*

"Amanda is calling me."

Grace doesn't finish filling in the word. Her eyes cut to Phoebe, who is sitting bolt upright and staring at her phone as it buzzes.

"What are you doing?" Grace says. "Answer the phone."

Phoebe does.

Amanda is obviously calling to tell Phoebe she's made the sHeroes roster, but you wouldn't know that from Phoebe's side of the conversation. She seems like an entirely different person. Spine locked straight, easy smile nowhere to be seen. She only responds in *uh-huh*s and *yes, ma'am*s.

Of course Phoebe made the sHeroes roster. Amanda wasn't going to call Grace in, so a midfield spot was open. It doesn't mean Grace is getting replaced, even if she feels that way. It doesn't matter. Whatever they're saying on the phone to each other has nothing to do with Grace. She tries to refocus on her crossword, but she's forgotten what answer she was filling in.

"Yes, ma'am," Phoebe says, still not a trace of a smile on her face. "I can't wait."

They say their goodbyes, and Phoebe ends the call.

And immediately launches herself at Grace.

"I made the sHeroes roster!" she screeches.

Grace barely has time to open her arms before Phoebe is somehow folding herself into her lap, her own arms snaking around Grace's neck.

Grace awkwardly pats Phoebe's back with the hand still holding on to the newspaper.

"I made the roster and Amanda said she wanted me to get some playing time? Like, she wants a look at me, a real look, an in-game look, and she said the World Cup roster wasn't decided yet, and yeah, maybe she said that because she didn't want me to get my hopes up, like just because she wants an in-game look at me doesn't mean I'm gonna make it, but if she knew she didn't want me for the World Cup, why wouldn't she just say that? She totally could've said I'm going to this tournament because you're injured but you'll be well by the World Cup, but that's not what she said." Grace tries not to cringe. If Phoebe notices, she must think it's about the volume of her voice, because she's quieter as she finishes her rant. "That's not how she put it. She might actually be thinking of putting me on the World Cup roster!"

At what point is Phoebe going to realize the spot she should take is Grace's? Grace would think she already knows, but Phoebe seems to share every thought in her head, and never once has she so much as hinted that Grace won't make the roster.

Maybe Grace should encourage Phoebe to lean into that defensive midfield position she wants. At least then they wouldn't be competing for a spot. Grace's natural position, her favorite position, no matter where she plays on the Krewe, has always been as more of an attacking midfielder. Amanda knows that, even if Eric doesn't seem to.

The sHeroes roster is not the World Cup roster. There are still three months before that comes out. Grace needs to stop feeling sorry for herself. That's never gotten anyone anywhere. All she can do is sit around and wait. *Rest.* And try not to let her imagination convince her she'll never play again, try not to wonder if that would be better than the inevitable slow decline as she ages.

It doesn't help that the Krewe's first preseason game is Wednesday. Grace sits on the bench, doesn't even suit up. Kayla wears the captain's armband. Phoebe plays like she's been in the league for years. Which is good. Grace wants good things for her team. It's great to have such a talented new rookie.

It feels like there's a rock in Grace's stomach anyway.

Twenty-Four

Over the weekend, as Phoebe packs for camp, her heart races. There's less excitement to outweigh her nerves, less *Oh my God, I got called in* and more *I really gotta prove myself here.* Being on the same flight as Sorrell calms her pulse, at least a little. She knows people here, has made friends with some of them, even. Gabby didn't get called up this time, though, so while Phoebe isn't brand-new, she is the newest. And there's more pressure this time around. When she'd been called into January camp, she'd hoped but hadn't seriously believed that she had a chance at the World Cup roster. Now, there's a real possibility.

Phoebe knows what she has to do, and this is her last chance to do it. They have three games—in California, Texas, and then the final back in New Orleans. If she's going to make the World Cup roster, she has to earn playing time, has to prove her worth.

It's nice that Grace isn't there, even if Phoebe misses her. She can't waste time mooning over a teammate. She has work to do.

Phoebe's leg bounces in the van on the way to the hotel. Normally she'd just live out of her suitcase, but she unpacks to give her hands something to do other than shake. Being assigned Pants as a roommate is perfect because the other woman is quiet and focused. She goes to bed early, which means Phoebe does, too, or at least she gets into bed with the lights off to scroll her phone. Nine is too early for Phoebe to sleep, even if it is technically eleven in the time zone she woke up in. She turns her volume as low as possible and opens TikTok.

In the middle of a video where someone made their cat dance to Lizzo, Phoebe's phone vibrates in her hand.

Grace is texting.

> What time is training in the morning?

Phoebe smirks and texts back, why are you so obsessed with me? Then double texts, jk i think it's cute that you miss me already.

> When does the bus leave to take you to the stadium? 8:30?

9

> Ok.

why do you want to know?

> Just wondered if anything had changed from how they usually do things. Make sure you get to bed at a decent hour.

yes, mom, Phoebe sends back with an eye-rolling emoji.

She spends the next hour debating what she could send to keep up the conversation, but Grace doesn't text again. Eventually Phoebe turns on Do Not Disturb, puts on her eye mask, and tries to sleep. Pants has been snoring lightly since about two minutes after she clicked off the lights. Phoebe keeps her eyes fully closed and tries not to think about Grace or training tomorrow or the World Cup roster.

She imagines her first cap instead. A career appearance for the national team felt like a pipe dream for most of her life, but it's going to happen within the week. Amanda had said she wanted a look at

Phoebe. Thoughts of it, about how it will feel and how she'll play and how proud her family will be, usher Phoebe off to sleep.

• • • •

The next morning, Phoebe wakes to her phone buzzing.

That doesn't make sense. Her alarms are loud, some preprogrammed tune designed to be annoying enough that people don't hit snooze. Phoebe always *does* hit snooze, but that isn't the point. The point is her phone should have woken her up with an obnoxious jingle, not the double buzz that indicates a text message.

It's time to get up.

This is quite possibly the most Grace thing imaginable. A serious, no-nonsense message where she makes herself responsible for someone else's actions. It would be obnoxious if it weren't so ridiculously cute. Phoebe can imagine the way Grace's face would wrinkle in confusion if Phoebe actually called her cute for this, but that's what it is.

you're not the boss of me, Phoebe texts back, just to be sassy.

Tardy players don't make rosters.

Phoebe gets out of bed.

Pants must've already gone to breakfast, her bed empty. Phoebe, who always has trouble falling asleep, can somehow sleep through a train derailment once she's actually out. She goes to the bathroom, plays solitaire on her phone while she pees, and wonders if she can wear pajamas to breakfast. She slept in thin plaid boxers and a tank top. After the third game of solitaire, she finally gets up to wash her hands. Her nipples are visible in the mirror. Definitely not breakfast appropriate. But she'll be damned if she's putting on a bra this early in the morning. She tugs on a New Orleans hoodie instead.

The hotel room door is almost fully closed behind her when she catches it. She races back for the room key. As she leaves for a second time, her phone buzzes again.

Have you gone to breakfast yet?

This is why she likes to take care of Grace in bed. To normal people, their sexual dynamic probably seems unrelated to breakfast, and it is definitely too early for Phoebe to be thinking about this, but it's true. Grace takes care of everyone. She checks in with everyone, every practice. And she certainly doesn't have to do this for Phoebe. She does a lot for Phoebe she doesn't have to do—shows her around the city, buys her meals even when they haven't bet on them, tells her the wrong time for a workout so Phoebe won't be late.

It makes Phoebe want to take care of Grace, too.

The woman deserves to relax. And clearly she is never going to take it upon herself to do it. So even though it doesn't seem related to breakfast, Phoebe walks into the hotel dining room thinking about how she wants to tie Grace down and make her come over and over again.

• • • •

The sHeroes tournament is four teams, all playing one another one time. Whichever team ends with the best record wins the tournament. While US Soccer uses the tournament to raise money for women and girls in sports, winning the whole thing doesn't technically get you anything but bragging rights. It's about more than that—this is the strongest competition they'll have before the World Cup. It's a final tune-up of sorts. The next time the roster gets named, it'll be the team going to the World Cup.

Phoebe doesn't exactly keep her head down, because she's never done that in her life, but she tries to work even harder than she plays. Or—play harder than she plays—play soccer harder than she jokes around.

Grace keeps texting throughout camp. She texts Phoebe to wake up every morning, texts her to go to breakfast, texts her in the afternoons to make sure she doesn't get distracted during lunch and miss the bus back to the field. Phoebe never once says thank you. Acknowledging it feels too serious. Instead, she sasses and complains—always with a winking emoji—and whines about missing her first Mardi Gras in New Orleans.

Phoebe doesn't text Grace about Kelsey, but she watches the defender.

She doesn't want to be obvious about it, and she's already watched plenty of YouTube videos of her playing, but she wants to see her strengths. She wants to see where Kelsey fits at practice, how she interacts with the rest of the team.

Grace is the one to bring up Kelsey.

I thought the plan was to take Cleary's roster spot, she texts after the first game.

It is, Phoebe replies. She has her own seat on the bus, thankfully, so there's no chance of someone reading over her shoulder.

Well, the two of you sure seemed friendly.

Keep your enemies closer ☺

Not that they're really enemies. Rivals, maybe. They rode the bench together. Kelsey asked about Grace, actually, about her injury. Phoebe wasn't sure if she was fishing for information or simply asking after her—just because Phoebe has an agenda doesn't mean Kelsey does. Then Kelsey asked about whether Grace had paid up on the bet last camp, and Phoebe decided, agenda or not, she wasn't a big fan of the defender. It was kind of a shitty bet, even if Phoebe had been on board at the time. She's glad Grace didn't kiss her on the mouth back then, glad their actual first kiss was *real,* not for some bet.

• • • •

They fly to Texas the next day. Phoebe hangs out with a bunch of the veterans while they do recovery in the afternoon, then plays in the pool with Jess and Michi and Pants after dinner. It's a good day—even when there's no soccer, Phoebe feels like she fits in with these people.

She leaves the pool when Pants, normally reserved little Pants, starts challenging them all to breath-holding competitions. It turns out she gets a lot louder once you get her around the other two.

Phoebe takes her time showering, like she does any time she's not in her apartment's tiny stand-up stall. After, she swipes her hand through the fog on the bathroom mirror. Her cheeks are flushed from the heat of the shower, and she wrinkles her nose at her reflection. She's fucking cute. Back in middle school, there was a clique that tried to make her feel weird about having freckles, and she doesn't know why it never worked, but it didn't. She wipes at the condensation again and makes faces at herself in the mirror.

Her phone is on the bathroom counter. It only makes sense to take selfies when she looks this cute. Plus, Grace hasn't texted as much today, probably since it's an off day. Phoebe might as well start the convo with a tasteful nude.

No, not really—they haven't discussed if sexting is okay, so Phoebe isn't about to send an actual nude. Just something a little provocative. Maybe not *quite* safe for work, but nothing you could get fired for, either. She wraps the towel low across her chest—all suggestive swell where her freckles start to fade. She opts for the filthiest smirk she can muster—she's never been able to raise one eyebrow, and trying contorts her face all funny, but raising both gives a nice *You like what you see?* sort of look.

It takes six different shots before Phoebe finds one she likes. (She's hot, yeah, but that doesn't mean selfies are easy.) In the end, she chooses a shot of her reflection in the foggy mirror, curly wisps of hair framing her face. She doesn't caption it, because she's always been better with suggestion than words.

The cold air of the room prickles Phoebe's skin when she steps out of the bathroom. Since Pants is out, Phoebe doesn't bother getting dressed, just grabs the remote and flops onto the bed with the towel still wrapped around her.

She finds ESPN right as SportsCenter's top ten plays of the day starts. They never have enough soccer in this thing, and worse, this version doesn't have a single female athlete.

She rolls her eyes and flips to another channel. Her phone buzzes on the bed beside her. Oh right! The text!

Cold showers are better for your skin.

Phoebe cackles. Truly the greatest reaction to a sexy pic she's ever received.

Whatever would I do without your knowledge, oh wise one—no, that's not right. She backspaces the whole thing. Teasing doesn't always translate well over text. Before she can come up with the right way to respond, another message comes through.

> But it's a nice picture.

Phoebe giggles to herself. She holds her phone up for another selfie. The towel barely covers her ass as she angles the camera over her shoulder. She kicks her feet up and lets her smile be joyful instead of flirty. She includes a caption this time, too.

> Thanks, Hendy. What are you up to?

Before Grace responds, though, she's suddenly in front of her.

Grace is on TV, kicking a ball while a voiceover says something about a protein bar. She doesn't even really look like Grace—you probably *have* to wear makeup to be in a commercial, but it's jarring to see Grace's lashes painted, her lips darker than usual. She wears a hot-pink racerback tank Phoebe is 100 percent sure does not belong to her. The only normal thing about her is her hair, in two perfect french braids down her back. Phoebe wants to tug on them.

> What are you doing on my TV?

The Grace on her TV holds up the protein bar to the camera and smiles, and Phoebe can't help but laugh. Grace's polite, forced smile is fine—the vast majority of the people watching the commercial don't know her, and if you don't know her, the smile works fine. But Phoebe has seen Grace's real smile. It's rare and tends toward mischief and makes those brown eyes sparkle. To anyone who knows her, the Grace on TV looks like she would rather be literally anywhere else.

???

It's a commercial for a protein bar.
When did you even film this?

Oh, that. The day after Dawn
benched me for a month

Phoebe reads the message three times to make sure she understands it before responding.

You filmed a commercial *after* being
told you were injured and needed
to rest

It was already scheduled. I just
kicked a ball a few times. It wasn't
a big deal.

You're joking

No?

Did I say something funny?

Phoebe sets her phone on her chest and presses her fingers to her forehead like that will make her brain understand this better.

What else have you been doing when
you were supposed to be resting?

You come over almost every day. You
know I'm not doing anything.

Phoebe flushes red, though no one is around to see her discomfort.

You come over almost every day. Like she's annoying. Like she isn't welcome. She *always* asks first. If Grace doesn't want her there, she can say no.

This isn't about Phoebe, anyway. It's about Grace, and her stupid lying and even stupider decisions once she got caught.

Grace texts again before Phoebe can come up with the appropriate lecture.

> Honestly, Matthews, it wasn't that big of a deal.

Phoebe's thumbs fly over her screen.

> How are you possibly still trying to use that argument when you've been out for weeks? When you could be out more? You're missing a tournament because of this injury, and you're acting like filming that commercial when you were specifically told to rest is not a big deal?

> Well, it's not, is it? It doesn't matter if I miss games, because they have you now.

Right. Because a rookie who hasn't had one minute of playing time is the same as Grace fucking Henderson, who's been on the team a literal decade. Of course Phoebe could never replace Grace. She's not even trying to. But she hates the implication that Grace thinks that's the only reason she made the roster. Does she think that's why Phoebe got drafted too?

> You know what? I'm glad I told Dawn about your hip

Phoebe regrets the text as soon as she sends it. She's escalating this fight and she has a feeling Grace isn't going to back down. But Phoebe shouldn't have to, either. She's the one in the right, here.

> You what?

I didn't mean to, Phoebe types, because even if she isn't backing down, she does want Grace to know it was an accident. But yeah, I'm glad it slipped out, because it's clear you were never gonna tell her, no matter the incentive

> Oh yeah, Matthews, sorry to let you know that sleeping with you wasn't enough incentive

If Grace used emojis, there would be an eye-rolling one.

> It's so fucking stupid that you need to be forced into taking care of yourself, especially physically! You're a professional athlete for Christ's sake. How can you act like taking care of your body isn't important?

Phoebe has never understood why Grace kept her injury secret. It seems like everything she does is for her team, but this—playing injured, potentially injuring herself worse, not being at her best—that's all fine, apparently. Nobody likes to be hurt. Nobody likes to have to sit out. But ignoring an injury only ever makes it worse. If it were anyone else, Grace would understand that.

> Like I said, they have you now. On the Krewe and the national team. It'd be a lot less work to just cede my spot gracefully rather than try to

fight until the rest of my body falls
apart. It's not like I'll be missed

Phoebe is more upset about this than it warrants, maybe, but she wants to grab Grace by the shoulders and shake her. She hits her where she knows it will hurt instead.

You shouldn't be allowed to call
yourself a captain when you don't even
bother trying to keep yourself healthy

It's true. Grace always acts like she's ancient instead of simply admitting people get injured sometimes. It's like she's decided that and refuses to change her mind, no matter what Phoebe or Dawn or anyone else says.

When Grace still hasn't replied by the time Pants has not only returned, but showered, gotten ready for bed, and turned off the light, Phoebe wonders if maybe she went too far.

She texts one more time before turning her phone on Do Not Disturb.

I'm sorry. It just makes me mad that
you act like you being hurt doesn't
matter. You matter.

Twenty-Five

Phoebe wakes up to her alarm the next morning.

Her alarm, not a text. There are no notifications on her phone. Which is fine. She doesn't need Grace's texts to get to breakfast on time. In fact, it's patronizing that Grace felt the need to do that. Like Phoebe isn't an adult who can take care of herself. Grace is the one who can't take care of herself, obviously. Phoebe may not have meant to say anything to Dawn, but she's glad she did. She'd rather Grace be healthy than they be on speaking terms.

She's twenty minutes earlier than usual when she arrives for breakfast. She's even wearing a bra. The team has a conference room set up for a private buffet and personal omelet station, way better than the dry scrambled eggs the rest of the hotel has to deal with, except there's no waffle maker. Phoebe would like to slather a Belgian waffle in syrupy strawberries and whipped cream, but she's an *adult*.

They have a half day of training, then an afternoon of watching film to prepare for the game tomorrow. In between drills, Phoebe chews the inside of her lip raw.

She sits alone on the bus back to the hotel after training, her forehead pressed against the window. Grace probably wouldn't even sit next to her if she were here. God forbid anyone know they're friends.

Madeeha slips into the seat beside Phoebe, interrupting her self-pity. "You good, Matty?" she asks.

"Fine," Phoebe says.

"No jokes today?" She bumps her shoulder into Phoebe's. "Where's that new kid energy?"

Phoebe knows she should smile. On any other day she would, probably. On any other day, Madeeha wouldn't have noticed anything was wrong.

"Just focused."

Madeeha doesn't ask her anything else for the rest of the ride.

• • • •

Amanda wants to see her after lunch.

That's good, right? It's not like she's going to get cut halfway through a tournament. Unless, like Madeeha, Amanda noticed Phoebe's lack of personality today. How could Phoebe let this affect her so much? This is *her chance,* and she's wasting it worrying about her fuck buddy not talking to her? She's gotta get her head on right.

This hotel is wild. Phoebe is more used to motels, the type where the rooms open directly to outside, but this hotel has valet parking and an atrium with a restaurant inside it and so many rooms Phoebe might get lost if Yoni weren't leading her to the conference room where Amanda has set up an office.

Yoni knocks twice at a closed door, then opens it and gestures for Phoebe to enter. He closes it behind her, staying in the hallway. It's just her and Amanda then. The coach is standing at a conference table, looking down at papers spread across it. Her perfectly straight brown hair is half pulled back, like usual, her eyes sharp behind rectangular glasses. During games she dresses up, slacks and blazers—she cleans up incredibly well, if Phoebe's being honest. Phoebe's not on L Chat anymore, but there's probably boards devoted to Amanda and her outfits, too. Today, though, she's in jeans and a navy polo, four stars embroidered on the left side of the chest.

She looks up and smiles. "Matthews," she says. "Phoebe. Come in. Sit."

Amanda sits at the table and Phoebe sits across from her. The vibes feel good, but Phoebe is still a little afraid she's about to get cut.

Instead, Amanda says, "You're going to start tomorrow's game."

Phoebe blinks. Swallows. Asks, "Could you say that again?"

"I'm going to start you at defensive mid tomorrow."

"Yeah, uh. That's what I thought you said."

This was her plan. This is exactly what she had planned—play DM and earn herself a spot. She's been practicing—on her own, since Coach Givhan won't play her there—and doing research. This is exactly the chance she's been preparing for.

Amanda speaks slowly, like she knows Phoebe's brain isn't going full speed. "I know it's not where you played in college or where you've been training with the Krewe, so I understand there's going to be a learning curve."

"I can do it," Phoebe says.

Amanda nods. "I know you can. But France is a top-five team, Matthews. It's a lot for a first cap. There's a mental game, as well as a physical one, and I want you to be ready for it."

Phoebe bites at the raw patch on the inside of her lip. Even just practicing with New Orleans, the standard of play is obviously higher than what she's used to. The national team is another step up from that. This is a whole new level.

But she can do it.

Throughout her life, Phoebe has had a tendency to quit. She knows that. It just makes things a lot less frustrating. She tried to major in biology when she first started school but got a C minus in her first class. Switching to a sports medicine major made a lot more sense than struggling through four years when she already knew from high school that she wasn't really cut out for academia. Even in relationships—after the fifth breakup because Phoebe missed an anniversary or was late to meet a girl's parents or always made time for soccer but not for her girlfriend—Phoebe stopped trying. She wants a relationship at some point, sure, but she didn't need it in college.

She doesn't need it right now, while she's got the national team to focus on.

Because that's the thing: in soccer, Phoebe never quits. In soccer, Phoebe has always been willing to do the work. She can do this. She can play at this level. And this is her chance to prove it.

"Yes, ma'am," she says, and Amanda nods at her.

"Do you have any questions for me?"

Part of Phoebe wants to say no. *No questions, I've got it. I know exactly what I'm doing.* But she isn't about to miss this opportunity.

"What can I do to best increase my chances to make the roster for the World Cup?"

Amanda gives her a small smile. Placating might be a better word for it. "We'll go over the game plan tomorrow in the locker room as a team. But for now, you just focus on this game, don't worry about what might come down the line."

Easier said than done.

"That's what you're supposed to do, though, right?" Phoebe asks. "When your dreams come true, you have to dream bigger."

The coach's smile grows wider. "As long as you take the time to celebrate first. And anyway, if your goal was just to play, let's go a tiny bit bigger and say play well."

"Oh God, yeah," Phoebe says. "I'm not gonna fuck this up." She pauses. "Ma'am."

God, she has to stop swearing at this woman when she shares exciting news.

When Phoebe leaves the room, Yoni is nowhere to be seen. She's not even sure what direction to walk in, but she sees a sign for stairs and heads that way. She has way too much energy for the elevator.

She's gotta call Grace.

She has the full and complete thought before remembering. Grace doesn't want to hear from her. Or—Grace hadn't said that, exactly, but Phoebe's pretty sure. Because Grace wants the freedom to do whatever the hell she wants, damn the consequences for her and her body. It's such an immature outlook that Phoebe doesn't understand how Grace justifies it.

But whatever. Today is *not* going to be about Grace Henderson.

Phoebe opens the family group chat and tries to figure out how to tell them in a way that isn't just screaming. It takes two entire flights of stairs to draft the message.

Not surprisingly, Teddy tries to video call immediately. Phoebe hits the ignore button. He's *definitely* going to be screaming, and she hasn't made it back to her hotel room yet.

A text comes through.

> oh my GOD i can't believe you
> would tell me this then not pick up
> i'm going to kill you

Phoebe beams.

Her dreams are coming true.

As long as she ignores the pit in the bottom of her stomach.

• • • •

Phoebe has never gotten particularly nervous before games. Even now, in a US Women's National Team jersey with her name on the back, in the locker room of a sold-out stadium, forty-four thousand people in their seats or walking the concourse or still going through the ticket line, her stomach stays settled. Her energy is anticipatory, not anxious, one leg bouncing. She wants to play. Wants to get on the field and forget everything else.

Everything else primarily being Grace Henderson and the fact that she hasn't texted in a day and a half. Phoebe hadn't even expected to text with her very much during camp—Grace was the one who started that. She was the one who established it as something they did, who got Phoebe used to smirking at her phone, imagining the exasperation in Grace's voice. And then she disappeared.

Not that it matters. Phoebe is about to make her first career appearance for the US Women's National Team. That's what matters.

Still, she scrolls through her phone one last time. Thirty-seven new messages. People are coming out of the woodwork: folks she hasn't seen since high school graduation; Mr. Peters, who she used to dog sit for; her whole family—Mom and Dad and Alice and Teddy, yeah, but aunts and uncles and cousins on both sides, too; a couple of women who are in her contacts with their names plus whatever bar Phoebe met them at.

There is nothing new from Grace.

Phoebe tosses her phone into her locker and twirls her index finger in her ponytail, catching some strands and tugging. Kelsey did her hair tonight, a french braid into a pony. Fish gave her a look while it was happening, like maybe it was obvious how much Phoebe wished Grace was the one with her hands in her hair. The braid isn't half as good as Grace would've done, either, but it will keep Phoebe's hair out of her face.

She has to focus. This is her chance. She can't waste it being distracted by some girl. (A voice in the back of Phoebe's mind protests calling Grace just *some girl*.)

Phoebe fidgets throughout the pregame rituals—the pep talk from Amanda in the locker room, the walk to the field, standing with her hands behind her back for the anthem, since US Soccer will punish them if they kneel. It's the loudest stadium she's ever been in, the fans a blur of red, white, and blue. The starting eleven circle up before kickoff, and Fish gives a pep talk of her own.

And then it's time. Phoebe's first appearance for the national team. The ref blows their whistle to start the game, and everything else fades away. There's no Grace, no World Cup roster, no screaming crowd, no cameras. There's just this field, and these players, and that ball. Phoebe fucking loves soccer.

•   •   •   •

With Mapleton, Phoebe was the star. She was the best player on the field, and she loved it. She's always loved being the center of attention. It's a middle child thing—you either become okay with being overlooked, or you become so obnoxious you *can't* be overlooked. Phoebe always picked the latter.

With the national team, Phoebe is surrounded by stars. And defensive mid is neither a flashy position nor one she's used to.

It's better than she imagined.

When the final whistle blows, she's played a full ninety minutes, chased down a player on a breakaway, and assisted a goal. New position, higher level of play—none of it held her back. Beginner's luck, maybe, or maybe this is what she's meant to do.

It's the best first cap she could have asked for—except that Grace isn't here to share it with. Her absence exists again now that the game is over. What would Grace say if she were here? Would she compliment Phoebe? Begrudgingly, maybe. Calling her Phenom like it's offensive instead of affectionate.

The rest of the team congratulates her. Fish, the only one on the team who's taller than Phoebe, gets her in a headlock and rubs a noogie that messes up her hair. Sorrell hugs her hard enough to hurt a little.

Madeeha beams. "Good game, new kid."

Phoebe wishes Grace were here. She wishes her family were here. They're coming to her first game with the Krewe, but Phoebe wants them now. For some reason she wants her mom, like a little kid at their first sleepover.

• • • •

She does get her family, virtually at least. Her parents do a video call while the team is on the bus on the way to the airport, the two of them squeezed into the frame together, beaming. Phoebe's chest loosens at the sight of them. By the time they've passed the phone to Alice, and then on to Teddy, Phoebe isn't thinking about anything except how happy she is.

"Oh my God, am I talking to *the* Phoebe Matthews?! World-famous soccer star?" Teddy is so loud Phoebe turns down the volume on her phone.

"Oh my God, shut up, I am not."

"You're well on your way!"

"Hardly." One cap is not well on the way to being world-famous. Not that Phoebe cares about that. "Anyway, fame doesn't matter to me."

"Says the biggest attention whore I know."

Phoebe laughs and doesn't deny it.

"Also, can I say—Grace whomst?!"

Phoebe adjusts in her seat as a reason to move her camera off her face for a second. She swallows hard and considers pretending her phone died, which it's been doing at random lately.

"I don't have headphones on" is all she says.

"Right, right, you're probably, like, around everybody or whatever," Teddy says. "We won't talk about you taking their roster spot."

Phoebe doesn't want to talk about anything anymore. She should be happy—her first cap, her first start, her favorite person on her phone screen. She *was* happy, thirty seconds ago. But Grace's absence overshadows everything.

Teddy moons over her some more, but when it does nothing to improve Phoebe's mood, she pretends they've arrived at the airport and ends the call. It should be enough, to have played well. To celebrate with the people who love her most in the world. It's so fucking annoying that it's not enough.

An hour later, as they line up to board their flight, Fish hip checks her.

"Cheer up, buttercup," the captain says. "That face is much too sad for someone who got their first cap today."

Phoebe fakes a smile. She spent the last hour reading her text history with Grace.

The last sentence Grace texted sits like a rock in Phoebe's chest.

> It's not like I'll be missed

Grace meant it about the team, which was stupid in its own right, but now, less than forty-eight hours later, Phoebe is realizing all the other ways Grace is wrong. *Phoebe* misses her. She made training on time out of spite, but Grace's texts were always about more than tardiness. Phoebe likes talking to Grace as soon as she wakes up. She likes sending pics and Grace responding by talking about what's best for her skin. She likes playing with her; they haven't gotten a minute of actual game time together, but Phoebe likes doing drills with Grace and liked their one-on-one before their teammates arrived. She likes sleeping with Grace, and she wants to do it again, but she likes making Grace laugh even more.

Phoebe is used to quitting when things are hard. It's been almost four years since she last tried to be someone's girlfriend. She probably doesn't know how. Grace isn't even looking for a relationship, anyway. But for the first time in a long time, Phoebe wants to try.

Twenty-Six

Grace watches the game.

Of course she watches the game. She still isn't used to watching it on her TV instead of from the sidelines, but she has to watch. Of the team's last hundred games, Grace played in ninety-five of them, watched four of them from the sidelines, and watched one from her living room. Other players missed games during that time, either from playing overseas or family commitments or injuries, but not Grace. Not until now.

So, though she's furious at Matthews, she still watches the game.

Furious isn't the right word. Or perhaps it is, but the person she is furious at is herself. From the first moment she met Phoebe, she knew better than to trust her. But she let the other woman charm her. Of course Matthews told the trainer Grace is injured. She has nothing to lose and everything to gain. Grace can't believe she let her guard down so easily.

So she *is* furious, and embarrassed, and honestly a little hurt, which is even more embarrassing. She'd tried to box these feelings up and put them in a corner of her mind, but with Phoebe getting her first start, the box won't stay closed. The announcers talk about the World Cup roster almost as much as Phoebe does. They do a whole segment on Grace and her injury, which mostly boils down to "we don't know when she'll be back." Grace doesn't, either. Dawn hasn't even scheduled her follow-up yet, even though the three weeks were technically up on Friday.

The announcers talk about Matthews, too, and the cameras seem to follow her every move. Even when it's a wider shot, Grace immediately finds that red hair. It's a simple french braid to a ponytail today. With Grace out, they don't have anyone in the locker room who can do more complicated braid styles.

Matthews looks at ease, not like a rookie in her first cap. Grace swears she's smiling every time the camera is on her, even midgame. She smiles taking throw-ins, grins after tackling the ball away from a forward who had gotten past everyone else. She's positively beaming when Kelsey scores a goal, then wraps Phoebe in what the team refers to as a koala hug to celebrate.

Those two certainly seem friendly. First laughing on the bench last game, now this. Grace doesn't know which is worse—if Phoebe isn't going for Kelsey's spot, it means she's been lying to Grace; if she is, it proves just how adept she is at manipulation. If she can convince Kelsey they're friends, what can she convince Grace of?

• • • •

Grace hates postgame press conferences. She always does them— because she's expected to, whether as captain of the Krewe or a star of the national team. By now, they're routine; she knows what to say and when, has some go-to phrases she can rely on. But she would always rather be anywhere else. Sometimes having an unimpressive game doesn't feel so bad if it means the media would rather talk to someone who played better.

Of course, after her first cap, Phoebe does the press conference.

Of course, she looks perfectly at ease, happy to be the center of attention, as usual.

Her hair looks freshly washed, slicked back into a tight ponytail. She wears a navy T-shirt with the typical US Soccer crest with four stars above it on the upper left side of her chest, but somehow she makes it look stylish instead of boring. Maybe it's the way she cuffs the sleeves. Grace doesn't want to think she looks good. She doesn't want to think about Matthews at all.

But then Phoebe grins on the television screen, and Grace bites the inside of her cheek to keep from smiling. It isn't fair for someone untrustworthy to be so disarming.

· · · ·

Grace tries to go to bed early. She does her entire routine: checks that her front and back door are locked, changes into pajamas, then comes floss, toothpaste, mouthwash, face wash, toner, under-eye cream, moisturizer. Her blackout curtains are pulled, her white noise machine set to ocean waves. She changed her sheets a day ago, but when she lies in her bed, they feel full of crumbs. She kicks her legs. The thread count is too high for the sheets to scratch her, but they seem to. She rolls onto her stomach, but the pillowcase against her face is scratchy, too. She rolls back over. Turns up the noise machine.

The day has been exhausting. Before she got into bed, her limbs were heavy, like she was tired to the bone even though she hadn't exercised in three weeks. Now everything is tense, jerky.

This happens sometimes. Not always at night, but usually. It's never worth trying to suffer through; she knows from experience she can't force herself to sleep. So even though she's completed her nighttime routine, Grace gets up and changes into the softest clothes she owns, thin joggers and a tagless T-shirt.

It's the darker side of dusk, streetlights glowing at fixed intervals. Grace follows their path toward the park one block over. It's shrouded in more darkness—inviting to Grace, rather than foreboding. Technically the park is closed, but there are no gates. She lets herself be enveloped. Far enough in, the vegetation blocks out almost all light. There's a bench Grace likes to go to when she feels like this. It is nothingness, but not. She doesn't need silence, just quiet. Maybe if she'd taken high school biology, she'd know what animals make the sounds that surround her.

This is as close as Grace has ever been to camping. Maybe she should try it. She could try anything now, has no reason to be in the city, no obligation to make her set an alarm in the morning.

Sometime this week Dawn could tell her she's cleared for exercise, but it's easier to imagine not being allowed back. It's easier to imagine this is never going to get better. She is going to be like this forever. One little muscle that twinged, and her life as she knew it was gone. One muscle twinge, and she's been replaced by Phoebe Matthews.

Grace shakes out her limbs.

She comes to the park to clear her mind. This place is supposed to calm her. Thoughts of her leg make her anything but, and thoughts of Matthews are even worse. So instead, Grace is simply not going to think. She breathes in, smelling an azalea bush she knows is only a few feet behind the bench, even if she can't see it at night, and listens to the wind rustle through leaves. The bare skin of her forearms prickles in the breeze. She doesn't think about working out after sunset.

She sits motionless long enough that her butt hurts, but the rest of her is finally like the night around her—dark and calm, peaceful, even. Finally, she starts toward home.

The city lights creep in as Grace leaves the park and has to remember the world around her. The moment she's back on the sidewalk, she's not alone. Half a block down, there's a woman lugging a suitcase. Her ponytail is long and her legs are longer. Though she's too far away to see freckles and the yellowish glow of the streetlights distorts the color of her hair, Grace would recognize her anywhere.

The last however many minutes Grace spent quieting her brain were apparently wasted. One look at Phoebe Matthews, and her heart is pounding inside her chest. Her shirt itches like there's a tag on it.

"Matthews," Grace says, enforcing distance with the surname. "What are you doing on the street with a suitcase at"—she checks her phone—"ten o'clock at night?"

Phoebe stomps up the block, dragging her suitcase behind her.

"I couldn't remember what street you lived on!" she yells, like this is Grace's fault.

It isn't. And Matthews hasn't even answered the question.

"Okay?" Grace says.

Phoebe comes to a stop finally, close enough Grace could touch her if she wanted to. Which she doesn't.

"You can't just stop texting me and think that's it. We're talking about this."

"You still haven't answered my question," Grace says. "Why are you here?"

"Because I like you!" Phoebe shouts it, then groans. "I came from the airport because I wanted to talk to you, since you decided to stop texting, which is just—ugh! I was trying to get a Lyft but my phone died—remember I told you weeks ago how it was doing that—before we ever—before the rest of the team arrived. So my phone died and I had to take a regular cab, and I don't know your address, I only have it in my phone, which, again, was dead, but I remembered the name of the park, and I was pretty sure I could find your house from there, but it's all different in the dark and so I haven't yet, okay? So that's why I'm here. That's what I'm doing in the street with a suitcase at ten o'clock at night. I'm trying to find your damn house so we can talk."

It isn't cute that Phoebe came to Grace's neighborhood even though she couldn't remember where she lived. Some people might have liked it, but Grace doesn't. It's everything Matthews always is: ridiculous and over-the-top and, yeah, maybe a little obsessive. Grace has half a mind to march back into the dark of the park and leave Phoebe lost on the sidewalk. She scratches at the back of her neck.

"Did you ever think maybe I stopped texting because I don't want to talk to you?"

"Yeah, Grace! Obviously I know you don't want to talk to me! I'm not an idiot!" Phoebe takes a deep breath and lowers her voice. "But you don't get to decide that. You can't just *stop talking to me* because I told Dawn about your hip. It was an *accident,* but even if it wasn't, you don't get to stop talking to me for it. Because someone needed to tell her. Someone needed to care about you, since you care about soccer more than anything."

Grace gapes at her. That is so off base. Grace *wishes* she cared about soccer more than anything. She *misses* caring about soccer more than anything. Back when she was a kid and played because she loved it.

Phoebe's still in that mindset, has gotten to be in it a lot longer than Grace ever did. Phoebe doesn't have to deal with captain duties and sponsorships and strangers thinking they know everything about her. Grace hasn't been able to care more about soccer than anything else since she was eleven years old. Matthews doesn't know what she's talking about.

Grace doesn't even bother saying anything before walking off. Phoebe follows her, because of course she does. Grace probably shouldn't lead Phoebe to her house, but if she went back to the park, Matthews would still just follow her, and she doesn't want her sanctuary ruined. Thinking about the girl every time Grace sits on the bench in front of her locker is bad enough.

At least Phoebe has already been in her house.

They're barely a block from Grace's, and on the way, she relives the goal celebration all over again. The way Kelsey leapt at Phoebe. How she wrapped her legs around Phoebe's waist. The way Phoebe threw her head back and laughed. Grace can feel her face flush the same way it did when she watched it live. Missing out on a camp and the tournament was bad enough. Knowing Kelsey took advantage of her absence to get close to Phoebe makes it worse.

Or maybe it's better, actually. Grace would rather know Phoebe is friends with Kelsey earlier rather than later.

As much as Grace doesn't want Matthews to come inside, she wants to have this conversation on the sidewalk even less. So she jerks her head, as much invitation as she can muster, and stomps up her porch steps.

Lilly doesn't greet them at the door. He's probably still in Grace's bed—*he* didn't have any trouble sleeping.

"I still don't know why you're here," Grace says, stopping with only enough room to close the door rather than moving into the living room.

Phoebe drops her suitcase onto Grace's floor like she's staying for a while. "You can't just stop texting me. We're talking about this."

"There's nothing to talk about."

Grace crosses her arms, and Phoebe shakes her head.

"I'm so mad at you!"

Grace huffs, half scoff, half laugh. "*You're* mad at *me*? When you're the one who's been gossiping about me to get a spot on the roster?"

"I have *not,*" Phoebe says. "I told someone who needed to know, and I didn't even mean to tell them in the first place. It was an accident. I haven't said anything to anyone else, even when Kelsey was clearly fishing for info on your injury."

"Oh, what a surprise." Venom drips from Grace's words. "You and Kelsey are buddies, huh?"

"What? No. I literally just said I didn't—"

"You sure seemed close on the pitch."

Grace narrows her eyes at Phoebe, who's looking back at her like she has no idea what Grace is talking about.

"Do you mean when we celebrated her goal?" Phoebe asks. "Because I celebrated with Kayla when she scored, too."

"Whatever." Grace stalks to the kitchen. "The company you keep says a lot about you."

Matthews follows like a lost duckling.

"I swear we're not even close. Is this about how she didn't kneel for the anthem when they still let us do that? Because I know. That was at best ignorant and at worst—"

"Jesus. No. It's not about the anthem. It's about how she used me to—"

Grace cuts herself off. She's never told anyone what Kelsey did. The anthem stuff went down soon thereafter, and that had been enough to keep anyone Grace cared about from getting too friendly with her ex. She isn't sure Kelsey even counts as an ex, but it's easier to think of her that way than just as some woman who led Grace on until she got what she wanted.

"Used you to what?" Phoebe asks.

"It doesn't matter."

"It does to me."

Phoebe's voice is so fierce Grace turns to look at her. Her eyebrows are slashes, her mouth a snarl. Grace has seen Phoebe playful and laughing. She's seen her serious and focused. She's never seen her angry before.

The absolute gall. Matthews doesn't get to be *mad* that someone had used Grace when that's exactly what she's doing.

"Don't pretend like you give a damn," Grace snaps. "She used me to get to New Orleans just like you used me to get on the national team."

"What? Grace, that's not—"

"It's exactly what's happening. You 'accidentally' telling Dawn about my leg is just like Kelsey deciding 'it's not you, it's me' right after I got her drafted by the Krewe."

"You got her drafted by the Krewe?"

God, does this girl ever listen?

"*Yes.* I was playing in the W-League in Australia and she was still in college, but we met at her first camp, and we kissed, and then we started texting. And yeah, maybe we never said anything official but it was—it was something." It *was,* even if Kelsey now acts like they don't have history. The kisses counted, and the texts counted more. Grace rubs the pads of her index fingers against the pads of her thumbs. "And she talked about how great it would be to play with each other in the AWSA and I talked to Eric and, yeah, they drafted her. Then she broke up with me or whatever."

Phoebe's brows are still furrowed in anger.

"No," Grace says. "You don't get to act like you're mad about that. Not when you're the same. Not when I should've known you were the same from the beginning. I *did* know, I just—I shouldn't have cared that you're hot or good in bed. Shouldn't have let it distract me."

Phoebe's mouth falls open. Her face shifts, but Grace looks away. She's not gonna try to figure out whatever Phoebe's facial journey means. She doesn't care.

"So, whatever," she says. "There. Now you know what she did, since supposedly it mattered so much to you. Now can you get out?"

"Grace," Phoebe says, and her voice is so gentle.

Grace doesn't want gentle. She doesn't even want to fight anymore. She wants to be left alone.

"I'm not using you to get on the national team."

Grace doesn't care what Matthews says. She gets herself a glass to fill with water.

"I would never do that. I want to make the roster, yeah, but I want to *earn* my spot. It doesn't mean anything to cheat your way onto it."

It's a nice sentiment, but Grace knows better than to trust Matthews.

"But also, I would never do that *to you*. You deserve so much better than that, Grace. It's really awful that she did that to you." Phoebe Matthews, who usually talks a mile a minute, who usually cuts herself off in the middle of sentences because she thinks of something else she wants to say, whose brain always seems to work faster than her mouth. Phoebe Matthews is calmly and clearly stating things like they're facts. "What Kelsey did was wrong, and shitty. Honestly, I wish you had told me sooner because I would have been a lot meaner to her. But she's the one whose spot I wanted to take before I knew this, and I do even more now. No one should treat you that way. No wonder you were so wary of me trying to be friends with you."

Grace is still standing in front of the sink, holding her empty glass. Phoebe takes the cup out of her hand and holds it under the already-running water. She turns the water off, holds the glass out to Grace.

When Grace reaches to take it, Phoebe doesn't let go until Grace makes eye contact.

"If I had wanted to get you off the team to make room for me," Phoebe says, "I would've told someone much closer to the World Cup."

Grace can't argue with that logic.

Phoebe turns away from Grace then, paces to the other side of her kitchen island. She tugs on the end of her own ponytail. Grace takes a sip of the water.

"I learned in college that I wasn't a good girlfriend," Phoebe says. Grace has no idea what that has to do with anything. "Might've learned earlier but there weren't exactly a ton of out queer girls at my high school." She tilts her head back and forth, drums her knuckles against the counter. "Then again, there weren't a lot at my college either, but— anyway, I'm not good at being a girlfriend. I forget anniversaries and prioritize soccer and flirt with other women, even when I don't mean to. Sometimes I've slept with other women, because I didn't know I wasn't supposed to. I've done a lot of crappy things to girls I was, you know, not necessarily officially *with* but not *not with,* either."

Finally, Grace gets why Phoebe is talking about this. She might be a bad girlfriend, apparently, but she wouldn't be as bad as Kelsey.

"I would *never* do that to you," Phoebe says. "I would never do anything like that. To you or anyone. No one should be used like that. That says nothing about you and everything about her."

Grace knows that, of course. But just because it says more about Kelsey than about her doesn't mean it doesn't affect her. It doesn't mean Grace is wrong to be more careful, trust people less.

"I'm not friends with Kelsey, I promise," Phoebe says. She looks down, shifts on her feet. "And in terms of officially saying something, I like you and I want you to know that I'm not sleeping with anyone else."

Another statement that has nothing to do with anything they're talking about. It isn't like Kelsey slept with someone behind her back. The betrayal was about emotional vulnerability more than any sexual intimacy. Then again, Grace probably wouldn't have sent those pictures if she'd known what Kelsey really wanted. But regardless, Phoebe can sleep with whomever she wants. She and Grace aren't dating. Grace has no idea when Phoebe would have the time to juggle sexual partners, anyway.

She mentioned dental dams the first time they slept together. Maybe that's what she means here. And honesty and communication were obviously not pillars of whatever had happened between Grace and Kelsey. So it makes sense that Phoebe wants Grace to know.

The redhead keeps talking. "Honestly I'm not even really flirting with other women. Like, I don't even want to, except to make you jealous, because, like, that's fun, honestly. Okay, I started and ended that with *honestly,* but I guess I'm just trying to be clear that I'm different from Kelsey."

"Right," Grace says.

She wants to believe her. She does believe her, at least a little. This whole thing does actually make her trust Phoebe a little more—not completely, of course, but Phoebe's right: if she really wanted to sabotage

Grace, she could've waited until right before the World Cup to reveal her injury. The facts of the situation demonstrate that she is different from Kelsey.

"And you?" Phoebe asks, tracing shapes on the countertop with her finger and only looking at Grace out of the corner of her eye. "Do you wanna sleep with anyone else? Or flirt with them or whatever?"

"No." Grace doesn't have to think about it.

She's never been much of a flirter to begin with. Even with Phoebe, Grace hadn't meant to flirt so much as to one-up her—that was why Grace turned the bet on its head. When she'd suggested Phoebe arrive early at practice to get her hair braided, it wasn't about flirting, really, it was about getting Matthews to practice. Not that she doesn't want to flirt now—she isn't quite sure how, but she likes making Phoebe laugh, or blush, or both. It makes her chest feel warm.

Like now, it's almost like she took a shot of bourbon, heat sliding all the way down to her belly at the way Phoebe is beaming at her.

"Really?"

Grace nods.

"What about the whole 'I'm not looking for a relationship' thing?"

Grace isn't, but she doesn't need to harp on the fact. She shrugs. "What about it?"

Phoebe giggles. "So, we're really, like—"

She covers her face with her hands for a moment. Grace doesn't understand why she's turned so red, but it's cute.

"Sorry, I just—I don't know, I guess I kinda figured out how much I care about you and when you stopped texting, I was afraid I had fucked everything up." She tugs on the end of her ponytail. "I'm really glad I didn't."

"I'm glad you came over," Grace says.

She wasn't at the beginning, but she is now. Their misunderstanding was more easily corrected. Plus, she isn't sure she would've ever gotten to sleep without clearing the air. Now, though, she loses the battle to a yawn. She could definitely sleep.

Phoebe takes a step closer, slides her hands around Grace's waist. "Are you too tired for makeup sex, or . . . ?"

Grace could sleep a little later.

Phoebe kisses her deep and slow and all of the anger, resentment, embarrassment, all of the *everything* seems to leach out of Grace's body. Grace is always in her head, thinking too much, about the past and the future and any number of little anxieties, but Phoebe kisses her and she is suddenly *present*.

Phoebe's hands slide to the backs of Grace's thighs and—oh. She picks her up. She picks Grace fully up off the ground. Grace wraps her legs around Phoebe's waist—instinctively, maybe, but somehow also desperately. She rolls her hips and Phoebe's fingers tighten.

"You're so fucking sexy," Phoebe murmurs like it's an observation. A fact. Like she's not even trying to get Grace worked up by saying it, but she gets Grace worked up anyway.

Grace has always been short but has never felt particularly small. She's thicker than most soccer players, especially midfielders. It made her insecure when she was a teenager, but she likes it now. She's harder to take down, can stand her ground and win a ball in the air. She can fuck another player up if she needs to, but she can usually beat them in some other way.

In Phoebe's arms, Grace feels small. She feels little and soft and delicate. Phoebe holds her like she weighs nothing. She keeps her mouth on Grace's neck while she walks them down the hall to the bedroom. Grace squirms in her grip, but Phoebe doesn't falter one step. She carries Grace to the bed, and Grace is so, *so* ready. She wants Phoebe to toss her on the mattress, to yank her to the end of it and strip her.

Instead, Phoebe slowly bends to set Grace on the bed. Carefully. Gently. Like she's precious. Phoebe looks down at her. Grace is still in her joggers and T-shirt, but Phoebe is looking at her like she's sexy. Like she's perfect.

Sex has always felt like a big deal to Grace. Maybe it's because she's never been friends with benefits with anyone before, but sex always felt heavy. Like it was *important*. Formal, almost. She's never been with anyone like Phoebe, who lets sex be whatever it is in the moment. In most of her life, Grace follows rules—not only rules like *don't disobey authority* but rules for interactions, for conversations. So much of the world seems like it has to happen a certain way. Then there's Phoebe, who throws all that out the window.

While sex with Phoebe can feel heavy, it can also be silly, or lazy, or rushed. Tonight, it's different from any other time they've slept together. Softer. It's still just sex, of course. That's what they had agreed on. So, it's not like there are feelings, not like that. They're just becoming better friends, that's it. Because Grace can't be catching feelings for her friend with benefits. Absolutely not.

Even while it's different, a lot is the same. Phoebe is still so sexy Grace is reduced to a thing that wants. Phoebe is still the one in charge; Grace gives over that control more easily by this point. She knows Phoebe will make her feel good. She *trusts* it. Maybe that is the difference—that there is more trust between them now. Phoebe has convinced her, has given her rationale, *facts*. Grace can't even find it within herself to regret sharing the story of Kelsey. Sharing it has quelled her anxiety. If sharing it means the sex gets even better, what's the harm in Phoebe knowing a little more about her?

That's a thought so out of character for herself, Grace does a double take inside her own head. Before she can worry too much about it, she's distracted by Phoebe lifting her cat from the tangled comforter.

"Lilly, baby, I'm sorry," Phoebe murmurs. "But I wanna wear your mama out, and you're gonna get in the way."

Grace snorts. Phoebe carries Lilly out of the bedroom and closes the door to keep him out. Then she flings herself back on top of Grace, who lets out an *oomph*.

"Now back to our regularly scheduled programming," Phoebe says, then kisses her.

They know each other's bodies by now, know what each other likes. Grace has elbowed Phoebe's hands out from under her enough times that the redhead knows it doesn't matter that she has more than enough strength to hold herself up, Grace wants to feel her weight. Grace takes a deep breath, hampered by Phoebe's body, and loves it.

Phoebe knows exactly how to push Grace's buttons. And Grace knows enough to let her. Because even when Phoebe is teasing, even when she pulls away right before Grace comes, the orgasm just ends up better. So Grace matches the soft way Phoebe is kissing her. She doesn't speed up or get greedy. Even though Phoebe seems to be spending an inordinate amount of time on the kissing. She keeps smiling, too; Grace can feel it when their mouths connect, the way Phoebe's lips are always turned up.

"Why are you smiling so much?"

Phoebe pulls away to look down at her. She's still smiling—those dimples digging into her cheeks. "Is it so shocking that I'm happy?"

When Grace thinks about it—is that what this is? There is a weight off her shoulders, having told someone about Kelsey and been affirmed. Does that count as happiness?

She offers a small smile up to Phoebe, who beams in response, then reaches up to pull the scrunchie out of her hair. Thick red waves cascade down, a veil between the two of them and the rest of the world. The smell of nectarines fills Grace's nose, and she inhales deeply. Her teeth dig into her bottom lip. Happiness has always seemed like an abstract concept to her. If this is it, it's a lot easier than she thought.

Phoebe leans down and captures the lip Grace had been chewing. She bites it harder, and Grace can't help the whimper she lets out. That's all it takes for Phoebe to finally move beyond kissing. She pulls Grace's shirt over her head.

Grace misses the weight of Phoebe, even if she would never stop her from moving that wicked mouth down her body. There's some kind of joke in her head about how Phoebe's tongue is so good because of how much she works it out by talking, but it's not fully formed, and then that tongue traces the line of Grace's hip bone, and Grace stops thinking about jokes.

Twenty-Seven

When Phoebe wakes up the next morning, she buries her smile in Grace's sheets. It's her too-big, too-excited smile; she can tell from the way it stretches her cheeks. She can't help it.

Grace Henderson is her *girlfriend*.

She played in her first game for the US Women's National Team and Grace Henderson is her girlfriend. Neither thing seems real. Her literal dreams are coming true. Who gets to date someone whose poster they tacked to their bedroom wall as a teenager? God, she has to find a way to take that down before Grace comes to visit.

She's getting ahead of herself. It's not like Grace is boarding the next plane to meet Phoebe's parents—it's been less than ten hours since they agreed to be exclusive. Phoebe doesn't know what she expected when she told Grace she isn't seeing and does not want to see anyone else, but it certainly wasn't the casual way Grace confirmed the same was true for her.

She just wanted to be honest with Grace, especially after what Kelsey had done. She wanted to be open and honest and communicate so they were on the same page.

She didn't expect the easygoing way Grace agreed.

Last night, Phoebe wanted to ask so many questions. Rather than talk too much, like usual, she limited herself to the most important ones—*Really?* and *What about not wanting a relationship?*

"What about it?" Grace said, all cavalier.

Phoebe has always been better with actions than words anyway. She poured herself into Grace last night. *Worshipped her* sounds a little too intense and Jesus-y, but Phoebe kind of worshipped her. Grace has been hurt, badly. But she likes Phoebe enough to try. Trusts her enough. Phoebe doesn't wanna fuck this up. She tried to say all that last night, with her mouth and her fingers and some words, too, yeah. She wants to say it again this morning, but Grace isn't beside her in bed.

Of course Grace gets up before Phoebe does. That's, like, the least surprising thing in the world. Lilly, on the other hand, is still sleeping beside her, stretched out on his back in the mess of the comforter. Phoebe moves him, ever so gently, to detangle the top sheet so she can wrap it around herself. She's not about to walk stark naked into Grace's living room the morning after she spent the night for the first time.

Grace is in the kitchen, fully dressed, making scrambled eggs.

"Oh my God, cooking me breakfast?" Phoebe says. "What a romantic."

Grace swallows so hard Phoebe can see it. "Well . . . I was hungry."

God, she's cute and awkward and Phoebe wants to kiss her. She would, too, except she hasn't brushed her teeth. So she leaves Grace to the stove and finds her suitcase where she left it last night, just inside the door. It feels so long ago that she met Grace on the sidewalk, frustrated and nervous but certain of her feelings. This is what she wanted to happen, but it boggles her mind that it actually did. She's dating Grace Henderson, exclusively. Grace Henderson is her girlfriend. Grace Henderson is making her scrambled eggs while she gets dressed in Grace Henderson's bedroom.

It's possible Phoebe needs to get it together.

She tries. Brushes her teeth then drops a kiss on Grace's mouth when she returns to the kitchen, *good morning* and *thanks for breakfast* both.

"Gotta eat quick," Phoebe says as she sits down in front of scrambled eggs and a piece of buttered toast on a blue plate. "I got a half shift this morning."

"You scheduled work the day after your first cap?"

"Well, I didn't know it'd be my first cap, did I?" She shovels a bite of eggs into her mouth, barely remembers she should chew and swallow before continuing. "But yeah, when we got the schedule and I saw we wouldn't have to go in until the afternoon today, I let my manager know I was available. Gotta make extra money where I can, you know?"

Phoebe is used to playing off her lack of money, but obviously Grace *doesn't* know, actually.

"Let me drive you," Grace says it forcefully, like she expects Phoebe to say no.

"Okay." Phoebe beams. "Thanks."

Her girlfriend wants to drive her to work. Her girlfriend made her breakfast. Grace Henderson is her girlfriend. Phoebe has definitely not gotten it together.

Grace is quiet, and at first Phoebe assumes it's just because she's processing everything. A lot has changed in the past twelve hours. But after Grace is silent the whole ride to the diner, Phoebe's leg is bouncing with nerves. She can't leave without checking in. She needs to make sure they're good, that Grace isn't regretting anything she told her or agreed to last night.

"Last night was . . ." How should she describe it? A lot? The best? Surreal enough that she's still not sure she can believe it this morning? Can she really be dating Grace Henderson?

"Nice," Grace finishes for her.

One bark of a laugh bursts out before Phoebe is able to swallow the rest. "Yeah. It was. Nice. I just wanted to see, like, how you're feeling about it, today."

"Good," Grace says like she doesn't have to think about it at all.

"Yeah?"

Grace takes a moment, then nods. "None of this is typical for me, but I'm good."

"Good," Phoebe echoes. "Awesome. Yeah. Me too."

So what if she's screaming inside of her head? She can keep her cool. Grace is good. Grace is her girlfriend, Grace shares vulnerable stuff with her, Grace lets her sleep over, and Grace is good. Phoebe is fucking great.

There's no one on the street, and anyone in the diner probably can't see them in the car, so Phoebe reaches across the center console and pulls Grace closer by the shirt. She kisses her girlfriend goodbye, then is off to work.

• • • •

Just because they're back in New Orleans doesn't mean Phoebe's life goes back to normal. (In more ways than just the whole Grace-Henderson-is-her-girlfriend thing.) She's busy as hell, which isn't unusual, but she doesn't mind. Sure, her life can be exhausting and overwhelming and she definitely doesn't get enough sleep, but she doesn't trust her brain when it gets time to think about things. It always picks the worst-case scenario, looking at situations in the worst light possible. Given enough downtime, Phoebe's brain can convince her that none of her friends like her, that she only learned to be charming and funny to make up for how annoying she is, and it doesn't even things out—she isn't charming or funny enough to outweigh how annoying she is. Her brain tells her that her worst traits are her most innate. On especially bad days, it can convince her that she's bad at soccer. In reality, she learned to be funny because it was better to joke about barely passing ninth grade than cry over the straight Cs on her report card reminding her how she was the stupidest of her friends. Though that doesn't really feel much better than what she thinks while spiraling.

Her spirals never make sense once she's out of them. Of course her friends like her. And she's fucking hilarious, thank you very much, no matter why she learned to be the class clown.

Anyway, she's fine being busy. After her half shift, she has recovery, then watching film with the team. It's wild, seeing herself in a jersey for the national team, *Matthews* and the number 17 across her back. Then she notices her messy ponytail, and God, she can't believe she let Kelsey do her hair. Phoebe has avoided her all afternoon—did recovery on a stationary bike instead of in the pool, then sat in the corner of the first row to watch the film. She's never letting Kelsey do her hair again.

Never letting her touch her again. Is that why Fish looked at her funny while it was happening? Does she know everything Kelsey did?

Then again, Phoebe still doesn't know if Grace is out to anyone but her family. Phoebe is such an open book she tends to forget that not everyone likes to share everything about themselves. Every time Grace reveals a new personal fact, it feels like a nugget of gold.

Phoebe doesn't want to ask Grace who she can tell. Not that it would be—she isn't, like, *afraid* or anything, it's just. Grace is Grace. She likes her privacy. She never wants to be tagged on socials. She doesn't seem to want people knowing her dating history—Phoebe certainly didn't know anything about Kelsey until Grace said something.

So the next day, when she gets Thai food with Gabby after their respective trainings, Phoebe doesn't mention anything about Grace.

Not even when Gabby chews a tapioca pearl from her boba and says, "I, uh, kinda have a crush on Kayla."

"Sorrell?" Phoebe only realizes she shouted because Gabby cringes beside her. "Sorry," she says more quietly. "That's, like—well, like, how do you feel?"

The smile that sneaks onto Gabby's face answers before she does.

"She's just so fucking *cute,* and passionate, about, like, so much. The Eagles and cheesesteak and really everything having to do with Philadelphia, and also any team she's on—the national team or the Krewe or even just at the bar trivia night she's been going to every Monday for, like, three years. She makes me smile, like, all the time."

"How do you think she feels?"

Gabby shrugs. "We've hung out a couple of times, and she seems—I don't know. Maybe?"

"She seems what?"

"Like super, I don't know, gentlemanly? Like I don't know if she'll make a move if I don't?"

"Oh my God, chivalry isn't dead."

Gabby gushes some more about Kayla. Her cheeks flush and she gets giggly, and Phoebe still doesn't say anything about Grace, even though she knows exactly how Gabby feels.

Eventually, Phoebe asks, "Is it a good idea to date a teammate?"

Whether it is or not, Phoebe is already doing it, but she wants to know what Gabby thinks.

Gabby snorts. "Literally every queer woman in this league has dated a teammate at some point or another."

Okay, that's probably true. Still, Phoebe worries. Her relationships have never worked out very well, so it was easier to just not be in them. But Grace makes her want to do the hard stuff.

Dating Grace feels like taking a penalty kick.

A PK is a great opportunity. The odds are in your favor. It's as close as you'll get to an easy goal. The mechanics of penalty kicks are simple: kick the ball into the goal. That's all you have to do. Occasionally you might make a mistake, but ninety-nine times out of a hundred, a professional soccer player will nail the mechanics of a penalty kick.

It's the mental aspect that trips people up.

There's the goalie, standing as tall and as wide as she can on the line—maybe she'll even come out a little while you get set up, she'll *loom* like a towering beast, huge and threatening. There's your team behind you, counting on you, fingers crossed as they make silent wishes. There's the knowledge that you're supposed to make it. As close as you can get to an easy goal, right? So you better not fuck it up. It'll be embarrassing if you fuck it up. You'll let everyone down.

Penalty kicks make Phoebe want to throw up.

Which—obviously, dating Grace doesn't make Phoebe want to throw up, and it isn't really like there's anyone like a goalie, trying to force her to miss, but whatever. It gives her the same nerves, the roiling in her stomach about all the ways she can mess this up. Dating Grace is wonderful— well, it's new, but if it's anything like being friends with benefits with Grace, it's gonna be amazing—but messing it up would crush Phoebe.

She tries to do what she does with PKs: not overthink it. It doesn't have to be a big deal. Sure, it was unexpected. Surprising. If you told Phoebe three months ago that Grace Henderson would be her girlfriend, she would've laughed in your face. But a lot can change in three months. A lot has changed. And Phoebe is happy about it. That can be enough. She doesn't need to psych herself out.

Easier said than done, of course.

Twenty-Eight

Normally, an injured player is evaluated for return by their club team's trainer. They might talk to Ilse, the national team trainer, if it were a long-term injury or some other unique situation. Apparently, the national team playing their last sHeroes game at Krewe Stadium is unique enough to change the regular procedure. So instead of seeing Dawn on Monday after waking up with Phoebe in her bed, Grace has to wait until Wednesday, three-and-*a-half* weeks after she's been benched, when Dawn and Ilse can take a look at her together.

Grace arrives a half hour early. Sits in her car in the parking garage for twenty minutes, fiddling with her fingers.

Of course her leg is still going to hurt. The only reason it hasn't is because she hasn't been doing anything. Not that it matters—Phoebe told Dawn about it; the trainer never even noticed on her own. And she won't today, either. Nor will Ilse. Grace will fake it like she's faked it since last season. She'll lie her way through this check-in and start getting back to work.

"Let's see how you're doing," Dawn says after the standard small talk.

"I'm fine."

It's reflexive, but true. In fact, Grace was fine *before* sitting out three weeks.

Rationally, she understands rest is necessary for an injury, but this doesn't even count as an injury. This is a joint problem, caused by playing soccer for more than two decades. Bodies have limited warranties. Hers is nearing its expiration date.

The trainers don't know any of that. And don't need to. No one needs to. Grace takes a breath and does what Dawn tells her to do.

They start with standard exercises—jogging and butt kicks and high knees. Grace steels her face for the last one.

"Huh."

Her hip doesn't so much as twinge as she runs, pulling her knees to waist level with each step.

"Good huh or bad huh?" Ilse asks.

"Neutral," Grace says.

She's not looking at the trainer, but from her voice, she'd guess Ilse rolls her eyes. "I mean, how does it feel?"

"Fine," Grace says. This time she continues, "No pain."

"No? You're not just saying that so you can get back on the field sooner?"

Grace shakes her head. "I thought . . ."

"You thought what?"

Grace doesn't want to admit it. She doesn't like being wrong.

"It doesn't hurt," she says instead. "At all."

"Wow, you must have actually rested," Dawn jokes. "Let's try some other movements."

Grace is silent as she follows Dawn and Ilse's instructions. Nothing makes her hip hurt, not even in the slightest. After the trainers have run her through everything, they consult, heads tilted toward each other, voices no more than murmurs. Grace doesn't try to eavesdrop, her brain too busy helicoptering around the apparent fact that her leg has healed.

"We're clearing you for practice starting tomorrow," Dawn says. "With a lot of restrictions. We're taking this slow, so you don't overexert yourself and get hurt again."

Grace nods. "Okay."

"I would've thought you'd be a little more excited," Ilse says.

"I am," Grace says. "Of course I am. Big news."

From the look Dawn and Ilse share, Grace isn't faking the emotion correctly. But she doesn't have the energy to do better right now.

She's not fully faking, anyway—she *is* excited. All she's wanted this whole time was to get back, and she's doing that. But she had expected to. She had expected that after this check-in, she'd be cleared to play. She hadn't expected her leg not to hurt. She hadn't expected Dawn to be right. Grace *had* been injured. It wasn't her body falling apart.

Ilse takes her to go tell Amanda, even though the coach almost certainly doesn't need to know tonight. She has a game to focus on. But when Ilse shares the news, Amanda grins and even looks for a moment like she's going to hug Grace. She doesn't, thankfully.

"Can't wait to have you back," Amanda says.

"Still gotta get game ready," Grace says.

Ilse sighs. "Just because being cleared for practice is step one doesn't mean it's not a step, Henderson."

"I know," Grace says. "I know."

There's still plenty of time before the game—gates haven't even opened yet—but ads are already running across the jumbotron, and the teams are beginning their warm-ups. Grace tries not to look at anyone. It's weird not being on the field.

Weird enough that she wants to leave as soon as she's done talking to Amanda. Not *leave* leave—she's staying for the game, of course—but head up to the suite she'll be watching from with some of her Krewe teammates.

Fish spots her and jogs over before Grace can make her escape.

"How'd it go, Baby Spice?"

"Cleared for practice."

Fish lets out a *woohoo* that gets the attention of the rest of the players. Grace rolls her eyes at the exuberance.

"Good news?" a shout comes from closer to midfield.

Grace knows the voice, would know exactly where Phoebe is standing even if she'd said nothing. Grace's eyes always gravitate to that red hair.

"Hendy can practice!" Fish yells.

"Fuck yeah!" Phoebe shouts. Then, "Heads up!"

She lofts a ball down the field.

Grace doesn't think before lifting her leg, pulling it back just enough upon impact that the ball drops to her feet. She instinctively toes it out of Fish's reach and puts her body between the defender and the ball.

But Fish isn't defending; she's simply standing there, grinning wide.

"That's what I like to see," she says. "Baby Spice back in her natural habitat."

Oh. Yeah.

Grace has a soccer ball at her feet for the first time in almost a month. It feels like an extension of her body, more natural than she's felt for weeks. She taps it back and forth between her feet, dances around with a little fancy footwork. Nothing hurts.

When Grace looks up, Phoebe's smile is so wide, Grace swears she can see her dimples from across the field.

"For real," Fish says. "I'm glad you're on the mend."

"Yeah, yeah." Grace brushes off the attention. "Get back to work. Shouldn't the captain lead by example?"

"Of course. Wouldn't want to make you uncomfortable by talking about feelings," Fish says, and heads back onto the field.

With the national team taking over their stadium, the Krewe has the day off from training. Grace's first official practice back will be tomorrow, but now that she's got a ball at her feet, she can't bring herself to leave. This is the feeling Dawn and Ilse were probably expecting from Grace. Her mouth wants to spread into a smile so much she bites the inside of her lip. Three nights ago, Phoebe had made her think about happiness. Maybe it really is this easy. A field and a soccer ball.

She's not in cleats, but she dribbles around a little anyway, flips the ball off the top of her foot and into the air to juggle. It doesn't feel weird to be on the sidelines anymore. Grace doesn't even notice there are people on the field; she doesn't notice the field at all.

It's not until someone says, "Excuse me," that Grace notices anything other than the ball and the pain-free way her body moves.

Grace settles the ball on the ground, stands with one foot on top of it. The person who interrupted is wearing a matching red blazer-shorts combo.

"Hi, I'm Clarissa Fields, new media director for the national team, pronouns she/her," she says. "I know you're not technically here with the team, but a couple of journalists are asking if they could get a quote."

Grace glances to where Clarissa came from but doesn't recognize the two people hovering with cameras.

"Sorry," Grace says, not sorry at all. "My next media appearance is an exclusive with Megan Thrace."

"No problem," Clarissa says. "Have a good day. It was nice to meet you."

That's the entire interaction. Nothing big, nothing special, but it dampens Grace's mood anyway. It felt so good to have a ball at her feet, she forgot that her return to soccer also means a return to other responsibilities. She wonders how long she can put the exclusive off.

• • • •

The game is better in person than watching from her living room— though maybe not being furious at Phoebe improves it, as well. Grace would still rather be on the field, or at least on the bench.

Phoebe subs in for Kelsey in the sixtieth minute. They high-five as they pass, but Grace can see on the jumbotron Phoebe doesn't even look at the defender. It's immature, but Grace's chest flares with warmth. The New Orleans crowd hasn't seen Phoebe play yet, but she gets applause by virtue of being on the Krewe.

Then she gets more applause by playing out of her cleats.

This is what makes Phoebe different from every other class clown Grace has encountered. She set her sights on proving her worth to Amanda, and she's doing it. Grace gets the feeling that if Phoebe had decided she wanted to play forward, or goalie, even, she'd prove that to Amanda, too. The girl is everywhere she needs to be, pickpocketing opponents and crossing up defenders with some of the best footwork

Grace has ever seen. The rest of the Krewe in the suite hoot and holler and talk excitedly among themselves about their club teammate. Grace can't wait to play with her.

• • • •

Grace joins her team on the field after the final whistle. Her team. For once, she feels like she'll actually be a part of them again soon. Like she said to Ilse and Amanda, it still takes a lot to get game ready, but it doesn't feel impossible like it did this morning.

She dreads getting older, but maybe Phoebe has been right, and she isn't aging quite yet. If her body isn't letting her down, she can do this. Getting game ready is not what she's worried about in her return; it's all those other responsibilities that come with playing.

The team has cooldown and media and interactions with fans, but Grace doesn't mind. She nicks a ball from the sidelines and takes it far enough onto the field that she can't hear anyone calling for her autograph. Fans are wonderful, but she's not here for them right now. She's here to remind herself what this feels like, dribbling around on a soccer field. The stadium is still full, but it might as well be empty, the way Grace's focus narrows.

In fact, she doesn't realize most of the crowd has trickled out until Fish interrupts her solitary play by trying to steal the ball. Grace keeps it at her own feet, and she can't stop herself from grinning.

"If I hadn't just played ninety minutes, I could get this from you."

"Sure you could," Grace says.

"Love that you two are having fun but c'mon, let's go," H says.

Grace looks up to find H, Madeeha, Sorrell, and Phoebe have also wandered over. In her distraction, Fish gets the ball away from her.

"It's time to celebrate the new kid's first tournament win, right?"

There's a chorus of agreement but Phoebe tries to beg off.

"I don't know," she says. "Don't you want to go see your kid?"

"She's with Nani for the night," Madeeha says.

Grace remembers their night at Algiers Point, Phoebe's lecture about being aware of other people's financial situations. Sure, Phoebe will get bonuses from being rostered for the tournament, and more for two wins, but Grace doesn't presume to know where that money may go. And regardless, it won't hit her bank account immediately.

"We're going," Grace says. "Drinks are on me."

"Buying us drinks is an excellent way to celebrate your return from injury, Baby Spice," Fish says.

"Maybe we could celebrate by you not calling me Baby Spice ever again."

Fish's laugh booms. "For the rest of the night is the best I can do."

Grace will take it.

They separate to get ready—those who played need to shower and do media, which Grace does not envy. It means she gets to the bar first. She's not going inside by herself, though, waits on the corner with her hands in the pockets of her leather jacket instead. Everyone else arrives within a few minutes, at least. Phoebe, no surprise, shows up last. She's substantially less dressy than anyone else—Madeeha favors big gold hoop earrings and Fish does winged eyeliner almost as well as she plays defense—but somehow Phoebe fits in just fine.

She's wearing the same camo joggers she wore to the Mardi Gras parade, plus an orange Mapleton College soccer shirt she's cut the sleeves off of, the armholes open all the way past her waist, the black sports bra she wears underneath on display. On top of her head is a denim-colored snapback with US Soccer's logo on it.

The outfit works, somehow, even if none of the colors match, but what Grace can't stop looking at is her hair.

Phoebe's hair is down. She never wears her hair down, is constantly tying it up with a scrunchie. The only time Grace sees Phoebe's hair in all its glory for any actual length of time, Phoebe tends to be naked. She takes it down to shower, and sometimes, but not always, to have sex. Sometimes she takes it down to have sex and then puts it back up because it gets in her way.

Phoebe's hair being down seems to activate some sort of instinctual response from Grace—she doesn't want to go out anymore; she wants to go straight home with Phoebe and get her hands in that hair.

The way Phoebe is staring at her, Grace is pretty sure she's thinking along the same lines.

"So . . . are we gonna actually go inside or just stand here?" H breaks the spell between them.

"Right," Grace says, ignoring the way her face heats. "Yeah. Let's go."

Once they're all crammed into a booth, conversation, as always, turns to soccer.

Grace appreciates that about her friends. When she was younger, there were people who would get annoyed that all she wanted to talk about was soccer. That never happens anymore.

Everyone is more animated than is altogether necessary, riding the high of the win and the drink and a half they've made it through so far. Grace has already switched to seltzer with bitters.

"Givhan plays you both as an eight, but I don't think it's ideal for either of you," Fish says.

"Oh God, not the numbers," Phoebe groans. "I never remember the numbers when I'm sober. How the hell am I supposed to do it now that y'all have bought me drinks?"

Grace learned the numbering system US Soccer uses to describe each position so long ago she forgets it isn't universally known. With New Orleans she always plays as an eight, center midfield, going box to box playing both defense and offense. It's never been her favorite position, but it's what her team needs, and she's their captain. She'll always do what they need from her.

"Which one is for somebody who likes to be able to see everything that's happening but also get to be a part of a lot of different plays?" Phoebe asks.

"This is what I'm saying!" Fish says. "You're a six. Defensive mid."

"Is it bad that I don't know the numbers?" Phoebe sticks her lower lip out. "I swear I'm working on it but I've never had a very good memory."

Grace stirs her straw in her drink just to stop looking at Phoebe—that hair and those freckles too much for her even without the pout.

"You don't have to know them all," Fish says. "But learn six. That's where you should play."

"It's where Amanda has you playing because she actually understands more than one strategy," Sorrell mutters.

Grace's eyes cut to the blonde. "You think we should change it up on the Krewe?"

"Yes, God. Maybe not always, but Jesus, we need some fucking variety. And Fish is right. Neither of you are eights. It's ridiculous that Givhan won't play you as a ten."

"I'm not a good center mid?" Grace can't help but ask.

Fish cuts in to answer. "You're both fine at center mid, but that's not the point. Givhan has one of the best players in the world and he's limiting you by playing you outside of your natural position."

"Worse, he's been limiting the way other people see you, too. Like, Amanda is only beginning to figure out where you belong when you should've just always been there." Sorrell is as fired up as Grace has ever seen her. "Of course you do fine in a different position. You're a world-class athlete. But there's a reason we've won the shield back-to-back and he's never won coach of the year."

"Kayla knows what the hell she's talking about," Fish says, tipping her glass to clink against Sorrell's.

"Maybe once Grace comes back from injury and is captain again, you can take over the head coaching job instead," Madeeha suggests.

The conversation moves on, but Grace doesn't. Sorrell sounds good, and looks good too, arguing about what's best for the team. She was the obvious choice to fill in as captain, but maybe it should be more than temporary. Grace is the captain because she's a veteran. She's been the responsible one on every team she's ever been on. She's played with the Krewe for her entire AWSA career. She knows how to execute Givhan's game plan. But she's never pushed back about it. Yes, she'd rather play as a ten, would rather be an attacking midfielder who gets to score goals, but that isn't what he asks her to do, so she doesn't.

She's still wondering about it when H drags everyone else to the dance floor. Grace stays put. She loves her teammates, but not enough to dance in public. They need someone to guard their table and belongings anyway, and, after all, Grace is the responsible one.

Barely one song has gone by when the *irresponsible* one flings herself into the same side of the booth as Grace, her knobby knee thunking against Grace's as she sits close enough for their entire sides to press together. Her foot comes to rest on top of Grace's, and she doesn't apologize or move it away.

"Hi," Phoebe says.

She's so slouched that, for once, Grace looks down at her.

"Hi."

"Thanks for coming. And buying drinks. I don't think you should buy me any more, though, or I might start doing stuff I'm not supposed to." She stares at Grace's mouth as she speaks, so Grace doesn't have to ask what she means. "I've been trying to be good. But—" She glances around. The rest of the group is still on the dance floor, the music loud enough that Grace has to strain to hear Phoebe's next words. "You're, like, stupid hot."

A laugh bursts out of Grace's chest. It's such a Phoebe way to give a compliment, is all. Phoebe's eyes sparkle and her dimples come out. She's still looking at Grace's mouth, which is curved into its own smile.

"You're drunk." Grace tries to sound admonishing.

"Yeah, but I'm still right."

She looks like she wants to lay one on Grace right there, but Grace hopes she doesn't. If Phoebe tries to kiss her, Grace might do something absurd like let her.

"Hey."

Grace jolts at the voice. Sorrell has returned from the dance floor. Phoebe is still sitting with her hip against Grace's.

"I'm taking off," Sorrell says. "There's only so much after-party I can handle."

Grace certainly understands that. Phoebe, on the other hand, boos. Sorrell responds by smacking the brim of the rookie's snapback backward, sending the hat off her head.

"I'm surprised you've lasted this long actually," Sorrell says to Grace as Phoebe giggles and scrambles to put her hat back on. "Isn't it past your bedtime?"

Phoebe's head snaps up. She's clearly invested in Grace's answer.

Sorrell notices, if the little smirk on her face means anything, but Grace pretends not to.

"I'm the one paying the tab," she says with a shrug. Phoebe's shoulders relax.

It's true. Grace isn't staying for Phoebe. She just hasn't cashed out. Maybe when the others get back from the dance floor she'll tell them they're responsible for their own drinks now, but for the time being, she'll stick around.

"Have a good one," Sorrell says. To Phoebe, she adds, "Drink some water before you go to sleep, okay?"

"Yes, *Mom*," Phoebe grumbles but follows it up with a laugh.

Once Sorrell saunters off, Phoebe crowds into Grace's space once more. Grace wishes she hadn't taken off her jacket; the ends of Phoebe's hair tickle her bare arms.

"You know," Phoebe says, "maybe Kayla had the right idea. Should we get outta here?"

Before Grace can say *yes*, their friends come barreling into the booth. Phoebe gets jostled even closer to Grace, one hand landing on her thigh. She doesn't move it away.

Conversations flow and overlap—about the drink selection and the music playing and back around to soccer again, congratulating Phoebe on a good game and lamenting her shot that went just wide—until Grace makes a decision.

"I'm taking off," she says.

"Me too," Phoebe says, barely a breath later. "Will you make sure I take the streetcar the right way? I'm bad with directions."

Grace watches for any suspicion from their teammates, but rather than any knowing looks, they simply complain.

H groans. "Come on, the night's just getting started!"

"Matthews, you don't have to go just because the boring one is!" Fish says.

"Excuse you, I've been buying your drinks," Grace says.

There's a grumble of acknowledgment.

"Both of you get home safely," Madeeha, always the mom friend, says.

"You wanna buy one more round before you go?" H says.

Grace does it to keep them from thinking too hard about her and Phoebe leaving together.

• • • •

"Grace," Matthews drags out the vowel loudly.

They're sitting across the aisle from each other on the streetcar. Grace didn't trust herself to be any closer.

"Grace, I want beignets."

"Of course you do," Grace mutters under her breath. "Morning Call's closed, Phenom."

"Grace." She's stage-whispering now, which is somehow more conspicuous than when she was too loud. "Maybe it's time for my Café du Monde *experience*."

The person sitting in front of her chuckles. Grace lets herself think it's funny, too, instead of annoying or embarrassing. It *is* funny, and maybe even cute. Plus, there's something to be said about Café du Monde after midnight. They're going completely in the opposite direction, but that's fixable.

• • • •

They get one order of beignets and two cafés au lait. Phoebe gets hers iced even though there's enough of a chill in the air that Grace pulls her leather jacket tighter around her body while they wait for the donuts.

Phoebe doesn't take any pictures this time. Nor is she nearly as careful, taking a first bite that sends a cloud of sugar dust everywhere. She moans about how good it tastes, and Grace feels like a cliché, but her skin warms at the sound.

Phoebe doesn't notice. She doesn't seem to notice a lot of things when it comes to Grace. Not in a bad way—the opposite, in fact. Grace usually feels like she has to behave a certain way, *be* a certain type of person. She feels like she has to perform, like everyone is expecting something from her but no one tells her what, so she has to guess at it and hope she's right. But with Phoebe, she can be herself, and Phoebe never acts like that's not enough.

"Everyone talked about how I almost scored but honestly, I didn't even care that much," Phoebe babbles. "Scoring's fun and all, and like, yeah, obviously it would be a big deal to score for the national team, but defense is just better."

"But you love to be the center of attention."

Grace doesn't realize until after she says it that it might sound rude. But thankfully, Phoebe bursts out laughing.

"Sorry," Grace says anyway, just in case.

Of course different players need to like different parts of the game, but she can't understand how Phoebe, of all players, prefers defense to scoring goals.

"No, you're right," Phoebe says. "I do. But I don't know—when I went through the roster with Teddy to see whose spot I should take, there were options, you know? Like of course there were options. It came down to whether I wanted to focus on offense or defense, and that answer was easy. Defense has always been better."

Grace's position should've been an option. Box-to-box midfielder, which from Grace's research back during January camp seems to be where Phoebe played most of her college career.

"And, like, tonight felt so right, Grace," Phoebe continues. "Obviously playing for the national team has always been my dream. But I don't know—it's even better than I imagined. It's . . . exhilarating. Even just thinking about it now, my heart gets all fuzzy-like."

"Fuzzy-like?"

"Soft," Phoebe clarifies.

There aren't many things Grace's heart feels soft for. Her friends, sometimes. Her family, as long as Harmony isn't annoying her. Khadijah. This evening before the game, kicking a ball around by herself on the sidelines. Sending the ball into the back of the net, her teammates racing toward her to celebrate, the crowd going wild.

"I like scoring."

She didn't mean to admit it, but it's out there now. And it's true, even if Grace doesn't know why she said it, even if Phoebe didn't ask.

"Maybe Kayla was right—I'm a six and you're a ten and our coaches should play us there." Phoebe's smile goes wide. "Then we could actually play together. Like, I know I got drafted to fill your spot when you leave for the World Cup, but what if we both left instead? We could be, like, a dynamic duo."

During the game, Grace imagined playing with Phoebe. She knows they would work well together. She knows they would have fun.

She also knows Givhan won't do it. Like Sorrell said at the bar, there's a reason they've won the shield but he's never been a coach of the year nominee. He hasn't changed their strategy since Grace has been on the team.

But she doesn't like the idea of crushing Phoebe's spirits when her voice is so dreamy.

"Maybe," Grace says instead.

Phoebe goes quiet then. She finishes her beignet, sips at her iced café au lait.

When she finally breaks the silence, it's to ask: "So, like, can I help in your recovery at all?"

Grace's first thought is of sabotage. Phoebe is only offering to help so she can see how far along Grace is, how close she is to being 100 percent. Maybe she'll push Grace too hard to try to set back her recovery.

Grace takes a deep breath through her nose. Why does her brain do this? They're having a nice night. Phoebe isn't like that. When Grace told her what had happened with Kelsey, Phoebe was furious—at Kelsey. She was mad at how Grace was treated. Grace is trying to trust that, trying to believe Phoebe cares about *Grace,* not just about soccer.

"How?" Grace asks, instead of dismissing the idea.

"I don't know, like, if you need a partner to do certain exercises or whatever. Or just as motivation—I've been told I give a good pep talk."

"You want to motivate me with a pep talk?"

Phoebe smirks. "I'll motivate you any way you want, baby girl."

Grace rolls her eyes because that's less embarrassing than blushing. Then: "This would be a pretty good first date."

Grace blinks. "What?"

"I mean, like, if either of us were looking for a relationship."

Phoebe giggles, then, and leans fully into Grace. Grace didn't realize Phoebe was drunk enough to almost fall out of her chair, but—oh. She isn't falling out of her chair. She's leaning in to capture Grace's lips with her own.

The kiss is soft. Sweet. Different. Grace doesn't understand why it feels different, but it does.

She hasn't been counting the number of times she and Phoebe have kissed, but it is high. High enough they aren't distinct—not that they aren't *memorable,* but some blur together. Every time Phoebe came over after a practice Grace had been banned from, she kissed Grace hello. During sex, she'll press their foreheads together and kiss Grace between breaths. She can kiss when they're both fully clothed in a way that makes Grace want to be naked.

This kiss is none of those. It's not routine or seductive or desperate.

Grace forces herself not to tense up. This happens sometimes— things change but she doesn't know what, exactly. It usually feels like she's done something wrong—missed some social cue or let someone down in some way—but that's not what this feels like.

It feels nice, actually. Grace tries to let it, instead of overthinking.

This wouldn't even be their first date if they were looking for a relationship. They went for breakfast tacos after their run more than a month ago. Though maybe that wouldn't count either since they hadn't slept together yet by that point. But surely the ferry would've been their first date. Then again, Phoebe had said that was romantic, too.

Grace supposes maybe she'd be a good girlfriend, if that were something she wanted to be.

Twenty-Nine

Phoebe has no idea how, with all the relationships she's messed up in her life, dating her childhood idol is easy.

Like, sure, they could probably communicate a little better about, like, what they're doing, but Grace has never been much of a talker. Besides, they established after the fight about Kelsey—or about Grace not texting, really, but tangentially about Kelsey—that they both want to be exclusive, no matter what they'd said when they started this thing.

Still, it surprises Phoebe, how easy it is. They just . . . get along. Grace, who was so wary at the beginning, keeps letting Phoebe in. Phoebe knows she can be a lot of company, but Grace never complains about how much she comes over, just unlocks the door and asks what they should have for dinner.

The first practice they have together, Phoebe plants herself next to Grace when Givhan tells them to find a partner. She can't flirt that much, not in front of the team, especially with Dawn still keeping a close eye on Grace and her hip. But she wants to partner with her girlfriend. The thought is like a little flame in her heart, warmth flickering inside her chest.

Of course, Grace can't just let them have this.

"You can't claim you're doing it this time because I'm so good you want to learn from me," she says quietly.

"Maybe I just like being your partner."

"Obsessed," Grace mutters, but she's smiling.

Phoebe giggles.

See? Easy.

Even so, Phoebe is a little nervous about asking anything. She doesn't want to upset the groove they've fallen into over the past two weeks.

And that's another thing. It's only been two weeks—just under, actually. No one would ever introduce a girl to her family after just under two weeks, but that's when opening day is, and Phoebe's family is coming for it.

With the bonus money she got from sHeroes, she bought them plane tickets. None of them have ever been on a plane before. Their last vacation was piling into her dad's beat-up old car to go to Baltimore, where the national championships were. Phoebe wishes she could bottle the memory of the end of that game. Scoring the winning goal in the eighty-ninth minute, the green of the pitch beneath her cleats, her teammates crashing into her in celebration, her whole family screaming from the sidelines. It was even better when she'd intercepted the other team's pass and took it to the corner to waste the last few seconds of stoppage time. She'd rather have the ball at her feet than anywhere, even in the back of the net.

The home opener feels bigger even than her first game with the national team. This is her career. Obviously, the national team provides more money, more recognition, but it's not what she'll be doing day in and day out. And to have her family there—she's so freakin' excited.

Nerves only come into play when it comes to introducing Grace to her parents. In the end, she waits until the day before they arrive to finally mention it while she and Grace are cleaning up from the pizza dinner they just finished. Friday night is always pizza night at Grace's, even the day before a game.

"I know we're not, like, public with this, but would it be okay to tell my family when they're here, or no?"

Grace turns away from the sink where she's washing their plates to stare at her. "What?"

"I don't know." Phoebe picks at some scraps of chopped basil on the cutting board. "I had just thought of, like, telling my mom."

"You want your mom to know who you're sleeping with?"

Grace doesn't joke often, but she can be hilarious when she wants to be—managing to sound so bewildered at the thought that Phoebe can't help but laugh.

"Okay, fine," she drags out the word like she's pouting, even though she's not. "I won't say anything. You don't have to be an idiot about it."

She softens the name-calling by flouncing over to plant a kiss on Grace's cheek.

• • • •

Phoebe should be focused on the game that's about to start. One of her favorite things about soccer is how it makes her focus, how, when she's playing, there's nothing but the ball and the field, her teammates and her opponents. Her thoughts that jump around like someone is playing whack-a-mole inside her head finally settle when she plays. But they're warming up for Phoebe's first professional game, and she's not focused at all.

It's no single thing—it's everything together. Knowing her family is in the stands. The fans, a whole stadium's worth, getting concessions and finding their seats and shouting to get players' attention. A lot of it is Grace, who still isn't cleared for games so she's not suited up, except that she is *literally* in a suit: a charcoal-gray three-piece. Phoebe's tongue practically falls out of her mouth at the sight.

To make things worse, they're playing the Phoenix Chix. Kelsey's team. Kelsey, who maybe didn't break Grace's heart but at least broke her trust. Kelsey, who offered to braid Phoebe's hair before the last sHeroes game, and didn't seem to notice the vitriol in Phoebe's rebuff.

Phoebe isn't used to feeling animosity toward a girlfriend's ex. Well, she isn't used to having a girlfriend, period, but in general the breakups that she's been around tended to be amicable—there wasn't much of a choice given the size of the queer community at her college.

You were bound to date a friend's ex or an ex's friend or both. Sure, some girls claimed their exes were horrible—possessive or gaslighting or whatever—and maybe they were. But Phoebe has never felt this before, this burning rage under her skin, like her blood is simmering. She can't think about it. She can't think about the way Grace's brow, mouth, shoulders turned down as she talked about Kelsey. She can't think about the way Grace stands on the sidelines at an angle as the teams warm up, like she can't even look at her ex.

As they line up before kickoff, Kelsey smirks across the centerline.

"Good luck, Matty," she calls.

Phoebe wants to flatten her.

She's can't, obviously. She can't let Kelsey get under her skin. They have ninety minutes to play. There's a game to win. Not just any game: Phoebe's first professional game. That's more important than her girlfriend's bitch of an ex.

And Phoebe can be professional. If she happens to get a yellow card in her first game, well, it'll probably endear her to the home crowd. Once the game starts, she'll be able to get out of her head.

Except no.

Every time she gets close, every time the noise of the crowd somehow goes muted, and her focus narrows, every time she almost loses herself to the beautiful game, Givhan's voice pierces the bubble around her.

"Get *forward*, Matthews! Push *up!*"

She's *tried*. She knows how he wants her to play—it's how she played most of her college career—be everywhere, all the time. Get shots on goal and win midfield battles in the air and tackle the ball away from their players on a run. She can play like that. She knows how. She's good at it—great, even. That's the style of play that got her drafted. It's the style of play she did in practice. It's what she's supposed to do.

But it isn't working in the game.

Her teammates don't need her pushing forward, leaving the back line vulnerable—or worse, Colleen will already be forward, and they're left with only three defenders. Phoebe slides over to cover, offer an outlet for back passes, fill the space to prevent a counterattack—and Givhan screams at her.

Toward the end of the first half, still tied at zero, Phoebe forces herself farther up the field than she wants to be. She needs her coach to like her. She needs to keep getting playing time, even after Grace returns. And he is the coach, after all; maybe he's seeing something she can't. She doesn't let herself disappear into the focus she loves—*Forward,* she reminds herself whenever the Krewe push the ball up. *Attack. Pressure.*

"Good, Phoebe, good!"

Even finally getting praise, it doesn't feel good. She's too far forward to see the field as a whole. What's that saying—can't see the forest for the trees? She's a part of the attack, but she doesn't know what's going on behind her.

That's not your job. She hears the thought in Givhan's voice.

Kayla passes Phoebe the ball and there's space in front of her. *Advance. Attack.* Phoebe dribbles forward. She jukes around a defender before finding Gabby open on the wing.

"Give her options in the box," Givhan yells, and his players listen.

They crash the box, playing it almost like a corner kick. Gabby's cross is too low for Phoebe to get her head on, and Kayla's outstretched foot just misses it. One of the Chix clears the ball instead.

Phoebe turns around and sprints.

She should have been paying attention. She should have known that Colleen was pushed out too far—Givhan always likes her to play a role in the attack—but now Phoenix has four against three. Phoebe's legs aren't carrying her fast enough. She isn't gonna make it. She left her team vulnerable. Their defense is strong, but they're outnumbered.

By the time Phoebe makes it to her defensive third of the field, the ball is in the back of the net. Phoebe can't do anything but offer Ash a hand to get up from where they dove for the shot.

"I'm sorry," Phoebe says. "I should've gotten back."

"Not on you, Matthews," Ash says.

"Not on you, either," Phoebe insists.

Ash gives her a grin. "First thing you learn as a goalie is there's ten people who had to fuck up in front of you first. I'm good. Get back out there."

Givhan doesn't yell at all in the five minutes between the goal and the halftime whistle. Phoebe thinks that's a good thing until they get into the locker room.

"We cannot be caught out on a counterattack like that," he says finally. "Matthews, what were you doing so far up the field?"

Phoebe blinks. "What?"

"You're a *box-to-box* midfielder, not a get-inside-their-box-and-get-caught-out-of-position midfielder."

She *knew* she had been too far forward. Still. To hear him say it, to call her out in front of the entire locker room? Her chest clenches like her lungs haven't recovered from the sprint back. Her first professional game and she not only isn't able to focus because Grace's ex is on the field, but she's put their team behind.

"Sorry, sir," she mumbles. "Won't happen again."

"If it does, I'm benching you immediately."

Phoebe swallows the rock in her throat and stares at the floor.

"With all due respect, Coach, blaming that on Matthews is bullshit."

Phoebe glances up to see Kayla, stone-faced, looking at their coach.

"With all due respect?" Givhan parrots scathingly.

"Yes, sir." Kayla gives a nod. "You spent the entire half telling her to push forward. You can't then blame her for playing forward."

"That captain's armband seems to be giving you some misguided idea that you can tell me what I can and can't do," Givhan sneers. "I can and will blame a player for being out of position and not making it back in time on the counterattack."

"And I, captain's armband or not, can tell you when you're wrong," Kayla says.

"Kayla, it's fine," Phoebe mutters.

It's nice of her to say something, but she doesn't need to get in trouble for Phoebe's sake. Phoebe was out of position, that's true. She's never had a coach so willing to lay blame on a player, but she isn't in college anymore. This is the big leagues. She has to play like it.

Kayla makes eye contact with Phoebe. "It's *not*." She turns her attention back to their coach. "We played better with Matthews in more of a defensive role. If you let her play that way instead of yelling at her, she would've been there to stop the counter. You can't have it both ways."

"I can bench you both, if you'd like."

"If getting benched is the consequence for standing up for my teammates, I'm happy to do that, sir."

"Give the armband to Johnson."

Kayla tugs the band down her arm and hands it to her teammate, never looking away from their coach.

"If Henderson were fully healthy . . . ," Givhan mutters, shaking his head. "Since Sorrell here seems to know best, she'll give you the half-time speech."

He marches off to his office, not quite slamming the door behind him.

Phoebe wants to disappear.

Kayla doesn't hesitate before launching into a pep talk—or what Phoebe assumes is a pep talk. She's still too humiliated to think straight. Why did she even get drafted?

Before they head back to the field, Phoebe pulls Kayla aside.

"Maybe I should sit, though."

"Come off it, Matthews," Ash, who apparently overheard, scoffs.

"I'm serious," Phoebe says. "I don't know what I'm doing out there."

"Yes, you do," Sorrell says. "I've watched you do it already. Ignore him. He's wrong."

It's what everyone had said when they went out after sHeroes—not just Krewe players, but Fish and Madeeha and H, too. Phoebe tries to believe it. She tries to remember how soccer feels when she's playing well.

It's just—it's a bad game, made worse by how much Phoebe desperately wants it to be good. Everyone has bad games sometimes, but this feels bigger than that. This feels like her dreams are slipping through her fingers, like her dream that was so close to coming true is gone now. Amanda is too smart to make a roster decision based on one bad game, but Phoebe only has so many chances to impress her.

Maybe she'll be impressed by the yellow card Phoebe gets fouling one of the Chix midfielders barely three minutes into the second half to prevent a breakaway. Givhan certainly isn't, even while Sorrell tells her it was a good foul.

"Doesn't seem like you're making your coach very happy," Kelsey says as they line up for the free kick.

Phoebe ignores her, but Kelsey keeps going.

"Did Grace give a rousing half-time speech?" she asks. "I know she likes to think of herself as the rugged veteran leading the team into war or whatever."

This is what Kelsey has always been like—teasing, but with a mean edge. It's not something Phoebe likes in the best of times, but it's worse now that she knows what Kelsey did to Grace. Phoebe is no longer willing to joke with her.

The Krewe settles in as the half goes on. Givhan is yelling less, at least, even though they're doing what Kayla suggested and Phoebe is playing as DM. She's playing well, is the thing—the game is going better, the whole team is playing better. Phoebe has actually been able to focus.

Then the ball goes out of bounds, and Phoebe wants a quick restart because Sorrell is open, but as she goes to take the throw, Kelsey grabs the ball instead.

"No way," Phoebe says. "It's ours."

When the ref signals that it is, indeed, Krewe ball, Kelsey flips the ball in Phoebe's direction, but just out of her reach. She smirks.

"Oops."

Phoebe clenches her teeth together, focusing on the pressure instead of on Kelsey's stupid face. The best revenge is winning. Phoebe gets the ball and restarts play.

Later, on a boot from the Chix goalie, Kelsey comes over Sorrell's back to head the ball to one of her teammates. Kayla ends up on the ground, Phoenix with possession, and no whistle to be heard. It's a bullshit no-call. The teammate—Phoebe doesn't even know who, she's so focused on Kelsey and her unsophisticated braided ponytail—the

Phoenix player passes back to Kelsey, and Phoebe doesn't think, doesn't care, isn't going to let her get away with any of this. She goes for the ball, she does, but she also slams her hip into Kelsey's and sends the blonde flying.

Now there's a whistle, which—obviously. Phoebe knew she'd get called for that.

She turns to make a wall for the free kick, but the ref calls her back. The ref reaches into their pocket, and Phoebe's stomach bottoms out.

She already has a yellow. Two yellow cards means—

When the ref shows the red card, the rest of the world floods back in: Givhan on the sidelines shaking his head in disgust, Kelsey still on the ground clutching her shoulder. Kayla is up now, pleading Phoebe's case to the ref. The crowd is booing, but Phoebe doesn't know if it's at her or at the call. It has to be at the ref, right? Surely her home crowd isn't booing her in her first game.

Jesus, her family is here. Why couldn't she have kept it together?

That's it. Phoebe is out, ejected from the game. Her team has to play down a player for the last thirty minutes. They're already losing, and her lack of thinking just ruined their chances of a comeback.

God, she wants to die.

Phoebe has to walk past her bench on the way to the locker room.

"What the fuck were you thinking?" Givhan mutters as she passes.

Phoebe doesn't answer. She wants to disappear. How the hell is she supposed to make the World Cup roster when she can't even get through a single professional game without losing her cool? Her team has to play down a player, and it's her fault. She's so fucking stupid.

"Keep your head up."

Phoebe doesn't have to look up to recognize that voice. She can't look at Grace right now. It doesn't even make sense that Grace would say that. Grace, of all people, should be disappointed in her. She only ever wants what's best for the team, and here comes Phoebe and her temper, fucking things up.

"Why the hell are you telling her to . . ." Phoebe is glad to get out of earshot rather than hear the rest of Givhan's tirade at Grace.

It's silent in the locker room; even the noise from the crowd is gone.

What's Phoebe supposed to do? She has to stay, right? The last time she got a red card, she was fourteen, and Alice had driven her home immediately. Surely this is different, though. Even if she wanted to abandon her team—which she doesn't, she wants to stay till the end of the game, she just wants to avoid the lectures she's bound to get, from Givhan and Grace both—but even if she wanted to leave, her whole family is still in the stands.

Phoebe doesn't bother to turn on the lights in the film room. She grabs the remote and slumps into one of the chairs. Here's hoping they don't lose by more than one, though it seems unlikely for her teammates to survive a third of the game down a player without giving up another goal.

Except when she finds the broadcast—the game is tied.

The game is tied.

It hasn't even been five minutes since Phoebe left the field, but somehow the Krewe scored.

Maybe she hasn't irrevocably fucked everything.

She tries to focus on the game instead of her inability to control her temper. Nothing about today should've been about her, really. It should've been about the team. She refuses to be so self-centered. Her team has rebounded from her bad decision, and they're tied. That's what matters. They just have to hold on.

In the seventy-eighth minute, the door to the film room opens, making Phoebe jump.

Grace comes into the room, the yellow rectangle of light from the hallway disappearing as the door closes behind her. She says nothing. Phoebe just watches her, the TV casting shadows across her face as she approaches. She sits down and still doesn't say anything. She isn't even looking at Phoebe. Grace's suit looks black in the low light. After a moment, Phoebe turns her attention back to the game, but she keeps glancing over.

She doesn't know what to say. *I'm sorry* or *I'd do it again* or just *Please tell me what you're thinking.*

Please tell me you still like me.

She fucked up the first game of her professional career—she

shouldn't care about what Grace thinks. It shouldn't be important. But she can't even fuck up right.

She and Grace watch the game in silence. When the final whistle blows, Phoebe lets out a breath. They did it. They held on. Managed to wrangle a tie out of this mess of a game. It's not a win, but it feels like one anyway. They finally replay the Krewe goal—it was Sorrell, a rocket from outside the box. Phoebe wants to celebrate with her team. She wants to never leave this room.

She has to face her teammates and her coach and her family, but she doesn't move. Neither she nor Grace has said anything. Her team might've survived Phoebe's dumb impulsiveness, but what if her relationship doesn't? What if Grace is embarrassed of her? Phoebe simultaneously wants to plead her case and wants to never talk about it.

They both stay silent until the door opens. It's still dark in the room but for the light of the TV. Stuart stands in the doorway, haloed by the hallway light.

"Matthews? Your family's here."

"Right," Phoebe says. "Thanks."

She pushes herself to her feet. Her whole body aches. She should've cooled down before throwing herself into a chair.

"Do I get to meet them?" Grace asks.

Phoebe turns and stares at her for a moment before replying. "Do you want to?"

"I do."

Thirty

"Well, look who it is," someone says, then nothing follows it as Grace rounds the corner.

There is a clone of Phoebe, exactly the same except shorter in stature and hair, staring at Grace, mouth hanging open. Grace doesn't have to have seen a picture to know that's Teddy. Phoebe's hand snakes out and hits him in the stomach, breaking his reverie.

"Wow, violent," he says. "No wonder you got a red card."

Grace doesn't like that—no one needs to tease Phoebe about the ejection, but especially not fewer than ten seconds into the conversation. Phoebe rolls her eyes exaggeratedly and pulls her brother into a hug like she didn't smack him a moment ago.

"I'm so glad you guys are here," she says. She steps back, glances at Grace with an inscrutable look. "This is Grace. Henderson. Obviously."

Grace only took in Teddy at first, but the rest of Phoebe's family is there, too: Alice, with pin-straight posture and even straighter light brown hair; Phoebe's mom, the shortest of them, faded red hair tied back in a low ponytail; Phoebe's dad, whom she must have gotten her height from and her smile, too, dimples appearing as he grins at Grace. They're all in various shades of purple and yellow—none in the exact team colors, like they don't have the right gear but wanted to be supportive.

Mr. Matthews has a strong handshake.

"You look familiar," he says.

Grace doesn't understand why Phoebe groans in response.

"Dad."

"Ah yes, I remember now. Your poster is above my darling daughter's bed."

"I hate you," Phoebe says, face as red as her hair.

Grace's own face flushes. She wants to kiss Phoebe. She's wanted to kiss her all day, or at least since Phoebe asked her to braid her hair.

It's a problem, really. Grace should have been focused—on the game, on how to help her team, even if she was on the sidelines. She came back to the film room because she'd told Eric she would "deal with Matthews." That was supposed to mean lecture her, tell her all the ways she messed up in the game. It wasn't supposed to mean sit silently beside her and do everything you can not to kiss her.

Grace is trying to ignore these—these—*feelings*. She's not good at having feelings. Feelings never help anything. And she *cannot* be getting feelings for Phoebe. Phoebe is her teammate and her friend and her fuck buddy, for lack of a better word, but they've been clear on what this is from the start. So she can't be having feelings for Phoebe. She can't be wanting to protect her from the way her family seems to like embarrassing her.

Proving Grace's point, Alice says, "Phoebe has been obsessed with you pretty much forever."

"Alice, oh my God."

"What? As someone going into social work, it's my duty to tell her she might have a stalker."

"I changed my mind, I'm not glad any of y'all are here."

Grace wishes her family was there. She told them not to come, but she wishes all the same.

"Of course you are, Pheebs," Mr. Matthews says, slinging an arm around his daughter's shoulders. "You're just mad because we're right."

To Grace, he says, "She hasn't shut up about learning from you since she got drafted. But couldn't you have taught our girl some restraint?"

Grace remembers her hands on Phoebe's hips, the first practice she was out.

"Grace has mostly taught me about restaurants, and y'all are gonna benefit from that knowledge this weekend," Phoebe says.

"Seriously, though, what were you doing?" Teddy doesn't let her change the subject. "I know we said you should take Kelsey's spot on the roster, but not by breaking her!"

"She's *fine*," Phoebe snaps, and Grace tries not to wince.

"There's that temper," her mom says, running a hand down Phoebe's arm like that will soften the comment.

Phoebe smiles at her mom, but Grace can tell her teeth are clenched. Grace changes the subject for her.

"It's nice to meet you all."

"You don't have to lie," Phoebe mutters, and it's Teddy's turn to poke her in the sides.

"I know you were worried about us embarrassing you, but you kind of handled that yourself tonight, didn't you?" Teddy asks. "Getting kicked out of your first professional game."

"Come on, Teddy, be nice," Alice says, and Grace is glad someone is the voice of reason. But she adds, "You know she's sensitive. You wouldn't want to make her mad and have her shove you to the ground."

Phoebe rolls her eyes. "You're hilarious."

There's a wrinkle between her brows, and Grace isn't always great at reading facial expressions, but she's never seen Phoebe like this. She doesn't like it.

"You're not too mad to take us to dinner, are you?" her mom asks.

Grace interrupts, but she can't come up with the words fast enough, all awkward pauses between each one. "Actually, can I—there's a—team-related—thing—that I need to, um, talk to you about. Before you go, I mean."

Phoebe tilts her head. "Okay."

Grace pulls Phoebe to a stop as soon as they're out of the hallway, before the corner that would lead them fully into the locker room. Their teammates' voices mingle with the sound of running showers and Colleen and Ash's postgame playlist. The noise should be enough to keep anyone from overhearing, but Grace speaks quietly anyway.

"Are you okay?"

She hadn't asked in the film room. They'd spent twenty minutes in silence because Grace hadn't known what to say.

"I'm fine, Grace, I've been kicked out of games before."

That's not what Grace is worried about.

"It's not that big of a deal," Phoebe says. "Like my family said, my temper gets away from me sometimes. I was stupid, but it's fine. We tied, so. No harm, no foul, I guess."

"You weren't stupid," Grace says.

Phoebe responds like she needs to defend herself. "It wasn't like I just randomly decided to hip check her. She'd been bitchy the whole game, and she kept making sarcastic little comments about you, which just reminded me how shitty she was to you. I had actually done a really good job of restraining myself for the entire game up until she took out Kayla."

It doesn't matter why Phoebe fouled Kelsey. That's not what this is about. It doesn't matter that Grace's heart suddenly feels weightless, that even with how much she's wanted to kiss Phoebe all evening, she's never wanted it as much as right now. She's never understood love triangles in movies and media, never thought people fighting over you would be romantic, but the idea of Phoebe knocking over Kelsey to defend Grace feels like the best thing anyone has ever done for her.

Grace shakes the distraction out of her head and tries to continue like Phoebe didn't say anything. "You're not stupid. And honestly, you're not that short-tempered usually, either. It's okay to be emotional and get upset sometimes. That doesn't mean you're too sensitive."

Phoebe's cheeks pinken.

"I don't know," Grace says. She scratches at the start of her braid, careful not to mess it up. "I feel like your family is being kind of—I don't like the way they're talking to you."

Maybe that's too personal, but Phoebe doesn't need to get down on herself for this, and Grace is pretty sure her family isn't helping.

"That's just what we do." Phoebe shrugs. "Give each other a hard time. It wasn't a big deal."

"Okay, but you're obviously upset."

"I'm not upset," Phoebe snaps, sounding very upset.

"I'm not judging you," Grace says. It's not her business, but Phoebe wanted to tell *her mom* about them, so getting personal is probably okay. Phoebe fouled Kelsey for her. "That's what I mean—I don't feel like they should give you shit about being sensitive or impulsive, though. It's not okay to tease someone for a symptom of their disorder."

"What?"

"If it's something they're actually worried about, maybe there's a conversation to be had about how well your meds are working, but—"

"My meds?"

Phoebe's eyebrows are up by her hairline, and there's outrage in her voice, which is probably loud enough to be heard over the showers, but Grace isn't about to shush her. Apparently getting personal is *not* okay.

"It sure sounds like you're judging me," Phoebe says.

"Look, I didn't mean to get into anything you don't want to talk about. That's between you and your doctor. I'm sorry."

"What the fuck, Grace?"

Grace cringes. "I'm sorry. I—"

"I *know* I'm impulsive and overly sensitive. They might be my worst qualities, but that doesn't mean I'm *disordered*." She spits the word with vitriol. "Jesus, that's so much worse than anything my family said."

Ash appears before Grace can defend herself, defend *Phoebe* from herself. They round the corner from the locker room, skin glistening damp. Grace is certain they overheard.

But Ash gives a grin rather than a frown.

"There she is!" they exclaim.

Their towel is tucked around their waist. It's how they've worn it since before they got top surgery, but Grace is glad they're no longer in their *tits-out era,* as they used to say. Phoebe probably is, too, with how Ash decides to pick her up. They wrap an arm around her and lift.

"Hero of the hour!" they yell, and Phoebe squawks.

The towel falls then, but Ash doesn't seem to mind until they only make it three steps before almost tripping over it. Phoebe lands roughly on her feet. Grace wants to catch her, but she's not sure Phoebe would take her hand right now. Then again—all the frustration seems to have left her face. A moment ago, she was almost in tears, but one small interruption by Ash and she's fine?

"You're so dumb." Phoebe laughs at the goalie. "And wrong. In what world is getting kicked out of the game being a hero?"

"Uh, this one? You lit a fire under our asses," Ash says like it's obvious. "It was less than two minutes after play restarted that Kayla sent that rocket in. You being sent off did more for morale than anything else could've."

"Whatever you say, goalkeep."

Ash finally wraps the towel back around their waist. Phoebe sends the briefest of glances at Grace.

"Anyway," she says, addressing Ash and pointing her thumb over her shoulder toward the door, "I'm gonna take my family out for a late dinner. Have a good weekend, yeah?"

"I want to meet the fam!"

"You're naked."

Ash preens. "Oh, would they be uncomfortable being around someone so handsome and half naked?"

"Full naked, Ash. As we've seen, that towel isn't exactly secure."

"Fine, fine. But next time."

"Sure, next time. Tell everyone they kick ass, okay? I'm sorry I gotta go."

She doesn't even say bye to Grace.

What just happened?

Grace isn't really asking herself the question—she knows what happened. What happened is she got too personal and Phoebe got offended.

Some people think medical issues are rude to discuss. Grace certainly didn't like talking about her hip with most people. But it's different with Phoebe. Everything is a little different with Phoebe, in a way Grace doesn't think about too often, because she can't explain it. She likes things that make sense, and Phoebe doesn't, a lot of the time, but her reaction was even more confusing.

Grace considers. Phoebe has been spending a lot of time at her house lately, and the only pills Grace has ever seen her take are fish oil capsules she steals from Grace's bathroom cabinet. Is it possible she's unmedicated? But her ADHD seems out of control. Then again, maybe that's why. Maybe she doesn't even know she has it.

If Phoebe doesn't know she has ADHD, no wonder she didn't know what the hell Grace was talking about.

Grace's sister Harmony almost failed out of college. She'd been fine in high school, top of her class, actually, but when she went to college, her grades plummeted. It wasn't that she was lazy, or not smart enough, or anything like that. Harmony desperately wanted to do better in school, but she floundered. Halfway through sophomore year, on academic probation, she was diagnosed with ADHD and medicated.

She graduated with honors.

Of course it's not the same situation, but Phoebe has always reminded Grace of Harmony in a lot of ways—her constant struggle to be on time, the way she launches into conversations with no preamble, how she accommodates herself by setting multiple alarms or writing down directions to the equipment room. Grace simply assumed.

Just like she had assumed Phoebe could pay for dinner. Just like she assumed Phoebe wanted to use her. Grace is twenty-six years old. She thought she knew how the world worked by this point. Phoebe keeps proving her wrong.

Grace takes a step toward the door, long closed behind Phoebe, but is stopped by Ash's voice.

"You look good, Cap," Ash says. "Love the suit. Not as good as my birthday suit, but still pretty good."

Grace glances at Ash, then back at the door.

"She's going out to dinner with her family," Ash says.

They did overhear, then. Enough to know that something's going on, at least. Enough to tell Grace she isn't allowed to follow Phoebe right now. Those aren't Ash's actual words, but Grace gets the underlying meaning, for once.

Grace follows Ash farther into the locker room instead. She can apologize to Phoebe later.

It's just a fight. A misunderstanding. They happen. Between friends, even, so of course they happen between friends with benefits, too. Phoebe needs some time to cool down, and Grace needs to pick her words more carefully next time, and they'll be fine.

More of their teammates have come in from the field, all big smiles and sweaty jerseys. Grace sticks out in her suit. If it were a normal home opener, she would still be on the sidelines, signing autographs for as many kids as she could.

If it were a normal home opener, she'd join everyone in recounting the best parts, thriving on the high that comes from playing with her team. They undress around her while she stands between her locker and the bench she first straddled Phoebe on. Sorrell rounds the corner, then, and the room bursts into raucous applause.

"O Captain! My Captain!" someone shouts.

Grace's skin feels too tight. She hasn't been cleared for game play yet, obviously, but if she were—she wouldn't have stood up to Givhan like Sorrell did at halftime. She wouldn't have given the speech Kayla gave. If she were captain tonight, the team probably would've lost.

If it were a normal home opener, she would meet up with her family afterward. Instead, she's halfway to her car when her dad calls.

Grace doesn't want to pick up. She doesn't want to *have* to pick up. Normally her family is *here* for the opener. It's the few days every year the family gets together outside of holidays. Grace told them not to come, she's the reason they didn't, and yet her heart aches looking at her dad's picture on her phone. She doesn't want to talk to him on the phone. She wants to hug him. She wants him to tell her it will be okay.

Her dad always calls after a game. He called after every game of sHeroes, too, and never even seemed put off by the one-word answers she'd give to his questions. She does pick up, in the end, because she didn't last time he called, after the sHeroes final, and she can't ignore him twice in a row.

"Hi, Dad."

"Hi, sweet'ums." Her dad greets her with the nickname he only ever uses on her, and Grace feels bad that she considered not answering. "How you doing?"

"Fine." Grace hates small talk. She'd rather they get to the point of the conversation. "You watch the game?"

The sooner they talk about this, the sooner she can hang up. She loves her dad, but all she wants to do right now is build a nook of pillows on her bed and pull the comforter fully over her head.

"Missed seeing you out there," he says. "What was it like to watch from the sidelines?"

Horrible. Fine.

"Different." Grace doesn't particularly want to say more. "Weird."

"They looked different without you there, too," her dad says. "But not to worry, you'll be back before you know it."

He doesn't know that, of course, because no one does. She's been practicing, but there's still a long way to go. Coming back from an injury is about more than healing; it's about recovering fitness lost in the time off, too. She's done with the rest part, but there's still plenty of work.

Right now, Grace can't even decide if she *wants* to be out there. The team might've looked different, but they still managed a tie even while they were down a player. Sorrell was a better captain that Grace has ever been. It'd be a lot easier to never come back.

Grace's car is ten yards away, but she stops to untie and retie her shoes. She's in tennis shoes, even with the suit, because dress shoes always pinch her feet. But her sneakers are too tight. Her bra is, too. It's a sports bra, like she always wears. Suit or not, she went with what is most comfortable and it still didn't work. Normally she'd pick a sports bra over any configuration with hooks and an underwire, but right now it's digging into the skin of her shoulders, constricting around her ribs.

She plucks at it through the vest and her dress shirt, right there in the middle of the parking garage. If this were a normal home opener, she wouldn't be leaving yet. She wouldn't have to worry someone might see her tugging at her clothes.

If this were a normal home opener, she'd be talking to her dad in person. It doesn't matter that Grace told them not to; they should've come anyway. Except of course they hadn't insisted. Why bother going to a game if Grace wasn't playing, and why bother visiting if they weren't going to a game? What would they do if she never played again?

Right when Grace thinks it can't get any worse, her dad says, "That Matthews sure is something."

"She's a good replacement for me." She kneels to adjust her shoelaces again.

"No one could ever replace you."

It doesn't matter how much she loosens the laces; her feet feel pinched. "Why not? She can play the position. I could just stop playing."

"Grace, what are you saying?"

Grace doesn't even know. This thought has hovered in the back of her mind, but she's never actually thought it through, and she isn't now, either—it's just coming out of her mouth like she doesn't have control over it.

"What's wrong?" her dad says.

Grace tries to inhale, but it ends up more of a hiccup, tears pooling in her eyes. She doesn't understand why she's this upset—she didn't even *know* she was this upset.

Grace makes it to her car because she has to. No one can see her like this. These episodes have happened all her life. Grace doesn't always voice her disagreement or discomfort. She's uncomfortable most of the time; it'd be too much if she always brought it up. But times like these, she can't hide it. It's like crying when she gets mad—the worst, most embarrassing reaction. She hates when she gets like this. Overwhelmed and anxious and unable to even make words. She can barely grunt at her father on the phone, and it's easier to say nothing. She almost chokes on the stale air inside her car.

Her family is used to Grace going silent, even if it doesn't happen that often. They've all learned through experience that trying to bring her out of it does nothing but make it worse. They simply have to wait it out. Grace rocks back and forth in the driver's seat, rubbing her fingers together. Her dad is silent on the phone.

Grace could never quit soccer, not fully. But maybe if she retired, after a few years, she could join a rec league or something. That would be enough. A small voice in the back of Grace's head tells her it might even be *better*. She wouldn't have to be a captain or a role model. She could just be what she wanted to be when she was a kid: a soccer player.

Maybe Dawn will agree to say her injury is worse than originally thought, or that she exacerbated it or something. Grace can't retire for no reason. There will be questions—accusations, even. Abandoning the team in a World Cup year? It's unthinkable. She would need an excuse.

She needs an excuse now, to explain why she's reacting like this. She rubs her fingers together faster, but it doesn't help. Why is she like this?

It's stupid, but Grace thinks about Phoebe. About how she always wants Grace to let herself feel good. Phoebe doesn't put pressure on her to come, or to regain her senses once she has. Phoebe just lets Grace be.

Grace tries to do the same now. Berating herself to get better doesn't help. Being embarrassed doesn't help. She closes her eyes and breathes through her nose and lets herself be.

When Grace comes back to herself, she has to look at her phone to see that the call is still going. She clears her throat. Swallows. And finally speaks for the first time in minutes.

"Daddy?"

"Hey, sweet'ums." Her dad's voice is tender. "You okay?"

Grace's knee-jerk reaction is *yes*. Of course she's okay. She's fine. She's always fine. Just like her leg was fine. Nothing anyone else needed to worry about, certainly. She could take care of herself.

But she went nonverbal. *Fine* is usually a bit of a stretch, but especially right now.

So she avoids the question.

"I'm sorry," she says instead. "A lot of things were happening."

That isn't right. All that was happening was she'd been walking to the car and talking on the phone. Somehow that overwhelmed her.

"You don't have to apologize, Grace," her dad says.

She always does. Apologizes and explains, if she can. Anything that could help stop it from happening again.

"Do you want to tell me what's going on?"

Her dad's voice is so gentle that Grace actually answers.

"Every phone call, the first thing you ask me about is soccer. Like you care about the team more than you care about me."

"Gracie, *no*." He sounds horrified. "I ask about soccer because that's what *you* have always cared about the most. I want the team to do well because I want *you* to do well. If you quit soccer, I'm sorry to your teammates, but I don't know that I would watch another game."

"What? But you've been watching the AWSA since I was a kid."

"Sweet'ums." Her dad sighs. "I'm not—when you and your mom moved so you could train, I started paying attention to the AWSA because it was a way to connect to you. It was something I could text you about that wasn't just your dumb old dad texting that he missed you. Your whole life, I've asked you about practice and games and teammates because it's the easiest way to get you to talk. You and me, we're not always sparkling conversationalists."

Grace chuckles at that, even while everything else he's saying feels like her world turning sideways. Or maybe like it's always been sideways and is finally getting turned right side up.

"You're my kid, and I love you, and you've always loved soccer," her dad says. "If you loved horses, I would've taken you to the Kentucky Derby. If you loved the stars, I would've sent you to Space Camp. Or if instead of astronomy, you loved astrology, on every call I'd ask about Mercury in retrograde or—I don't know anything else about astrology really, but I would if you loved it. And that's what I'd ask about. That's all it is. If you don't love soccer anymore, quit! We'll come up with different conversation topics."

"I can't quit in a World Cup year, Daddy," Grace says. "And even if it weren't, I'm still captain of the Krewe. What kind of role model would I be if I quit?"

"It sounds like you're putting a lot of pressure on yourself," her dad says. The sentence hangs in the silence between them for a moment before her dad sighs and continues.

"When you and your sister were kids, we tried to teach you that you could be anything you wanted when you grew up. We never wanted you to think anything was impossible. But maybe we pushed too far in that direction. If all you want to be is Grace, that's enough." Grace feels wrong even thinking it. "The corollary to *you can be whatever you want* is *you don't have to be anything you don't want*," her dad says. "If you don't want to be a soccer player, don't be a soccer player. It's your life, Gracie."

She could quit? She could just . . . stop playing.

That's what her dad is saying. She can do whatever she wants.

Grace thought she already was. She loves soccer. She's always loved it. How can playing soccer professionally not be what she wants?

She thinks of her career. Of the most beautiful game. Of everything that comes with playing it—interviews and sponsorships and fame. Fake friends and strangers' judgment.

It's not soccer that's the problem.

"I don't want to quit," she says, voice quiet but sure.

"Well, then don't. But figure out what you do want to do," her dad says, like it's that simple. "Because I want you to be happy, and it doesn't seem like you are, sweet'ums."

Thirty-One

When Grace was eleven, her travel team had a seven-hour train ride to a tournament. The train was way better than the bus—faster, more comfortable, you were allowed to get up and move around. The bathrooms were on a separate level. There was an entire dining car. Grace's team had players from all over the country who had come to train in Southern California. There were three girls from the Midwest—two from Michigan and one from Chicago—and they got the whole team hooked on some card game called euchre.

Grace had spent the first part of the trip listening to music by herself, so when she finally got bored and wandered into the car where everyone was playing, she'd missed the explanation of how to play. She watched instead. For an hour and a half straight. Then she volunteered for the next game.

That's how she's always gone through life: learning the rules by watching.

Which makes being secret friends with benefits incredibly difficult.

Grace has a vague understanding about how friends with benefits works, of course. Friends is self-explanatory, and the benefits are sexual. That much is simple. But there are more rules than that. There are always more rules than anyone admits, unspoken rules, and Grace doesn't know *any* of them in this situation.

Since sHeroes, Phoebe has been spending more and more time at Grace's house. It seems normal in that Phoebe never makes a big deal of it, but it's a change from how they first started, so Grace isn't sure. When she looks at the rules she knows, though, the situation seems to follow them. Phoebe is around more, but friends hang out. And she and Grace usually end up in bed—or on the couch, or, memorably, on the kitchen counter—together, so it follows that part of the rules, too.

The spending-the-night thing, that's what really throws Grace off. She wouldn't have agreed, at the beginning, to friends with benefits if she knew Phoebe was going to be sleeping over so often, because she doesn't like people in her space. But once it actually started happening, Grace found she doesn't mind it—though Phoebe has, indeed, been in her space, given the redhead's tendency to go spread-eagle in the middle of the night. It's just confusing. If it's okay for Phoebe to spend the night, is it okay for Grace to clear out a drawer for her to keep clothes in? Grace had always thought that was something people did for their significant others, not for their friends with benefits. Is getting her clothes out of a drawer somehow more intimate than the duffel bag Phoebe normally brings over?

Grace hasn't offered, not yet. Now she might not even get the chance, depending on how mad Phoebe is at her.

She reminds herself that it's fine. People fight. But Grace doesn't like uncertainty. Phoebe hasn't texted her, and who knows if she will? Grace would like to know, not just that she will, but when. Grace would like to be prepared. She's already gone over a variety of ways of how the conversation might go, how she might apologize and do better and not hurt Phoebe this time. She's ready, for whenever—*if* ever—Phoebe does text.

But in the meantime, she has other things to do. Plans to put in motion.

She considers sending Sorrell a meeting invite, but it seems a little formal. This is formal, though. It's about their jobs. It's about Sorrell being good at hers. But Grace knows an official invite would come off weird, so she texts instead, asking if Sorrell is up for grabbing a cup of coffee or a smoothie or something, just the two of them.

> Sounds good.

> Though I'm pretty sure you're not asking me out, just in case: I'm dating Gabby.

> I am NOT asking you out.

> I figured.

They meet for smoothies that afternoon.

"I paid, but this is not a date," Grace says.

"We've established that."

"I didn't know about you and Rodriguez. Congratulations."

Sorrell gives a small, private smile. "Our rookies this year sure are something, huh?"

Grace blinks. "What? What do you mean?"

They're talking about Sorrell and Rodriguez—what does Matthews have to do with that?

"Nothing. Just—" Sorrell shrugs. "They are, right?"

Grace supposes she can't deny that. "Sure," she says. "Anyway . . ."

"Right. Since this is not a date, what is it? I assume you didn't randomly want to get a smoothie with just me for the first time in our friendship."

"I'm almost back at full strength," Grace says.

A side effect of spending so much time with Phoebe: Grace has grown to expect to be interrupted. Kayla, though, just nods.

"I assume Eric will want me to take over the armband again," Grace continues. "Especially given what happened last night."

Sorrell still says nothing, but her eyebrows pinch down and in like she's still angry about it.

"I don't think I should."

It's Sorrell's turn to blink. "What?"

"You're a better captain than me," Grace says. "You stand up for the team instead of going along with whatever Eric wants. That's what we need from a captain. I've been the default by being a veteran. And I thought I was doing it right, but I haven't been. You're actually good at it."

"I . . ."

She doesn't say more.

"I haven't told anyone else about this," Grace says. "If you don't want the armband, I'll keep it. But you should have it."

Grace says she'd keep the armband, but she no longer knows if that's true. She wouldn't force it on anyone, certainly, but after the conversation with her dad . . . it's like he gave her permission to imagine what her life could look like without the parts of it she doesn't like. And now that she's considered the possibility, the thought of keeping her captain duties itches like a stiff tag on a T-shirt. Grace rubs at the back of her neck even though she's cut all the tags out of her clothes for years.

If Kayla doesn't want to be captain, Grace will figure out someone else to ask.

"I've enjoyed being captain," Sorrell says. "But I hadn't thought about keeping the armband. I hadn't expected it to be an option. You really don't want it?"

"I don't."

It feels simple now, even if it was complicated getting here.

"I don't know if I would've spoken up so much if I had known it was something I could keep doing," Sorrell admits. "I figured it didn't matter if Eric liked me, because you'd be back soon enough, and then we'd both be gone for the World Cup."

For once, the idea of the national team roster doesn't stress Grace out.

"I still don't know that it matters if he likes you," she says. "You sort of changed my understanding of what being a good captain is."

Kayla ducks her head, hiding a sheepish grin. After a moment, she says, "You know you could just adjust how you captain, rather than offering it to me."

"I don't want it," Grace says. "Being sidelined has made me realize what I like and don't like about playing. Mostly that I like playing, and not the rest of it."

"So you gonna stop doing press, too?" Sorrell asks.

"What?"

"If you're no longer doing stuff you don't like to do, I just assumed you'd give up press, too. You always look like you hate doing media after the games and stuff."

Grace hadn't considered that. Is that an option?

"You think I could?"

Kayla chuckles. "I think you can do anything you want, Grace."

That's what her dad said, too. Along with the corollary—she doesn't have to do anything she doesn't want to. What if she never had another interview? Didn't have to worry about saying the right thing, or how someone might quote her out of context.

"Maybe?" Grace says.

She never used to admit to being unsure, especially not to a teammate. She was the captain, the veteran. She was supposed to know what she was doing. But even if Sorrell doesn't want to be captain, Grace won't be, either. And now that she's suggested it, of course Grace is going to pull back from media. Why wouldn't she?

"Yeah, okay," Kayla says. "I'll be captain."

Grace exhales. Thank God.

"You're gonna be great," she says. "I've known it should be you since that conversation at the bar after sHeroes, to be honest."

Kayla raises her eyebrows. "You think I can convince Givhan to put both you and Matthews in the lineup?"

It sounds like a dream, but: "Probably not."

She chuckles humorlessly. "Yeah, you're probably right."

When they're done, Kayla grabs a Lyft and Grace gets into her car. She doesn't start it. She doesn't even put the keys in the ignition. First, she pulls out her phone and emails her agent right then and there.

The exclusive with Megan Thrace will be her last interview.

She won't be doing media after games anymore.

She's taking a step back, even as she returns to the game.

Normally, when Grace makes a decision for herself, it makes her anxious. It feels wrong. But when she presses send on that email, a weight lifts off her shoulders.

No more media. It doesn't mean no more fame, of course, but it's something. She considers deleting her social media next, opens Instagram. She'd posted for their first game and should see how the post is doing, if anyone commented with something she should respond to, or maybe delete, because that happens sometimes. That's why she's on social media. That and deciding whether or not she should delete it. She hates social media; obviously, she wouldn't be on it if she didn't have to be. If she happens to ignore the red bubble of notifications in the upper right in favor of scrolling her feed until she finds Phoebe's most recent post—well, she's simply checking on her teammate who had a rough game.

It's embarrassing, lying to herself this much. She knows that's what she's doing, but it somehow feels easier than admitting the truth. Than admitting, even to herself, that she misses Phoebe, that she's worried about her, worried about them, not that there is a *them*, really, but even if they don't keep being friends with benefits, they have to keep being teammates. Though maybe Phoebe will be like Kelsey, and even after whatever this is ends, she'll act like it was nothing. The thought makes Grace recoil.

If Phoebe were here, Grace wouldn't believe that. She can only think the worst of her while she's gone. It's easier then, when Phoebe isn't right in front of Grace, proving her wrong over and over again.

Phoebe seems to be having fun with her family, if the picture of her at the aquarium with Teddy in a headlock is any indication. That's good. She deserves the break. And clearly everything that happened Friday night didn't ruin her weekend. Grace doesn't need to worry. They're fine. They'll be fine.

Thirty-Two

I'm outside your building. Will you
let me in so we can talk?

Phoebe's family left this afternoon. She's not really in the mood to be
lectured by Grace, but what's she going to do, ignore her forever?

It makes sense to talk tonight, otherwise practice tomorrow is going to be awkward as hell, and Phoebe doesn't need everyone noticing.
That would probably make things worse with Grace, anyway, since
she's never seemed to want anyone to know they're dating. Though
that turned out to be a good thing, in the end. Imagine if Phoebe had
introduced Grace as her girlfriend right before Grace told her she was
disordered.

Does this count as their first fight? They had a fight about Phoebe
telling Dawn about Grace's leg, but they weren't officially dating at that
point—that's what, like, started the whole thing. So this is technically
their first fight, right? Who knows if they can even make it through?
Maybe this is it. Maybe they're breaking up. Maybe that's what Grace
wants to talk about.

Phoebe texts her apartment number and buzzes her in.

She immediately regrets it. She should have gone down to meet her. They could've gone somewhere to talk, anywhere but Phoebe's apartment, which is small and messy and embarrassing. Maybe one of the symptoms of her *disorder* is messiness, since that's another thing Phoebe hates about herself. Whatever. She's not cleaning up for Grace.

Except then Grace is there, at her door, looking as beautiful as she always does, brown eyes so dark they're almost black, hair in one simple french braid down her back. Grace is at her door, Grace is following her inside, Grace is in her living room and why did Phoebe not clean up?

There's still a suitcase on the floor. Phoebe only took the time to flip the top closed. She should've made Grace wait, should've cleaned, made her apartment look like somewhere an adult human lives. A normal one. Not a *disordered* one, or whatever Grace sees her as.

It's easier to stay mad at Grace. Easier for Phoebe to know she's in the right than allow herself even a second of doubt. It doesn't matter if Grace didn't mean to be cruel; she was. Phoebe doesn't have to be polite, or kind, or forgiving.

"What do you want?"

"To apologize," Grace says, and Phoebe wants to forgive her. "And talk and explain myself better."

"Fine," Phoebe says. She drops into the chair that looks comfortable but in fact is hard as a rock, then gestures for Grace to take the couch. "Go ahead."

Grace sits, right on the edge of the cushion. Phoebe wants to hand her a pillow, wants to go out and buy a variety of pillows, because Grace has so many on her own couch, and Phoebe knows playing with the tassels helps her think. But she's mad at Grace. She's supposed to be holding on to that. Easier to be mad at Grace than hate herself for getting kicked out of her first professional game, even if Ash insisted she's the reason they tied.

"I'm not good at this," Grace says. "I haven't really had any practice, not in a situation like ours."

Normally, Phoebe doesn't mind that Grace doesn't want to be public about the two of them. It's special, and not anyone else's business, and anyway, being out or not out—especially when you're a public figure—it's an individual thing. It's personal, and it's Grace's choice, and Phoebe is totally fine with it normally. But Grace can't even say the word *relationship*? She calls dating Phoebe a *situation*?

Suddenly it's not so hard for Phoebe to hold on to her anger.

"So I'm sorry for not explaining myself well," Grace says.

"You know, often explaining oneself while apologizing is more like offering excuses."

"That's not what I—" Grace cuts herself off. "Why did you let me in if you weren't going to let me explain?"

Phoebe can't remember. Why did she let Grace in? She supposes she thought it would go better than this.

"Maybe I wanted to yell at you, Grace," she snaps. "Maybe my *terrible temper* got the best of me and I wanted to take it out on you. Maybe I thought I was going to listen but I'm *sensitive* and I remembered how you said I needed to be on meds and that hurt my feelings. Maybe I just didn't think it through, like I don't think anything through."

"I didn't say you needed to be on meds," Grace says. "I assumed you already were."

"Oh, since that's so much better? What the fuck? Is that really how you see me, like some little fucked-up girl? Like my bad qualities are symptoms of some disorder?"

"They're not even bad qualities!"

Phoebe has never heard Grace yell before. The look on Grace's face seems like she didn't expect it either, but she recovers quickly.

"It's not bad to feel things with your whole heart or do things you want to do. I love that as soon as you arrived in New Orleans you decided to see the stadium, even though it was nine thirty at night. I love that you jumped the fence to come talk to me. And I love that you knocked Kelsey down—both as retaliation for her foul on Sorrell and as . . . well . . . the idea that it had anything to do with me. I like that, too."

It's very hard to stay mad at someone while they quite literally yell at you about how much they love the things you hate about yourself. *Love.* The word ricochets around inside Phoebe's head.

"But whether they're bad qualities or not"—Grace lets out her breath—"I do think some of these characteristics are at least partially symptoms of ADHD."

ADHD is a thing middle school boys have, not adult women. But honestly, Phoebe doesn't even care about that right now. She wants to throw herself at Grace.

Grace keeps talking like Phoebe is thinking of anything other than fucking her brains out. "My sister has it. And medication helped her symptoms so much. I could—"

"Grace," Phoebe says, slowly rising out of the chair, "I'm really going to need you to stop talking about symptoms and kiss me instead."

"What?"

Phoebe takes a step toward the couch. "I suppose I can do the kissing, huh?"

Grace leans back as Phoebe gets closer, which only means she ends up mostly lying down, and Phoebe crawls on top of her instead of straddling her. Her eyes are dinner plates.

"You're not mad at me anymore?"

Phoebe shrugs. "Your heart was in the right place."

Grace gets this hint of a smile, a barely there turn of the corner of her lips, and Phoebe might die if she doesn't get her mouth on it. "So, we're okay?"

"We're okay," Phoebe says. "Can I *please* kiss you now?"

Grace kisses her first.

They've done it on a couch before—a much more comfortable couch at Grace's. Not that Phoebe doesn't want to fuck Grace on her couch—she wants to fuck Grace everywhere, pretty much, and kind of all the time—she just wants to make sure Grace is comfortable. So they're not gonna fuck here. Phoebe is gonna take Grace to bed. She is. In a minute. She just needs to kiss Grace a little longer. She just needs to slide her hands under Grace's shirt to stroke at the soft skin of her sides.

Grace pulls the shirt over her own head.

Okay, yeah, no, Phoebe needs to spread Grace out *now*.

Thank *God* Phoebe changed her sheets when she cleaned up before her family arrived. While her bed isn't made and there are already dirty clothes on the floor, at least when she sets Grace on the mattress, the sheets beneath her are clean.

"You're the prettiest girl in the world," Phoebe says, and it's not even a line, it's the *truth,* even more so when Grace's cheeks go rosy at the compliment.

Grace is sitting on the edge of the bed, her feet still on the floor. Phoebe goes down on one knee to roll Grace's pants down her legs. On the way back up, she kisses her ankle, her calf, her knee.

"You're perfect," she murmurs.

The first few times they slept together, Grace always tried to take control. She trusts Phoebe now. She doesn't say it, but Phoebe can tell just by the way Grace sits, waits, lets Phoebe do whatever she's going to do next.

What she's going to do next is lay Grace back on the mattress and lean over her, holding herself up with one hand, her face inches from Grace's.

Grace usually closes her eyes during sex. Not necessarily, like, all the time or anything, but a lot. Which is fine—Grace can do whatever she wants during sex, in Phoebe's opinion. Again, Phoebe just wants her comfortable. If eyes closed is what makes her comfortable, great.

That said, Grace looking up at her as Phoebe slides a hand between her legs? It kind of feels like everything.

"You're so fucking perfect," Phoebe says.

Neither of them look away or close their eyes. Phoebe rubs at Grace through her underwear until the fabric is as humid as the air between them.

Phoebe can focus just fine. She focuses on Grace's skin, soft and tan and perfect. She focuses on telling Grace just exactly how perfect she is. That perfect skin and those perfect tits and her stupid perfect face, eyes, mouth, lips, *tongue.* Maybe Phoebe should come up with an adjective other than *perfect,* but she's never been particularly good with words. While her mouth can open without consulting her brain, other times her thoughts spiral too quickly for her to actually figure out what she wants to say. And right now? This? She has no idea how she would say this to Grace. Phoebe has been afraid of fucking things up just by being herself, just because she always has before, from the beginning she's been afraid of it. And then Grace has to go and basically write poetry about the worst parts of her?

Yeah, she has no words for how that makes her feel.

So, she focuses on making Grace feel good. Not on making her come—Phoebe wants to, sure, but sometimes Grace is too in her head, and that's okay. An orgasm isn't the ultimate goal here. This is about making Grace feel as good as possible for as long as possible. This is about how Grace made Phoebe feel, saying what she said. Grace *loves* the parts of her that Phoebe hates about herself.

Phoebe wants to do everything to Grace. *Everything.* But rubbing at her is so nice, Grace's underwear so wet her fingers are already sticky, Phoebe can't bring herself to stop. She presses their foreheads together.

Eventually, Grace breaks the reverent silence between them.

"I—" she says. "Your mouth."

"What about my mouth, baby girl?"

"Please," Grace says. "Put it on me. I wanna come on your tongue."

Phoebe doesn't need to be told twice. She keeps Grace's underwear on still. It's a mess, warm and wet and so delicious Phoebe goes light-headed as she sucks the fabric.

Grace can handle a lot through her underwear—Phoebe uses her teeth, licks hard enough the underside of her tongue hurts. Grace rolls her hips, a surefire sign she wants more. Phoebe finally tugs her panties down, leaning back in to lick, to taste, to have her tongue against Grace with no barrier. Normally she pulls back a little once the underwear is off, but she loves Grace's cunt so much, she doesn't think, she's not careful, she goes a little too hard.

Grace pushes her away.

"Too much," she gasps.

"I'm sorry," Phoebe says. "I'm sorry."

A shudder runs through Grace, and Phoebe hates that it's not a pleased one.

"It's fine," Grace says, her voice practically businesslike. "But I lost it. I'm not gonna come right now. Let me touch you instead and we can try again after."

Phoebe shakes her head, her cheek resting against Grace's thigh.

"It's okay," she says. "I'm sorry. I can be gentle."

Grace's eyes go soft. "I know you can."

"Let me keep going? Please?"

Grace takes a deep breath and lets it all out. After a moment, she nods.

Phoebe nips at her inner thigh in thanks. She keeps her mouth there, for a while, first one thigh, then the other, kissing and sucking and the occasional bite, never breaking eye contact.

"You have a perfect pussy."

Grace presses her lips together, but her eyes are smiling. Phoebe wants to open her up, blow a stream of air across her clit, but she's being gentle. She's going slow. She licks up Grace's leg, to where her hip flexor is—Phoebe isn't great with anatomy, but she looked it up when she learned that was why Grace was out—she licks up to Grace's hip flexor and then presses light kisses there. Grace spreads her legs wider.

"Yeah?" Phoebe asks, still kissing Grace's hip.

Grace nods.

Phoebe kisses her cunt instead. She keeps her eyes on Grace's, her mouth closed and soft. She wants to taste her again, but her tongue stays tucked away. This isn't about her. She avoids direct contact to Grace's clit until Grace slides a hand into Phoebe's hair and holds her there.

"Please," Grace says, and Phoebe complies.

They both moan when Phoebe finally lets her tongue dip between Grace's folds. Phoebe's eyes close in ecstasy at the taste, and when she opens them again, Grace has finally closed hers, her head tilted back, chin pointing toward the ceiling.

It doesn't take long from there.

• • • •

After, there's no choice but to snuggle, given the size of Phoebe's bed.

Grace shifts in her arms. "Would it be okay if we . . . continue our conversation from earlier?"

Phoebe doesn't need to anymore—when Grace first arrived, Phoebe was sure she needed an apology and groveling and Grace to fully understand why Phoebe was hurt. Now, stretched out in the twin bed that came with the apartment, nowhere to be but pressed up against Grace's bare body, Phoebe doesn't care about their fight.

"Sure," she says, even though it doesn't matter. "I didn't mean to distract you with sex. I just really needed to kiss you."

"I am not complaining," Grace says. She presses her lips against the skin of Phoebe's shoulder. "But I really do think you have ADHD. And getting medicated would help."

Phoebe shrugs. "But I'm not hyperactive."

"You once told me you're like a dog and if you don't get to run around every few days you go stir-crazy."

Okay, fair.

"Okay, yeah, but like, I can focus on stuff."

"As soon as you realize a TikTok has a part two, you stop watching it."

"Well, I can focus on some stuff. Like, if I have ADHD, then why can I focus on eating your pussy for as long as you'll let me?"

"Phoebe," Grace says, "people with ADHD can focus on stuff that interests them."

Phoebe doesn't know enough about ADHD to debate this.

"I'm not trying to make you feel bad," Grace says quickly. "I just think medication could really help you."

It's nice that Grace wants to help her. But Phoebe has enough to deal with.

"Honestly, I have so much other stuff to worry about right now," she says. "Maybe when things die down a bit, I can look into it, but right now I gotta keep working to try to make the roster."

Especially given her performance on Friday, not that she's going to mention that. She doesn't understand how Grace thinks she knocked Kelsey down because she has ADHD, but whatever. It doesn't matter. She did it, regardless of why, and it probably set her back in Amanda's eyes. She has to work twice as hard to make up for it.

"Okay but Phoebe, this is something that can help you with that," Grace says.

Annoyance tickles the back of Phoebe's brain. She doesn't want to talk about this. She wants to snuggle with her girlfriend who loves things about her.

"C'mon." Phoebe shrugs, and Grace's head, which is on her shoulder, moves with her. "Where am I supposed to get tested? How am I supposed to pay for it? Even if I'm diagnosed or whatever, how am I supposed to pay for the medication?"

"The team gives us health insurance," Grace says.

"Yeah, I've had health insurance most of my life. That doesn't mean health care has ever been affordable."

It's embarrassing to talk about this with Grace, who obviously didn't grow up poor. ODP is technically free if you qualify, but to do that you need gear and to be part of a good program, a.k.a. a travel team, which means money on gas and hotels and food while you're on the road. Plus, Grace was getting sponsorships when she was, like, sixteen—even if she was poor once, she isn't now. Phoebe doesn't mind being poor, most of the time. She doesn't mind having two jobs when one of them is playing soccer. She knows she and her family aren't somehow "bad" people just because they aren't well-off. You can't budget your way out of minimum-wage jobs and cut hours and a union-busting employer. Especially not when your youngest kid needs puberty blockers and then hormones, and your health insurance pretends it's all "elective." Phoebe hates dealing with health insurance. It's always too expensive while trying to make you feel like you should be grateful to have it at all.

"The prescription coverage is comprehensive," Grace says. "I could help you—"

"Look, I appreciate your concern, but I'm not really interested in taking meds that slow me down."

"That's a misconception. It's—"

"Grace, c'mon. Let it go."

She doesn't need Grace looking after her. Even if it does make Phoebe's chest warm that Grace wants to. It makes her want to be gentler in her dismissal.

"You're very sweet, okay? I just can't think about it right now," she says. "Maybe I'll get to it, but there's already not enough time in the day for me to do everything I want to do. Pretty much every minute I'm not with you I have to devote to one of my two jobs—I mean, obviously you're with me at one of them, too, but—you know what I mean. My dream of playing for the national team might be coming true, but I can't quit at the diner because there are no guarantees. If I don't make the roster for the World Cup, I'm gonna need hours at the diner. My phone dies at random and I can neither afford to get a new one nor do I have any time to. You would think I could, with money from the sHeroes tournament, but I bought my family plane tickets and sent the rest of it home. My parents have whatever crap insurance they can afford, and it's not covering top surgery for Teddy. Even if I do make the roster and get bonuses and allocation money—I mean, I don't even know how much I'd need to quit, to feel comfortable quitting. I can't imagine that. And yeah, I guess I could take a look at my finances and my family's finances and try to figure it out, but that's work in and of itself. It gets overwhelming. There's only so much time in the day. I appreciate that you think this is something that might help me, really, but I don't have the time. I don't have the money. I don't even have the energy. So it's easier not to think about it. Okay?"

Phoebe hates being vulnerable about money, but it's easiest to be honest. And anyway, she doesn't want it to seem like she doesn't appreciate that Grace cares about her. It means a lot that Grace is trying to help her, even if Phoebe isn't going to take the help.

"Okay," Grace says quietly.

Phoebe tightens her arm around her girlfriend's shoulders and thinks about *love*.

Thirty-Three

Those feelings Grace told herself she couldn't have—she has them.

She's getting stronger each day in practice, except for the way her knees go weak around Phoebe.

Not literally, of course, but she's beginning to understand the phrase. She's gone soft.

She's still herself—particular and introverted—but something's different. Like she used to have an exoskeleton but she grew out of it, and now there's nothing to protect her. After Kelsey, Grace didn't date. She didn't let anyone in. She told herself it was about trust. She told herself people would use her, would hurt her if she let them in. For some people, certainly, she had been right. It was a good reason and it worked. But with Phoebe . . .

With Phoebe, something even worse has happened. Grace should've kept Phoebe away, because at least then she wouldn't have fallen for her. They could not have been more clear with how this whole situation began—neither of them looking for a relationship—and now Grace's heart has to betray her by fluttering when Phoebe smiles at her.

Phoebe is where Grace has gone the softest. Grace used to require alone time to recover from being around people, but now when she's home alone, she's lonely. She used to prefer her house quiet, but it feels silent without Phoebe there, talking or laughing or scrolling through TikTok. Thinking of Phoebe makes her insides—and she hates that word, it's vague and unscientific—go all floaty. She doesn't spend much time thinking about where her organs are inside her body, but when she thinks about Phoebe they all seem to go up, like there's a helium balloon attached to each one, like she could be lifted off her feet if she didn't shake her head to clear it. That feels silly, too: that she has to physically do something to stop . . . *daydreaming* about Phoebe. It's embarrassing even though she will *never* tell anyone else.

That's why Grace can't let the ADHD thing go. Because thinking about Phoebe's ADHD is easier than thinking about Phoebe in any other capacity.

Plus, this isn't about Phoebe. It is, quite literally, about Phoebe, but it's not because she's *special*. Grace would do this for any of her teammates. She helps them be their best. Even if she's giving up the captainship, she's not giving up that. Phoebe is her teammate and her friend, and getting diagnosed with ADHD could make her life easier. That's enough reason for Grace to do this. There doesn't have to be anything more behind it.

The first thing Grace does is download TikTok. She needs to speak Phoebe's language. The week Phoebe wouldn't stop talking about D. B. Cooper, she'd even found some TikToks about it. So there must be ADHD TikToks, too.

Grace has never really understood the app. The team does "Game Day Fits," filming players as they arrive at the stadium. As soon as that started, everyone's fashion changed pretty dramatically—honestly the *shoes* some of the girls wear—but Grace still shows up more often than not in black joggers and a white T-shirt. That's the extent of her experience with TikTok.

She underestimated the app. There is a video, multiple videos, for anything she wants to find: how does ADHD medication help, what are lesser-known ADHD symptoms, how can ADHD manifest, what's it like for women, what's it like to be diagnosed as an adult. She collects the most illuminating videos in her likes. If she can't convince Phoebe to see a doctor herself, these will help.

Grace was already rather certain Phoebe has ADHD, but after perusing ADHD TikTok—she's *very* sure. But still, she needs to figure out how to handle this. Her opinion on the situation is just that: her opinion. She can't really know what's best for Phoebe. She doesn't have ADHD.

Hence, step two: calling her sister.

"I need your help." It's Grace's turn to skip the small talk.

"One second, I'm getting another call," Harmony says. "Yeah, it's from the weatherman, apparently hell just froze over."

"Shut up. I've asked you for help before."

"You literally have *never*."

"Well, if this is what you're like when I ask for help, maybe you can understand why I wouldn't do it."

Harmony sighs. "Okay, okay, fine, what do you need?"

"I've researched ADHD, but I still have some questions I'm hoping you can help me with." Grace has a pen and paper in front of her, ready to take notes on her sister's answers.

"Okay?"

"What was the process for getting diagnosed? Was it difficult for you?"

"Well, like, once we actually got to the diagnosing part, no, that wasn't very hard," Harmony says. "But everything leading up to that kind of sucked."

"You mean like your grades?"

"It was about more than grades, Grace. Obviously I'm proud of myself for graduating with honors, but I don't even have friends from freshman year, because I was such a flake. I forgot people's names and was bad at both making and keeping plans. I had such a hard time adjusting to college because it was such a big change and I couldn't self-regulate my emotions to save my life. My self-worth was in the toilet. Getting medicated helped me get my life together."

That sounds familiar. The way Phoebe is certain there are parts of her that are inherently *bad*.

"Okay look, I've been waiting for you to explain this to me at your pace," Harmony says, "but you haven't, so." They haven't even been speaking for two minutes. "You gotta tell me why you're asking all this shit. You don't think you have ADHD, do you?"

"No," Grace says.

ADHD is not and has never been her. Though ADHD TikTok did lead her to autism TikTok, and that's . . . something she might look into more when she has some extra time, but for now, this isn't about her.

"There's this girl, Ph—"

"There's this *girl*?" Harmony screeches.

"I'm never asking you for help again."

"Grace, come on, it's only fair that I'm excited about this. You've never talked to me about a girl before!"

That can't be true, can it? There's been nothing to talk about in years, but surely when they were younger—except Grace didn't come out until she was eighteen, and she was already playing for Lyon by then.

"Well. Anyway. Yeah. Phoebe. She's a teammate and—"

"Oh my God, you have a crush on the girl who they drafted to replace you."

Every once in a while, Harmony does something that reminds Grace she doesn't hate soccer like she likes to pretend.

"She's not going to replace me," Grace says.

"No, I mean—like obviously I just mean for the World Cup. Not like you're getting replaced."

Grace wonders if their dad told Harmony about his conversation with Grace, if she's being delicate because of that or just because she's feeling nice.

"I think she can make the World Cup roster," Grace says it out loud for the first time.

She's been worried about Phoebe making the World Cup roster the whole time she was out with her injury, worried Phoebe would take her place on the national team. But this is the first time Grace thinks about them *both* on the World Cup roster.

Phoebe suggested it at Café du Monde, but Grace hadn't actually thought it was an option. Eric wouldn't play them in different positions; that was all she'd thought then. He still won't, probably, but regardless.

"I think she should make it."

"Shit. Really?"

"Really. She's working really hard for it, except she very obviously has undiagnosed ADHD and she's refusing to get diagnosed."

"Well, that makes sense," Harmony says, even though it doesn't. "Look, I had so much going on I never would've gotten diagnosed on my own. I was desperately trying to not fail my classes. I didn't have any brain space to figure out getting diagnosed. Dad was the one who set up the appointment, put it on the family calendar, drove me there. I had no idea what to do by myself."

"So I should make Phoebe an appointment," Grace says.

That's easy. She knows Phoebe's schedule by now. As long as the doctor doesn't have too long of a wait time, Grace can get this taken care of quickly.

"Uh, do you want her to know you like her?"

Grace's thoughts stutter to a stop. "What?"

"That's kind of a big thing," Harmony says.

"What? No, it's not. That's the point. It's not a big deal to someone without ADHD, that's why I can do it."

"I'm just saying. She's probably going to think it's a big thing."

Well. Maybe that's not the end of the world. Maybe this could be a two-birds-one-stone sort of thing.

"We'll see," Grace says. "Anyway, I appreciate your help, and you only being a little bit of a dick about it."

"That's me, only a little bit of a dick."

They talk for a while longer, Grace asking about Harmony's life and then feeling guilty that she isn't closer with her sister. Maybe that's something she can change, now that she's doing the things she wants to do.

Setting up the appointment for Phoebe is *not* a big deal, really. It takes thirty more minutes of research, two phone calls, and a short conversation with the receptionist explaining why Grace doesn't know the patient's birthday and would it be possible for that to be filled out later? All that's left is to tell Phoebe.

If Phoebe is awkward about it being too much, Grace can play it off. But if Phoebe is . . . open to it, maybe Grace can explain how she's gone soft.

Grace doesn't want to explain that, but not in the same way she usually doesn't want to do things. No, instead it's worse, because it's like what happened when Kayla asked if she was pulling back from media: Grace hadn't thought of it before, but as soon as she thinks of it—she doesn't want to do it because she's scared, but she *does* want to do it rather desperately. She wants it to already be done. She wants to be on the other side of it, to have it already be over. She doesn't know how to do this, and even if it goes well, she doesn't know how to do what comes after, either. She's never been in a relationship as an adult. Not anything real. But if she can get through this part, the scary part, the admitting things part—if this does go well, she'll have Phoebe to help with what comes after. She's pretty sure she'll be able to handle that.

Thirty-Four

Wednesdays are Phoebe's rest day.

Well, not really, because they still have practice—and she's been working extra hard to make up for the fact that she was suspended for last weekend's game, given the whole red card situation. Givhan still hasn't spoken directly to her since she was sent off in their first match, a full week and a half ago.

But the point is, Phoebe never takes a shift at the diner on a Wednesday. It's a good little midweek break.

It's especially needed this week, given that she did an overnight on Tuesday. She doesn't usually do overnights anymore, but they needed someone, and she knew she'd be able to sleep away the next evening, and anyway Dallas was working, too, which means they took turns sleeping through the shift as long as no one was around.

Grace knows Phoebe takes Wednesdays off but does *not* know that she still does overnights sometimes. So when she stops beside Phoebe to retie her laces and asks if she's coming over after practice, what's Phoebe gonna do except say yes?

It's probably going to be a problem eventually—not Phoebe doing overnights, but the fact that Grace only says something about them dating when no one else is around. She's never used the word *girlfriend*. Phoebe is gonna slip up. It's only a matter of time. That, or there will come a point where she can't take this anymore. Phoebe is loud and affectionate and incredibly out. She isn't built for secret relationships, not like this, not long-term.

But that's a problem for future Phoebe.

Current Phoebe's main problem is how fucking tired she is.

"Lilly, I know your mother doesn't nap, but surely you'll nap with me," Phoebe says the moment she's inside Grace's house.

The cat, as usual, is much more focused on yelling at Grace until she gives him treats than on anything Phoebe has to say. Phoebe hurls herself onto the couch without moving any of the pillows, then has to writhe around a bit to get them out from underneath her so she can get comfortable. She piles them all on top of herself instead. God, lying down feels good.

After an indeterminate amount of time—just enough time for Phoebe almost to have fallen asleep—Grace clears her throat. Phoebe cracks an eye open. Her girlfriend is perched on the edge of the armchair beside the sofa.

"I want to talk to you about something," she says.

Phoebe feels like someone dumped ice water over her head. Any time someone has to warn you they want to talk instead of just talking to you—it's never good.

"It's not bad," Grace says like she's reading her mind.

She's probably reading her face—Phoebe probably looks as terrified as she feels. She shrugs to disguise the way her shoulders have crept toward her ears even though she's lying down.

"What's up?"

"I know you told me to forget about the whole ADHD thing."

Phoebe sighs. She supposes she's grateful Grace isn't breaking up with her or anything, but she can't imagine this conversation is going to go much better than the last one they had on the subject.

"I did some research," Grace says. She's playing with a loose string on a pillow rather than looking at Phoebe. "And I talked to my sister—I told you she has ADHD. I wanted to know how to help."

"Grace, I told you, it's fine. I'm—"

"Let me finish. Please."

Phoebe stays quiet.

"You said you didn't have time to think about it," Grace continues eventually. "Which makes sense. I can see why it would be overwhelming. But again, I wanted to help. So . . ." She changes tack. "It's okay if you don't want to do this. I won't be offended. It's your life, of course, and I don't want to assume anything. I mean, I did assume, earlier, with the thought of you being on meds to begin with, and I don't want to do that again. I don't want to—"

"Grace," Phoebe says. "Just tell me."

Grace takes a deep breath. She rubs the loose string from the pillow between her fingers. "I looked into our insurance, and it does pay for testing and medication. So I made an appointment for you, two weeks from today, with a doctor who takes our insurance. You can get diagnosed. If you want."

Phoebe sits up, ignoring the seven pillows that fall to the ground. "Wait, what?"

"I made an appointment for you to potentially get diagnosed with ADHD," Grace says. "If you want."

"You did all that for me?"

"It's not *all that*," Grace says. "I know it would've been hard for you, but it wasn't for me. It was simple."

"But not just like—like you did more than just call one random doctor. You researched to make sure testing was covered and that the doctor took our insurance?"

"Well, there were a variety of ADHD specialists who took our insurance, so I looked at patient reviews, too."

"Grace."

"I can show you the reviews, and the TikToks I found, and—"

"The TikToks you found? About the doctor?"

"No, about being diagnosed with ADHD as an adult."

"You looked up TikToks for me?"

Grace nods.

This *girl*. Phoebe can't help the smile that takes over her face.

"God, I love you," she says, and Grace freezes.

She freezes. Fully. Her fingers stop playing with the pillow, her face goes blank and white, all the blood draining from it. Phoebe's brain catches up with her mouth, and she panics.

"I mean, like, you don't have to—I know you're not looking for a relationship." She tries to wink, can tell it's one of those ridiculous, over-the-top, exaggerated winks cheerleaders do. Her face feels like it's on fire. "I just meant—you know. Anyway. Thank you. That's what I was trying to say."

It's just an expression, except it's not. Or—it *is*, obviously, but Phoebe didn't mean it like that. She *meant* it. She loves Grace Henderson. Given the look on Grace's face, though, she doesn't love her back. Which is fine! It is! She loves things about Phoebe—she told her that, yelled at her, really, about all the things she loves about her. So it's fine. As long as Phoebe hasn't scared her off with the words.

"Right," Grace says, her voice flatter than flat. "You're welcome. Like I said, the appointment is two weeks from today, at five, so you don't have to miss practice."

Okay, Phoebe has to fix this. Grace looks shell-shocked. But she hasn't kicked Phoebe out of her house or anything. And she went to all the trouble of setting up the appointment and everything. That isn't something you do for someone you don't care about. Phoebe just has to not be awkward about this and everything will be fine. She can't take it back, but she can distract from it. She switches from her place on the couch to sit on the arm of Grace's chair.

"Hey," she says, and she forces herself to look away from Grace's hands and maintain eye contact instead. "Lemme thank you in a better way? A way that isn't my stupid mouth embarrassing me and making it awkward."

"You didn't—" Grace swallows. "You're fine. Your mouth didn't do anything."

Phoebe takes the opportunity for innuendo, waggling her eyebrows. "How about I show you what it can do, though?"

Grace rolls her eyes, but a smile peeks through. Phoebe kisses her. Yeah. This is better. She'll thank her this way and they can both forget she said anything, or at least pretend they've forgotten, and it'll be fine.

Phoebe has other things to focus on, anyway. Their next game is Saturday. There's not long until the next national team camp, the final one before the World Cup. And now she's got a doctor's appointment in two weeks. There are so many more important things than whether or not Grace loves her.

As she starts carrying Grace toward the bedroom, though, that doesn't feel true. For the first time in Phoebe's life, something feels more important than playing in the World Cup. She wants Grace more than she wants to make the roster.

The thought hits so hard Phoebe has to stop and set Grace on the hall table. She presses their foreheads together. Inhales shakily. She is in so much trouble.

But like she'd told Grace about ADHD—it's easier not to think about the stuff she can't change. She kisses Grace, mouth betraying her desperation, then picks her up again and carries her the rest of the way to the bedroom.

Thirty-Five

Grace has been reintegrating into practice, step by step, for more than three weeks when Dawn tells her, "I'm clearing you for game play."

Somehow it still comes as a shock.

After almost two months on the sidelines, desperate to get back in a game, suddenly she's in the lineup for Saturday. Two-and-a-half days away. It couldn't happen at a better time.

Last night, Grace was ready to tell Phoebe she has feelings for her. Thank God Phoebe stopped her before she fully lost her dignity. Phoebe said *I love you* the way she says it all the time, the way she loves Rodriguez when she shares prewrap for a headband or Stuart when he gets grass stains out of her jersey, even though that's literally his job. She said *I love you,* and Grace froze. She couldn't breathe.

Phoebe noticed—how could she not?—and made one of her jokes about not looking for a relationship. Grace doesn't know when those jokes stopped being funny—or, well, she'd never found them particularly funny. But now they seem almost cruel. They seem designed to make Grace feel stupid. Any time she gets some vague romantic notion about her feelings, Phoebe really hammers it home that they aren't reciprocated.

Which is fine. Grace and Matthews are teammates with benefits, and that suits Grace fine. She likes their relationship as it is. No need to change a good thing.

None of that matters, anyway. What matters is Grace is going to be back on the field. What matters is her agent finally schedules that interview with Megan Thrace, Grace's last interview. What matters is when Eric says, "Welcome back, Captain," Grace realizes that now's the time. She was going to have to tell him eventually.

"You know, Coach," she says, stalling, "I've been thinking."

"That's never good."

She laughs because that's what he wants, because he thinks he's funny. He thinks a lot of things—that he's a good manager, that they never need to change their tactics, that he knows better than everyone else.

"What if you played Matthews at DM, and me more in an attacking role?"

It isn't what Grace means to say. She means to tell him she's passed on the captainship officially, completely, for good, but what comes out is a suggestion she knows he won't take.

She's right, of course—he chuckles.

"And why would I do that when I finally have the chance to bench her ass for what she pulled in the opener?"

Grace ignores him. "I'm game ready, but you know what coming back from injury is like. Fitness is always a concern."

"Dawn said you were fine."

"I am," Grace says, and for once, it's true. "Box-to-box is a big responsibility for someone who hasn't played ninety minutes in months. If Matthews slots in at DM, I have an opportunity to do my job but get fewer miles on the field."

"Why would I change something that has been working for years? Or did you forget we're back-to-back winners of the shield?"

"Being able to succeed in a certain style of play is different than excelling at it. Just because it's worked in the past doesn't mean it's what's right for the team now." Grace takes a breath. "Relatedly, I've talked to Sorrell. She's going to remain captain."

Eric gapes at her. "You're really telling me you're quitting on me while asking for a favor?"

"I'm not quitting on you."

"On the team then."

She's *definitely* not quitting on the team.

"This is what's best for the team," Grace says. "And playing Phoebe as the six and me as the ten is, too."

Eric rolls his eyes. "According to you."

He's so unprofessional, Grace doesn't know why she thought he'd care about what is best for the team anyway.

"What about this?" she says. "You give me one game. Have us both in the lineup. If it doesn't work, I'll stay on as captain."

It's the last thing Grace wants, but that's how confident she is. They can do this. She knows they can.

"So, what—does Matthews have some dirt on you or something? To get you to advocate for her like this?"

Grace isn't advocating for Phoebe; she's advocating for herself. She doesn't explain that to Eric. She doesn't need to explain anything to him.

"Do we have a deal?"

"Fine," Eric says. "Whatever. I can't wait for this ridiculous experiment to fail."

Grace is going to make him eat his words.

• • • •

She doesn't tell Phoebe she talked to Eric. No reason to put pressure on the girl. Grace recognizes now the effect pressure can have on a person. The way it can shape them and their lives into something they never wanted.

Things with Phoebe are surprisingly normal. She partners with Grace in drills, sneaks a kiss goodbye after practice before flouncing off to her Thursday night shift. Nothing has changed. Nothing has been ruined. Not like it would've been if Grace had actually admitted her feelings. Instead, they pretend they weren't on the precipice of something new and keep going the way things have been.

They both have other things to focus on, anyway. Phoebe has her job and the roster and her doctor's appointment in a couple of weeks. Grace has her first game back, two days from now, her one chance to prove she and Phoebe should play together, and her last-ever interview the next morning. Grace has Amanda, calling that evening to congratulate her.

"I never had any doubt you'd be back and better than ever," Amanda says. "Dawn has been keeping Ilse up to date, and I want to say how proud I am of you for taking the time to rest and recover. I can't wait to watch you play Saturday."

"About that," Grace says. "You should watch Phoebe, too. Matthews."

In the second of silence that follows, Grace wonders what the hell she's doing. But then Amanda responds.

"Should I?" she says, tone curious, not judgmental.

"She'll be in at DM." Grace doesn't give herself a chance to second-guess. Nor does she explain that she'd had to bribe Givhan into setting this lineup. "And I know you're the coach. I know that roster decisions are up to you. I know that you don't have to listen to me on this at all, and I will understand if you don't. But we should take her to Australia."

She pauses for a breath, and when Amanda doesn't immediately reject the idea, Grace takes it as permission to continue.

"She is so talented, and she keeps getting better. I don't know where her ceiling is. I know Eric drafted her to fill in for me while I was out this season with national team duty, but she is so much more than a stand-in for me. We haven't gotten game time together yet, but in drills, in scrimmages, playing with her feels like playing soccer did when I was a kid, when I did it for fun and didn't have so much pressure on myself. When it was just a game."

That's too personal, too emotional. Grace should've stuck to the facts, listed Phoebe's skills, told Amanda everything she can bring to the team. A rational argument can't be denied. Her feelings shouldn't be a part of this. She tries to rein them in.

"Matthews is a target on set pieces. You've seen firsthand what a good tackler she is, how fit she is. I've seen her chase down people on a breakaway who she never should've been able to catch. Ask anyone on the Krewe, she's the hardest-working player on the team. She would be an asset for the national team."

Grace's nostrils are flaring when she's finished, her heart pounding like it's the end of the beep test.

"I like this," Amanda says eventually. "You speaking up about this. You've always been a bit of a yes-man. I like seeing you stick to your guns."

Grace swallows. She doesn't know what she's supposed to say to that.

"I'll keep my eye on both of you this weekend," Amanda says. "And congrats again on your return. I have a feeling it's going to be triumphant."

"Thank you, ma'am."

Grace hangs up the phone. Her chest heaves with each breath.

What did she just do?

Grace doesn't have feelings about rosters.

Grace doesn't talk to coaches on behalf of other players.

But she's already broken all her rules when it comes to Phoebe. She said she wasn't interested in casual sex, and then they started having it. She said she wasn't interested in a relationship, and then she went and caught feelings. She said getting close to her wasn't going to give Phoebe a boost when it came to making a roster or getting playing time, and now she's talked to not one but two coaches about her.

When things happened with Kelsey, Grace told no one. It was embarrassing. She felt stupid. And it was no one's business, anyway. So she'd kept it to herself.

She's done that with Phoebe, too, of course. No one knows they're friends with benefits. No one but Harmony knows Grace has any sort of feelings, and even they haven't really talked about them.

Things with Phoebe still might not be anyone's business, but Grace needs advice.

She writes out the text three different ways before finally sending it. Just to Madeeha, the gentlest of her friends. When they talk about teammates, last names are common, so first Grace calls her *Matthews,* but it feels too distant. The whole point of telling Madeeha is that Grace has gotten too close. So she switches it to *Phoebe Matthews,* but that's worse, like it won't be clear who Grace is talking about without the full name. Just *Phoebe,* then.

> I'm sleeping with Phoebe.

Grace might vomit.

Hopefully Madeeha will tell Sarah, since they're married and probably tell each other everything. It will be good to get advice from the married couple. Obviously, they know how to be in a relationship with a teammate.

While Grace is waiting on a text back, she gets a FaceTime call instead. It's Madeeha, which is *rude,* frankly. You're supposed to respond in the same way someone reached out to you. A text begets a text.

Worse still, when Grace picks up, it's not just Madeeha—H crowds into her screen as well, and not only that, but there's a third person on the call: Fish.

"Wilson, that message was in confidence," Grace snaps, as though she hadn't hoped Madeeha would share it a mere thirty seconds ago.

"I haven't said anything!" Madeeha says. "But this conversation is going to require more expertise than I have."

"Would somebody tell me what the hell we're talking about?" Fish says.

"You don't have to," Madeeha tells Grace. "I just thought more opinions might be helpful."

That's probably true. But Grace isn't sure she can say it out loud.

Madeeha nods on her screen, and Grace takes a breath, and: "I'm sleeping with Matthews."

Shit, she forgot she's supposed to call her Phoebe. Too late—Fish is already screaming *what* on repeat.

"I cannot *believe* you didn't warn me what this was about," H says to Madeeha.

Her wife ignores her. "Courtney Trout, if you wake our baby, I swear to God."

Fish cackles. "So turn your phone down! You cannot prevent me from yelling about this. This is gold."

Grace does not understand what about the situation is *gold*. You win gold for first place, so gold implies *good*, and this is not *good*. Except it is, maybe. That's the problem. It seems like it's good, lately, really good, good enough Grace wants to do something about it.

"I can't believe you're sleeping with Matthews," H says.

"How did this even happen?" Fish says.

"Do the two of you pay any attention at all?" Madeeha asks.

"What?" Sarah says, and Grace isn't sure if she's joking or proving her wife's point.

"Grace and Phoebe have been circling closer since the moment they first laid eyes on each other," Madeeha says. "And how did you miss whatever happened during sHeroes?"

"What happened during sHeroes?" Fish asks.

"Matthews spent a day and a half depressed, then returned looking like she was going to murder Kelsey," Madeeha says. "And when we went out to the bar after, she barely did anything but stare at Grace like she hung the damn moon."

Grace doesn't like people speculating on her relationships. She should be annoyed. But her main reaction is:

"She was staring at me like that?"

Madeeha gestures to her wife like *See?*

"If you're already sleeping together, what's the problem?" Fish asks.

"I want to . . ." Grace rubs her fingers together. "Date her."

Madeeha and H make sounds of understanding. Fish still looks confused.

"So . . . tell her?" she says. "As the token straight, am I missing some reason you can't just say, 'Hey, Matthews, I wanna be your girlfriend'?"

Grace's heart swells at the word *girlfriend*.

"We both agreed, when this started, that we weren't looking for a relationship."

The other three listen as she lays out the details. Actually, she lays out the vague overall facts rather than the details, which she prefers to keep between Phoebe and herself. But it's enough so they understand.

She explains how she tried to say something and Phoebe shut her down, how she wants to try again anyway. The fact that she's talked to both Givhan and Amanda about playing Phoebe—Grace has to try again. She's scared, but . . .

She doesn't admit it to her friends, but if she had to pick between dating Phoebe and being on the World Cup roster . . . it wouldn't even be a hard decision.

"Here's the thing," Fish says once Grace has finished her explanation. "She's definitely into you."

"Obviously she's into me. We've been sleeping together for months."

"No, like, romantically," Fish says.

Grace shakes her head. "But she always reminds me that neither of us want a relationship."

"Yeah, probably to throw you off the scent of how she's obsessed with you."

"Fish, you can't just say that," H says. "You want Grace to declare her love and get her heart broken?"

Grace didn't say anything about *love*.

"No one spends that much time with a fuck buddy," Fish says.

"It's not that simple when you're sapphic," H insists. "We actually like spending time together outside of sex. I know you and Cam do, too, but that seems rare for the hets."

Fish rolls her eyes. "Are all sapphics this dumb?"

H scoffs like she's offended, but Madeeha winces and nods.

"Don't you remember how long it took Sarah and I to figure it out?"

"Lord, yeah." Fish shudders. "That was embarrassing for y'all."

"Wait, Madeeha, does that mean you think Phoebe is into me, too? Romantically, I mean?" Grace asks.

Madeeha's deep brown eyes look so soft, even through the phone screen. "Grace, I'm telling you, the way she looked at you at the bar—she's been into you—romantically—for a long time."

Grace lets out a breath. She's still not sure she believes it, but it feels more possible, suddenly. Maybe Phoebe has feelings for her, too.

"Okay so you gotta do something big," Fish says. "Really hit her over the head with the fact that you wanna date."

"But make it Phoebe-specific," Madeeha says. "Not just a generic declaration."

"That's a good idea," H says.

"Oh, so now you agree that Phoebe likes her," Fish says.

"I trust my wife," H says. To Grace, she adds, "Like, if there's something she really wants or needs that you could get—that shows you pay attention and care."

Grace didn't tell them about the doctor's appointment she set up for Phoebe. At least this is confirmation it was a good thing for her to do.

"Maybe you should go buy poster board and some markers," Fish says. "Do it like a high school science project."

"Are you so old you've forgotten Grace didn't finish high school?" H says.

"If we were in high school, I'd shove you into a locker."

Grace ignores their playful bickering and considers.

Phoebe needs a lot of things, really. Her brother needs top surgery. Her parents need better health insurance. Grace could do all of that. She's not hideously wealthy, but she's got money, even if she doesn't take another sponsorship again. But that all feels stale. Impersonal. Grace wants to spend her money on Phoebe and her family, wants to help, and she will, but that's not how she wants to . . . woo her, for lack of a better word.

It takes money to provide those things, that's all. Grace wants Phoebe to want *her*, not her money, or her stardom, or her talent. Grace wants to show Phoebe that there's more to her than that. That stuff is all she's let most of the world see for so long. Phoebe has always seemed to recognize that Grace is more than that—maybe even before Grace recognized it.

Back at the beginning, when they first spent time together, when Grace took Phoebe to Morning Call, Phoebe wanted her to be in a picture. She wanted to tag Grace on social media. At the time, Grace thought about Kelsey and being used and strangers thinking they knew her life from the small slice that made it to the internet.

"I should come out," Grace says.

Fish and H are still giving each other shit, but the statement stops them in their tracks.

"What?" H says.

"Phoebe is publicly out, and that's important to her."

"Grace," Madeeha says. "I don't know that coming out for someone is a good idea."

Grace shakes her head. "I wouldn't be coming out *for* her, but it would show I'm serious. Hit her over the head with it or whatever Fish said."

"This sounds like a great idea to me," Fish says.

"Coming out is nuanced," Madeeha says. "If you want to do it, Grace, of course I support you. But I want to make sure you're thinking through what it means. How many articles and columns and everything it will set off."

"Oh, but I'm not doing media anymore."

There's a general chorus of *Wait what?* Grace forgot she hadn't told them that part.

"Yeah, uh, this is all part of a bigger, like, thing." That sounds stupid but she doesn't know how else to explain it. "Where I'm not gonna be captain or do media anymore."

"You're not gonna be captain?"

"Sorrell is going to keep the armband."

"That's a good choice," Fish says. "She's gonna captain the national team someday."

"Yeah, whenever you finally retire," H says.

"This call is about Grace," Fish says. "Could you maybe stop being a dick for one second?"

"I don't know, that sounds hard."

"Seriously, shut up, both of you," Madeeha says. Then, to Grace: "I'm proud of you. For setting boundaries to protect your happiness. For going after what makes you happy."

Phoebe. That's what makes her happy. Phoebe and soccer. It really is that simple.

"You really don't ever do anything halfway, do you, Baby Spice?"

"What do you mean?"

"Some people make incremental changes to their lives," Fish says. "But you're going all out."

Grace shrugs. "These are the changes I want to make."

"You're really just done doing press?" H asks.

"I have one commitment to follow through on, and then . . ." Grace trails off as a light bulb goes off in her head. "Of course. I have my last interview on Sunday, with Megan Thrace. I can use it to come out."

"Grace, are you *sure*?" Madeeha asks.

"I'm already out to anyone who matters. It's not as big of a deal as you're making it seem."

"It will be a big deal to a lot of people," H says.

"Yes, you're right," Grace admits. "I don't mean to act like it won't matter. I get that it will. For a lot of reasons, to a lot of people. But the way in which it will matter to me is that it's my best chance to be with Phoebe."

"You really got it bad for this girl, huh?" Fish asks.

Grace looks away from her phone to the other side of the couch. Phoebe's side of the couch. She usually doesn't spend the night when she has an evening shift, but Grace wants to text her, tell her to come over afterward.

"Yeah," she says quietly. "I guess I do."

Thirty-Six

Playing soccer has been Phoebe's favorite thing since she learned how to kick a ball.

Playing soccer with Grace is even better.

Givhan puts them in the lineup together for Grace's first game back. He puts Phoebe in as defensive midfielder! She has no idea why, but she doesn't ask—don't look a gift horse in the mouth and all that.

Playing soccer with Grace feels like . . . like . . . Phoebe doesn't even know. She's never been that good with metaphors, or similes, or whatever. It feels like the best thing she's ever done.

Eleven minutes in, Grace takes a corner kick and Phoebe stays still, one, two, three seconds longer than she wants to before taking off. A diving header makes a pretty cool first professional goal. Celebrating by hugging her girlfriend isn't half bad, either. Better still? Six minutes later, when Phoebe intercepts a pass and then starts the counterattack, sending the ball to open space ten yards ahead of Grace, who beats her defender and the goalie to put the Krewe up 2–0. She koala hugs Phoebe after, and it takes everything Phoebe has not to kiss her in front of the entire stadium.

Grace scores again in the second half, and Gabby adds a fourth goal in stoppage time.

Even though it's her first game back and she's undoubtedly the MVP, Grace doesn't do media after the game. She doesn't wait for Phoebe to, either, so Phoebe celebrates with Gabby and her margarita glasses instead of her girlfriend. It's fine. Grace isn't pulling away because Phoebe declared her apparently unrequited love. She just needs space to process her return from injury. Phoebe doesn't need to worry.

Except then Grace is fucking weird. For days.

• • • •

Phoebe goes over to Grace's Sunday afternoon, once Grace is done with her interview, and of course she asks how it went.

"Why?" Grace says, eyes darting to Phoebe then away.

"Uh, just wondering?"

It's been a long time since Grace was so suspicious about Phoebe asking questions.

"Fine," she says. "The article publishes on Thursday."

"Nice," Phoebe says, then kisses Grace instead of asking anything else.

• • • •

At practice Monday, Grace announces Kayla is taking over as captain. She doesn't explain why, just says it's been an honor to serve, and Sorrell's gonna take it from here. Phoebe is thrilled for Kayla, but isn't wild about not knowing in advance.

She waits until they're in Grace's car on the way home to complain. "I can't believe you didn't say anything!"

Grace shrugs. "I wanted to tell the team all at once."

Phoebe almost claims that as Grace's girlfriend, she should get special treatment, but they've still never used the phrase out loud. Even though yesterday was officially their one-month anniversary. Not that Phoebe is counting or anything.

She opts for something lighter, something teasing. "What other secrets are you keeping from me?"

It's supposed to be a joke, but Grace ducks her head.

"My interview—" she starts. Stops. "It was my last interview. Ever."

"Wait, what?"

As she drives them to her house, Grace explains that she had a conversation with her dad and decided to only do the things she wants. That's why she isn't captain anymore, and why she's not gonna do media ever again, either.

"I talk more about why in the article, which comes out Thursday," Grace says.

"Right."

Phoebe already knew that. She wants to ask about what she doesn't know: What are the things Grace wants to do? Why is Grace acting weird? Except Phoebe *doesn't* want to ask, because what if it's her? What if it's her and her stupid mouth and how she told Grace she loved her last week? So Phoebe stays quiet and lets Grace be weird.

• • • •

It all makes sense on Thursday.

They're gonna watch film of their next opponent after lunch, and Phoebe is early—only because she rode with Grace, who had a check-in with Dawn beforehand. She's still with Dawn when other people start to join Phoebe in the film room, Colleen and Ash, then Kayla and Gabby. Phoebe's trying to subtly make fun of Gabby for having clearly had some afternoon delight—seriously, there's a hickey on Kayla's neck—when Colleen says, "Holy shit. Did y'all know Grace was coming out?"

Phoebe's head snaps to look at her. "What?"

"An article just dropped."

Phoebe scrambles for her phone. The article was posted three minutes ago.

GRACE HENDERSON RETURNS:
Her injury, her identity, and her rediscovered love of the game

Holy shit is right.

Phoebe's eyes skim faster than her brain can make sense of the words. She forces herself to breathe. To focus. To slow down enough she can actually read the article.

It talks about Grace's conversation with her dad in more depth, discusses how her injury made her reassess the role soccer plays in her life. About halfway through, it says:

"I'm a lesbian," Henderson says frankly. "My friends and family have known that for a long time, but it's reached a point where I wanted to say it publicly for a lot of reasons."

"What's going on?"

Phoebe looks up to find the subject of the article at the door to the film room. Every single other person in the room is on their phone.

"Your interview," Kayla says quietly.

Grace's eyes go wide, and they land directly on Phoebe. She looks terrified. Phoebe wishes she could hold her—wait. Maybe she can? If Grace came out, does that mean—Phoebe looks back to her phone and skims on purpose this time. Did Grace mention her?

Before Phoebe can figure it out, Grace's fingers are closing around her wrist.

"Come with me," Grace says.

Phoebe does.

Grace marches them out of the room, down the hallway, and into the equipment room, the one she'd shown Phoebe the night they started, the night they played keep-away until they couldn't keep away from each other. Finally, she lets go of Phoebe's wrist.

"Have you read it?" Grace asks.

"Some. Why didn't you tell me—"

"Read it. The whole thing."

Phoebe doesn't know what's going on. She does as she's told.

Grace, perfect, private, independent Grace, talks so freely on the page. Sweet and vulnerable and honest. She talks about the pressure she's always put on herself, and about how coming out and stepping away from media and the captaincy will lessen that. Phoebe loves her so much it's stupid.

But coming out now is about more than representation and pride for Henderson.

"We're not together, currently, but there is someone who I'd . . ." She trails off. "Who is really important to me. And part of this whole doing-what-I-want-to-do thing is going to be telling her how I feel."

There's one paragraph after that wrapping the whole thing up, but Phoebe barely processes it. She's too fucking confused. *We're not together, currently, but . . .*

Phoebe looks up at Grace, who looks like she's in more pain than she ever was with her hip.

"Grace," Phoebe says. "Is this last part about me?"

Thirty-Seven

Grace takes a deep breath. She knows what she wants to say, actually wrote it all out by hand last night.

"It is," she says. "I know that when we started this neither of us wanted a relationship, and I understand if you still don't. We can keep doing what we've been doing, or if you're uncomfortable with me having feelings for you, we can be friends instead. But I had to say something."

She takes another breath, goes to run her hand through her hair before remembering it's braided. Her fingers find the end of the braid to play with instead. She's staring just over Phoebe's shoulder; she wants to look at her, but actual eye contact is too hard.

"I really like you, Phoebe," she says. "You're funny and passionate and gorgeous. I've kept people at a distance for a long time, but you walked right through all of my defenses. You're confident and unapologetic about the space you take up in the world. The joy you take in playing soccer is infectious, and reminded me that I used to feel like that, too. You've helped me find that joy again. Even if you don't feel the same way, I'm so grateful to know you."

She finally makes eye contact. They need to invent new words to describe the green of Phoebe's eyes. Grace looks away.

"You're pretty special," she says quietly.

"Baby girl," Phoebe says, and usually that's a good thing, but it's also usually a sex thing—it's what Phoebe calls Grace when she's about to make her come. Grace doesn't exactly know what to do with the term in this situation. Before she can panic about it, Phoebe has her up against the wall and is kissing her.

She kisses her and kisses her and kisses her until they're both gasping.

"Jesus, you made me cry." Phoebe wipes at her eyes. Her hands drop to Grace's hips afterward, her phone still clutched in one of them. "But also, this makes no sense at all."

Grace's chest heaves. She shakes her head to clear it. "What do you mean?"

"Haven't we been dating for, like, a month?"

"*What?*"

"I literally told you I loved you last week."

Grace gapes like a fish. "That was—you followed it up by reminding me we weren't in a relationship!"

"Oh my God." Phoebe sounds *delighted*. "That joke is only funny because we *are* in a relationship."

Grace has always prided herself on being levelheaded. She is good in a crisis. Calm. Pragmatic.

And yet in this moment, her voice comes out as a shriek. "Since *when?*"

"Since sHeroes," Phoebe says, like it's obvious. "Like, we had the exclusive talk and everything."

"We did not."

"We did!" Phoebe insists. "I told you I wasn't interested in sleeping with anyone else and you said the same."

"I thought that was about STIs or something."

"Are you serious?"

Grace shrugs. Rather violently. "We had talked about dental dams!"

"Yeah, but we'd never used them! Even before then!"

"I don't know! I was confused!" Grace slips out of Phoebe's grasp, paces to the end of the room and back. This conversation is going too fast for her brain to process. "You're saying you thought we were dating since then?"

"You're saying you didn't?"

"Obviously!" Grace gestures to the phone still in Phoebe's hand. "I just told a reporter I was single. Clearly I did not think we were dating!"

"Baby girl," Phoebe says softly, dimples digging into her cheeks.

So much makes sense now. Everything Phoebe said after Grace told her about Kelsey. Why she wanted to tell her mom. Every time Phoebe said something about not wanting a relationship, she'd giggle or wink— the laughter used to make Grace hopeless. And all along, it was because Phoebe thought she was in on the joke.

Grace takes a breath. If she understands this correctly . . .

"So," she says, "when you said you loved me and then joked about it . . . it wasn't because you realized I was about to tell you I had feelings for you?"

"Jesus, no," Phoebe says. "I thought you were freaking out because I said it and you didn't love me back. Which, I'm realizing you probably don't, given that you didn't even realize we were dating. But that's fine, like, totally fine. It doesn't have to be weird. I'm used to—"

"I think I might love you," Grace says.

"Oh," Phoebe says. "Okay. Wow."

Shit, should Grace not have said that?

"Is that . . . okay?"

"Fuck yeah."

Phoebe says it so vehemently, Grace can't help the giggle that escapes.

She's dating Phoebe. Phoebe *loves* her. Grace's entire life this last month just got turned on its head, but she doesn't even care. She had considered a lot of outcomes of the article, prepared for a lot of potential conversations with Phoebe afterward. Never in her wildest dreams would she have come up with this.

She takes a step closer. Phoebe mirrors it, grinning.

"So," Grace says. "You're my . . ."

"Girlfriend?" Phoebe offers. "If you want."

Another step. "And I'm yours?"

"If you want."

"I want."

"I'm gonna kiss you now."

"I want," Grace says again.

Phoebe's mouth is soft, and warm, and perfect. But she pulls away too soon. Grace wants to keep kissing her; they can talk later.

"You know," Phoebe says, "this is going to be a story we tell at our wedding that people aren't going to believe is true because you are so ridiculous."

Okay, maybe they can talk now.

"Our wedding?" Grace cocks an eyebrow.

Realization dawns on Phoebe's face, and she shakes her head frantically. "No. No, I did not just say that. Let's go back to literally anything else."

Grace is not about to propose. That would be really advanced U-Hauling, to go from not knowing you were dating to proposing within five minutes. But Phoebe's embarrassed smile is so damn cute Grace can't help herself.

"I think *this* is a story for our wedding," she says, "you talking about our wedding two seconds after we are officially dating."

"No way. We've been officially dating for a month."

"I don't think we can be officially dating for a month if I didn't know about it till today," Grace says.

Phoebe doesn't even pretend to consider it. "I don't know," she says. "That sounds like a personal problem."

"You're a personal problem."

Grace digs her fingers into Phoebe's sides. Tickling will hopefully distract her so she doesn't notice how Grace's response doesn't make sense. Indeed, the redhead squeals with laughter and squirms to get away.

She doesn't get away, but she does eventually catch Grace's hands in her own. Her cheek presses against Grace's temple.

"Should we go watch film now?"

"Eh," Grace says. "They can wait."

"Wow, you really have changed. Grace Henderson, late for a mandatory team activity."

"Didn't you hear? I do what I want now."

What she wants is to nose under Phoebe's chin and kiss the same patch of skin she'd first put her mouth on. Phoebe tilts her head, giving Grace more access.

"Unless you think we should go," Grace says.

"No, it's okay." Phoebe is breathless. "I'm used to being late."

Epilogue

In the locker room, while she waited for her turn to have Grace's hands in her hair, Phoebe told herself she just needed to get on the pitch and her nerves would settle. But she's on the field now, her hair in two french braids leading to a ponytail, and it doesn't matter that this is all she's wanted for her entire life, it doesn't matter that she never usually gets pregame nerves, she feels like she might throw up.

She shakes out her limbs, joining the rest of the starting eleven circling up near the eighteen.

"Who wants to do this?"

Fish always asks who wants to give the pep talk before kickoff. Normally Phoebe likes that—that they're all equals, that every voice carries equal weight, no matter their position or tenure with the team. But today, a minute before the whistle blows to start her first game in a World Cup, Phoebe wants to hear from a veteran. She's the only who hasn't been here before, but she wants to hear from one of her teammates directly across the circle: Fish or Madeeha or H, the three most capped players on the team.

The player who speaks up, though, is right beside her.

"We got this," Grace says.

H lets out a *whoop* while Fish yells, "Okay, Baby Spice!"

Phoebe shares their enthusiasm, but her heart continues to race behind her sternum. Even the shock of Grace volunteering to give the pregame speech for the first time since she'd abdicated all responsibilities can't quite overtake Phoebe's nerves.

"We already did the hard part," Grace says.

Phoebe knows she shouldn't interrupt, and in any other situation she wouldn't—her ADHD meds have helped her rein in that impulse—but she can't help herself.

"Is winning the World Cup somehow the easy part?" she asks.

"We got here, Phenom."

Grace doesn't talk about injuries or roster spots or their own self-worth holding them back. She doesn't have to. These women took the journey together.

"Now all we gotta do is play," Grace says. "Hands in."

"You always were a woman of few words," Fish says.

"Everyone's a woman of few words compared to you." H's eyes find Phoebe's across the circle. "Except maybe Matthews."

"Hands *in*," Grace says again, and they listen this time, crowding closer together.

Phoebe's hand is layered between Kayla's and Becky's.

"*Play* on three," Grace says, focused on the team even while she catches Phoebe's other hand, tangling their fingers together between their bodies. "One, two—"

"Play!" they shout as a team.

Grace squeezes Phoebe's hand.

They all break off, then, and head to their positions. Phoebe does a couple of high jumps, pulling her knees to her chest, like her blood needs help pumping.

She's not nervous anymore. All she's gotta do is play.

The whistle blows.

ACKNOWLEDGMENTS

There are so many people I couldn't have done this without:

Vicki Lame, who let me push and push and push deadlines, and believed in me the whole time.

Patrice Caldwell, who is everything I could've hoped for in an agent.

Trinica Sampson-Vera, who keeps me on top of everything I forget about.

Mary Roach, who first conceived of Grace and her prickly self.

Rosiee Thor, whose amazing thread of takes on the phrase *meet-cute* gave me a title.

Mary Randall, who read and yelled and made me feel like I'm good at this thing.

Christina Cheung, who has probably read more of my words than anyone else.

Keena Roberts, who gave the first-ever feedback and instantly made this book better.

Jen St. Jude, who is so damn good, and the thirstiest sports queer, and who gave me info about NWSL.

Charles Olney, who also gave me soccer info that I didn't use as much as I should've.

Avery Friend and Tabitha Edmondson, who answered my every question about New Orleans.

Courtney Kae, who is a supportive delight.

Tash McAdam, whose friendship and belief in me is what started me on this journey.

Becca Mix, who convinced me to go to my first writing retreat (and who drove me there!), and Andrea Hannah, who hosted it and just makes me feel all warm inside.

Aimée Carter, who let me talk to her about my plot for two hours when we had just met. She is the reason there's any external conflict at all.

Zabe Doyle, Emma Patricia, Mary Roach (again), Christina Tucker, and Ashley Blake: finding a group as queer and unhinged as y'all is one of the best things that has ever happened to me. Zabe, you're basically my ride or die. Emma, there are things about me that you get that no one else does. Mary, I wanna be like you when I grow up (don't remind me how young you are). Christina, until you see how great you are, I'll believe in you enough for the both of us. The best thing *The Morning Show* ever did was make us friends (also: the fires episode). Ashley, I didn't even know I could love MILFs as much as I love you.

And of course, my Brooke. Life has taken me places I never imagined I'd go. I'm so glad I get to spend it all with you.

CREDITS

Macmillan/St. Martin's Publishing Group/St. Martin's Griffin

Editor
VICKI LAME

Editorial Assistant
VANESSA AGUIRRE

Publisher
ANNE MARIE TALLBERG

Marketing
RIVKA HOLLER
BRANT JANEWAY

Publicity
MEGHAN HARRINGTON

Designer
GABRIEL GUMA

Jacket Designer
OLGA GRLIC

Mechanical Designer
SOLEIL PAZ

Managing Editor
CHRISINDA LYNCH

Production Manager
JOY GANNON

Production Editor
LAUREN RIEBS

Copy Editor
MICHELLE LI

Proofreader
DAKOTA GRIFFIN

Cold Reader
MORGAN MITCHELL

Creative Services
BRITTA SAGHI
KIM LUDLAM
TOM THOMPSON
DYLAN HELSTIEN

Audio Producer
KATY ROBITZSKI
CHRISSY FARRELL

Audio Marketing
SAM GLATT

Audio Publicist
DREW KILMAN

New Leaf Literary

Agent Team
PATRICE CALDWELL
TRINICA SAMPSON-VERA

Foreign Team
VERONICA GRIJALVA
TRACY WILLIAMS

Film Team
POUYA SHAHBAZIAN
KATHERINE CURTIS

MERYL WILSNER writes happily-ever-afters for queer folks who love women. They are the author of *Something to Talk About* and *Mistakes Were Made*. Born in Michigan, Meryl lived in Portland, Oregon, and Jackson, Mississippi, before returning to the Mitten State. Some of Meryl's favorite things include: all four seasons, button-down shirts, the way giraffes run, and their wife.